Gabriel

By: Jennifer Cross

Dedicated to:
My mother, Lynn Silvers, and sister, Rhea Bennett, for always giving me the strength to do the things that seem the hardest.

The storm had settled over the Colorado Mountains, sending the clear message that winter had come to stay for the year. The snow muffled the sounds of the world as it blanketed everything, the silence only disturbed by the popping and creaking of the trees under their burden. The snow was quicky sent flying back upwards to flurry down through the wind as the man's form hit the powdered ground. The clearing's white expanse was tainted now by the red droplets falling from between his fingers where they clenched at his chest. He struggled to lift himself up and out of the drifts, tumbling and falling as his legs refused to obey and sent him falling back down into the wet cold. His skin was flushed and pale, exposed to the elements, nothing but a thin piece of leather around his neck that donned a plain and tarnished cross.

The cold was eating away at him quickly as he sunk deeper into the snow bank, startling blue eyes blank as he lifted them upwards towards the heavens. He knelt like that, becoming a frozen statue as the blood that was now beginning to thicken and congeal on his chest steamed with the remnants of his body heat. His eyes focused again, a tremor running through him though not from the chill as the clarity of his situation seemed to cut through to him. The pain and cold were suddenly thrown into the turmoil of feelings that ran over his face; betrayal, fear and pain, all of them ripped out and thrown into the world with an agonized scream aimed at the cloud heavy sky.

- Chapter One - Gabriel

The morning had turned bitter cold in the aftermath of the storm, the first heavy fall of snow claiming the ground and wiping it of any trace of roads or trails. The storm threatened to dump more, waiting for the day to progress far enough along that it could abandon more moisture over the mountain range. Amongst the quiet of the early morning there was the sound of excitement cutting though the air, joy-filled barking peppered with calls of encouragement. The sled dashed forward at full speed behind the line of five dogs, its rider sharing in the enthusiasm of the huskies who were filled with pure happiness at their first run of the winter season. They knew the path well, no need for direction from the woman as they traveled along until a wayward scent caught their attention. The lead dog veered suddenly, and the rest followed despite the corrective call that came out from their rider. The woman's voice called out in a commanding tone when they failed to get back on track, their curiosity seeming greater than the training they'd gone through over the years.

Despite her frustration as she tried to slow the team, there was no hint of panic or concern at the sudden detour. Her trust in her team was deepened by the years spent running with them, and she doubted they would lead her too far off course. Still, she shifted her weight, preparing to step on the track brake to stop them, applying just enough pressure to make them slow slightly. She was about to let her full weight drop down on the brake when the team came to a sudden standstill, forcing her to put her foot on the spike brake to keep the sled from wanting to continue forward. She shook her head after assuring herself that her team wasn't going to start up again, a mumbled curse passing her lips over their moments of disobedience. She called to her lead dog, watching the team's attention stay strictly forward with their ears perked and their muscles taunt. A tug of apprehension hit her then, eyes moving to scan the trees in front of them for some sign of trouble.

"Hike!" The call was usually all that she needed to send her team off in a flurry, but despite the command the dogs continued to stand in their place. The lead dog tilted his head back, looking at the woman with a soft whine before returning his attention to the seemingly empty clearing. The message was being made obvious that they weren't going to leave until she figured out what lead them here, and with uneasiness she followed their line of sight. It took her a few moments to see it lying in the snow obscured as it was by the drift. It made it impossible for her to tell just what she was looking at from her spot on the sled. She pulled the goggles up off her eyes, nerves making them darken to a forest green with pupils wide as the adrenaline started creeping into her. She stayed focused on the shape in the snow as she leaned down to fish out the snow hook with one hand, setting it in place before she stepped off the runners. She paused beside the sled, leaning down to grab the shotgun she kept with her just in case protection was needed. It had only ever been used twice in the six years that she'd owned it, and not once had she taken aim at something but only scared off an animal with the noise. She proved that she knew well enough how to use it though as she loaded it and aimed without once taking her eyes off the huddled shape ahead of her. She started up along the line of her team; the lead dog's tail beginning to wag just slightly, a twitch of acknowledgement as she passed.

"Easy Yakone." Her tone was hushed now, breath fogging in front of her face as she stopped just ahead of the dogs. She didn't want them trying to rush off without her if something startled them, though the snow hook would hold them back from going very far. She stood, trying to figure out what she was looking at before she tried to get closer. It was large, bigger then her in mass from what she could tell, though the snow had built up around it. That made her relax slightly, knowing then that whatever was there had been there overnight. She took a few steps forward as she let the shotgun drop a little. She was still a few feet from it when the movement made her snap back to attention, gun lifting up smoothly as she stared in disbelief. The hand had twitched just slightly, but it brought the form to focus and forced her thoughts into overdrive. After the initial fight response that had gone through her, she started towards the man with hands tight on the gun as she imagined the worst. She stopped beside him and nudged him with the toe of her shoe as she kept the barrel of the gun aimed firmly at his center. When there was no response she dropped down to her knees, her mind trying to take in what was happening. It was clear he wasn't a threat now that she looked at him as he lay there still and pale, and a dread filled her as she wondered if he was dead. The decision to act came quickly out of desperate need to help him, even if the life had already left the man. She started to dig then, trying to pull the snow away from him so she could get a good hold. The snow turned a ruddy brown color around him after she cleared the first layer away, and it took her thoughts a while to catch up with what it meant. The blood wasn't fresh anymore, though the source was obvious as his bare chest came into view. She wrapped her arms around his frame, pulling and dragging him now towards the sled. The dried blood cracked, allowing a fresh trickle to start seeping through sluggishly from the wound as they reached the sled.

"Shit." Blood soaked into gloves, and she tried to push the knowledge into the back of her thoughts to keep a wave of nausea from rolling through her. The dogs watched with apparent interest, heads turning as she fought and tugged him along though they made no move to investigate their newfound passenger. She heaved him into the sled's basket with effort, having to try several times before she could get him situated right in the rigging. Once he was in she stilled for a moment, half lying on him as she caught her breath from the exertion. He was young, maybe about his early twenties, much too young to be found dead in the snow though she knew it happened more then she liked to think. The unexpected spasm from the man's chest as he started coughing sent her back into frightened motion as the sign of life startled her. She dug rapidly for the solar blankets that were packed down under him, managing to free one and pull it from its package. She laid it over him, trying to tuck it down around him in an attempt to keep the cold from continuing to steal away his warmth. She stumbled through the snow to retrieve the shotgun, hearing Yakone give an uneasy whine as she passed the dogs once more. She gripped the gun tightly feeling the need for the sense of security it offered as she held it close. She wanted to be gone from there, and the dogs seemed to agree as they started to shift and pull at their harnesses. The anxiety was starting to eat at her and her heart was racing now that the adrenaline had taken hold, the feeling of fear spiking when Yakone's growl started to rumble behind her. She turned sharply, running and stumbling back to the sled as the rest of the dogs joined the chorus. The curious but calm disposition of the dogs had given away to one of hostility and fright as they pulled at their leads in an attempt to leave. She looked behind herself trying to find some sign of the threat her dogs perceived, but was only met with the wall of trees and the white expanse.

As soon as her feet hit the footboards of the sled, she yanked the snow hook up and called to her dogs to run. They rushed forward, turning back towards the familiar path as they fled the area with the common sense of trepidation. They didn't want whatever had injured the man and left him there to come back and do the same to them. She glanced back, staring at the empty clearing before dropping her goggles back down over her eyes and peering forward. Silently she willed her dogs to get them away from there and back to the safety of home as quickly as possible.

The temperature had changed enough for snow to start falling again outside the small house that nestled itself on the fringes of the mountain town of Edenspoint. Despite the flickering fire on the hearth, the mood inside the house remained a somber one tinged with a deep concern and suspicion. She was pacing back and forth as she nervously worried her thumb nail with her teeth, watching the doctor as he leaned over the man from the snow. Blankets had been piled over his bare form with hot water bottles tucked in-between in an attempt to warm him.

"You need to call your brother, Anne." She stopped at this, narrowing her eyes slightly as the doctor gave her a look from over his shoulder. They were about the same age, both in their early thirties, but even though he was only a couple of years older than her he had a way of making her feel like a child when he wanted. The grey blue eyes turned back to his patient, and she started pacing again with a bit more agitation to her step. She gave the dark brown hair on the back of his head a look of her own, crossing her arms over her chest. "Anne..."

"I'm not calling him, Blaise. Leo will just make a big deal about it, and think he has to rush out here immediately." The doctor's long fingers pressed the medical tape in place over the bandage that covered the fresh stitches in the man's chest, holding it there for a few seconds before letting go and placing the blankets back around him. If he had believed in them he might have thought it was a miracle that the guy was alive after being left naked and bleeding in the snow, but he felt more comfortable saying it was luck. His eyes paused for a moment on the cross the man wore around his neck, the small item managing to make the man seem less bare with its presence. He stood, pulling the gloves from his hands carefully and placing them in a plastic bag with his other used supplies before giving Anne a steady gaze.

"Of course he's going to make a big deal about you finding a guy half dead in the snow. Even if he wasn't the sheriff, he would make a big deal about that. However, he does happen to be the sheriff and he needs to know about this. Anne...what ever did this wasn't an animal. Someone sliced this guy open pretty good, and then left him out in the snow to die." He stepped over to Anne as he rolled down the sleeves of his sweater, blocking her path to stop her pacing. She tried to stare him down, but she knew he was right in the end. The sheriff did need to be involved, even if dealing with Leo when he was in job mode was far from her favorite thing. Blaise lifted a hand and gently tugged her wrist to pull the thumb she had started to abuse again away from her lips. She sighed as her shoulders slumped in defeat as she leaned closer to him, though they kept enough distance they didn't touch. His hand lingered for a few seconds on her wrist before letting it drop, and he pulled away. "I can call him if you'd rather, though you know he'll worry more if it's me asking. He'll think something happened to you."

"No, I'll call. Would you mind starting some tea and coffee though. I have a feeling we'll need it." They stepped away now with their own separate tasks, both avoiding their unconscious witness now that there was nothing more for them to do but wait.

The coffee and tea were forgotten once the sheriff arrived, storming in once Anne opened the door. He stepped past her, followed by his deputy who paused by the door and gave Anne a sheepish smile as he took off his coat.

"I'm afraid you may be in for it a bit, he was worrying the entire way here that something had happened to you," he said as he hung his coat on one of the wooden hooks by the entrance, side stepping out of the way for Anne to close the door.

"Thanks for coming with him, Mackenzie," Anne said, watching her brother with narrowed eyes as he did a once around the living room, and probably would have taken up Anne's position of pacer if he hadn't caught sight of Blaise just then.

"You should have called me as soon as she called you out here." Blaise had just stepped out of the kitchen with a cup of tea in hand when Leo let his worry and frustration out, getting uncomfortably close to the other man to jab a finger into his chest. If the outlash was unexpected, Blaise did a good job of hiding it as he stood there calmly.

"I would have if I had known what it was about, Leo. She told me she thought she'd sprained her ankle, I didn't know it was anything more until I got here." Blaise set the cup down on the counter behind him as he spoke, though he knew Leo had a handle on his temper. It was obvious that the sheriff was trying to hold back on his stress and concern, his jaw muscles were clenched as he stared Blaise down with eyes that were almost mirrors of Anne's.

"Leo, I know you're a bit pissed off, but you know Blaise can hit back fairly hard. Anne's fine as far as I can tell, she's not hurt at all. Reel it in there, Sheriff." Mackenzie stepped in, setting a hand on Leo's shoulder and rolling his eyes to Blaise behind Leo's back. Leo stepped back a little at this, pinching the bridge of his nose for a moment as he closed his eyes. He had a better hold of himself when he looked up at Blaise again, the worry behind his eyes enough of an apology for the two of them.

"All right Anne, mind telling us what happened?" Leo turned, removing his coat now as he let himself slip back into being the sheriff instead of the worried older brother. He let the coat rest on the back of a chair as he moved to look down at the man lying on the couch. Anne shook her head, preferring the angry brother to the professional sheriff that was now surveying her living room. As she sat she was joined by Blaise and Mackenzie, the two men taking their own seats as she explained how she had found the man in the snow. Leo let her talk, but at the end he turned to Blaise instead of her.

"How long was he out there for, Blaise?" A flash of annoyance went through Anne's eyes at this, knowing that her brother didn't believe her full story. He knew she wouldn't flat out lie, but he also made it obvious that he felt she had missed something or exaggerated due to the shock of finding the man. She felt Blaise's hand settle on her knee though he didn't look at her, and she realized her leg had been bouncing tensely as she glared at her brother.

"It's impossible to tell for sure, but it couldn't have been for too long with how cold it is out. Hypothermia has set in, but I'm not seeing any signs of frost bite yet. With nothing on to protect him he probably would have died in a matter of minutes from exposure considering he was wounded as well. My guess is someone dropped him there just before Anne got to him." Blaise paused for a moment, feeling Anne's gaze turn on him. She felt a little betrayed by him for going against her word even though she knew deep down that he was probably right. She didn't see how someone else could have been there without leaving any tracks behind though, or how the man had ended up under a layer of snow. "As for the injuries themselves, the cut's deep but not life threatening at this point. He had to have lost quite a bit of blood, but the cold may have saved him in that case since it would have slowed things down a bit."

Anne was shaking her head slowly; the messy tumbling curls of brown hair dark enough to seem black shivering with the movement. She had crossed her arms over her chest as she stood, feeling the need to be moving. She stepped close to the sheriff, making the resemblance between them easier to pick out. They shared the same forest green eyes with speckles of brown and the same dark hair among other things. At that moment there was also the same stubborn set in the two sibling's jaws as Anne spoke her disagreement.

"I don't see how he could have only been out there for a few minutes. There were no signs of anyone going in or out of that clearing, not even his own tracks left. He was half buried in the snow too. That couldn't have happened if he wasn't out there over night." Anne caught Leo shooting his partner an annoyed look at his sister's protest, and her eyes narrowed as she stepped up closer to him. Mackenzie just gave Leo a shrug in return, moving a hand through his red hair as he sighed. An argument was coming, something not uncommon between the brother and sister, and if you could stay out of the line of fire it could be an amusing battle of wills. Blaise and Mackenzie shared the common interest of staying well out of the way while the two of them argued this out, and when the doctor motioned towards the kitchen for tea Mackenzie followed. Leo and Anne didn't even seem to notice their departure, and the conversation trickled in after them as the two settled in the next room.

"Anne, there's no way he was out there for long. I know you didn't see any tracks, but that doesn't mean there weren't any. You were never the best tracker."

"Oh, so now I'm just a silly girl who can't recognize a trail when I see one? Leo, you know better than that. I use to out-track you when we were younger, and there was nothing but fresh untouched powder around him." Leo gave a growl of frustration as he set his shoulders back. Being the sheriff was on the back burner again now as his sister pushed at him, and he turned and did a short pace towards the couch and back as Anne continued. "There was no one. There were no tracks. If anyone was there, I would have seen them." Anne spoke in a deliberate and pointed tone from between clenched teeth. Her words slow like she was explaining something simple to a child, or perhaps to someone with a mental deficiency.

"He would have died if he'd been there overnight, and you said yourself that the dogs acted like someone was out further in the trees," Leo said with frustration, his voice raising just slightly though he was trying hard to keep it under control.

"I didn't hear anything."

"I think the dogs have better hearing than you." The tense silence returned as Anne's anger all but radiated off of her, bouncing back and echoing off of Leo's. Mackenzie shook his head as he leaned against the counter, watching as Blaise got the kettle going for more hot water again. Blaise settled across from him as they waited, the two of them listening to the siblings in silence for a few moments.

"Really, the guy could have been dropped there by aliens for all I care. Either way, we have an injured man who was left abandoned at our backdoor."

"Exactly, an injured man that was obviously left there by someone else. A man that we know nothing about, and have no idea what kind of shit he's in. And here you are dragging him back to your house, and not even calling me. What would have happened if the people who left him out there showed up when you were by yourself, or if he'd woken up? You put Blaise in danger too." Mackenzie gave Blaise a small grin as the other winced at the mention of his name.

"Better hope they change course or your going to be wishing you were unconscious like our friend out there, Doc. I don't think this is one you want to end up in the middle of."

"I'll just drag you out there with me, Deputy," Blaise replied with a bit of sarcasm as he crossed his arms. "You're the best at handling Leo when he's like this. Maybe you should have stayed out there."

"Well, you're the best at getting Anne to calm down and I don't see you out there throwing yourself to the wolves yet." Blaise laughed quietly, pushing off the counter as the kettle started to whistle softly. "You know Leo doesn't mean it, don't you?" Blaise looked over his shoulder with a frown as he pulled the kettle off the burner and grabbed a fresh mug and tea bag. "He knows you'd take care of Anne, he knows how you feel about her even if you two are still dancing around the subject."

"I know that he knows Mackenzie, though I'm not sure if he approves even if I'm his friend. He seems to think that I couldn't protect myself from a fly though, so I doubt he really trusts me to protect his sister."

"I think being his friend makes it less likely that he'll approve of you going after his sister. And, considering your first week in town you managed to get yourself knocked out by the town drunk it's no wonder he doesn't think you can protect much." Mackenzie gave Blaise a teasing grin as he was handed his cup of tea, holding it between his hands for the warmth as Blaise gave him a look of mock anger.

"I still say Barry had an unfair advantage that night. I don't normally drink whiskey and it had gone to my head a little fast." They both heard the argument grow louder out in the living room again, and went silent to listen for a second as Blaise's name was mentioned again.

"The guy's unconscious for Christ's sake, Leo. Maybe we should wait until he wakes up before we decide he's some kind of serial killer. Even if he had woken up, Blaise would have dealt with him just fine. I knew it was a mistake to call you in." Anne's voice was still clear and crisp though it had dropped to a quieter tone in her anger, though where she had gone quieter Leo had gotten louder.

"Blaise wouldn't have been able to do jack shit if that man had woken up and come at either of you!" Mackenzie gave the doctor another apologetic look as Blaise just shook his head, taking a long sip of his tea despite it still being a bit too hot for comfort. "That's it, we're taking him down to the station right now."

"What! You can't be serious, he can't be moved like this. Blaise!" The two men in the kitchen got resigned looks on their faces at this turn, and Blaise moved away from the counter after taking another short sip.

"You're coming with me, Deputy. Don't think you're getting out of that."

"Wasn't planning on it. I'm assuming Anne's right that it wouldn't be good to move him right now," Mackenzie said, shifting to follow Blaise back out of the kitchen. Blaise just shook his head in answer, giving Anne and Leo a smile as he turned the corner to find them both shooting daggers in his direction. "Tell him he can't take the man in his condition, Blaise."

"Blaise, if you say he's stable then I want him out of this house now." The two of them had spoken at the same time, and Blaise slowed to wait for his back up. Mackenzie stepped around him, moving to put himself between Leo and Anne as a physical wall to separate the two furies.

"I'm sure Blaise can give him a once over to see if he's stable enough to move. If not, we'll just hang out here until he is. With the storm things will be quiet in town, and I'm sure Sheila will call us on the radios if they need anything," Mackenzie said with a reasonable tone, handing his untouched tea to Leo who seemed caught off guard by the suddenly offered cup but took it anyway.

"I'll take a look, though with the hypothermia we can't risk his body temperature dropping again. Let me see where he's at, and then we can make a decision from there. Anne, why don't you go get a couple more cups of tea ready? One for Mackenzie and yourself while I examine him." Mackenzie nodded with a wide smile, patting Leo's shoulder before turning to Anne. The tension was slipping away now that there was something they had to wait for, though Leo still looked a bit intense.

"Come on, Anne. I'll help you out, I think I want a bit of coffee instead of tea so we can get the pot going," Mackenzie said, getting Anne started towards the kitchen with a touch to her shoulder. Mackenzie gave Blaise a bit of a 'good luck' look as he passed, and Blaise turned to the couch to take a look at his patient. Leo paced for a couple of turns before taking a seat and watching as Blaise went about going over their unknown's condition again. They could hear the quiet noises of Anne and Mackenzie in the kitchen carry over as they sat in silence for a few minutes.

"I'm sorry, Blaise..." When Blaise looked behind him Leo was sitting in the chair, staring down into his cup of tea with interest and a hint of guilt. Blaise turned back to his work, shaking his head in response.

"No need to be sorry, Leo. She's your sister, and you're just worried about her. I should have called you even if I thought it was just a sprain like she said." He heard Leo shift uncomfortably in the chair behind him, waiting for the sheriff to get his words in order to speak his mind.

"That's not what I'm sorry about...though I shouldn't have gotten mad at you about that either. I'm sorry because....well, I know you would take care of her if something would have happened. I don't always say things the way I should, but I hope you realize that I know you'd keep her safe. Mackenzie's right, you do have a mean right hook when you get a chance to use it." There was a tentative hint of humor in Leo's voice, a hopeful sound that Blaise would take the bait to show he wasn't mad.

"Well, considering I'm sober tonight I'd like to think that I wouldn't be completely useless in a fist fight. Though you do still have the gun, so I guess I shouldn't tell you that I think Anne was real close to kissing me earlier," Blaise said, keeping his voice even though he was grinning as he checked under the man's bandage to make sure it hadn't started bleeding anymore.

"You may want to be careful, I don't appreciate people pining after my sister. Though, I'd only have to shoot you if she'd actually kissed you," Leo said with a light laugh, the last of the tension leaving the room as he relaxed. Blaise pressed the bandage carefully back into place with a light chuckle of his own, pulling the blankets back up into place. "He all right to move?"

"He still seems a bit cold, we may have to wait a while. His heartbeat seems strong though," Blaise leaned over the man, pressing his fingers to the side of his neck as he checked his pulse. He looked up with a frown as an eerie cry rose up from the side of the house, one of the dogs giving a mournful howl outside the door. It was followed by another, the dogs raising their voices together for a few seconds before fading back out.

"That's odd, Anne's dogs don't usually howl," Leo said, staring at the side door near the kitchen that led out into the dog run. The dogs had been out when they'd gotten there, enjoying the snow the way only huskies seemed able to, appearing impervious to the cold. Blaise was about to answer in agreement as he looked back down at the man, startling as he saw the dark black-blue eyes looking back up at him. He pulled back, but the man moved surprisingly fast and in one swift movement he had thrown the blankets off with one hand while the other closed around Blaise's throat. Blaise tried to break loose, giving the man a kick which the other took advantage of and knocked him off balance and flat on his back, leaving Blaise pinned to the floor by the hand pressing down on his windpipe. The knee buried into the pit of his stomach stopped his next kick just short, and Blaise was left struggling to get some hold on the man's hand to force it loose.

The cup shattered just above his head as Leo dropped it in favor of drawing his gun, the second of stunned immobility passing from him as he stood swiftly. The sound drew Mackenzie and Anne back out of the kitchen, though Anne was quickly pushed back in by Mackenzie before he drew his own gun a bit hesitantly.

"Let him go and back away now," Leo demanding, the harsh tone in his voice straining to stay low causing it to come out in a growl. The man didn't waver though, looking down at Blaise as the doctor struggled under him. Blaise gave up on prying the man's hand off of him, and reached up to try and get enough force to push some of his weight back. His lungs were starting to burn though, and his vision was starting to spot in front of him. "Let him go now, or I'll shoot." Leo cocked his gun taking a step forward to attempt getting close enough to get hold of the man. Mackenzie was coming in on the side, reading his partner's intentions without taking his eyes off the two struggling on the floor. Leo was about to move, not willing to wait any longer to get Blaise free, when the man's hold suddenly loosened and he looked up at the two cops.

The blank stare on the man's face changed to one of confusion and then fear as he looked between Mackenzie and Leo, though he was suddenly upended as Blaise managed to get some purchase with the loosened hold and shoved him off of him. Blaise rolled onto his side, coughing and trying to gulp in large breaths of air. Leo leaned down next to him, keeping his eyes and gun trained on the stranger as he took Blaise's arm, pulling him back away from the other. Mackenzie moved forward, hand moving to take the cuffs off of his belt as he did.

"Where am I?" The man's tone was harsh and quiet as he spoke, the words sounding strained as though he hadn't spoken in a long time. He didn't struggle as Mackenzie pulled him to his feet, cuffing his hands behind his back before unceremoniously dumping him back onto the couch. Anne stood in the doorway of the kitchen with wide shocked eyes, not moving until she got a nod from her brother that it was okay. When she got this she moved quickly to Blaise's side, her hand rubbing his back as he put his head between his knees to try and get control over his breathing. "Where am I?" Mackenzie shook his head when the man asked again, moving to sit down on the footstool to face him. The man was eyeing Leo's gun warily, and Mackenzie gave Leo a stern glance.

"I think you can put your gun down now." Leo seemed to hesitate on this, his jaw working as it tensed. He was struggling between what he wanted to do, and what he knew he should do with his anger. "Leo..." Mackenzie sounded calm, and he lightly kicked one of the discarded blankets back from his foot to join the pile that was at the stranger's feet. Leo's gun lowered, the sheriff's shoulders easing back as he put it away into its holster.

"You okay, Blaise?" Leo turned his back on the man, working on calming himself until he was ready to bother asking some questions. Blaise nodded, leaning back against Anne as his body started to relax and stop complaining as oxygen returned. Leo nodded softly, running both hands through his hair to smooth it though only managing to gain the opposite effect. "Anne, why don't you go get Blaise some water? We'll need to clean up the broken glass as well before someone gets hurt on it." Leo rested a hand on his sister's shoulder for a moment before offering Blaise a hand to get up.

Mackenzie kept his focus on their visitor, giving him a tense grin that didn't seem to comfort the man any. He was looking around at his surroundings with a nervous air until he appeared to realize for the first time that he was naked, and he shrunk back into the couch. He tried to find a safe spot to stare, but there weren't many with the others around him. He accidentally caught Blaise's gaze as the man stood up, and shifted with sudden guilt.

"I'm sorry...I didn't....I don't know where I am or what's going on. I didn't mean to hurt anyone."

"Hey, you don't need to be talking to him. You talk to me or my partner, no one else," Leo spoke strictly, making the man turn to look at him with his tone of voice. Mackenzie leaned forward, elbows resting on his knees as he studied the man. He didn't seem hypothermic, and the injury across his chest didn't seem to even register to him though Mackenzie could tell that it was bleeding a little again. Leo paced across the room a few times; a habit that had driven Mackenzie insane when they'd first started to work together.

"You don't know where you are now, but where do you come from? Where's home?" Mackenzie would ask the questions for now, starting simple until Leo would take over if they didn't get the answers they needed.

"I don't know...I don't remember. I can't remember anything..." His eyes fell to the floor as he tried to search for some hint or clue, any memory that he could stir up. He remembered basic things, names of items and things that seemed to pertain more to knowledge, but there were no memories of him or his life mixed in amongst it all. "Why can't I remember any of it? What's happened to me?" The question came out in an accusatory tone as he panicked, looking between the four strangers that were staring at him.

Mackenzie looked over at Blaise for a second where the man had taken a seat in the empty chair, asking the man a question with his eyes. The emotion seemed genuine enough from the man, but it could have just as easily been some ploy to avoid their questions. They didn't know what exactly had happened to him, and as such they couldn't say that he was lying flat out. Blaise shrugged slightly in answer, unsure himself at this point whether the man was acting or not. The stranger scanned between them, searching for some hint as to what was going on and finally settled his eyes on Blaise. Despite, or perhaps due to, the fact that the two of them had their clash before he felt most comfortable focusing and addressing the doctor instead of the two officers. It may have been Leo's looming presence staring down at him with a cold hostility, though even Mackenzie's curious and calculated look made him feel uneasy. Blaise stared back in a cool manner, but it was calming and controlled.

"Please, it's like its all been taken from me or that there wasn't even anything there to begin with. I just want to know what happened to me." Anne finally reappeared from the kitchen having taken the time and care to calm herself down and erase any signs of her distress. She didn't want the others knowing she had shed tears while getting a glass of water for Blaise, and she emerged now looking pulled together and relaxed. She had the glass in one hand and the broom with a roll of paper towels dropped around the handle in her other. She'd been listening from the kitchen to what had been going on out here, though seeing the man brought a fresh wave of fear and anger. She pushed it down as she leaned to hand Blaise his glass with a small, private smile. Leo finally stopped pacing, standing near his sister as she bent to clean up the tea and sweep the broken mug away. His own feelings were more obvious then his sister's, he could hide his thoughts as well as Anne, but at the moment he didn't feel like doing so. He wanted it made very clear that he didn't think the man should be looking to Blaise for understanding right then.

Blaise took a sip of the water, taking the few seconds that it gave him to think over things. He cleared his throat in an attempt to make his voice come out strong the first time even though his vocal chords felt bruised. "Your name? Can you remember your name, at least? With that, we should be able to figure out a lot for you and maybe you'll start to remember once we dig some things up." Despite his efforts his voice still broke in places, his throat strained and causing a bothering tickle to rise in an attempt to make him cough. He took another quick drink of his water, giving the man some time to think over his options. It may lead to nothing, but it couldn't hurt either. If the man remembered his name, and told them his real name, it may help them out. If they got a fake name it would at least be something to help them pick apart the man's act, though it seemed real enough to Blaise. He knew it could happen, but people rarely lost their memories. The knowledge of basic functions or the ability to make new memories, yes, but to lose memories was something different. They were all staring at the man as they waited, even Anne had stopped what she was doing to see if they'd get anything from him. A look of uncertain relief had come to the man's face, and he looked up to meet Mackenzie's eyes for just a second before looking back at Blaise with a small smile.

"Gabriel, my name is Gabriel."

Chapter 2 - Calm before the Storm -

Leo stifled a yawn as he sat behind his desk, working on some papers that he'd been putting off the last week or so. The winter was slow for them, but even with the boredom of just sitting he found it worse to be working on signing and filling out the documents. His lips quirked upward when he saw his salvation arrive in the form of a styrofoam cup set down in front of him.

"That bad, huh?" Mackenzie asked as he sat down across from Leo, a cup of his own in hand as well as a pastry from the local cafe. Leo lifted an eyebrow, taking his cup to pull in a long sip of the spiced latte his partner had brought him. Mackenzie set his pastry bag on the desk to eat off of, managing to sprinkle crumbs over some of the papers.

"You're a little late today. Is it really that hard to get over here on time for work? And, don't tell me it was because you had to go out of your way for the coffee. You live above the cafe, I haven't forgotten that fact," Leo said after he was satisfied. He tried to brush the bits of pastry off of his papers before straightening them and setting them aside.

"Gabriel was there. I stayed to chat a bit, I figured you wouldn't have room to complain about that." Mackenzie talked around the piece of coffee cake he popped into his mouth, leaning back in his chair. Gabriel had been working at the cafe for the last month, and Mackenzie had been making a point of talking with the man each time they ran into each other there. He was at the point that he no longer doubted Gabriel's story about not remembering his past, but he knew Leo was far from accepting it. He'd probably still have Gabriel locked up in one of their few cells if he'd been able to find cause, but with Blaise refusing to press charges for the assault he'd only been capable of a week of lock down and even that had been pushing it.

"I'm assuming it's the same story as usual." Leo didn't really have to guess on the fact that Gabriel probably still said there was nothing new in his memory bank. Mackenzie would have told him first thing if there had been, and it still caused the same twist of frustration on Leo's part. He had tried everything he could think of to find some hint of who the man was, but nothing had shown up on any of the databases or questioning emails he had sent out. So far, no one knew anything about a man fitting Gabriel's description. Even Leo was starting to feel that there might be nothing to find.

"Still blank, though he does make a damn good vanilla latte. He did also say that Blaise's cooking was terrible, so we now have a fourth person who can keep that man out of a kitchen." Leo's brow furrowed, though there was a small glimmer of amusement in his eyes at the comment. Blaise's cooking had always been something to write home about, mainly to give warning never to eat it.

"I still don't know why Blaise is letting that guy stay in his spare room." Leo took another draw from his cup before letting it rest between his palms to warm his hands a bit. Blaise was never one to hold a grudge, but Leo had thought the last thing he'd do was invite Gabriel to stay at his place. It had become a bit of an issue between the group of friends, and it was at the point where Leo barely got a hello from Blaise if they passed on the street. He knew he was partially to blame since he couldn't keep his mouth shut about his thoughts on the matter, and had insulted Blaise more times then he liked when he got heated about it. It was wearing on his patience though, and seeing how Anne was reacting to the sudden distance between their group only made it worse. Mackenzie was the only one that Blaise would really talk to at the moment, and it was through him that Anne and Leo got their information. "You hear anything from Blaise?"

Mackenzie's look answered the question before he shook his head. "I think he's gotten the hint that I've been relaying to you. He's been a bit quiet the last few days, even when we met up for a beer the other night. He doesn't look good though, something's eating at him. I asked, but he just said he hadn't been sleeping well. I managed to pry out of him that he's been having those disturbing dreams again the last week or so, but he still won't elaborate on them. I'm getting a little worried about him." Mackenzie crumbled up the pastry bag as he took his last bite, taking aim and tossing the wad of paper at the trash bin. He gave a triumphant smile when it landed in the bin with nothing but net.

"Maybe I should have Anne give him a call. I know things are a bit rocky there since she has the same foot in mouth syndrome that I have, but she may be able to get a better feel of what's going on. I think it would do her some good to get in touch with Blaise anyway, she's been moping about like a teenage girl who's been dumped right before prom." He shifted to pick up the phone, dialing his sister's number with hopes that she'd be home. It was her day off from the diner, but she might have taken the chance to go running with the sled. He wasn't sure she'd listen to his suggestion, but even with the slight rift between them all she was still the best one to talk to Blaise. It helped that Blaise had been carrying a torch for his sister since the day they'd met. It made him soft where Anne was concerned, and Leo had no doubts that Anne shared those same feelings for the doctor. Despite their best efforts, Leo knew the two of them had something going on though they wouldn't admit it and he hoped that the current trouble between them wasn't ruining things.

It took until the fourth ring when Leo was just about to admit his sister wasn't at home when he heard her pick up the phone sounding a bit breathless. She'd been out with the dogs earlier, but had been working on getting them settled and put back in their large run when the phone had started to ring. They talked for a bit about the dogs, the small talk to catch up with their days before Leo broached the subject with a touch of care.

"I was thinking you should give Blaise a call today, see if he wants to meet for lunch or something." He tried to toss it casually in amongst a pause in their conversation, but the drawn out silence after the comment spoke volumes to him. "Anne, I know things are a bit strained right now. But could you call him, and try not to start an argument with him right off the bat this time? I'd do it, but you know how I am and Blaise isn't as willing to forgive me for voicing my opinion as he is for you."

"I don't know Leo. I want to, but at the same time we fought pretty bad last time we talked a couple of weeks ago. I just...don't like it, and I don't want to deal with another argument today if it gets brought up." There was a hint of defeat in Anne's voice, and it made Leo feel a tug of anger towards Blaise for causing it. It made him feel like they could leave Blaise to deal with things on his own even if he ended up getting strangled in the middle of the night by his 'house guest'. He pushed it down though knowing that the ill-wishing would be regretted a moment later, and even more so if something did end up happening to his friend.

"Mac's worried about him Anne, but Blaise won't talk to him about it. You're the only one that can pry him open when he gets like this. You know I feel the same way as you do about this whole thing and I'm even worse about keeping my mouth shut, but do you think you could try just for a short time to not argue even if it gets brought up? Try to get him to talk, make sure he doesn't need help." He heard Anne's sigh over the phone laced with frustration and concern. Mackenzie was sitting and listening idly to Leo's half of the conversation, rolling his cup between his hands.

"All right. I'll give him a call and see if he'll meet me for lunch this afternoon."

"Thank you, Anne. I'll come by for dinner tonight? I'll bring some whisky."

"Okay, but only because you're bringing whisky," Anne responded, making Leo smile before he hung up. He hoped he wouldn't be called for a domestic later that day if Anne couldn't manage to keep an opinion to herself for the afternoon.

Anne had hung up with Leo, her fingers hesitating to dial Blaise's number. Part of her was excited, eager even, to have the chance to talk with him, but there was a part of her that was still angry and frustrated towards the man. She wasn't as bad as Leo when it came to saying hurtful things, but she had done it the last time they'd talked. She hadn't really meant it when she told him that no one would want a fool like him and that if he wound up dead she wouldn't care, but she had said it in the middle of their argument. She'd managed to hit two points with it, both in telling Blaise that she basically didn't want him but more so in calling him a fool. Blaise didn't take offense to much, but being called a fool was one of them due to his father. Blaise and Anne didn't fight very often, but that didn't mean they didn't know what spots to hit. She had the heated sharp jabs that hurt; Blaise had his calm and cold words. She sat with her elbows resting on her knees, the phone dangling between her legs as she fought back her nerves.

Yakone gave her a nudge, pulling her back and she gave the dog a smile as she lifted a hand to scratch behind his ears. She'd stepped back into their run while talking with Leo, and her dogs were around her happily lying in the fresh hay now as she hesitated.

"I suppose I should call him, huh boy? Leo will be mad if I don't, and I have a few things to apologize for that I can't keep on avoiding," she said to

Yakone who seemed more interested in sniffing at the ear of Subine as the other dog came to sit near them. Anne gave the two dogs each another pat before dialing Blaise's number. As she heard the rings come back at her over the line she hoped that it would be his voicemail to pick up. When she heard the click on the other end, and Blaise's voice giving a questioning 'hello' she knew she didn't have such luck. "Hey Blaise."

"Hello Anne. How are you doing?" There was a tentative note in his voice, though no anger that she could detect. Blaise didn't hold things against people, but he obviously didn't just forget about them either as he was now waiting to see what Anne planned on saying. Still, just hearing his voice made her smile, glad to know he would talk to her at least.

"I'm doing all right. Just finished taking a run, and thought maybe I'd see if you want to meet for lunch?" Despite her concerns and apprehension that had built up before she'd dialed the phone, she was hoping that he would agree to meet with her. There was always the chance that he was busy, or had to go into work soon and wouldn't be able to meet up with her even if he wanted to. There was also the chance that he wouldn't want to meet her in the first place though.

"Sure. I have to head into town in a few hours anyway to pick Gabriel up from work, we can meet early before he gets off," Blaise said, voice casual though Anne knew well enough that he was waiting to see if she'd get upset over the mention of the man who'd come between them lately. Anne didn't jump though, deciding that it was enough to be happy to see Blaise and ignoring the drop of Gabriel's name.

"That sounds great. How about around one-thirty? That will give me time to clean myself up a bit. No need to come into town smelling like wet dog." She could hear Blaise relax over the phone, the subtle change in the tone of his voice like he'd just been made lighter by some invisible force. They agreed where to meet for their meal, and then once they'd hung up Anne leaned to give Yakone a big hug before dashing off to get in the shower.

They met outside the small deli, having chosen to forgo the diner since Anne spent enough time there for work. It also gave them a touch more privacy, though there wasn't really any of that in their small town. People tended to know what everyone else was doing at any given moment in Edenspoint. Blaise got there first, freshly shaved in an attempt to look less bedraggled then he felt. He hoped it was enough to cover up the fact he'd been losing sleep the last week or so, but Anne was a tougher audience than the other doctors and nurses at work.

The smile slid naturally to his lips when Anne pulled up, a bit late as usual as she parked her jeep next to his truck and climbed out. She hardly looked like she'd spent the morning out in the cold on the back of a sled, dark hair shiny and full bodied as it curled in small waves around her shoulders. She was wearing the leather bomber style jacket that had once belonged to her mother with some worn jeans and a scarf thrown haphazardly around her shoulders.

"Sorry I'm late. I never seem to time it right to get out of the door on time," she said as she pulled him into a hug, and they squeezed each other tightly for a few moments before reluctantly letting go. "Leo called after we talked and told me to tell you hi." That part was a lie, but not a complete one in Anne's mind since Leo had told her to ask Blaise to lunch in the first place.

"You'll have to tell him hello back for me," Blaise said, still smiling though Anne caught the double meaning. Blaise was willing to trust she might make it through a lunch without causing an issue, but Leo was another story. Her brother had a hard time not speaking his mind if something got brought up, and it was hard to talk around a roommate that had been the cause of several problems in Leo's mind. They turned to head into the diner, fingers brushing though neither of them worked up enough nerve to take the other's hand in theirs. Mackenzie had told them both that they acted like teenagers dancing around the subject of their first relationship several times before when he caught them sharing a moment.

They took turns ordering at the counter though Blaise managed to pay for them both before Anne realized he was doing it. She protested more for the show then anything else, she'd learned long before that Blaise wouldn't budge. Once they'd gotten their food they settled down in a booth beside the window, sitting opposite each other as they fell quiet. Both of them knew that getting to this point meant they'd start talking less about the weather and more about the personal matters going on in their lives. Usually Anne would start by asking about things Blaise had told her last time, but it'd been long enough since they'd talked she didn't know where to begin. They sat at a loss for a few moments like strangers unsure how to start the blind date they'd awkwardly been set up on.

"How have things been? It's been a while since we've really sat down and talked," Anne said, deciding they couldn't sit around in silence the rest of their meal.

"It has been a while. Things have been all right. Work's the normal for this time of year, a lot of colds and flus and then the usual bumps and bruises from people slipping on ice and things. A snowboarder from one of the resorts got sent down to us last week because he'd taken a bad tumble into a tree, but luckily it was just a case of a few cracked ribs. It's been quiet. How have things with you been? The dogs doing good?" Blaise was very skillfully stepping around anything personal in his answer, and that only managed to make Anne worry. Looking at him now as she took a bite of her turkey on dark rye she could see the telltale signs of wear on him, things most people wouldn't notice or would attribute to his work. There were circles starting to form under his eyes which were usually clear and alert, but seemed a bit dull and unfocused now. Blaise still had his probing gaze that made you want to just spill everything to him, but it only seemed halfhearted at the moment as he worked extra hard to guard his own secrets and weaknesses that he usually could hide with no effort. On top of it all, he had picked up his own sandwich a couple of times only to set it back down still intact, not seeming to have any appetite.

20

"They're doing real good. They always perk up this time of year with the weather, and I've been taking them on at least two runs a week. You should come out with us some time, take a break and just enjoy the speed and freedom of it. You look like you could use a little time away..." Blaise's focus on her seemed to get a bit steely for a moment, but then she watched him relax back into his seat as the exhaustion and trouble came seeping through. She'd been afraid he was going to close up completely for a moment, an uncommon shock to her when she'd seen those seconds where the walls were going up instead of down at her acknowledgement that she knew things weren't exactly good with him. "What is it, Blaise?"

"I don't really know, a number of things I think. I'm tired of feeling a bit like I'm the outcast of our group to start with, but I can't change your minds and I know that. I've gotten a little irritated with your brother sending Mackenzie to play telephone too." Though part of her felt a bit of anger rise in her throat like bile, she pushed it down. Blaise wasn't laying blame despite how the words sounded. He seemed more regretful that it was like this rather than feeling upset at them for how they'd been acting. "I get that you guys don't understand why I'm giving him a chance. If it was one of you I'd probably be feeling confused and upset myself that you'd invite that sort of potential trouble into your home. Hell, I was fairly upset at you for bringing him to your house when you found him instead of leaving him and calling one of us to come get him. If you'd been alone when he'd woken up, who's to say you wouldn't have been the one he dropkicked to the floor?"

"If you understand why we think it's such a bad idea Blaise, then why are you still letting him stay with you? That's what I don't get is why it seems so important to you to be helping him out so much. You've said that it's the right thing to do and that you trust that he's telling the truth, but you've never said why it has to be you that risks all the unknowns that he comes with." Anne tried to keep herself pulled back, not wanting this to turn into an argument when they were finally managing to discuss the situation head on.

"Because, who else is going to do it Anne? Leo would have just kept him locked up if he could, and like hell any of us were going to let him stay out at your place. Mackenzie has offered a couple of times to have him take up his couch, but there's not really enough room for two people in Mac's apartment. We have a lot of great people in this town, but most of them aren't going to take in a stranger who's first appearance was being taken in with handcuffs by the sheriff. Besides, I sort of know how he feels being the new guy in town. I had that honor before him, and it's hard to fit in when no one wants you to."

"Blaise, you can hardly compare him to you when you first got here. First off, you were the new doctor in town, not the new amnesiac who was found naked in the woods." She managed to get a brief smile out of him, but he shook his head lightly at her.

"My first week here I got taken out of the bar in cuffs by your brother, people see that as being about the same even if I only fought back in self defense. It was one of their own that I was fighting, so in the eyes of everyone else I was the one to blame for that. If it wasn't for Leo and Mackenzie befriending me, followed by you, I probably still wouldn't be fully accepted here," Blaise spoke plainly of thoughts that had been shared before. Things had been different when he'd first moved to Edenspoint; the biggest difference was Leo's attitude. It was before he'd lost his wife and Leo hadn't lost his general trust in the world, it was different now.

"I think everyone knew that your fight with Barry was self defense. You were both drunk, but he's the one that threw the first punch that night," Anne said with a small smile, watching Blaise finally take a bite of his sandwich. He chewed slowly for a few moments, waiting until his mouth wasn't full to respond even though Anne talked around her food when she spoke.

"How would you feel in that situation, Anne? You wake up surrounded by people you don't know, in a place you don't know and with nothing on but a pile of blankets. Add in the fact that when he went unconscious his last thoughts, whether he remembers them or not, were of a fight or flight instinct and I was reaching down to put my hand on his neck you can't blame him for reacting in a defensive manner," Blaise said calmly, though there was a touch of caution in the way he spoke. Anne wanted to say that she definitely wouldn't react by attacking the person standing closest to her, but she knew better than that. If it had been her waking up in that sort of situation she would have fought her way out, and then ran as soon as she had an opening.

"I probably would have fought, but that doesn't change everything Blaise. It was eerie to me...how calm he seemed during it all. And, from what Leo says, the way he took you down was with skill. It wasn't luck and you being unprepared, Leo said he probably would have even gotten him down if he'd been in your place. It worries me that he remembered how to do that, but not anything else other than the name he gave us," Anne said, keeping her own tone of voice carefully controlled and even. She didn't want the tension that had settled in Blaise's shoulders to creep any further down his back, and she knew neither of them wanted this to be another argument.

"Well, I'm glad that even the mighty Leo will admit that he'd have ended up on his ass," Blaise said, though there was a gentle humor in his voice that made it clear he was teasing. "The thing is Anne, you can forget who you are or end up losing the ability to form new memories but still remember skills. Skills are formed through different means than memories are, and they can remain intact while your memories can be damaged. I think with Gabriel that his memory loss is more psychological than an issue rising from injuries. Despite what movies would have you believe, when someone loses their memory due to a stroke or other ailment it's usually either their learned skills or the ability to form new memories that take the hit. Since Gabriel doesn't remember his past at all, I have a feeling it's linked to him suppressing something that's caused psychological damage." Anne's lips pressed into a thin line at this, not feeling much relief at the explanation.

"Doesn't that make you worry more? That whatever happened to cause that will find him?" Anne spoke quietly enough that it was hard for Blaise to hear her even in the near empty silence of the deli. Blaise managed to work out what she had said though over the soft sound of Susan, the deli's owner, humming to herself in the back room.

"It's a concern, but it also gives me more reason to help him. If whatever happened to him was bad enough for him to have that sort of break, then I can't reasonably push him out into the world with no way of protecting himself or knowing if he's even in danger. It's been a month and a half, whoever left him there has either moved on thinking he's dead or feels that they can't give another try at him a go with him living and working in town now. That doesn't mean that if he was on his own they wouldn't try to kill him again. It'd be on my hands if I made him leave and something happened because of that."

"What if something happens to you because of him though?" Anne was having a hard time biting back the twinge of anger that had settled in her chest; trying to push the worry and fear she was feeling back. It was easier for her to deal with anger than fear, but she didn't want to push Blaise away with the unease.

"That's a risk I have to accept to help keep him safe. I know you don't think its worth that risk Anne, and at first I wasn't really sure either and did it more out of guilt than anything else. He's not a bad guy though, who he is now at least since I can't speak for before. If you gave him a shot you might realize that, and I would appreciate it if you did try to get along with him and get to know him." Anne narrowed her eyes at Blaise, though a smile tugged at the corners of her mouth that she hid by taking a drink from her straw.

"That's a low blow, asking me to do it for you. That will work on me, though Leo's going to take more work than that if you try to get him to ease off. For you, I will try to give the guy a chance now that I know better where you're coming from and since you asked nicely. The moment he so much as steps out of line though…"

"Please, I can't even get the guy to drink. I doubt he's going to be in bar brawls anytime soon. I'm starting to fear that he's some sort of prohibitionist."

"If that turns out to be true then I'm afraid all bets are off. You can't trust a man who doesn't drink, Blaise. I mean, come on, even priests drink," Anne said with a grin. Blaise seemed more relaxed now as he finally dug into his sandwich with some heart, just in time for Anne to have finished hers. There was still the tiredness around the edges, but he seemed lighter than before now that they'd settled the issue between them at least to an extent. Anne wasn't thrilled to get to know Gabriel and still couldn't say she trusted him further than she could throw him, but she at least understood where Blaise was coming from and was willing to give it a shot. She felt more relaxed herself having that conversation over, but she knew there was still more they needed to get out from between the two of them. She relished the comfortable silence between them for a few moments before she broke it again. "I'm sorry for what I said last time we talked. I didn't mean it, and I shouldn't have said it."

"I think we both said things we didn't mean, Anne. I should apologize too," Blaise said to her, shaking his head to cut her off from continuing her apology. Anne sighed, worrying a nail slightly until Blaise took her hand in his and pulled it away from her lips. "Don't worry over it, Anne. I know you didn't mean it, and I didn't mean any of the things I said either."

"The things you said were true though, I was being cold-hearted. And, I do only know how to really relate to my dogs, I'm not that great when it comes to people. I think most of the town thinks I'm just as loony as they saw my grandfather being." Anne let her hand rest in Blaise's, his were a bit rough around the edges from the work he did outside the hospital though they had the long-fingered grace that helped him be such a good doctor. Normally they'd hesitate to make a public show of their affection, but just then they felt secluded with the streets empty due to the cold and Susan tucked in back as she worked on making bread and slicing meats and cheeses.

"Anne, you don't have a cold-hearted bone in your body and I can assure you that as a doctor that you're not loony," Blaise said with a teasing pull on her fingers that she returned as her nose wrinkled with amusement. Their hands separated out of habit as the bell above the door jingled, announcing the arrival of Paul, Susan's husband. Blaise let his hand slide to his cup naturally, lifting it to his lips to help brush off any suspicion of their lingering touch. They both knew that Paul and Susan realized there was something between them from the previous lunches they'd had at the deli together, and though the two hadn't ever spread the rumor about the town they still reacted with fluid secrecy when in view of them. Paul gave them a smile, stomping his feet on the mat to clear off the snow clinging to his boots as Susan came out to greet him. They were both in their late fifties, though managed to hardly look their ages most the time. The winters wore on Paul though, the cold making him stiff and sore as he limped in.

"It's colder then a witch's teat in a brass brazier out there," he complained, giving his wife a quick kiss as she moved to help him out of his coat and to take the bag he carried. "How are you two doing?"

"Well, how are you Paul? Joints aren't acting up too bad, are they?" Blaise said in response, probing at the man in a fatherly way even though Paul was more the age for the behavior.

"Oh, I'm fine. They aren't bothering me too bad, though I may stop by for some of that medicine you gave me last year in case that storm they're expecting blows in. It's still the worst when a front comes over from the peaks," Paul said, stretching now that he was free from the burden of his outerwear.

"That's fine, just stop by in the next couple of days and I'll get the prescription to you." Blaise gave the man a smile as he headed into the back with his wife, the sounds of their affectionate jibes over whether Paul had gotten the right kind of beans for the chili they'd have that night carrying over to the table. While Blaise finished up his sandwich they talked of more normal things again, falling back into the ease of conversation with the tension gone. Anne prodded at Blaise about the dreams the man had been

24

having, trying to get him to tell her about them but he refused and denied remembering what they'd been about. Blaise had always had strange dreams, many were disturbing though usually amusing at the same time. They didn't normally keep him awake other than a few times during the years they'd known each other. The last time he'd had trouble sleeping was back before Marie had died, and he wouldn't speak about them then either. She had learned a long time ago that pushing about the subject never helped, and she let it drop with ease for the time being.

She felt a twist of regret when they're lunch was over, and Blaise had to leave to collect Gabriel from the café. Blaise kept coming up with simple questions, half of which they'd already talked over earlier, to keep her there, but it became obvious after a few minutes that they weren't going to get a moment of pure solitude for him to slip her a kiss. Once they stepped outside they lingered over goodbyes before finally parting ways, Blaise turning to walk up the street to the café while Anne took the few steps to her car so she could head back home.

Gabriel had gotten off a few minutes early and had decided to sit out on the cafe's porch with a cup of coffee as he waited for Blaise to arrive. It was cool out, but it wasn't so chilly that it made sitting inside seem a better option for him. The family that ran the cafe were friendly enough to him and their daughter, Lisa, who worked with him the most seemed to have decided he'd be her confidant. The other people from town that came in were polite, but he still heard their whispers behind his back. There were the few that accepted him, though they were mostly the nurses or the few other doctors that came in for their coffee which meant it was Blaise's influence on them. In the end, he found it simpler to sit outside on the days he could after work where the townspeople could spread their gossip without him overhearing.

He stretched, letting his feet prop up on the chair across from him and wondering where Blaise was. It was now about ten minutes past his shift, and he had discovered that Blaise was one of those people who managed to always be right on time. He looked up the street, searching for some sign of the man's car heading down the road and rather hoping that he hadn't gotten called into the hospital unexpectedly. He usually would call the cafe if that happened, and set it up for Mackenzie to take him home though.

He took a long draw from his cup, the air cooling the coffee quickly to a drinkable temperature and his eyes landed on a man that was standing across the street. He paused, feeling a strange tug at the back of his mind though he didn't think he'd ever met the man before. He was being watched in return, and he couldn't quite ignore the warning bells that seemed to be going off in his head. The man smiled at him, however it seemed far from friendly and more like the man was baring his teeth as he lifted a hand to wave at Gabriel. The alarms seemed to get louder and Gabriel felt tense as he pulled his feet down to the ground, feeling the need to run for a reason his mind couldn't tell him.

"Hey Gabriel, sorry I'm late." The voice right next to him startled him, making Gabriel jump and sloshing his coffee onto his hand and jacket. "Shit, sorry. I didn't mean to startle you, I thought you saw me. I'll grab some napkins real fast." Blaise stepped into the door quickly, going to the small counter that held the straws and napkins. Gabriel looked up, searching across the street for some sign of the man but he was gone now. Part of Gabriel asked if he had even been there in the first place, and he sternly told that section of his brain to go to hell. He had wondered if he was crazy for the first month or so after waking up in the town, and had firmly decided that he wasn't though that didn't stop the doubt from coming through from time to time. Blaise returned, handing the stack of napkins to Gabriel while taking the cup of coffee to hold for him as he dried himself off. "It didn't burn you too bad."

"No, it had cooled off quite a bit," Gabriel said, answering even though he knew it wasn't a question. He knew Blaise had probably assessed whether Gabriel was badly burned before Gabriel had processed he'd spilt the drink on himself. Gabriel finished getting the lukewarm coffee wiped off, and when he looked up Blaise gave him one of his apologetic looks that always came off as a guilty wince. "I was distracted, wasn't your fault. I didn't even hear you pull up."

"I walked. I'm parked down by the deli, I met Anne for lunch down there. Everything all right? What had you distracted?" Blaise handed him his coffee back as Gabriel stood up, dabbing a little at the front of his coat still to try and catch a few drops that had escaped his notice.

"The guy across the street, I don't think I've seen him before but he waved at me. Did you know him?" Blaise nodded towards the cafe door, signaling that he wanted a cup before they would head down the street themselves. They stepped back in, Gabriel noticing the couple of women towards the back that fell silent when they walked through the door.

"I didn't notice him, so I can't say. Afternoon Mary, Shelly," Blaise said, smiling pleasantly though his eyes were conveying disapproval enough the two managed to look abashed. "Why? Did you recognize him?"

"No," Gabriel said with a shake of his head, "He waved at me, and that's uncommon for most people in town." Gabriel didn't want to make something out of nothing, after all the man hadn't been acting strange really. It had just unnerved him how it felt like he was being watched, he was sure that was all that had brought about the tension. Even now he could feel the muscles in his neck tense under the gaze of the two women in the corner, and he'd seen them almost every day staring at him for the last few weeks.

"The horror. The people are now being friendly, what terrible attack will they plan next?" Blaise said jokingly, patting Gabriel on the back before turning a smile at Lisa who was giving Gabriel a look over from behind the counter.

"You got a hole in your lip today, Gabriel," she said teasingly, laughing when Gabriel just shot her a look. "Maybe you should wear the apron all the time, even when you're not working."

26

"That would be an interesting fashion statement, though I don't think I could pull it off. Now why don't you serve the doctor," Gabriel said flatly through the hint of a smile in his eyes. He and Lisa got along well, but she liked to pass the time by ribbing him. By the end of his shift some days he was ready to be away and in silence, though never truly upset with her for it. She was one of the few people who treated him like he wasn't some monster come from the depths.

"Fine, grump. You want your regular, Doctor Fairholm?"

"Yes please, Lisa. Not having any trouble with your newest employee, are you? I've heard he's some ruffian that is sure to burn the town down around us," Blaise said, faking a serious and concerned expression though the slight twitch at the corner of his mouth ruined the effect. Gabriel sighed loudly at the two of them as Lisa proved she was most skilled with her fake terror, her eyes growing wide as she leaned in close to them over the counter as though she was afraid to be overheard.

"It is surely the most terrifying thing, having to work with that man. I'm afraid he'll just snap and start throwing the sugar and sweet'n'low around. I have to watch my every step with him," she said loudly, a slight southern accent that she'd inherited from her family slipping through in her exaggeration. Blaise put his hand comfortingly over hers, patting it gently.

"It will be all right, child. Just keep him away from any condiments or creamer, and you should be safe. It's the half and half that's the most dangerous with a man like him." The two women who had been gossiping in the back both got up, making disapproving noises at the joking going on at their expense. The two of them huddled out into the cold, no doubt going to spread news of the rudeness of their doctor and café workers. Lisa gave a laugh of delight, pulling back to make Blaise his latte with an overflowing air of amusement.

"Yeah, that will help with my popularity with the locals," Gabriel said with a shake of his head, though he smiled in appreciation. Blaise had done more than his fair share of sarcastic remarking and disapproving looks on Gabriel's behalf the last month or so, and though it didn't always make people accept him it often got them off of his case for a while. He had worried that it would make the townspeople treat Blaise differently, but he'd discovered that no one managed to stay mad at the doctor for long.

"Don't worry about it, Gabriel. You have to stand up to the busy bodies sometimes to get them to stop. Besides, it will be at least dinner time before everyone has heard about it."

"You should do as the doctor prescribes, Gabe. It would be better if you stood up for yourself then continuing to mope around in silence. They just want to know that you're human, after all. Shout a little or something, grow a pair," Lisa said over the sound of steaming milk.

"I doubt that it would make their hearts grow fonder if I followed Blaise's example. Besides, getting punched out by one of the locals hardly sounds more appealing than the gossip and stares," Gabriel said, raising his voice as well. He saw Blaise shake his head beside him, though the man waited until the milk was finished steaming before he spoke. Gabriel had found very little that could be used to jibe at Blaise, but the bar fight he heard about through Lisa always seemed to do the trick. That, and Anne, though he didn't bring her up since he felt it was far from his place. Lisa seemed to think differently about that though.

"One bar fight, and it seems to be the only thing that people ever bring up even after all this time."

"It's the only exciting thing you've ever done, other then seeing the sheriff's sister behind his back," Lisa said, waggling her eyebrows at Blaise suggestively. "I heard the two of you were making eyes at each other over at the deli just a short while ago. Better be careful, Leo might find out and shoot you."

"Who told you that? I remember meeting a friend at the deli for lunch, but I don't believe we were making eyes at each other," Blaise said, raising an eyebrow with a look that plainly said that the discussion was over in his opinion. Lisa feigned innocence, handing Blaise his cup.

"Oh, I don't remember. Just someone that thought they saw you and your friend holding hands over the table." Blaise didn't dignify that with an answer, taking a sip of his latte as he handed his card towards Lisa. Lisa shook her head, refusing the payment. "It's on the house today since you helped me scare off those two old betties. I was getting a bit tired of hearing how irresponsible my parents were for letting me work with someone like Gabriel." Blaise chuckled, slipping the card away and dropping several dollars into the tip jar instead.

"Fine, though I do ask that you don't go around spreading rumors about my love life," Blaise said as they turned to make their way towards the door.

"Oh, I won't. I don't want people finding out that your one true love is really me," Lisa called after them, making Blaise laugh into his cup as his next sip was interrupted.

"Yes, please do keep that a secret," Blaise said with a shake of his head while getting a horrified look on his face. "I wouldn't want to deal with your father if he heard something like that." Lisa grinned, crossing her heart in a promise to keep the 'secret' quiet. Gabriel gave her a final wave as they stepped outside and turned down the street. They walked along in silence for a few moments, Gabriel curious about Blaise's lunch with Anne though hesitant to bring it up.

"Did you have a good lunch then?" He kept it as an open question, letting Blaise bring up how things were with Anne if he decided to. Gabriel knew very well that he'd been making things rocky between the group of friends, and it bothered him that he was the cause of the problems. The guilt was worse when it came to Anne because he knew he was coming between something a bit more than friendship there, though he hoped that since Blaise was in a good mood that meant things had gone well.

"I did, it was nice. We got to talk over some things, and I think we're all right if that answers your whole question," Blaise said, and Gabriel was forced to wonder if he was really that easy to read. He had thought it was just

Blaise at first who was able to pick up on his thoughts and feelings so quickly, but Lisa had been doing it to him as well while they worked together. He was starting to think that he couldn't keep a single thing to himself since his face gave it away so simply. "I will warn you, she may try to talk to you sometime. I asked her if she'd give you a chance, and she agreed this time. I can't promise instant friendship between you two, but I think you two may manage to get along."

Blaise shifted to cut across the street to where his car was parked and trusted Gabriel to catch the change in direction. Gabriel followed behind him, glad for the moment that Blaise had his back to him. He couldn't say that he wasn't glad Anne was willing to ease off and give him a chance, but he didn't have as much faith in it as the other man seemed to. He wanted to trust in Blaise's judgement that it would be a sincere attempt, but he didn't want to put any faith in someone who'd already shown her dislike of him rather clearly. Part of him couldn't deny that he actually enjoyed the solitude that he had, enjoyed not having to make conversation and small talk with many people. Having less hostility would be nice, but having to handle more awkwardness and strained discussions was less appealing. He stopped besides the passenger side door of Blaise's truck waiting for it to be unlocked and both of them to get inside to answer.

"That's great." He even managed a smile.

Chapter 3 - Unsettled -

The next couple of weeks had passed by a bit slowly, though there was the appearance of Anne a couple of times. Today had been one of them as she'd met up with Blaise at the cafe to have some coffee while he waited for Gabriel to get off. It had been awkward, but it hadn't been horrible and Gabriel was able to distract himself with work when it got to be too much. Anne had ended up leaving a little before his quitting time, Gabriel watched her say a quiet goodbye to Blaise before she waved tentatively at him.

Afterwards Blaise hadn't said much about the meeting, and they'd gone home only to do more work. Gabriel found that he didn't mind the wood chopping that Blaise had him help with though. Since Blaise had a lot of trees with beetle kill in them through the woods on his property he'd started taking the logs felled by the logging crews to make into firewood.

He'd been selling the firewood for a reduced cost to the grocery store in town, and now was giving Gabriel a portion of the money for helping out. The two of them usually spent a few hours every evening in the fading light, and they worked even longer with the aid of the porch lights and some lanterns since they'd promised to bring a shipment in before the predicted storm at the end of that week. They worked with no conversation that night which gave Gabriel some time to think over things, and Blaise's inward expression showed that he was doing the same. There were several times once dark fell that Gabriel thought they were surely going to stop, but Blaise kept going so he followed suit.

Part of Gabriel wanted to be hopeful that Anne seemed to be giving him a chance to prove he wasn't the horrible person she thought. It might mean he would finally start being accepted as part of the town. That frightened him in a way as well though, afraid it meant that he really had lost his past completely at this point. He hadn't remembered anything about who he'd been other than his name, and it left him feeling untethered to the world. He never could say that he came from anywhere, he didn't know if he had family out there somewhere wondering about him. All he really had was his name, and that wasn't much in his opinion. He did have the things he had found here, his friendship with Blaise being the most withstanding. Gabriel felt almost brotherly affection towards the man, which was why it bothered him even deeper that his presence was causing a rift in Blaise's other friendships. He let the axe swing down, cutting the piece of wood cleanly in two at the thought of Leo's looks of loathing. It was a start...Anne could be a start. If he managed to prove to her he wasn't that bad, maybe she could then convince her brother. He hoped so, because Blaise seemed to be floundering slightly without the hold of the friends.

Gabriel realized then that with his last strike of the axe that it had fallen completely quiet over the woodpile, and he turned his attention to Blaise. The man had stopped, the axe resting on his shoulder as though he'd been about ready to swing at the stump of wood in front of him then decided to take a break. Blaise was staring off towards the trees, and Gabriel watched him for a moment feeling a bit disturbed by how still the man was. The entire world seemed still right then, no sounds rising from the forest around them, even the trees going quiet as though the earth had just stopped with Blaise.

"Blaise?" It took a moment for the doctor to turn towards him, and Gabriel managed to catch a moment of unguarded expression before Blaise gave him an owlish look that showed nothing of what he'd been thinking. What he saw in that moment troubled him, the unhidden fatigue and sadness mixed with something like fear. "You all right?"

"Yeah, sorry. I think I spaced out for a moment," Blaise said, shaking his head to look down at his watch. He winced slightly when he saw the time, giving Gabriel an apologetic smile that made Gabriel feel like was he apologizing for more than how late it was. "I didn't even realize the time, you didn't have to stay up with me. You could have left me chopping wood alone all night." Blaise lifted the axe off his shoulder and let if fall to split the piece of wood he'd had ready before wedging the blade of the axe into the chopping block.

"I was starting to wonder if it would be all night. We should both head to bed, I'm not leaving you out here to chop your foot off in a moment of forgetfulness," Gabriel said, his eyes flickering to the trees, trying to find if it was just his thoughts that had caused what Blaise was quickly trying to cover up for. Gabriel had caught Blaise in a few moments of unguarded thoughts and emotions, it would have been hard not to seen hints of it while they lived together, but he felt suddenly like he had intruded on a deeply private and concerning second. He wanted to push and ask what was really going on, what Blaise had been thinking about, but he kept the questions back. Blaise was very good at hiding things and evading questions, and if he didn't want to talk about it Gabriel couldn't push him into it even though he wanted to right then. Blaise laughed a little, taking Gabriel's axe from him to embed next to his before running his hands through his hair a few times, leaving strands sticking up in odd directions.

"You're probably right. We'll have to take the wood into town tomorrow anyway, and though it's my day off I'm on call in case they need me. The last thing I need is to get called in, and be too tired to do a simple stitch or exam." Blaise gave Gabriel a flash of a smile, though it didn't reach the man's eyes. He followed behind Blaise through the trail they had stamped out of the snow leading between the house and woodpile. Conversation lapsed again between them, though it didn't feel like the normal pause. Gabriel wanted to ask Blaise what was going on, and from the way Blaise stayed a few steps ahead of him it seemed the man knew that and wasn't going to allow him to. They did the normal routine of stomping the excess snow off their boats at the door, and then Blaise was heading towards the stairs. "I'm just going to head up. We'll want to get the wood over before noon tomorrow."

Gabriel nodded, watching Blaise pass through the kitchen on his way to the stairs. He sighed when the man was gone, hanging up his jacket in the mud room and kicking his shoes off before going right into his bedroom. He was tired, and it settled over him as he stripped off the work clothes until he was down to nothing. He felt most comfortable at these times, closed off in his room in only his skin. He'd started sleeping that way since he felt less constrained with just the feel of the blankets over him. His hand absently touched the rough leather of the cross necklace that he'd kept on, fingers moving to play with the cross for a moment as he pulled the covers back. He'd removed the cross once in his first few weeks in Edenspoint when he'd been upset and frustrated with his lack of a past. He'd thrown it across the living room, Blaise watching quietly as Gabriel's anger at himself and the world had gone through its courses. After it had faded, a sense of loss and panic had replaced it as he then tried to find where the cross had landed. Blaise helped him recover it from amongst the organized clutter of the living room, and Gabriel hadn't removed it again since then.

He debated taking a shower before climbing into bed, but decided he was too worn out to bother right then. He laid down, pulling the blankets over him neatly as he stared at the ceiling for a few moments before reaching over to turn off the light on the nightstand. He slid to sleep quickly, wondering how Blaise had stayed so patient with him through that first month when Gabriel had been at a loss on how to feel or act.

Blaise had tried to sleep, but it was only a couple of hours before the dreams had set in again. They left him lying in bed feeling cold and anxious, a gnawing worry in the back of his mind that he couldn't push down. He'd had times like this before, where his dreams felt real and tangible. Sometimes they were good dreams, like the times he'd dreamt back in his last few months in the city before moving to Edenspoint of the dark haired beauty that became real when he met Anne. There had been less pleasant times as well, like when he was only fifteen and he'd dreamt of his father with large exaggerated fists pummeling him down into the soil deeper with every hit, only to have his always verbally abusive father suddenly turn physical on him one day when Blaise had talked back. The dreams were always strange, a cluster of images that made no sense and always managed to leave him confused when they came out of nowhere. It'd been years since he'd had the last, the calm dreams of floating over a frozen sea with the woman who'd ran with the wolves.

He wished he could go back to dreaming of Anne running wild again, his current dreams were far less pleasant. They made less sense to him than any he'd had in the past, the images twisted and confused as they only made him feel fear and loss. He had started trying to avoid sleep despite knowing very well the results of sleep deprivation, but he'd managed it all right for the most part. The fatigue was getting to him though, that much was obvious since his friends were starting to question him. Still, when he'd woken again in a sweat feeling blood and hands on him he couldn't bring himself to just turn over and fall back into that hell.

He was sitting now in the kitchen, only the dim glow of the overhead light on the oven spilling in a small pool across the floor. He didn't want to

32

wake Gabriel who's room was just down the hall, so he'd been careful making the cup of tea that was cooling quickly between his hands as he sat at the kitchen island. He knew the best thing to do was to find the reason for the dreams, to try and decode it so that he could acknowledge whatever was being said to him and then get past it. Try as he might he couldn't find a single thread of thought that made sense, even now that the dream was lengthening with new events.

It always started the same, the door to Anne's dog run swinging open and a snarling, drooling creature stepping out with blood on its flanks. It was dog-like, wiry coarse hair over its body that was lupine in form but stretched and contorted. It's neck looked as though it'd been pulled and lengthened like taffy, the large head turning almost snake like upon it to look at him as the body followed. Legs long and disjointed, though no less elegant in their movements as it stalked. Suddenly as it stared into his eyes the world seemed to cut to black and white, and Blaise found himself out in the snow. His wrists were tied together as he was pressed against the trunk of a tree by some unseen force, the branches above turning to hands and gripping him tight against the bark while his friends were torn apart by some terrible force a small distance away. The man was the only thing that seemed almost normal in his dream each time he showed up, always standing just behind him as he managed to break free from the tree's hold. Blaise would hit the ground running, and the snow would rise up to envelope him and devour him all the while the man stood there watching with an almost adoring smile on his face.

The man was new in the dream, he'd only been making his appearance the last week and a half or so. Tonight Blaise had been startled awake by the voice, the only sound that had ever come through in the dreams. The words had seemed so close, as though they were being whispered in his ear and he'd awoken feeling like someone was in the room with him. He remembered the words, though they made little sense as well. 'Your eyes are mine, where is the key?'

"Blaise?" He jumped at the sound of his name, managing to spill the lukewarm tea over his hands and on the table. He hadn't even noticed the hall light switch on or Gabriel's door opening, and he cursed softly at himself as he got up to grab a paper towel. Gabriel seemed to hesitate at the end of the hall, not sure whether to come into the kitchen or not. Blaise noticed that hesitation was still a habit for Gabriel. He could hardly blame him though at the moment for not wanting to come into the kitchen with Blaise who had been sitting in the dark for no obvious reason.

"I didn't mean to wake you," Blaise said, drying his hands before moving to soak up the puddle on the counter with another paper towel. Gabriel stood still for a second longer just watching him with a concerned look before moving to help clean up the spill. Blaise was glad for the excuse not to make eye contact right away as he gathered his thoughts back into place after the unexpected interruption.

"You didn't. I just need a glass of water. Everything okay?" Gabriel tossed his wad of wet paper towel into the trash can once the counter was dry again. It was a lie, of course, he had noticed the light being switched on and the sounds of Blaise making tea. When it had gone quiet again he thought that Blaise must have gone back to bed, so he'd pulled on some sweats and a t-shirt to go turn the light above the oven back off. He shifted to the cabinet to get a glass for his water though, not wanting Blaise to feel bad for waking him.

"Yeah, just having trouble sleeping again. Was hoping some tea would relax me so that I could manage." Blaise discarded his own wet paper towels as Gabriel turned on the tap to fill up his glass. They switched places easily as Gabriel moved to give Blaise access to the sink then so that he could dump out what was left of his tea.

He could feel Gabriel's eyes on him, and he felt a twinge of unease at the dark gaze. Gabriel didn't make him feel nervous most the time, but every now and then he'd find Gabriel just staring. He'd watched him do it to other people as well, following them with his eyes as whatever thoughts were churning behind the black gaze turned and locked into place. Then the moment would be over, and whoever had been the target would be left feeling insecure and confused. There had been one morning that he'd watched Gabriel preform this on Mackenzie, who had tried to joke at first until his normal confidence seemed to diminish as the seconds wore on. It ended suddenly as Gabriel asked the deputy if Leo had sent him to check on the 'crazies', and the two of them had gone back to joking though Mackenzie seemed more tentative than before.

Blaise didn't like having that specific gaze fixed on him right then despite knowing that Gabriel was likely unaware that he had lapsed into staring. It made Blaise feel like the disturbing thoughts that had been plaguing him before Gabriel's appearance were all just riding around on his back in visible form, there for Gabriel to study and criticize. This feeling was only heightened as he heard Gabriel ask, "Was it the dreams again?"

Blaise set the cup down beside the sink, looking out the window for a moment as everything out there appeared flat and monochromatic. Gabriel didn't ask again, but he could still feel those eyes on him and Blaise got the point. Gabriel wasn't going to back down about it, wasn't going to let Blaise side step it as he'd been doing the last few days.

"Yeah, it is. They've gotten worse the last couple of nights," he said, turning to lean back against the counter. He at least wanted to face his interrogator if they were going to delve into this. Gabriel knew better than the others how much of an impact the dreams had on him, it was harder to hide it from someone who lived in the same house when you're woken by nightmares almost every night. Gabriel sat down on one of the stools as though preparing to be there for a while, and looked at him expectantly.

"Want to tell me about them? Maybe letting someone else know exactly what they are will help." Blaise felt conflicted as he both did and did not want to tell Gabriel about the dream. Having the burden of the images shared with someone seemed like it would be a relief, but Gabriel wouldn't understand the true reason they kept Blaise up so often. Blaise couldn't explain that he feared that it would come true, or that some interpretation of the dream would at least. He also felt almost protective about them, as though sharing them would be like giving them a life of their own.

Part of him wanted to keep just standing there, never saying anything. He knew that Gabriel would most likely give up, because he was always so careful not to overstep his boundaries. He was lucky it wasn't Leo sitting there, because Leo would have sat there for all eternity. Either that or he'd have already told Blaise to stop being a prick and just tell him already, that was a bit more Leo's style.

The silence dragged on in the kitchen, Blaise staring down at a spot on the floor with his face calm and passive, carefully kept unreadable. Gabriel didn't waver though, and Blaise mentally laughed as he told himself he deserved it. He'd sat there and made a lot of people, including Gabriel, cave in and tell him things with just a probing look and a single question. He was just getting some of his own treatment back, karma biting him in the ass. He sighed as he caved in, though his face was still a blank slate as he started to speak. Gabriel had started to wonder if he'd crossed a line, but he had asked the question and hadn't wanted to start back tracking when Blaise had gone quiet. He had his own sigh to breath when the man finally spoke again, erasing some of the awkward tension Gabriel had been feeling.

"They don't really make sense, they're mostly just flashes of things," Blaise started off, finding that once he started it all seemed to come easily. He told Gabriel about the dream, but hesitated to mention the real reason it bothered him so much. He didn't normally confide in others about the dreams at all, and he'd only ever told his mother about the correlation between them and reality once. She had simply looked at him in a frightened way, and told him not to tell others about it because they wouldn't believe him. Gabriel listened, and continued to look at him expectantly when he finished.

"It's a disturbing dream," Gabriel said, seeming apprehensive to continue with the thought. He'd watched Blaise as he spoke, and though the other guarded himself well there was undeniably something stirring under that calm exterior that made him feel there was something Blaise wouldn't say. "Are you sure it's all that's been bothering you though, Blaise? You've been out here almost every night lately…" He'd found the courage to poke his nose into Blaise's personal life, and now that he'd taken the first step he felt more confidence in pushing. The confidence faded as soon as he saw Blaise seem to close up before his eyes, and he wished he hadn't asked.

"It is other than how things are with everyone right now. That seems to be improving at least," Blaise said, giving one of those smiles that didn't quite reach his eyes again. Gabriel wondered for a moment how someone who was so in tune with everyone else's emotions and thoughts could feel the need to hide his own so often.

"That's true. Maybe things are getting easier, and maybe the dreams will pass when some of the tension has left," Gabriel suggested, no longer feeling secure in pushing matters. He felt almost positive that there was something more to Blaise's distraction recently, but he didn't think it was his right to push someone to talk. Blaise seemed to relax slightly when it became obvious that Gabriel was letting it drop, and Blaise ran his hands through his hair like he normally did when feeling a bit nervous.

"Hopefully so. I've had nightmares before off and on, and they usually don't last too long before they pass," Blaise said, though there was little relief in his voice. Normally the dreams passed because whatever they were warning or hinting to him about had come to pass as well. He told that gnawing anxiety in the back of his brain to go away, that this dream made no sense when applied to reality. That maybe this time it was just simply a nightmare, something his brain had cooked up due to stress. He could tell by the way Gabriel glanced at him that the man didn't believe that he was telling him everything, and he forced his smile to be more relaxed and questioned if he was being that transparent or if Gabriel was just getting to be a better judge of things. "I should try and head back to sleep. I'm sorry if I've been waking you with all this, I hadn't been meaning to. Tea's sort of my fall back drink."

"It's fine, you haven't really been waking me up that much. I've just been noticing all the cups that appear in the sink over night," Gabriel said, a hint of joking to his voice as he downed the last of his water. He waited until Blaise had gone back upstairs to head to his own room, unsure how easy he'd sleep now. He told himself that it was just the dream that was keeping Blaise up, it was disturbing for a dream, but he couldn't shake the feeling that Blaise was waiting for something. The times he let his guard down just enough for a glimpse of what he was feeling always gave Gabriel the sense that the man was just waiting for something unwanted to happen. It was as though he was biding his time, waiting for the world to drop out from under him.

Gabriel woke a little before noon to an empty house and a note on the counter. Still a bit blurry eyed he missed it at first, starting a pot of coffee and getting half way through his first cup while wondering how long Blaise was going to sleep before he noticed the piece of paper sitting there. He tilted his head to get a straight view of it as he read.

Got called in. Mrs. McGully went into labor, may be gone all day. Anne's coming by at noon to help you get the wood into town. Sorry. -Blaise

Gabriel glanced at the time, and almost choked on his next sip of coffee as he realized it was already eleven-forty. He set the cup down, going to jump quickly into the shower so that he'd be ready when Anne got there. The last thing he wanted to do was to ruin his 'new' first impression by being completely unprepared and making her wait. He didn't take the long shower he'd been contemplating for the ache in his muscles, and instead settled for a quick burning hot one. He was in and out within a matter of minutes, and managed to pull on clothes and be back to sipping coffee by eleven-fifty. He made himself some toast after a bit of debate, deciding that working through the day without any sustenance at all wouldn't go well. He realized fifteen minutes later that Anne didn't have Blaise's knack for getting there right on time as he glanced at the clock. When five more minutes passed and there was still no sign of Anne he began to wonder if Blaise had misunderstood what time she was coming, or if she was coming at all.

He was finishing the last bite of toast when he heard the car pull up outside, an excited bark following the thud of a door closing. He set his dishes into the sink and made it to the door only a few seconds after Anne's knock. He opened it for her, finding her standing there in jeans and a navy blue sweatshirt. One of her dogs was sitting at her feet, grinning up at him with tongue hanging from his mouth.

"Sorry I was late, this one was throwing a fit about being left behind today." Anne tried a smile, but didn't quite make it work as it felt more like a grimace to her. Yakone hadn't actually cared about coming with her or not, perfectly content on hanging back with the rest of the team, but Anne had spent too long debating if she wanted to take him as a comfort. When it had gotten to be noon and she still hadn't left her house she finally just brought him along, wanting the protected feeling he'd give her if she was to be alone with Gabriel. She silently cursed Blaise for calling her instead of MacKenzie when he'd gotten called in, especially knowing what day it was. She knew the man had done it on purpose though, taking the first chance he'd gotten to pin her with Gabriel's company. If he wanted to give her a pop quiz she'd just make sure she passed it with flying colors. She tried for a smile again, and this time felt like she managed pretty decently. "Ready to get the wood moved?"

"Yeah. You want some coffee first, there's still half a pot left," Gabriel said, thoughts not too different from Anne's. He felt like he was on trial though, impress the judge or there would be no more chances after this. He couldn't bring himself to feel upset with Blaise for setting him in the situation so unexpectedly though, he knew Blaise's intentions were in the right place. He managed a smile as well, shyer but less forced then Anne's as he stepped back to let her in the house. When she stepped in the dog followed, and it seemed like some silent signal was given to the dog that set him free then. Gabriel quickly found the dog's nose pressed against his jeans as the dog sniffed at him, and then jumped up to try and lick at his face.

"Yakone, down," Anne said strictly in a tone that Gabriel could only call motherly. Yakone listened, but still stared at Gabriel expectantly with his tail wagging. Gabriel relax a notched at the friendly greeting, and bent down to scratch behind the dog's ears.

"It's all right. I don't mind him saying hello." Anne watched the two of them as Yakone basked in Gabriel's attentions, eyes closing in a look of ecstasy as the man ruffled the fur on top of his head. Part of her wanted to call her dog traitor for being so easily swayed, but she felt another part of her ease back. If Yakone approved then she most likely had nothing to worry about from this man, her dogs were good judges of character. Gabriel straightened up and looked at her, reminding her of a dog for a moment with his dark eyes expectant and hopeful of her approval. The honesty of the look caught her off guard for a moment, and she found herself just staring back at him until he seemed to grow a bit nervous. "Ready?"

"Yeah, I pulled the jeep around as far as I could so we should be set." Gabriel nodded and turned to head back through the house to go out the back door. Anne followed a little more slowly, allowing herself to soak in the feel of the place. The house was full of Blaise, the books and pictures along with trinkets that were set around. She'd always loved coming to his house, because all the different bits of clutter fit him just right. She noticed now that here and there new things had cropped up that hadn't been there last time. A few of those things didn't quite fit, and she had a feeling they were part of what little Gabriel had acquired during his time there. She realized she was a bit far behind when Gabriel opened the door to go out back before she'd even cleared the living room, Yakone rushing past the man's legs to dash out into the snow with an excited bark. Gabriel didn't comment or even pause at her lagging behind, instead just starting down along the well tread path to the woodpile. Anne reluctantly pulled herself away from her exploring to get the back of the jeep opened up for them.

The work allowed them a break from the awkwardness between them as it eliminated the need for talk. The two kept their distance from one another as they carried the wood to the jeep, mindful of each other in a way that made it seem there was some bubble between them that kept the distance. The space eroded slowly though as the woodpile started to dwindle down, and some of the nervous energy was wearing off as well. By the time there was only a couple more bundles of wood left the two felt comfortable enough to walk side by side with only a couple of feet between them. Anne loaded her last bundle into the back of the jeep, and turned towards the house.

"I'll go lock up while you get that last one," she called from over her shoulder, and Gabriel gave a quick wave in acknowledgement on his way to grab the last stack of wood. Yakone had been lying in the snow and dashing about in intervals while they'd been loading up, but now the dog was standing by the woodpile at attention as he stared towards the trees. Gabriel ruffled the fur on the dog's head as he bent to grab the final cords, but stiffened when he heard Yakone's nervous whimper. Gabriel straightened up, and looked over at the edge of the woods along the back of Blaise's property. He didn't see anything at first until the other man moved, and Yakone gave a quiet woof as the hair rose along the dog's back.

"Easy boy," Gabriel said softly, though he felt anything but at ease as he watched the man. It was the man he'd seen on the street outside the cafe the day before, and he was just watching Gabriel again as he had done then. Gabriel lifted a hand to wave at the man, fighting the feeling that something wasn't right. He could tell even from there that the man smiled at the greeting, and waved in return which seemed to upset Yakone as the dog gave a growl. As the man finished his wave he lowered his hand, and Gabriel couldn't tell but it appeared he made a gesture as though aiming a gun at him and firing it. Nerves shot down his back and coiled around his gut like a snake preparing to strike. When the hand touched his shoulder he jumped, turning quickly to face whoever had snuck up on him.

"Gabriel?" Anne was looking at him tentatively, taking a step back as though she was afraid he was about to lash out at her. He tried for a reassuring smile as he attempted to shake off the adrenaline that was making his heart pound loudly in his ears.

"Do you know that guy? Does he live around here?" Gabriel turned to point back at the man, but found there was nothing but the trees there. Anne scanned, trying to find who he was talking about before looking questioningly at him. If it wasn't for the fact that Yakone was still standing at full attention towards the trees she would have been deeply inclined to believe that Gabriel was seeing things or making something up. As it was though, Yakone appeared just as agitated as Gabriel did, fur standing on end and a quiet rumble going through his chest.

"Closest place is a few miles up the road or down in town. The park surrounds Blaise's property for the most part, it might have been someone who got a little off track while on one of the park's cross country skiing trails though," she suggested, looking back towards the trees uncertainly. Blaise had a large bit of land, and the man would have had to wander pretty far off course to get this close to the house. There weren't many rational reasons for someone to be happening past the back of Blaise's place, but there were a few. She made a note to tell Blaise just in case Gabriel chose not to. "Come on, we should get going. It's getting kind of late."

Gabriel nodded, reluctant to turn his back on the trees but he forced himself to as he adjusted his hold on the wood. Anne called for Yakone as she walked towards the car, the dog slowly backing up before turning to bound after her and jump up into the back seat. Gabriel closed the back hatch of the jeep before moving to get into the passenger seat just as Anne turned the engine over. He glanced in the side view mirror, watching the trees as they pulled away for any sign of movement.

The drive into town was quiet, mainly filled with small talk until Gabriel had brought up the dogs. Anne opened up with the conversation, and soon the two of them were discussing the details of how to run a team. Gabriel actually found it rather fascinating how Anne was able to read her dog's moods and how they seemed to do the same in return. He was also surprised to find that they could be worked during the summer by having them pull a four-wheeler behind them instead of the sled to give them the exercise and experience during the months without snow. While they talked, or more while Anne explained, Yakone sat in the backseat with his head poking out between them with his tongue hanging out as he watched the trees pass the car. He would turn every now and then to place the tongue on Anne's shoulder in an affectionate lick before going back to staring out the windows. As they reached the edge of town Gabriel had just asked how many dogs Anne's grandfather had use to keep when they passed by the small church and graveyard. Someone was out visiting graves, and Gabriel turned as he thought he recognized the man though it was hard to be sure.

"Is that your brother? Who is he visiting?" He knew he shouldn't have asked the question as soon as the words passed his lips, Anne falling quickly silent without answering. He turned to look back at her, and saw she'd returned to staring strictly forward at the road. "I'm sorry, it's none of my business."

"No, it really isn't." The short answer sounded guarded and defensive, and was all that Gabriel got for the rest of the drive. They made their way further into town until they reached the grocery store, Anne backing up into a space near the entrance so that they could unload.

Yakone stayed in the car, watching them excitedly over the seat as Anne opened the back hatch of the jeep. They set to work with the help of the son of the store owner. The kid's name was Jeff and he managed to get Anne talking a bit again, though if Gabriel chimed in she went decidedly cold once more. He was apparently not the only one to notice her attitude towards him since when she went inside to settle things with Jeff's father the teenage boy teased him about it.

"Boy, what did you do to get Anne's panties all in a bunch? Or; is it that she just doesn't like you? I heard she's not really fond of you living with her boyfriend," Jeff said with a smart-ass grin on his face. The younger generations in the town weren't nearly as wary of him as their parents, and Jeff apparently had no issue with Gabriel's mysterious origins.

"I noticed that her brother was at the cemetery and asked her who he was visiting. We were actually managing to get along before that." Gabriel was hoping the kid would be able to shine some light on what he'd done wrong, and sure enough Jeff took the bait quickly with a sober expression on his face.

"Oh that…Leo goes to visit his wife every year on the day of her death. I'd forgotten that was today, no wonder she's a bit testy. It's not personal this time buddy, Leo's mood gets ten times worse than usual this time of year and Anne, Blaise and MacKenzie usually get the brunt of it. We all get a bit depressed, Marie was a great lady. Hot too," Jeff said, a hint of his grin returning at the end as he gave Gabriel a light punch on the shoulder. Gabriel was tempted to ask more, but Anne reappeared just then with keys in hand.

"All right, let's get going. I need to get back." Gabriel got a pitying look from Jeff as he turned to head back to the car. He tried a few times on the ride back to get Anne talking again, but she seemed set that they were finished conversing. In the end he sat staring out the window as they drove back to Blaise's house, his hand scratching behind Yakone's ears idly. When they pulled up she made no move to get out of the car even though Blaise's truck was sitting in the driveway by now, and Gabriel climbed out. He turned before he closed the door, giving Yakone one more pat on the head while looking at Anne.

"I'm sorry I asked. I didn't mean to upset you." He closed the car door, feeling a soft twist of happiness when he caught a guilty expression flicker over Anne's face. She stayed until he was inside, but then he heard her pull away. The sound of running water from upstairs let him know that Blaise was most likely showering, so he headed into the kitchen to grab something small to eat before disappearing into his room. He'd talk to Blaise later, but right then he wasn't in a very good mood and he'd rather just relax alone for a while before having the other man ask how things had gone.

This day had been the same for him for the last two years ever since Marie had died. He would always rise early to get to the cemetery with some fresh lilies from Ms. Harold's greenhouse, and would spend the entire day there with her. No one would bother him other than Mackenzie or Anne, one of them would bring him lunch. At the end he had driven out to Anne's place, though this year there had been a distinct difference in their night of drinking and reminiscing, Blaise didn't show up.

He was thinking of that now as he lay in the bed of Anne's spare bedroom. The house was quiet other than the normal creaking of settling homes under the snow and Mackenzie's snores coming from the living room couch down the hall. He had just assumed Blaise would be there like usual that night, and when the man was absent upon his arrival he'd felt a flare of anger at first. Mackenzie, being the only one who had no reason to suspect he was the cause of Blaise's absence, had been the one who finally ask Anne where the man was.

"He said he didn't feel too welcome this year, and that he was going to stay home. I tried to tell him to come, but he wouldn't..." That was Anne's answer, his sister's voice going a bit quiet as she tried to hide her own guilt and hurt from her voice. Leo had a feeling that, despite Blaise being willing to do most anything for Anne, in this case she wasn't the one the man had needed to give him the okay to show up tonight. Leo shifted in the bed to try and find a more comfortable position, finding himself staring up at the ceiling. Things hadn't been this bad between Blaise and him since the year Marie had died. Leo had partially blamed Blaise for his wife's death since he was the doctor who had tried to save her when she had arrived at the hospital that night. He shouldn't have, Blaise had blamed himself enough for the both of them for Marie and the two teenage boys who had been in the other car involved in the accident. Leo's blame was completely self-focused now, he shouldn't have asked her to come into town to meet him for dinner so he wouldn't have to leave work.

Leo was pulled from his thoughts at the sound of a floor board creaking with someone's step, and he looked towards the closed door of the room. His eyes were adjusted to the darkness of the room by now, and he could clearly make out the silhouette standing in front of the door though no features. He shifted to sit up in bed, his head reminding him that he was still pretty far gone with the whiskey and beer they'd all been drinking a few hours before. His first thought was that it had to be Anne, she was the only woman in the house. He hadn't heard her come downstairs though much less open the door to his room. The figure started towards the bed until she was close enough for him to see her face. He must have fallen asleep without realizing it, and this was a dream. It was the only way to explain it rationally as he looked into the eyes of his dead wife.

"Hello Leo." She gave him a knowing smile, moving to sit on the edge of the bed besides him as he stared. He didn't want to move in fear that it would break the illusion and he'd wake from his dream to find himself alone again. She laughed as he just kept staring at her though, and lifted her hand to his cheek to cup it gently. "It's okay, Lion. I won't disappear." She used the nickname she'd given him in high school to annoy him, and that had grown to be a term of endearment between them as they'd gotten closer and through their short marriage. He moved his hand to hers finding it solid under his touch as their fingers linked.

"Thank god for whiskey," he muttered under his breath, causing her to laugh again which lit her brown eyes with amusement. She was just as he remembered her, soft blonde curls framing her face that held delicate yet strong features around large burnt amber eyes. She was also completely bared to him, skin white and seeming to glow in the darkness. She leaned into him, their lips making contact hesitantly at first but then rougher as need overcame him. "I've dreamt of you, but never like this before..." He whispered the words quickly between kisses as he pulled her into his lap, arms wrapping around her.

"Shhh...then let's not waste it with a lot of talking, hm?" she mumbled back against his lips, a sly smile playing at the corners of her mouth. Things went fast yet seemed to slip by slowly at the same time like water rushing under the stilled ice of a frozen creek as they made love. She pressed him down into the bed as she straddled him, joining them together as the quiet of the night continued through the rest of the house as though their whispered murmurs were a part of it.

Gabriel had drifted off without realizing it until he woke a couple of hours later to the scent of barbeque in the air. He ran a hand through his hair as he sat up and tried to rid himself of the last few tendrils of drowsiness before shifting out of bed. It was almost midnight at this point, and he frowned in confusion as he found a fresh shirt to pull on before stepping out into the hall. The door to the back was open, and he could hear Blaise out by the grill where the pleasant aroma was drifting in from. On the counter was a bottle of Jack that had a good third missing from it. Gabriel eyed the bottle for a second before stepping out into the back porch to join Blaise. The doctor was standing over the grill with a glass of the Jack Daniels in hand as he turned what looked like a couple of steaks over.

"Smells good." Blaise looked up when Gabriel spoke, and gave the man a quick half-hearted smile. It was cold out, but Blaise wasn't wearing more than jeans and a long-sleeved undershirt as he cooked. Gabriel leaned against the railing, watching the other man with a bit of concern and wondering if the bottle inside was all that Blaise had been working on so far. He'd heard the stories of Blaise being drunk, mostly that he was good natured but a few where he'd ended up in bar brawls and fights. He wondered which mood the man was currently in, and if it may be best to leave him be other than the fear of him burning the house down around them.

"How'd things go with Anne today?" He was caught off guard by the clarity in Blaise's voice, and relaxed a bit that Blaise didn't sound as though he was too far gone at all.

"It went well for the most part, but I sort of ruined things around the middle part. I don't know if she's going to be all that willing to put up with me again." Blaise finished his glass and set it aside as he closed the lid on the grill to let the steaks cook for a while longer. He nodded for Gabriel to follow him as he turned to head back inside after reclaiming the empty glass. He started to pour himself another dose of the whiskey before offering the bottle towards Gabriel, who merely shook his head in response.

"What happened?" Blaise drained half the glass in the first sip, and Gabriel felt the bit of doubt creep back in. He slid the bottle towards himself in the guise of reading the label, noting that the whiskey wasn't all Blaise had had so far. There were about five empty beer bottles sitting on the counter besides the fridge where he had missed them before. He didn't know if it was because he didn't drink himself that made him uncomfortable with the amount or if it really was leaning towards excess. He debated on whether he wanted to broach the subject at hand, or if he wanted to avoid it in case it set Blaise off as it had with Anne. "Gabriel...what happened?"

When he looked up Blaise was giving him that steady look that Gabriel knew well by now to mean that the man wasn't going to drop it. He hesitated still though, not wanting to touch a sore spot only to have Blaise react worse than usual because of the alcohol. In the end he decided it may be best to throw all his chips into the pot though, accepting that Blaise would just keep asking him more questions if he didn't answer.

"I didn't know Leo was married before. I asked her why he was at the graveyard, and she got upset." For a moment he thought he'd made the wrong decision in telling the truth instead of trying to come up with some lie in hopes that Blaise wouldn't pick up on it. It went silent in the kitchen other than the distant sizzle of the steaks cooking outside the door, and he had seen Blaise tense slightly. The tension went as soon as it had arrived as Blaise lifted the glass and finished off the whiskey that was sitting in it.

"I should have warned you. I was too distracted this morning with everything though, and I guess I was hoping it wouldn't have come up between the two of you. She told you about it?" Blaise sounded a bit surprised about this, and Gabriel shook his head a little guiltily.

"No, Jeff did while we were at the grocery store. He noticed that she was pissed, and asked what I had done. He filled me in after I told him we saw Leo at the grave..." Blaise nodded, reaching for the bottle again and seeming to realize for the first time that Gabriel still had it nestled between his palms on the other side of the kitchen island. He seemed ready to ask for it, but then set his glass down between them instead. Gabriel wasn't completely sure if he was expected to fill it for Blaise or not, but Blaise appeared to forget about the glass in a matter of seconds.

44

"Did he tell you everything, or just that she died?" Blaise was looking in his direction, but his eyes weren't focused on him but instead seemed to be staring past him at something distant.

"Just that she died..." Gabriel didn't know if he wanted to continue on the subject, something had settled over Blaise that made him feel a little ill. He couldn't tell if it was the distance in the man's eyes or some other little difference, but it made the man seem darker and closed off.

"Guess he didn't tell you that I'm the one that killed her then, huh..." Gabriel startled slightly, eyes going wide as he stared at Blaise. The doctor started past him to head out onto the porch again, taking the bottle from between Gabriel's hands as he passed so he could start drinking straight from it. Gabriel was still standing at the counter when he heard Blaise continue from out on the porch, apparently oblivious to the fact that Gabriel hadn't followed him out there. "It was a car accident, a couple of kids were coming through town on their way back from a ski trip. They lost control a few miles out near where Leo's place is, and Marie happened to be driving home just then. They hit head on, one of the boys died instantly, but Marie and the other kid came into the hospital still alive. I was the one on duty, the one who should have been able to save them but I panicked for just those few seconds. I ended up not being able to save either of them, I killed them both because I froze up at my first big trauma."

Gabriel had moved out onto the porch slowly as Blaise talked, the man standing at the grill again though the spatula hovered over the steaks with no intent of turning them. Gabriel recognized the darkness now that had engulfed Blaise so quickly. It was self loathing, the feel of failure and loss mixed in with a overwhelming sense of responsibility. Blaise gave a quick bitter sounding laugh as he lifted the bottle again.

"Leo punched me that day when I told him she was gone. I deserved it, probably deserved a lot more. They always tell you never to make it personal, to keep some distance and to know when to recognize when there was nothing you could do. You can't do that when it's your best friend's wife that you just let slip away on the table..."

Gabriel wanted to tell Blaise that it wasn't his fault, to try and find the right words to express to him that would make him feel better. He couldn't though, there was nothing he could say because he wasn't there. Anything he said, no matter how much care he took with his words, would feel insufficient at the moment. Instead, he moved to stand besides Blaise and took the spatula from him along with the bottle of whiskey.

"Don't want the steaks to burn," he said, flipping one before lifting the bottle to his lips. The alcohol burned as it went down, making him cough and sending a chill down his spine. He heard Blaise chuckle, not a full laugh, but it was at least something.

"You really aren't a drinker. Here, give me that. I'll go grab a couple of plates for those," Blaise said, taking back the bottle as he nodded at the steaks. He went inside to retrieve the plates, and Gabriel pretended not to notice that it took longer than it should have. They ate out on the porch despite the chill of the night air, the whiskey going down a bit smoother with each sip until Blaise ended up having to help Gabriel into his bed before heading upstairs to his own. Blaise would dream that night of Marie as she devoured Leo, swallowing him whole while the man who stalked Blaise in his sleep stood in the background watching.

Gabriel was up first in the morning with a hazy feeling in his head, but otherwise not any worse for wear. He'd gotten some breakfast started for the two of them, thinking over what Blaise had told him the night before. It seemed like Blaise was changing over the last few weeks, and Gabriel couldn't assure himself that it was the memory of his guilt over Marie that was causing it. Dark spots were appearing in Blaise's normal confident attitude like bruises darkening the flesh. Gabriel frowned down at the bacon as it sizzled at him, trying to remember if Blaise had told him anything else after they'd been drinking for a while. The alcohol apparently affected his memory similarly to whatever had brought him to Edenspoint in the first place though as he couldn't recall much past a few dim words of their conversation.

Blaise groaned as he entered the kitchen looking a bit like he was hit by a train. He sat down on one of the stools before giving Gabriel a narrow-eyed look. "You seem to be feeling pretty well for having helped me finish off a bottle and a half of whiskey last night. Close the blinds." Gabriel did what he was told, and pulled down the shade over the kitchen window. Blaise relaxed his stare a little, but was still eyeing Gabriel with a bit of envy. "How are you not hung over? You've never touched a single thing alcoholic during your time here, and yet you apparently handle it like an alcoholic."

"Maybe I was an alcoholic," Gabriel said with a shrug, taking the batch of bacon out of the skillet before dumping the scrambled egg goop into it to start cooking. Blaise made a bit of a non-committal noise, his attention focused now on grabbing a cup of coffee from the pot that Gabriel had brewed. He snatched a piece of bacon while he was at it, giving a quiet curse when it burned his fingers slightly though not bad enough to make him let go of his bounty. "I'm surprised you want to eat if you're hung over."

"I handle my alcohol extremely well. It's just the head that hurts, I mixed a bit too many types of alcohol last night."

"I thought you just had beer and whiskey," Gabriel said, turning around once he was sure the eggs were just fine on there own for a few minutes. Blaise gave him a slightly guilty look over the edge of his coffee mug.

"You were out for a few hours. I drank some vodka and rum before I moved on to the beers. I know I should know better, but I was pretty focused on my intent," Blaise said, biting into the bacon and finding it crispy to the point of almost being burnt. Bacon was the one thing that Blaise could manage to cook better than most people, everything else he was easily beat at though. He didn't really care at the moment, he would have happily ate it even if Gabriel had burnt it black. Gabriel was currently giving him a look

46

mixed between amusement and concern, and Blaise raised an eyebrow at him in question.

"I'm amazed I didn't have to call an ambulance for you," Gabriel said dryly, and Blaise rolled his eyes dramatically.

"You need to work on your nagging skills, mom. Besides, like I said…I handle my alcohol well. You didn't see me running out naked into the woods at any point in the night, did you? And, who had to drag whom to bed last night because they couldn't walk the few feet themselves?" Gabriel was about to respond when a knock at the front door interrupted him, and he motioned for Blaise to stay where he was as he moved to answer it. When he swung the door open he was met with a slight scowl from Leo, though to the man's credit he tried to cover the look up quickly.

"Blaise still in?" The question came in a short clipped tone, and Leo was already stepping into the house as he asked it. Gabriel just let him, though he had a moment's thought to shut the door in the other man's face instead.

"Yeah, he's back in the kitchen right now." Leo gave a stiff nod, but didn't turn to head back to find Blaise like Gabriel thought he would. Gabriel closed the door and looked at Leo a bit expectantly for a moment before the other spoke in a quiet tone.

"I still don't like or trust you, and I probably never will even if you continue to be in this town for the next fifty years living your amnesia-rich life. Blaise trusts you though, and he's my friend. I'm not letting you ruin a perfectly good friendship, got it?" Gabriel stared back at Leo for a moment, wondering if this was as close to acceptance he was going to get from the man. Leo didn't look like he had slept well the night before either, and Gabriel checked himself before he said something he'd regret.

"Got it." He kept it at that, watching as Leo turned to walk towards the kitchen with familiar ease and seeming more relaxed now that that topic was closed. Gabriel paused a few moments to let the tension in his shoulders ease before he followed, moving to slip into his room instead of hanging around. Blaise gave him an apologetic look, and Gabriel had a feeling that Blaise may have overheard despite Leo's effort. Gabriel just gave a quick shrug of his shoulders before closing the door to his room as Blaise turned to offer Leo some coffee as he removed the skillet with the eggs in it from the burner.

The unease in the air lessened once Gabriel was out of sight, though Leo took several seconds to start the conversation still. Blaise and him sat in silence while Blaise got Leo a cup of the coffee Gabriel had brewed, the Sheriff taking a piece of bacon from the plate as he sat.

"Missed you at Anne's place last night. Where the hell were you?" Blaise couldn't help the wry smile that pulled at his lips as Leo cut straight to the point, and he set the mug down in front of his friend before finding his own seat again. A sense of familiarity settled over them as Leo took a sip of the coffee, the previous times they had sat in just these places talking masking some of the distance that existed between them now.

"Wasn't really sure if I was welcome to come around. Besides, got called into work yesterday for a delivery." Leo kept a steady gaze on Blaise, and found it returned in part by the other man. They broke it at the same time as though some unspoken agreement had passed, and Leo rested his forearms on the counter with his mug between his palms.

"I should have asked you to come. I know things haven't been right between us, but part of me figured that it hadn't gotten this bad. I don't like how its been the last month, and I know the biggest part of the blame lies on me. You got some cream for this?"

"Yeah, let me grab it," Blaise said, getting up from his seat to grab the half and half from the fridge. "It's not just your fault, Leo. Its not like I was tracking you all down to try and get things settled between us. Even if you had called me up to tell me to come last night, I don't know if I would have." Blaise handed Leo the carton before finding the sugar without his friend needing to ask. The conversation lulled again as Leo made up his cup to his liking, and then Blaise tucked everything back away in its place.

"Still should have asked, even if you wouldn't have come. I want things to be better though, that's why I came by. Last night made me realize how far apart all of us have gotten, not just you and me. I can't promise love and acceptance for your roommate there, but I guess at this point I have to accept that he's here to stay for a while. If I try, think you could find it in yourself to try too, Doc?" Blaise nodded his head, studying Leo and noticing that he seemed a bit more pulled together today than he normally had after the anniversary of Marie's death. Leo pulled him from the speculations of whether his friend was finding closure or not by moving the conversation on to his next point. "You been doing all right? I heard the others say that you haven't seemed right lately, a little run down. I didn't think things had gotten busy enough at the hospital yet this year for them to have pulled you over to the ER more than once or twice."

"No, things have been relatively quiet at work so far. Some of the other doctors have decided its just the calm before the storm, though I'm hoping it just means its a slow injury and accident year. We've had a lot of colds come through, a bit more than usual so I've been keeping busy with my regular patients."

"Then what's been going on?" Leo cut to his point again, and Blaise raised an eyebrow at him sardonically. Leo shot a deadpan look back at him before just shaking his head. "What's been going on other than what we've already discussed? I know its something more, we all do. Anne and Mac have mentioned it to me too that you've been getting a bit weird lately."

"Weird, that's an eloquent way of saying that you all think I've lost it a bit." A slight crease between Leo's brows belied the impassive glare he gave to Blaise at this, and his fingers tapped on the side of his mug in slight agitation.

"Don't try to use sarcasm on me, Blaise. I'm not going to let you sidestep around this like the other two have. Is it something to do with your visitor or has something happened that you're not telling?" Blaise ran a hand over his hair, managing to smooth some of it into place though a good portion of it still stuck up from his head.

"It doesn't have to do with Gabriel. I worry from time to time, but before you say anything its more for him than anything else. He still doesn't remember anything, and though its been almost two months there's still the concern that whoever left him out there may realize he isn't actually dead. It's mainly been that I just haven't been sleeping well. I told Anne and Mac both that, there isn't really anything else to it." Leo eyed him for a few moments as he tested whether he believed Blaise or not, and in the end lifted his cup to drain some of the coffee from it.

"Yeah, they told me you said you'd been having nightmares or something. I know you get your bad dreams from time to time Blaise, but you're not a five year old. If I believed that it was as simple as you say then I'd be a lousy cop, but I also get that you don't want to talk about it. However, that doesn't mean that I'm going to let this drop for long. Now, just how much did you drink last night and do you think you'll be recovered enough to meet me and Mac down at the bar later?" Blaise gave an almost thankful smile at Leo, though he mentally wished the other would drop it for good. He had talked a bit with Gabriel about the dreams, but that had only managed to make him feel more superstitious that something bad was coming. It didn't help that the dreams hadn't stopped yet or really showed any sign of doing so.

"I think I drank half a liqour store, though I had a bit of help. I'm certain I can manage to be back on my feet enough for a few drinks tonight despite it," Blaise said, and Leo looked back at Gabriel's door with a doubting look before just shaking his head.

"Meet you around seven then. I need to make sure I get caught up on all that exciting paperwork that comes around when you have little to do. May want to call Anne, she seemed a bit upset last night and if you ever plan on making a move on my little sister you'll need to be in her good graces." Leo smirked when he saw the flicker of emotion cross Blaise's face before he remembered to cover it up with his normal indifference.

"I don't know what you're talking about. You must still be drunk if thoughts like that are going through your head and you haven't threatened bodily harm yet," Blaise said, standing when Leo did so he could walk the other to the door.

"Well, don't think I won't shoot you if you break her heart. You may be a good friend, Blaise, but she's still my sister," Leo said as the two of them started to move towards the door. "And, I'd also appreciate it if you didn't act like I was blind and hadn't noticed you two fawning about over the years." When they reached the door Leo turned to look at Blaise, all joking gone from his face. "Seriously Blaise, I'm trusting you with her."

"It's a good thing I don't plan on hurting her then. I don't want to break your trust, much less find myself wishing I owned a bullet proof vest. I'll see you tonight, Sheriff." Leo smiled, opening the door for himself and stepping outside.

"I'm looking forward to it, Doc." Blaise waited to make sure Leo maneuvered to his car without slipping on the ice of the walkway and cracking his head open. He waved once more before closing the door, returning to the kitchen to find Gabriel there pouring himself a cup of coffee. Blaise felt a little over conversations about the state of things right then, but he waited to let Gabriel get things off his mind if he needed it nonetheless.

"I almost think he'd be more accepting of me if I could remember who I was, even if that someone was an axe murderer." Gabriel was stirring some sugar into his coffee as he spoke, and Blaise took a second to pour himself another cup before approaching the conversation.

"In a way its what he does, Gabriel. He's not naturally trusting in everyone he meets, and we've had a few rough characters up here over the years. Isolated mountain town seems to be the key words for the vacation those types like to take. He's more frustrated that he doesn't know who you are more than the fact that you don't know," Blaise said quietly, shaking his head when Gabriel offered the cream to him. "He'll come around when he feels there isn't any doubt left that you're not wanted for mass homicide."

"And if I am?" Blaise looked at Gabriel as though he believed that was the last thing Gabriel could be.

"I guess you'll find out if he trusts you more then or not. I know it doesn't seem like it with the way he acts, but he is going easy on you. From what I could hear of the conversation by the door you two had, he's starting to ease up even more though it probably doesn't seem like it. For now, just do your best to brush it off and try not to go around impaling people with axes. I have to head into town for a bit in a little while to check on how the McGully family is doing if you want to come along. I need to go clean up and take something for this headache first." Gabriel nodded as Blaise set down his fresh cup of coffee to return to later, a habit that Gabriel didn't fully understand. Gabriel nursed his own cup until it was gone before heading into his room to change before enjoying the rest of his breakfast while he waited for Blaise.

The day had felt too long to Mackenzie, and having to deal with Leo's moods throughout hadn't made it any shorter. At least now they were all sitting at the bar, the hangovers of the morning forgotten, or at least forgiven, as they worked on their beers. They had started off a bit awkward but with some prodding from him the other two were starting to relax a bit. He could see Blaise sitting on a question though, and try as he might to psychically tell the other to shut the hell up the man finally spit it out.

"You seem to be handling things well this year, Leo. Did something change or...?" Mackenzie read the sudden tension from Leo, though the man just took a drink from his beer. Mentally Mackenzie damned Blaise and his questions despite knowing that he had every right to ask them. They'd all been friends for years and if at this point they couldn't put each other on the spot about things they'd be in trouble.

50

"I've just come to realize that even though Marie's not here anymore that doesn't mean she's gone entirely. I still have my memories of her, and I'm sure that she wouldn't want me beating myself up every year," Leo said, his tone a bit short though measured. Mackenzie was glad they hadn't gotten far in their drinking, because the last thing he wanted was to break up a fight between the two of them. Blaise could get short tempered the more he drank, and Leo wasn't known for patience even when he was sober.

"That's good that you're starting to focus on remembering what you had with her. You two had a lot of good times," Mackenzie said, stepping in to try and keep any more questions from rising. Leo had told him a bit more about what had caused this epiphany during the day, and though Mackenzie would have liked Blaise's take on it this didn't seem to be the time.

"It is good." Mackenzie said a quick thank you as Blaise kept his answer short and simple even though there was the gleam of curiousity in his eyes. To Mackenzie's surprise though, Leo started up on the subject again without any prodding.

"I had a dream about her last night, that's what did it. It seemed like she was really there and when I woke up this morning a part of me that's been hollow over the last few years seemed to be a little smaller." Blaise was caught midsip as Leo said this, and Mackenzie saw a flicker of something in the man's eyes while Blaise thought his expression was hidden by the bottle. Mackenzie narrowed his eyes at Blaise, trying to get a feel for just what it was he had seen for that second before his friend had closed up but couldn't place it. Blaise now had his face under control, that calm and unreadable expression settled over his features.

"You have dreams about her before?" Leo shook his head, glancing at Blaise from the corner of his eye as he did, and Mackenzie knew he wasn't the only one that had seen that flicker of something.

"Nope, first time. I had nightmares about the crash right after, but it's been a long time since I had one of those and this one wasn't a nightmare. I'm figuring it probably won't happen again, but if it does it will be a pleasant surprise." Leo shrugged at this, and his tone seemed to be saying that was the end of the conversation. Blaise stared at him for a few seconds before just turning back to his beer, eyes a bit distant as whatever thoughts he was having worked themselves out.

"We got a call today from state patrol that the FBI is in our area, and may be stopping by our humble little county," Mackenzie filled in, putting an end to the silence that threatened to fall between them all. The phone call hadn't exactly been a high point in the day, but it was something different to talk about. Blaise's focus returned to them, and he raised an eyebrow at Mackenzie.

"What are they doing out our way in the middle of winter? I haven't heard about anything that the FBI would have to be involved in going on." Leo signalled for another round for them all, a crease appearing between his eyebrows at his frustration.

"There isn't anything as far as I'm concerned. They said they had some information on a case that involves a missing witness. The case apparently ended up jumping state lines, so they got involved and a tip lead them out this way. I'm rather hoping that something else leads them back out of our area. That's the last thing we need coming through here," Leo said as he crossed his arms over his chest, the irritation from the phone call coming over him anew.

"Could this missing witness have anything to do with Gabriel?" Mackenzie stepped in on the question from Blaise, giving him an apologetic look as he did. The only person who may have been more focused on finding out where Gabriel came from than Leo was Blaise, though they wanted to know for two very different reasons. Blaise was trying to help Gabriel remember, Leo just wanted to know whether he needed to throw Gabriel in jail or not.

"No, State knows we've been asking around about him. They have their description, so if the missing person matched at all they would have sent the FBI our way first thing. The fact that they're not here yet means that they don't feel Gabriel is related to their case at all."

"Unfortunately it still seems as though no one even knows Gabriel exists other then us, much less noticed that he's missing from wherever he's supposed to be. I'm starting to wonder if he didn't just appear out of thin air," Leo added, though there was no hint of his normal bitterness over the subject in his tone. Blaise just nodded, and they all made a silent agreement to move on to more neutral subjects for the rest of the night. The atmosphere relaxed further as the night went on, all of them managing to lose track of time sufficiently until the bar finally closed.

Chapter 5 - Loss of Feeling -

Leo lived in his parent's old house on the edge of town, and was glad that it was a short drive from the bar. He didn't envy Blaise with his drive through the cold, though he'd asked the other two to send him texts that they got back safe since they'd all been drinking. They all knew each other's limits, and he would have made them stay at his place if they'd gotten anywhere near it but they'd only had a few beers each over the hours they'd been out. That didn't mean he didn't feel a bit guilty letting them drive either way though.

He entered his house through the side door that attached to his garage, yawning as he tossed his keys up on the key rack. He was too tired and too far gone to really care about washing up before he headed to bed so he started down the hallway towards his room, stripping his clothes off along the way and leaving them on the floor to deal with in the morning. He like the cold and always kept his place a bit chilled, liking instead to pile extra blankets up on his bed for the nights than waste the gas and money. He was very ready to dive into these right away when he walked into his room, but stopped when he found someone had beaten him to it.

"Marie?" He hadn't been expecting to see her again, and this time he knew he wasn't dreaming even with the warm fuzzy feeling the alcohol had wrapped his brain in. She was sitting back against the headboard with her legs under the blankets and wearing her normal pajamas that consisted of one of his large flannel shirts. He had stopped in the act of removing his boxers and she watched him silently for a few moments, looking pissed off at him for some unknown slight. He snapped himself out of it long enough to kick the boxers off, wondering if he should just ignore her presence. Once was one thing, but this was something different and it made him worry he was losing it.

"I don't get why you're still friends with him when he let me die," Marie said coolly now that he had come out of his frozen state. He moved to the dresser to find some sweats suddenly feeling self-conscious about being naked in front of his own delusion. He wasn't completely sure that was the right word for this though, because he knew well enough she couldn't be real and that people didn't just come back from the dead. Maybe it was more like a hallucination then. "So now you're going to ignore me. You're going to side with him instead of me? You know he could have saved me Leo, but here you are acting like nothing ever happened."

Leo pulled on a pair of sweatpants and then stepped into the adjoining bathroom, deciding that maybe he did need to do his nightly routine after all. He was trying to ignore her even though that went against every fiber of his being. She was everything he wanted, always had been, and now she was back within his reach despite not being a reality. He started to brush his teeth, but could feel her eyes on the back of his neck. He knew she would keep staring at him too until he broke, it was something she often did during their arguments when he got to the point of not listening to her. It had managed to both start and end several fights between them. He could see her now in the reflection of the mirror, and a niggling voice in the back of his mind asked what the harm was in just talking to her. There was no point in denying himself a bit of joy with having her around, it wasn't as though she was showing up in public and disrupting his life.

He spat in the sink and rinsed out his mouth as he thought this over, eyes lingering back to her as he put his toothbrush away. There really wasn't any harm in it as long as he reminded himself that she wasn't really there, kept himself from falling into the belief that she was anything more than a figment of his own mind. He turned to head back into the room, meeting her stare as he did and giving her one of his own.

"Blaise didn't let you die, and you know that. He did everything he could to save you," Leo said, putting a strict tone in his voice as he sat down on the edge of the bed. He slid his socks off, glancing back at her to find her still staring at him but with slightly less malice. She waited until he slid under the covers, and then leaned against him and let her head rest against his shoulder. Her hair smelled of pomegranate like the shampoo she'd always used and he took a moment to relish it.

"He froze up. We both know he did, he knows he did. If he hadn't, I might still be here with you. We could still be like we were then." Her words echoed his own right after Marie had died when he was still angry and looking for someone to blame. He'd been a lot harsher in his delivery when he'd told Blaise how he felt though, and he still regretted how he'd acted. His friendship with Blaise never had truly fully-recovered after that, but the two of them never talked about it either. Leo had tried once, and he'd seen the damage that his blame had done when added to Blaise's own personal guilt. They all saw it from time to time still, though he seemed to have a better handle on it.

"I blamed him for long enough, Marie. He tried and I know that if anyone was going to be able to save you it would have been Blaise to pull it off. He has enough of his own guilt that he doesn't need more added to that." Leo slid his arm around her to hug her closer to him as he rested his cheek against the top of her head. He wondered if this was just him talking to himself since Marie was his illusion, if he was just talking with a part of his inner conscious that still blamed Blaise. He thought he had stopped long ago, but now he wasn't as sure. He felt her shift beside him, curling up against him.

He expected more arguments, but didn't get any from her. She just hugged him close, and he felt the need to relax into her take over. She tugged him down gently to get him lying besides her, and their bodies twined together under the covers.

"Come, let's sleep," she said in his ear, and he found he couldn't have fought the suggestion even if he wanted to as all his energy seemed to drain from him. He fell asleep with the warm feeling of her against his side seeming to melt into him.

Gabriel laid listening to the sounds of the empty house as it creaked and groaned while settling in the cold of the night. He'd been trying to fall asleep for almost an hour now, but he felt jumpy and on edge for some reason. Normally he enjoyed the quiet that having the house to himself gave him, and he had tried to sit up and read for a while but found himself rereading the same line over again and finally had decided to try and go to bed. He felt like his wires were drawn tight, ready to snap at any hint of friction for reasons he couldn't pinpoint. He heard a creak near the door to his room and looked towards it half expecting to see someone standing there, but he was still alone in the house as all he saw was the dark shape of the closed door. He'd been like this since Blaise had dropped him off earlier before going to join Mackenzie and Leo at the bar. He knew the other was likely to be out late and he wished that he'd asked to be left at the diner or the café until Blaise was on his way home.

He shifted onto his side, turning his back to the door in another attempt to fall asleep. He closed his eyes willing his mind to relax and let him drift into oblivion. He hadn't realized it was working until the sound of someone saying his name startled him back awake and he sat up in the dark room quickly. He didn't see anyone but he was sure he'd heard his name, and when his heart beat started to return to a normal pace he wondered if it had been Blaise getting home he'd heard. The house was still silent other than its own groans as the heater kicked on. He laid back down to stare up at the ceiling knowing he wouldn't be able to sleep now. It must have been one of those dreams that started before he was completely gone, but he still felt as though the voice had been there in his room.

"Gabriel." It came from near the window that looked out back, and he sat up again. He had looked at the window first thinking the voice was coming from outside, but he saw the man's shape soon enough as he stepped out from the corner of the room. Gabriel couldn't remember seeing him before, but he felt like he knew the man as the dim light of the moon hit him through the window.

"Who are you?" Gabriel had gotten up out of the bed without even thinking about it, some instinct telling him it was better not to be at a disadvantage. The air was cold even with the heater chugging away in the background, and the man stopped with about a foot between them. Gabriel tried to remember where he knew the man from and why his eyes most of all looked so similar. The man seemed to be studying him with a sense of sadness in his eyes though it was met with a flare of anger as his eyes stopped at the scar that was visible on Gabriel's chest

"You really don't remember.... I was half expecting that you would see me and give up the act. You were being foolish Gabriel, you shouldn't have done what you did. When you remember you must tell me where you've hidden it and then do as I ask. My patience is not the only you tried with your little stunt." Gabriel pulled back as the man reached towards him and this seemed to ignite the anger in the other's eyes again. He made a grab at Gabriel but missed as Gabriel ducked and then ran at the man to catch him in a tackle. Gabriel hit the small desk instead of the man and knocked the lamp to the floor where the bulb shattered. Before he could recover the man had him in a hold from behind, pressing a hand to Gabriel's forehead while Gabriel struggled to get himself free, trampling on the lamp shade and the cut glass. "You need to remember, Gabriel."

As the man spoke a dull pain started in Gabriel's head and then suddenly exploded through his brain, and he was lost into a jumble of voices and images. A flash seemed to go off before his eyes and he found himself in a clearing full of snow in the middle of the forest. The snow swirled around him in a frenzy so he couldn't see further than a few feet in front of him and as he looked around faces seemed to appear in front of him that he felt he knew. He reached for one while calling out for help and the man who'd shown up in his room suddenly rushed out of the blizzard at him in a fury.

"How can you choose them over me Gabriel?" Something clicked into place as he stumbled back from the man, he knew why his eyes had looked so familiar now. They were the same as his own, complete twins in their color and shape. The snow seemed to explode upwards between them as the man's voice echoed around him full of rage. "Can't you see that they're turning you against us?" Darkness plunged around him, seeming to swallow him whole, whisking away the snow and trees and the voice that roared in his ears.

Gabriel woke with a start to find himself lying in his bed, the light coming from the window hazy and grey as it announced the sun was starting to rise. His heart was pounding loudly in his chest, the sound drowning out all other noise until he forced himself to take deep breaths and get it back under control. He was covered with a sheen of sweat that made the sheets cling to him, and he pushed them back and swung his legs over the side of the bed. He sat there for a few minutes until he had calmed himself and he ran a hand over his face as he looked at the window. Too many things were going through his head, but he forced himself to glance at the clock to see what time it was. Being able to place himself now in time and space he let himself lie back across the bed again.

He'd fallen asleep obviously, but his dreams seemed too real and concreted into a place in his head. It confused him as he tried to sort through what had actually happened and then separate it from reality. He sat up again as he remembered the fallen lamp, but the floor was bare as it had been before he'd gone to bed. The lamp was sitting on the desk undamaged and there was no sign of a struggle in the room. He couldn't reconcile that with the set feeling that he knew the man, that he'd been right in front of him just moments ago. He knew that he was beginning to remember, but the memories must have come to him as dreams. They were only fragments that he couldn't make much sense out of other than he had a family, three siblings that he had somehow done something to betray them and the man he had dreamt was in his room was one of his brothers.

The mainstreet of the town was being turned into Christmas Lane outside by the town workers that morning as Leo had gotten into the station.

He felt weak and achy like he was coming down with a cold, and had at first thought it was the last remnants of a hangover. It was almost noon now though and he still felt like he'd been hit by a train when Mackenzie came in with two cups of coffee in hand. It was his partner's day off, but Mackenzie almost always made a stop at the station at some point each day. Leo accepted the coffee gratefully as Mackenzie sat down in the chair across from him.

"Merry Christmas, figured I'd drop it off before I headed over to pick up Rebecca from the hospital for our lunch date," Mackenzie said while giving Leo an eyebrow wriggle. Mackenzie had been out with every nurse in town on at least one occassion, and Leo didn't quite understand how he managed it without landing himself in the middle of a cat fight. Mackenzie most likely had taken every single girl in town out except for Anne, and they all seemed to understand that it was never anything serious. Mackenzie hadn't ever found someone that had made him even acknowledge the word commitment before.

"I thought it was Amber you were taking out this week," Leo said, taking a sip of his coffee and finding that it was still too hot to drink without risk of burning some tastebuds off. He figured they could deal though with the way he was feeling and suffered through a longer draw from the cup.

"We went out last week for dinner. I told Rebecca I'd take her for lunch on her break when I went and picked Amber up. Have to keep things even." Mackenzie leaned back in his chair and chose the smart route of setting his cup aside to cool for a few minutes before he drank any. Leo had always been bothered that Mackenzie liked his coffee lukewarm at best, but they'd long since come to the understanding that if he didn't make comments about it that Mac wouldn't comment when Leo managed to burn the skin from the roof of his mouth.

"I think it's a good thing you go to church each week, Mac. You manage to go absolve your sins this morning after two days of drinking and your lusty behaviour?"

"Of course, I wasn't that far out of it not to think of my own salvation. Besides, you go early in the morning during the middle of the week and you get the place to yourself other than Father Brandon."

"Maybe you should have waited until the end of the day to go seek your salvation. I didn't think God gave reprives before you've commited the sins," Leo said with a slight smirk, and he found he had to suddenly dodge a pen that was thrown at him from across the desktop.

"Don't go mocking my beliefs just because you seem to have none," Mackenzie said, neatly catching the pen when Leo tossed it back. The facade of being offended melted away quickly as Mackenzie gave him a smile. "You still seem in an unusually good mood, though your looking a little green today."

"Didn't sleep that great. I think I might be coming down with a cold," Leo said, avoiding the unvoiced question that was the 'good mood' comment. He wasn't sure he really wanted to answer it right then. Seeing Marie for a second time had given him an uneasy feeling once he was out of the house that morning. Part of him couldn't deny that when he woke up alone he was disappointed, and that seeing her had made him feel a whole lot like something that had been stolen from him had been returned for a short time. It didn't block out the concern that it all meant something was wrong with him, that something was causing the dreams or hallucinations, which ever they were. Marie's side of the conversation about Blaise didn't help put him at any ease either.

"Leo, don't make me ask it outright. I don't appreciate you hiding shit from me, especially when I can usually see right through it. I am your best friend after all, not to mention we're partners." Mackenzie spoke bluntly as he picked up his coffee to give it a test, but finding that it still had an iota of true heat left in it he set it aside again.

"Don't you have a date to be getting to?" It almost didn't work until Mackenzie glanced up at the clock and gave a quiet curse. He grabbed his coffee and pointed at Leo as he headed towards the office door.

"You're telling me later or I'll kick your ass."

"Fine, then you can tell me all about your date while we discuss my neurosis," Leo said with about as little enthusiasm as possible.

"Oh goody, we can paint our toenails and giggle like school girls while we're at it," Mackenzie said with a flash of a smile before disappearing behind the doorframe to avoid the pen that flew through the air where his face was a moment before. Leo shook his head and finished off his coffee before looking back at the paperwork on his desk. He was going to need to grab some cold medicine from the store if he was going to try and tackle all of that. He pulled on his coat and let Sheila know that he was going to be out for a few minutes, and to call him if anything serious actually managed to come up.

Despite no serious cases coming through the hospital, it had still been a busy day so far. Blaise was thankful as he got a moment to himself as he sat down in the small break room. He was still feeling a bit of the pay back for the night before, and he was going to be happy once the day was over. His shift had started early so Gabriel had tagged along into town with him, planning on getting the cafe ready for opening during the extra time so it would be ready when Lisa got there. Blaise had noticed that something had been off with Gabriel, but his prodding questions had been met with an emotional wall. Blaise tried to remember if he'd said anything that might have made Gabriel mad, but the other had been asleep when he'd gotten home the night before. He did his best to push it out of his head for now, intent that later he would be more persistant to know what was up.

Blaise pulled himself to his feet having one more task he wanted to do before he headed down to grab something to eat and take a true break. He stopped at the nurse's station in the small maternity ward, giving a smile in greeting to the three nurses that were chatting there.

58

"How are they doing?" There was only one family in the ward right now so he didn't have to specify for them to know he was asking about the McGully's. They would have been going home that evening except that the mother, Taylor, still had low blood pressure and it had made Blaise a little uncertain about her leaving quite yet.

"Fine. I checked on them about an hour ago and Taylor said she was going to take a nap. Her blood pressure has improved a little, but is still a bit low. The little guy is doing great other than still not having a name. Those two can't seem to decide which name they like best," said one of the nurses, Allison. Blaise gave a nod, glancing at his watch for a moment before he started towards the room.

"I'm going to check on them and see how mom's feeling. If one of you want to bring a bottle it's about that time so I'll stick around to see how much he eats." The nurses all nodded, and Allison moved to get a warm bottle prepared from some of the milk that Taylor had pumped earlier so if she was still too worn out and fatigued they could use it.

The door to their room was mostly closed, a small crack left open so that if the family had needed anything they could call down to the nurse's. As he got closer he could hear the faint cries of the baby inside though something seemed a little off. He pushed the door open while asking, "Is someone hungry in here?"

It took him a moment for things to snap into place as the sense of wrong grew. Taylor was lying in bed, and her husband Alex and the baby weren't visibly in the room. He took a few more steps inside, still able to hear the crying and he realized it was coming from the bathroom. For a moment he thought Alex had taken the kid in there so that the crying wouldn't wake Taylor. She was lying in the bed at an odd angle with her head under one of the pillows and the blankets were kicked up around her in turmoil. The crying continued as the sound of running water started up in the bathroom, and Blaise was moving before he even realized it. The door was locked when he tried it and the crying cut out for a moment before it started again at a more fevored pitch.

"Mr. McGully? Alex! Open the door now Alex!" Blaise heard Allison enter the room, the nurse giving a gasp and then a curse when she processed what he had. Blaise threw his shoulder against the door as he got no response from inside the bathroom but the baby's wails, and Allison was soon besides him as they both pounded and slammed against the door. One of the other nurses from down the hall rushed in, but he didn't take time to see which one as he told her to call security up to the room. The wood was creaking and groaning against their efforts, and the door was giving away quickly as it loosened with each blow. It went eerily quiet in the bathroom, and they both paused for a second before redoubling their efforts and finally getting the door to break away from its latch.

As Blaise pushed into the bathroom he found Alex McGully standing with his child in his arms, a knuckle in the baby's mouth for it to suckle. The water in the sink was running with the drain plugged, and both the baby and

Alex's arms were soaked with water. Alex pulled his hand away, and the baby started to cry once more as it lost its makeshift pacifier.

"Alex, give me the baby..." Blaise spoke calmly, trying not to startle the father into resuming what he'd been doing before they'd gotten into the room. He took a few careful steps into the bathroom aware that Allison was staying close behind him, ready to take the baby from him once he got a hold of it. Alex looked up at him for a moment and he seemed to try to say something as tears gathered in his eyes.

"I didn't do this..."

"Of course not. We don't think you did, we just need to take the baby to get looked at Alex," Blaise said after a moment of silence, afraid of upsetting Alex or saying the wrong thing. The man studied him for a few moments before starting to reach out towards Blaise to hand the child to him, and Blaise felt a moment of confusion as he read the loss and pain in Alex's eyes. The man really seemed to believe he hadn't just been trying to drown his child, that he hadn't smothered his wife. At the last moment all of that disappeared as Alex's eyes went pitch dark and empty and Blaise found himself looking at a completely different person than a few seconds before.

The baby's sobs had quieted for a few moments until Alex turned towards the sink to try and plunge the baby under once more. Blaise made a desperate grab, struggling with the baby's father to get it out of his hold without hurting it as the baby screamed like a banshee. As the water from the sink sloshed around them he finally landed an elbow to Alex's chin and stunned the man long enough to pull away with the baby in his arms. Blaise turned quickly to Allison, pushing the baby into her arms and he saw her eyes go wide just before Alex hit him from behind. Allison pulled herself sharply back and out of the way before the two men tumbled past before landing on the floor on the main room.

"Get him out of here, Allison!" Blaise yelled, trying to manage some sort of hit so he could get free of Alex who was keeping him pinned to the floor on his stomach while throwing blows. Allison hesitated for a moment before turning to head for the door, but that second had been enough. Alex was suddenly off of him and heading towards her with a scream, and he grabbed hold of Allison's hair and pulled her back further into the room. She lifted a hand and scratched across his face, twisting to get out of his hold while keeping herself between Alex and the baby in her arms. Blaise pulled himself up and forced himself between Alex and Allison trying to help her free herself from him. He managed to get her loose, but Alex was near the door now. Blaise kept himself between the nurse and the father, trying to judge if he could get Allison enough time to get out of the room if he attacked.

Alex just stood there studying them in turn, nothing but anger in his eyes now as they stared darkly at them. He slowly lowered himself then for a moment, hand dipping to his work boots from which he pulled a hunting knife that had been hiding there. It wasn't unusual for people in town to have knives on them, and it was less so for Alex who worked with the forest service and often carried one in case the need ever arose on the job.

Blaise pressed himself back so that he was shielding as much of Allison and the baby as he could between himself and the wall. He was starting to wonder what was taking security so long to get there, even though it had only been a few minutes it felt like it had been hours since he'd walked into the room. He threw an arm up when Alex suddenly lunged towards him again, and he felt the blade of the knife bite into his arm though he didn't feel any pain with the sensation. He swung with his other arm, trying to get a solid hit in that could stun Alex long enough for him to get the knife out of the man's hand. He realized too late that Alex had managed to make a quick upward swing, and as his blow hit he felt the knife skim along his ribs. Blaise kicked Alex back as hard as he could with what little ground he could manage. He started towards Alex hoping that he could force the other further across the room, but felt Allison take hold of his shirt from behind to stop him. Sounds of people running came from the hallway suddenly, and Blaise saw over Alex's shoulder that the security guard had appeared in the doorway followed quickly by Mackenzie. The guard stood in the doorway gaping at the scene before he realized that Mackenzie already had his gun drawn and he scrambled to get his taser pulled out as well.

"Alex, drop the knife." Mackenzie sounded steady and calm, though there was a slight twitch in the muscle along his jaw that spoke of the tension he was feeling. He'd only been at the hospital for a few moments, and had been getting ready to head out with Rebecca when the security guard that had been loitering in the lobby of the main entrance had gotten a call on his cell and taken off running. Mackenzie had followed without a thought, and then had picked up speed when the security guard had told him someone had been killed in one of the rooms. He met Blaise's eyes for a second and saw him give him a slight nod to let him know that they were okay so far in the room.

Alex stopped abruptly in a move that looked as though he was going to charge Blaise again, and he cocked his head to the side in a sharp movement that didn't seem right to Mackenzie and he wondered if the man had taken something. It seemed as though Alex was listening to something that the rest of them couldn't hear for a few moments, and Mackenzie saw the security guard shift uncertainly besides him. Alex seemed to catch the movement too as he turned slightly to look back at them, and any doubt that he was on something disappeared from Mackenzie's mind; Alex's pupils were dilated to the point of looking completely black, and though he looked at them he didn't seem to process what he was seeing.

Alex turned back towards Blaise, who's back straightened as he prepared for whatever Alex might do next. The knife was raised slowly into the air, but before Alex could take a step forward the taser went off in the security guard's hands and the prongs hit Alex squarely in the back. Alex jerked back a few steps as the taser gun cracked, but he managed to keep his feet under him. The security guard let off, but as soon as Alex started towards the others huddled in the room he pulled the trigger again. Alex continued moving towards them even with the electricity going through him, and Blaise turned to envelope the others to keep any blow from hitting Allison or the baby. Allison curled up against him, creating a cocoon around the baby, though he felt her lift her head from time to time to check on if Alex was still coming. Mackenzie was shouting at Alex now, telling him to stop over the crackling of the stun gun.

Blaise closed his eyes tightly when he felt Allison suddenly grab the front of his shirt in her hand with a frightened curse. All noise was suddenly drowned out by the sound of a gun shot, and silence followed other than a muffled thud through the ringing of his ears. Blaise felt a weight against the back of his legs and he opened his eyes to check on the baby before meeting Allison's wide-eyed gaze. He turned and looked down at Alex's body at his feet, and then met Mackenzie's stare. Mackenzie lowered his gun slowly appearing shell shocked as all tension seemed to drain out of him, leaving him looking shaken. The emptiness was filled with the sudden wail of the baby, and the curses from the security guard.

Mackenzie had kept it together long enough to get orders given on how the room should be handled, and that the two bodies would need to be left until others from the police department could arrive. He hadn't gotten a chance to do more than ask Blaise if he was all right before the turmoil of nurses and doctors came to try and sort out what they could do for who. Blaise had taken the baby from Allison and had carried it securely but almost absently in his arms until one of the nurses had said they could take the little boy and had gently pried it away from him so Blaise could get stitches. Mackenzie sat now in the lobby, staring at the floor between his feet as he listened to the conversations around him without really hearing any of it. Those that had been present were being interviewed, and questions were being asked of the nurses that had last been in contact with the McGully family before the incident.

Mackenzie didn't need to look up to know it was Leo who stopped beside him and set his hand on Mackenzie's shoulder for a brief moment before sitting down in the chair next to him. They sat in silence for a while, Mackenzie staring at the floor between his feet. He heard Leo sigh besides him and saw him hold his hand out palm up.

"It's just for now, Mac. You know its routine, we'll give you a replacement until the investigation is over. There's no question that you only did what needed to be done," Leo said quietly. Mackenzie leaned and pulled his gun, holster and all, loose from where he kept it on his belt at all times. It left him feeling oddly naked without it as he set the weapon in Leo's hand. He had carried it with him while both on and off duty since he'd become a cop, and though part of him didn't even want to look at the thing he also felt unease rise inside him by being separated from it. "It will be okay, Mac. Just keep in mind that he gave you no choice. He'd already killed his wife, he would have done the same to Blaise and Allison to get to the kid." Leo tucked the gun away into an evidence bag and handed it off to one of the few forensic techs that they shared with the rest of the county.

They fell into silence again as Leo stayed sitting beside Mackenzie. They had known each other long enough that Leo knew once Mackenzie was ready to he would talk. Leo knew how he felt, he'd been forced into shooting a man one summer when he'd taken his wife and daughter hostage for thirty-six hours. Leo had gone in as negotiator, and the man hadn't wanted to listen and moved to shoot the daughter. Leo had managed to get a shot off first though. It didn't make a difference that the man had the intent of killing his family, it had still left Leo feeling numb with the knowledge he'd killed someone. Alex McGully was Mackenzie's first, and Leo hoped it would be the only time his partner had to make that decision.

Mackenzie had his own doubts on whether he'd really done what was right. There hadn't been any room left for decisions or talk when he'd finally pulled the trigger, but he was left wondering if he should have done something else. He had thought at first that he should have tried to get the knife away from Alex, but he had judged that the distance between him and Alex gave too much time for the man to react and get to Blaise. Now he felt that he should have tried, felt now that the distance hadn't been as large as he'd thought or that he could have moved faster than he'd felt he could at the time. There were too many ifs and buts, and now in the aftermath he felt those choices were all better than the one he made. He had taken a life , and it was one that he knew fairly well. Alex had gone to high school with him and Leo though he was a couple of grades behind them. Mackenzie ran his hands over his face, pausing for a moment over his eyes in an attempt to still the thoughts of what if and to try and stop the scene from replaying in his mind again.

"I could have gone for a wounding shot…" He felt Leo lean back in his chair as he crossed his arms over his chest. Mackenzie leaned back besides him, and found Leo studying him with lowered brows. Leo seemed to think for a few moments, and Mackenzie felt uncomfortable under his gaze. Leo shook his head then though, looking back out over the waiting room.

"No, you couldn't have. Henry said that he got Alex with the stun gun, got a good hit that stayed stuck to his clothes so he was getting the full affect of the shock. Even with that he said Alex didn't go down, barely even seemed to notice it. If you had just gone for a shot in the leg or arm you ran both the risk of it managing to hit the others or that he'd still have gone for the baby and hurt more people." Leo scanned over by the entrance to the ER's main hallway, watching for Blaise to reappear. He was getting stitched up in one of the rooms, and no doubt still dealing with some things on the hospital end. They both knew that Anne would be showing up soon, and that she'd be on edge until she could see for herself that he was okay.

"I could have tried to get the knife away from him."

"And gotten stabbed yourself or worse? A taser's not going to stop him, but you're going to manage to disarm him by hand without getting yourself or another hurt in the process?" Leo wasn't being short with him to be mean, and Mackenzie knew that but it still stung a little that the other bit the words out at him. He looked at Leo, and got a steady look in return though it was softer than the words had been. "You did what was best for the safety of the people in that room. I know it doesn't feel that way, but all those other possibilities that you're going through…they aren't going to get you anywhere but doubting yourself. You did right, that's all you need to know."

Mackenzie looked down at the floor, and Leo gave him a gentle push with his shoulder. They both looked over when Anne came in the door, and Mackenzie was surprised to see Gabriel follow shortly after her. Anne looked panicked, and she didn't see them right away until Gabriel pointed them out sitting on the chairs.

"I told Anne to pick him up and let him know what happened." Mackenzie looked at Leo with surprise when the other offered up this bit of information.

"You did?" Leo shrugged and stood up to go meet his sister as she started towards them.

"Blaise thinks of him as a friend, he should know," came Leo's answer over his shoulder before he stepped away to meet Anne part way, pulling her up into his arms in a hug. Gabriel bypassed the two of them to come over to Mackenzie, giving him a worried look.

"Are you all right?" Gabriel sat down beside him, though Mackenzie caught him scanning the rest of the waiting room for Blaise as well. He was still wearing his apron from the café having forgotten to take it off when Anne had come in to get him. She had been in a flurry of anxiety and Gabriel had followed and gotten into the car without knowing what was going on until he'd gotten her to talk when they'd been parking at the hospital. Mackenzie nodded to answer his question, not feeling like going through it all again. He would prefer to never have to go through it ever again, but he had a feeling his memory wasn't going to be so kind. Gabriel seemed like he wanted to say something more, but he hesitated just a second too long and leaned back in his chair to stay quiet as Leo and Anne joined them.

Anne leaned down and wrapped Mackenzie in a hug, and she whispered quietly to him that it would be okay. He gave her a gentle squeeze back, happy for the comfort that she gave before she moved to sit down between him and where Leo sat down. She kept a hand on his arm even as she leaned to try to see if Blaise had appeared yet, her nerves seeming to make her vibrate with anxiety. Mackenzie glanced at Leo, knowing that usually the other would be taking statements instead of just sitting idle. It was obvious Leo was restless as he shifted in his chair, but he chose to stay close to Mackenzie and let the other's do the work. In stark contrast there was Gabriel, who was sitting as still as a statue beside him. It made Mackenzie feel uncomfortable since he couldn't seem to help but fidget in his chair, agitated. A nurse finally approached them after what felt like hours, but Mackenzie didn't bother to see which nurse it was. He wanted to leave and go home and crawl inside a bottle of whiskey.

"Leo, you can talk to him now," she said quietly, the entire staff was hushed as they seemed to walk on egg shells in the wake of what had happened. Leo nodded and patted Anne's knee before he got up to follow the nurse back to where Blaise was. Mackenzie felt Anne's hand slide into his, and he let their fingers link together tightly for a few moments before loosening his hold as he found her hand felt extremely delicate in his. She leaned over to him and placed a kiss on his cheek before whispering in his ear.

"It will be okay, Mac. Thank you for keeping him safe." Mackenzie nodded in response, not able to meet her eyes. He didn't feel like he'd done enough to keep Blaise safe and as such he didn't deserve her thanks. He looked away from her and found Gabriel looking at their joined hands on Mackenzie's knee, and when Gabriel looked up Mackenzie felt uneasy. For a second he got the feeling that Gabriel was able to see Anne and his entire shared past, including their short and awkward experience of dating in high school that had come to an abrupt end immediately after their first kiss revealed just how much they felt like brother and sister. Mackenzie broke the eye contact and looked down at the floor again, finding it to be far easier to stare at.

Anne jumped up from her chair suddenly when Blaise appeared following Leo into the waiting room. He had changed out of the clothes he'd been wearing that now were bloody and wrapped up in a bag under his arm and was wearing a spare pair of scrubs from the hospital. Every one of Blaise's defenses were up and it left his face blank from any of the emotions he was feeling. When Mackenzie looked up at him though there was a fleeting moment where they leaked through as they shared mutual acknowledgement of the whirlwind of nerves and guilt inside them both. That brief second gave Mackenzie an odd sense of relief despite still feeling the pain and the jumpiness. At least there was someone else that would understand.

Anne threw her arms around Blaise tightly when she reached him, breaking the second of eye contact between him and Mackenzie. Blaise winced but bit back any other sign of his pain as he just hugged her back the best he could with his one uninjured arm. That was something Mackenzie didn't have, someone like Anne to help him forget. When Anne finally released Blaise she started to dote on him; chastising him and examining the damage while never having a second where she broke contact with him completely.

"You helped save that." Gabriel's voice startled him slightly, having forgotten that the other was still sitting beside him. The slightly stone-faced and silent Gabriel had faded a little when Mackenzie looked at him. "Keep that in mind if you start to doubt that what you did was right. It's unfortunate that it came down to a life needing to be taken, but you saved more by doing so. You saved them, and you saved her too." Gabriel nodded back towards the nurse's station, and Mackenzie saw Allison standing there amongst a gathering of nurses. She was watching Blaise and Anne, but when she seemed to register that he was looking at her she turned to him and gave him a sad smile before returning to the conversation going on around her.

"I'm going to go make sure everything is set here. Anne, walk with me," Leo said after taking a few moments to survey what was left of his people at the hospital while letting his sister have enough time to know that Blaise was all right. Anne looked questioningly at her brother and something passed between them quickly and silently, Anne giving Blaise one more squeeze before she followed without protest. Gabriel nudged Mackenzie before standing up, waiting for the other to join him before heading over to Blaise.

"Are you all right?" Gabriel's concern was evident again as he stopped besides Blaise, glancing to make sure that Mackenzie had actually followed. He didn't seem willing to let either of them sit on their own, and he was trying to make sure they were corralled together. Blaise just nodded in answer, shifting his bundled clothes so that they hid the stitches down his arm from view the best he could. "Funny, you look like you've been hacked at with a knife." There was a bite to Gabriel's words suddenly, and Blaise's carefully blank expression broke with surprise at the tone. Mackenzie stood there watching the two of them for a moment as Gabriel waited for Blaise to say something in response.

Someone in the room started to laugh, a chuckle at first but it grew a little. Mackenzie suddenly realized it was him who was laughing, and he put a hand over his mouth as he tried to stop it. Every emotion inside of him though was trying to bubble out in unreasonable laughter, and his shoulders shook even as he fought to push it all down again. He gave up when Blaise started to laugh with him, and the rest of the waiting room fell silent.

Leo and Anne suddenly reappeared, drawn by the sound from the talk they'd been having around the corner. Anne moved to Blaise and pulled him to her gently so that his sobbing laugh was muffled by her shoulder. Leo took a more direct approach with Mackenzie as he slapped the other just hard enough that it stung and cut through everything so that he could manage to choke it all back. Blaise's own laughter died down leaving their little group now standing in the middle of the silence that followed.

"Come on, let's get out of here," Leo said, giving a short look to one of the deputies that was staring at Mackenzie judgementally. Anne nodded, taking Blaise's hand to lead him out through the front door. She was going to drive them back to Blaise's place while Leo took charge of Mackenzie. The siblings had discussed the fact that they didn't think either men should be left alone for the night until the shock wore off and they came to better terms with what had happened. Anne hadn't even thought for a moment about not staying with Blaise, she was too shook up herself with the knowledge that if Mackenzie had been a few moments later with the shot Blaise could be in worse shape if not gone completely.

When they reached Blaise's place, Gabriel retreated back into the kitchen as Anne took Blaise upstairs to help him change. When she came back down a few minutes later while he was making a can of soup for his dinner he was surprised that she had willingly left the other alone even for a few minutes. She leaned against the counter for a few awkward moments in silence before she caught Gabriel in a squared look.

"What did you say that set them off?" Gabriel paused before he took the pan and poured the soup into the bowl he'd grabbed down from the cabinet. He could feel her watching him, but took his time. He wasn't sure if it was because of the few memories he was getting back bringing out a part of the old him, but he didn't feel as willing to cave to her whims as he had before.

"I asked him if he was all right, and he said he was fine. I called him on it, said that he looked more like he'd been carved up with a knife. He needs to face what happened before it eats at him too much like the thing with Marie does." When he turned around with his bowl balanced carefully in one hand he saw that Anne's look had intensified, and he felt a stir of unease that he pushed back. The heat from the soup was seeping through the bowl and starting to burn his palm slightly, but he ignored it as he met her gaze.

"Don't you think that was a little harsh? It's not like it had been a few weeks, hell it had hardly been a few hours. People need some time to adjust before they can always just face things and move on. And where do you get off even mentioning what happened with Marie? You weren't around then so you don't know how it was."

"I know how it is. I sat out with him while he got wasted the night that the rest of you were all out at your place for the anniversary of her death. I saw how much it still eats at him, that's where I get off on mentioning it. The last thing he needs is to let something else fester inside him emotionally." He thought for a moment that she was going to hit him when she pushed away from the counter, but half way to him she seemed to lose steam and came to a stop.

"That was different than this. Marie's death hit all of us hard, and Leo needed someone to blame so he focused on Blaise and himself. I'm not going to let this tear at him, but he still needs time to deal with it before you can expect him to just move on. Don't push things." She ran a hand through her hair, looking flustered for the first time since he'd met her. They both jumped a little when Blaise came around the corner from the living room, and Anne gravitated to him. "I thought you were going to lie down. I said I'd bring the tea up."

"I…I thought I'd come down and make sure you didn't need any help," Blaise said, managing to cover up whatever he had started to say at first with nothing more than a slight hesitation. "We're not keeping you up, are we Gabe?" Gabriel glanced down at the bowl of soup in his hands that Blaise had apparently not noticed him holding, but he didn't comment.

"No, you aren't. I don't have to work tomorrow so I was going to stay up reading," he said, which was partially the truth. Blaise nodded as he set about getting the tea made himself despite Anne's insistence that she'd make it, but she dropped it after a few moments. Blaise seemed to need the activity right then, this becoming more evident when he had gotten to the point where he was just waiting for the water to boil but he still messed with the tea bags a bit restlessly. Gabriel set about finishing his soup, feeling awkward in the silence as he watched Blaise out of the corner of his eye.

He wanted to say something, but he didn't know what other than the things that had already been said. He had the urge to try and pop Blaise's defenses and make him let some of the emotion he was keeping bottled up boil over, but he wanted to respect Anne's feelings on it. He'd give Blaise some time to start facing things, but eventually he would feel the need to push to get his friend out of it. He felt more confident in doing it too. He knew that part of it was he knew Blaise better now, but he felt more at ease in asserting himself now that he was remembering more things than he had before. He was finding that with his memories came the assurance that he wasn't so different than he had been, he'd just been more assured of himself in the snippits of memory.

The kettle gave a whistle to let them know the tea was done, and Blaise stared at it for a moment before seeming to register what the noise meant. He poured two cups of water with a tea bag each, and let Anne add what she wanted while he did the same. Gabriel had a feeling Anne would have preferred coffee by the way she glanced at the maker on the counter, but she didn't say anything about it.

"See you guys in the morning," Gabriel said after them as Blaise started back towards the stairs without notice. Anne gave Gabriel a thankful look for keeping quiet before she followed him and left Gabriel alone in the kitchen once again. Gabriel finished his soup and set the bowl into the sink before heading into his room. He could hear their muffled voices above him for a while before they died down into quieter murmurs and then finally silence.

About four hours had passed when the nightmare tore him awake feeling disoriented and lost. For a few seconds he didn't know where he was, and when a dark figure rose up beside him he pushed himself away from it and hit the floor flat on his back. The thing leaned over him, a dark shroud covering its face as it said something to him. A light clicked on from the nightstand and Anne was looking down at him, her hair loose and wild as it hung around her face.

"Are you all right?" She looked at him with concern, doing a quick once over to make sure no stitches were pulled as she slid to the edge of the bed. She reached towards him for a moment, but seemed to hesitate since Blaise appeared so shaken. Instead she lowered herself down onto the floor beside him, giving him a few moments to pull himself together. Blaise was working quickly at separating reality from the dream, his brain finally catching up fully to the fact that he was awake. The strange man wasn't standing over him and writing on the walls in blood before Blaise found himself buried under the snow. The McGully's were dead though and it was something that echoed inside his dreams and out.

He wished he had understood when their deaths had been new fragments of his dreams that starred a faceless women's corpse crying out

68

with the screams of an infant. He wished part of him wasn't relieved when he had realized that the dream had meant them, and that Anne was still safe from appearing in the horrors of his visions. He had even naively hoped that it would be the end of the nightmares, but he'd just been proven wrong about that. Replacing the images of the crying corpse there was now buildings on fire, and Anne and the dogs racing through the trees trying to escape something.

Anne sat silent, leaning back against the bed and waiting for him to collect his thoughts. She was letting him speak first, and Blaise felt the urge to tell her the truth, all of it. He wanted to tell her about the dreams and how they were coming true, how he couldn't stop them even if he tried. He had learned that years ago when he was still in college and no matter what he tried to do he hadn't been able to save a friend from dying in a drunk driving accident. He tried to push away from the doubt and fear and focus on her, on what she would think if he told her and if it would even do any good for her to know. He sighed and ran a hand over his face to try and wipe away some of the left over haze before he sat up. He knew the answers to those questions; she'd think he'd lost it and it wouldn't do any good even if she didn't.

"I'm all right...was just a bad dream. It left me feeling disoriented for a few seconds," he said, his voice hushed and low as though he was afraid of waking some demon that slept in the corner. He hoped she took it as him trying not to wake Gabriel, though he highly doubted that he hadn't managed to do that already by falling out of the bed. Anne nodded silently with understanding, though amongst the concern he saw a hint of doubt in her eyes. He felt that internal tug to tell her again, but pushed it down as he stood up. "I'm going to grab a glass of water. I'll be right back."

"Okay...do you want me to come with you?" Blaise shook his head in response, and saw the urge to argue flicker across Anne's face. It flitted away though, leaving her with a slightly hurt expression as she pulled herself up off the floor next to him. He leaned to her and pulled her into a hug, ignoring the slight pull he felt on the stitches lining his arm. She rested against him, her arms slipping around his waist."Promise you'd tell me if you weren't okay?" Blaise placed a kiss on the side of Anne's head, lingering there in the scent of her hair.

"Of course...but I'm fine. A little battle scarred, a little sore, and still not quite registering everything that happened. But, I'm okay," he said quietly into her ear, and he felt her arms tighten around him for a second before she pulled away. "Be right back." Anne felt guilt pull at her, knowing that she should be the one comforting him and not the other way around. She made herself stand up straight, pulling herself together so that she could be the strong one for them.

When Blaise pulled away she nodded, waiting until he stepped out the bedroom door before climbing back into the bed. Blaise held in his sigh until he was down the stairs, pausing there for a moment. He mentally told himself he was okay as he glanced back up the steps. It was the future that troubled him the most, the question of if they'd all be okay by the time whatever was happening had passed.

He made his way to the kitchen, glad for the silence that greeted him as it gave him a few moments to try and push the images from the dream away. Unless he could take his mind off of it he wouldn't get anymore sleep tonight. He noted that the first floor was completely dark, and was relieved he hadn't managed to wake Gabriel up with his tumble. Blaise picked his way to the kitchen by feel and memory, not wanting to turn any lights on. By the time he reached the sink his eyes had adjusted and he reached up to pull a glass down, filling it once and draining it before filling it again.

This one he drank slower as he thought about the decision that had solidified in his mind without him even acknowledging it before now. With the deaths of the McGully's he had come to a conclusion, he was going to stop whatever else the dreams were leading up to. He had to at least try, there seemed too much at stake. He had to tell himself that it would work this time, that he'd change things even though he'd never been able to do so before. He had to try now, everyone he knew seemed at risk of some lingering presence that he couldn't pinpoint.

He dumped the rest of the water out into the sink before setting it on the counter to wash in the morning. He headed back upstairs to Anne, not realizing that Gabriel had opened his door and been watching him. Gabriel closed his door again having decided against interrupting Blaise's thoughts, surprised by the mix of emotions that could be read from the other's face when he thought there was no one around to hide them from.

Anne was still up when he got back into the bedroom, sitting and waiting for him with the light on. He climbed under the covers besides her and leaned back against the headboard as she watched him. He had hoped they could just try to go back to sleep, but Anne seemed determined to say something so he waited for her to speak her mind.

"You did good keeping them safe from him, you know that don't you?" She spoke quietly but with the conviction that the discussion was going to happen. She sighed when he didn't respond, instead choosing to wait until she'd said her piece. "Blaise, you managed to keep two people safe and alive today-"

"And, two people also died today. Anne, I know what you're trying to do and I know what you're going to say, but in the end that's what it comes down to. I missed something or overlooked some sign that could have helped me know this was coming. That little boy is going to grow up now without either parent and will eventually find out why. I may have saved two but I lost two as well." The words came out in a sharper tone than he had meant, and he saw the look of worry flicker over Anne's face. They sat for a second, Anne trying to think of what to say but Blaise's tone had caught her off guard. Blaise was acting like he had when Marie had died and he had done nothing but blame himself. Anne wondered if Gabriel had been right, if it was better to push Blaise to face things. It gave her stomach a twist thinking about it, she hadn't liked the Blaise she'd been confronted with after Marie and she didn't want that version of him to return. It had been the only time she hadn't known how to handle or read him.

It had gotten to the point back then that things had fallen apart between them, though they'd also been just starting out. They had come a lot further now and she wasn't sure she could handle starting over again if Blaise pulled away from her. She looked up when she felt his hand rest on top of hers, and she found the Blaise she understood looking at her.

"I'm sorry Anne. I just…right now all I want to do is lie down and try to go back to sleep. Don't worry about me though, remember I said I was okay and I meant it." Anne nodded and curled up beside Blaise, resting her head on his shoulder. She told herself it'd be like the other times where a patient hadn't made it. The times where, though far from easy on Blaise, he understood that he had done what he could and didn't carry it on his sleeve. "I want to handle this with you, I'm not going to push you away this time. I just can't help but feel that I should have seen something, but I'll deal with that and come to terms with it."

"You didn't fail me or anyone else." Blaise made a noncommital sound to this, but she felt him relax a little besides her. She only knew a little about what Blaise's family life had been before his mother had left his father, but she knew enough to understand that the voice that told Blaise he was to blame for failing belonged to his father. She shifted next to him, sliding down onto the bed and pulling him with her.

She would comfort him as she could, try to pour all the strength and forgiveness she could give into him while accepting his grief and anger, his guilt and pain in return. At one point he bit her shoulder and she pressed against him harder in response, refusing to let him go. Once they were exhausted she lay beside him with her arms around him, listening for his breathing to steady in the slow pattern of sleep before she drifted off as well.

"How could you chose them over me Gabriel?" They were standing in a small room that appeared to be someone's private room, though who's he still wasn't sure. "You're willing to tear our family apart for their sake."

"I told you I won't give it to you, Michael. It's my decision to make, and I've made it. Now leave, please."

Chapter 6 – Sugar-

Mackenzie had gone out to the church again in the early morning hours despite the bitter cold temperatures that settled over the town. It had been below zero for the last few days, and if you spent too long outside any skin that was exposed would start to tingle and then go numb within a few minutes. He had the meeting that morning about whether he'd be reinstated to full active duty or not, and if the shooting had been justified. He had been questioned by the woman sent by the state to do the investigation, and after that he'd been told he could be on desk duty. He had found that sitting at a desk all day was just as bad as staying home all day. He'd fallen into the habit of coming over to the church in the morning for some time alone to face how he felt that particular day, and this morning was no different. At first the Father had come out to talk with him, but a couple of days ago he had asked if he could spend the time on his own. He had assured the priest that he would come find him if he needed to talk.

He'd been sitting in the front pew before the altar for about fifteen minutes when he heard the sound behind him, but he didn't look up. From time to time another person would wander in to do their own silent prayers, and Mackenzie figured the footsteps belonged to one of them. When a man sat down beside him though he raised his head to see who had interrupted his thoughts. He didn't recognize the man and sat up straight to give him a questioning look.

"Are you feeling a bit lost again, Mackenzie? I don't think prayers are going to help much this time." The stranger's use of his name caught Mackenzie off guard, and he tried to place if he did know the man but hadn't recognized him at first.

"Do I know you?" The man gave him an amused look for a second, and Mackenzie felt a jerk of recognition but it was gone as fast as it came as the man fell serious once more. He looked up at the alter instead of Mackenzie now, staring at the form of Christ on the cross.

"Not personally, no, though most people know of me. Why are you here, Mackenzie? Looking for forgiveness for taking a life? Or are you hoping to cleanse yourself of all your other sins? The Lord knows you have plenty that you need to atone for." The man turned to look at him, studying Mackenzie like someone would study an interesting insect on the wall. He turned away leaving Mackenzie feeling strangely bare like he'd managed to strip away everything about him and leave it all out on the table. Gabriel had done that at the hospital when he'd noticed Anne holding his hand, and he liked it even less now that a stranger had done it.

"I'm coming to terms with what happened. I know I'm not perfect, but I don't think that I'm beyond his compassion. Again, do I know you? You seem to know quite a lot about me, but I can't place where I would have met you before." Mackenzie felt on the defensive, he'd been working hard on being okay with what he had done even if he couldn't ever feel right about it. The man seemed to be trying to chip that away, and his hold on things was still a bit tenuous.

"You have a chance to atone, I'm giving it to you. If you're interested you can find me here. He may not feel like forgiving you," the man nodded towards the crucifix, "but I'm not as willing to give up. He's sent me to give you another chance. You can't expect forgiveness just by convincing yourself what you did was right."

Mackenzie stared at the man waiting for the punchline, though when one didn't come he got the uneasy feeling that the man wasn't completely there mentally as he was talking about God giving him permission to help guide him. He sat back in the seat, and looked up at the alter again.

"So he gave you permission to prove him wrong about me. I always thought his word was final." The man stood from the pew, looking down at Mackenzie for a second.

"If you want to find your salvation then let me know, Mackenzie." Mackenzie shook his head, glancing down at the floor before turning to give the man a response only to find himself alone. He looked behind him, but all he could see was the door to the church closing quietly. A tight knot formed in his chest at that man's quick retreat, and he felt a weight drop in his stomach. He got up from the pew and left the church, all certainty that he had done the right thing back at the hospital shaken. He headed home to change, needing to be ready for the meeting he had that morning at the station.

Leo had woken up later than he had intended that morning, and was afraid he would be late for work. Marie wasn't helping as she stood in the doorway to the bathroom giving him a look from over his shoulder in the reflection from the mirror. She had gotten worse the last few days since Mackenzie had come over the night of the shooting. He had hoped she'd stay out of sight while his friend was there, but she had stood in the background the entire time. When Leo wasn't at home and wasn't in her presence he knew that it wasn't right, that things weren't good and she was influencing him to pull away from the rest of his life.

It was harder when she was standing there in front of him, when she guilted him about leaving and asked why he was choosing everything else over her. Afterall he had lost her once and now he was acting like it was no big deal that she had come back for him. That had been the line she'd given him that morning as he'd climbed out of bed. She made his head fuzzy and he felt like he couldn't focus on anything but her in the house.

"Are you sure you can't stay home? I'm sure the meeting will go fine without you if things are as you say." Leo was working on a rush job at shaving, wanting to make sure he looked as professional as possible. He wasn't the one at risk, but he wanted the best impression possible going into the meeting. It wasn't that he was worried Mackenzie wouldn't get reinstated, he'd been basically told that the day before when he'd been told the decision had been made and to set up the meeting. The woman the state had sent had been nice, her name was Jessica and she'd approached the shooting head on and quickly gathered the information she needed from all of them.

He was worried about making a good impression for the sake of his precinct. He knew that, as approachable as she seemed, Jessica would be taking her impressions of them all back to the state. Some of the guys that worked for him had hopes of getting onto the state force someday, and it would help if their boss didn't look like a slob.

He finished, coming out with only a couple of minor cuts left behind despite Marie's efforts to distract him. When he turned around she was staring at him through narrowed eyes and was blocking the doorway.

"Marie, I have to be there. I'm the sheriff and with that comes the responsibility to be around when one of my officers has something like this. I can't stay home and just expect Mac to tough it out, even if I know they found it to be justifiable." Leo tried to move past her, but she stayed where she was.

"It's another woman, isn't it?" Leo felt a jolt of nerves, wondering if she had somehow guessed that he'd been thinking about Jessica. He hadn't been thinking of her that way, though he had found her attractive when she had shown up a couple of days ago. He faltered for a moment, and Marie's eyes narrowed even more.

"Dammit, Marie, it's not another woman. What's up with you? You never acted jealous or even mildly concerned that I would stray before and now you're pissed because I'm going to work to support Mackenzie." He brushed past her, feeling her eyes follow him as he grabbed his shirt to pull on. He glanced at the clock and cursed silently as he saw he hadn't been as quick with the shave as he'd hoped.

"Well, before I wasn't dead because my good for nothing husband wasn't able to pull himself away from work to come home in time for dinner." She spat the words at him, and Leo felt like she'd slapped him. The sensible side of Leo was telling him he needed to leave now, alarms were going off in the back of his mind but it was pushed away by the sudden weight of guilt.

"Marie…I've told you I'm sorry about that. I should have been with you that night, and I know that. I'm not leaving you, but I do have to go. I want to stay, but I can't just stand this meeting up." Leo turned to face her, but his apology didn't seem to have any effect on her so he went to her instead. The meeting didn't start for another forty minutes, it was plenty of time for him to try and show her that he meant it when he had said she was the only one. He'd have to rush a little to get into town on time, but that was what four-wheel drive was for.

"You wish I never came back, don't you?" She looked up at him with sad eyes, sliding her arms around him when he pulled her to him.

Yes. The thought was there for just a second before it was pushed back again.

"No, of course I don't wish that. All I've wanted these last few years is for you to come back to me. I'm not going to push you aside now that you have. I don't have long, but I can stay a little longer." With that she managed a smile and she pulled him back to the bed, another victory under her belt.

By the time he got out of the house he was running late. When it came time for him to leave she had tried again to talk him into staying, getting in his way as he redressed and throwing more guilt at him. When he had finally made it to the front door she had stood in the middle of the small living room looking dejected.

"I'll be back this evening," he said, leaning to kiss the top of her head though that voice told him not to make eye contact or he wouldn't be making it out of the house. He started towards the door without looking at her, and paused when he heard her call after him.

"Love you, right?"

"Of course, love you," Leo said, instinctively looking back to give her a small smile and the frightened part of his brain all but failed him. He wavered with his hand on the doorknob as he stared at her sad eyes but his reason finally kicked back in and he turned to leave the house, walking faster than was probably necessary. He got to the car and climbed behind the wheel and just sat there for a few minutes to get a handle on himself. He had almost stayed, almost just gone back to bed with her and called in to tell work he wasn't going to make it.

When he finally started to drive he found that the further he got the more at ease he felt, and the more reasonable he seemed to be as well. The fog that seemed to sit over his mind when he was around Marie lifted, and it left him feeling relieved. He reached the end of the long drive up to his house, and sat for a few seconds at the crossroads. Turning right took him into town while left would take him out towards Anne's house. That painful pull tried to sneak in and tell him to turn around and go back to Marie again, but the rational side of him said that he needed to talk to someone.

He pulled out and headed towards town as he mulled this over. He didn't want to tell Anne, because he knew she'd tell Blaise who would suggest therapy or something equally ridiculous. Leo had gone to a therapist on the urgings of his sister right after Marie's death, and he'd found his feelings on them were founded. The man had done nothing but urge Leo to talk, and then sat nodding his head and acting interested in what he was saying despite Leo's suspicion that the man wasn't listening. Leo had just stopped going after their second session, and lied to Anne by saying he was still going each week.

That left Mackenzie, who did already know that Leo had seen Marie that first night though Leo hadn't shared with him that he'd continued to see her after that. Mackenzie had so much going on right now though that Leo didn't feel like it was fair to dump this on him. The last thing his friend probably needed was to hear that Leo was likely losing his mind. Leo pulled into the station, not even realizing he had already driven the entire way into town until he had.

He decided then as he saw Mackenzie getting out of his car a couple of spots down that he would wait until after the meeting today and see how Mackenzie was doing. He would talk to him then if he seemed to be handling things well enough. If Mackenzie seemed stable then Leo would ask him if he wanted to go out for drinks that night to celebrate his reinstatement and he'd bring it up there. This seemed to put his concerns for his own sanity at ease for the moment, and he got out to meet Mackenzie up at the door so they could head in together.

The meeting had taken longer then he felt it really needed to considering they all knew the outcome with the exception of Mackenzie. The other had seemed distracted through the whole thing, but when Jessica finally said that her conclusion was that he could return to active duty in the next couple of days he seemed to relax a little. He even took the stipulation that he attend a few therapy sessions with the local psychologist, the same one Leo had gone to, in stride which was better than Leo would have.

Everyone that had been involved filed out of the room, Leo saying thank you to Jessica and telling her to travel safely before she went. In the end it was only Mackenzie and him left in the small conference room that also served as their interrogation room when the need arose. Mackenzie stayed seated, seeming to guess that Leo probably wanted to talk to him before he was dismissed completely. Leo sat back down now that they were alone, the sounds of the station going back to its normal work flow picking up outside the room.

"How are you holding up, Mac?" Leo figured the best way to go about things was to be straight-forward with Mackenzie. The other had seemed better over the last couple of days the few times he'd talked with Leo, but today he seemed distracted and Leo wanted to know if it was more than the meeting that was making him that way. Mackenzie seemed to snap out of whatever thought he'd been having, and he looked at Leo with a quick smile that was almost normal.

"It's been a little rough with worrying about my job and just…dealing with things. At least I know I don't have to worry about the job part now, though the dealing part may take a bit longer. Hell, maybe I'll find that talking at the shrink will actually manage to help." Mackenzie tried to pull it off as a joke, but it fell flat between the two of them. Leo sighed as Mackenzie looked down at the table, going quiet on him again.

"It's okay to feel bad, Mac. I don't think you can avoid it, but I need to know that you don't feel like you're to blame for it. You seemed good yesterday, but today you're a little shaken. I want you to talk to me if you need to." Leo kept his focus on Mackenzie, watching his friend for any clue to what was going through his head. Mackenzie was usually a pretty simple read, but the other was staying focused on the table for the moment.

"It's just the meeting today. I guess it kind of brought things up again. I-" Mackenzie stopped, seeming to think better of saying something. Leo felt a little frustration, not use to Mackenzie hiding things from him and try as he might he couldn't keep some of that frustration from leaking out.

"Mac, I'd prefer you not keep secrets from me. If something is up, you tell me. You never kept things from me before." Mackenzie looked at him then for a second, but just shook his head.

"I just need a few more days, Leo. Give me that, and if you don't feel like I've pulled things together by then you can interrogate me all you want. I'm doing okay, today has just brought it a little closer to home than I've been keeping it the last few." Leo couldn't read any dishonesty from Mackenzie, though he still felt like he wasn't getting quite everything either. He didn't push though, leaning back in his chair and looking out at the squad room through the partially opened door.

"All right, I can do that. I know you know this already, but you did what was right. I am here if you want to talk, though I can't claim the same expertise as Doctor Crazy." Mackenzie managed a slight smile, and it put Leo at ease that the other wasn't so far gone in his guilt not to find humor in things. "Why don't you get going? I have some incredibly important filing to do, and I'm sure there's some woman waiting for her lunch somewhere."

"Actually there is, so I should get going." Leo raised an eyebrow at Mackenzie expectantly as the other stood. "It's Allison, the nurse that was there when…things happened. She came into the café yesterday and asked if I wanted to meet to talk. Said it may do us both some good."

"Good, I'm glad. It may help both of you a bit. Maybe you should see about talking with Blaise too. What I understand he hasn't really said much to Anne about it all, and he isn't doing that great. Though, that seems to have been going on longer than just the last couple of days. If you get a chance though…maybe check in with him," Leo said, a little surprised but glad that Mackenzie wasn't just meeting up with someone for a simple lunch and hook up.

"I will, I'll give him a call or grab him when he drops Gabriel off sometime." Mackenzie headed for the door but paused when he reached it to give Leo a quick look. "You don't look so good yourself lately, Leo. I haven't asked cause I've been so caught up in my stuff, but is there anything you need to talk about?" Leo's look must have faltered for a second, because Mackenzie pulled back from the door a little.

"No, I'm fine. It's just been a lot of late nights getting things sorted out." Leo almost spilled the whole thing about Marie, but the words didn't come. All that made it out was the excuses, and he saw Mackenzie's face tighten a little at the lie. They stayed like that for a few moments, Mackenzie letting the silence drag on to see if Leo would break and fill it.

"I suppose if you're letting me keep my secrets to my chest a little while longer I can do the same for you," Mackenzie said, pulling on his coat. It was Leo's turn not to meet his gaze and after a few moments Mackenzie was gone, leaving Leo alone in the room.

"I'm afraid she's taking control," Leo said quietly after a few moments, finally able to get the words out but the empty room didn't appear to have any suggestions.

Mackenzie was a few minutes late when he entered the diner though that was normal for him. He normally felt a bit guilty making people wait, but today it seemed magnified as he walked towards the booth that Allison was sitting at. She already had an iced tea and what looked like the remains of a cup of soup in front of her, and he wanted to kick himself. She had asked him to meet because she wanted to talk with someone who had shared the experience of what happened with the McGully's, and here he was showing up after she'd already ordered. He slid into the booth across from her, catching Anne's eyes from a couple of tables over where she was taking another order. She would already know what he wanted, and he was glad since it gave them a bit more uninterrupted time.

"I'm sorry I'm late," Mackenzie said before Allison had a chance to call him on it. Instead of giving him shit for it she just nodded, taking a sip of her iced tea before really looking at him.

"It's all right Callahan, I came early cause I had some time to kill. Did your meeting go okay? I heard that they were telling you their decision this morning." The use of his last name didn't phase him, the times they'd talked at the hospital she'd always used his last name. He didn't know why, but he'd accepted it fairly easily since they'd never really gone past simple small talk and work conversations when things brought them together.

"It went okay. They said it was justified like Leo thought they would, but I can't seem to make myself feel right about the whole thing. I was doing all right for the last couple of days, but this morning it hit me again that maybe I should have done something differently." Anne dropped off his coffee, and Mackenzie put his hands around it to absorb the warmth. She didn't say anything when she came, but she placed a hand on his shoulder for a second before she walked away again to leave them alone to talk.

"I don't think you're supposed to feel right about shooting someone, but you shouldn't let yourself feel guilt over it either. It was unfortunate, but it was what needed to be done to stop others from getting hurt. I've been meaning to tell you thank you, by the way. One of the people you helped keep safe was me." Allison nudged a few remaining pieces of potato around in her bowl as she talked, scooting it idly across to one side and then back.

"I know that what I did kept you safe, and I can appreciate that. But, what I did also put an end to someone's life. I don't know, it's hard to explain. I've only talked to Blaise a little, but he seemed to understand the best so far. You know that what you did was for the good of most of the people involved, but it wasn't for the best with Alex. It wasn't even really the best for that kid, cause now he's stuck with no parents and no explanations. He may never know what his parents were like or who they were." He could tell that Allison was studying him though he kept his eyes on his coffee. It seemed easier to talk to her about all of it than it was with Leo, and he had a feeling its because she was there to see what happened. She could tell him that what he did was for the best, and it meant a little more since she'd actually seen it.

"He'll know who his parents were, Taylor and Alex both have good families that will help take care of him if they ever can agree who should take him. There's a lot of hurt going on between the two groups, but I think in the end they'll come to understand its better if the kid knows what they were like together before this happened. Eventually he'll find out what his dad did, but before that he should know who his dad was for most of his life." Mackenzie nodded, turning the cup in his hands a couple of times until Allison reached out to stop him by putting one of her hands over his. "Hey, all you need to know Callahan is that you tried to get through to him and in the end when that didn't work you did what you had to in order to keep everyone else safe."

"In your opinion were there any other options that I could have taken?" Mackenzie finally met her eyes, and she gave him the same sad smile that she had in the hospital that day after it was all over.

"No. The taser wasn't stopping him, he wasn't even acknowledging it. If you had tried to just wound him he could have kept going, and then he could have done a lot worse than he already had. If you tried to physically restrain him he could have hurt or killed you, and then we'd have been left trying to fight him off ourselves. Alex had to have been on something, and we'll know for sure what it was once the tox-screen comes back. In my opinion you did all you could, and it was the only option left that would ensure everyone else's safety." Mackenzie nodded silently, and they pulled apart when Anne came over with two plates. Mackenzie had gotten a burger while Allison had ordered a turkey club, and they both started in on their food for a few minutes.

"How are you holding up?" Mackenzie asked, feeling like an ass for not checking with her. She'd been one of the ones dealing with the brunt force of the attack, and yet all they'd talked about so far was how he'd been handling things. She shrugged mid-bite, and he waited for her to be ready to answer.

"Not too bad. I still find myself feeling a bit jumpy every now and then, and I'm still having nightmares though I don't consider that too bad since it hasn't been that long. Mainly right now I'm finding that I get bored and end up thinking about it when I don't want to. They told Blaise and me both to take a week off before we came back in, make sure we feel better before we may have to deal with a stressful environment again. I'd rather be there though, working to keep my mind off of things. I heard from some of the other nurses that Blaise is still stopping by even though the other doctors tell him that he needs to be at home resting, so I'm guessing he feels the same way."

He appreciated that she was being straight forward with him with how she was doing after he'd been honest with her. They didn't know each other that well, but that may have been why it was so easy to talk to her. It wasn't that he didn't trust Leo or Anne's judgements, but they both had their minds made up and wouldn't listen to anything that was to the contrary.

"Has he seemed off to you lately? Not just since the thing with the McGully's, but before that?" He didn't know why he decided to ask, and he glanced to find where Anne was to make sure she wasn't in earshot. She'd be upset if she felt he was talking about something that should just be between their group, but he wanted to know if others had noticed it too.

"Actually, he has. Some of the nurses have mentioned it and so did Doctor Maycroft. He seems really tired lately, and preoccupied like something's on his mind that he can't seem to completely ignore. He doesn't talk to anyone at the hospital about anything overly personal though. A few of us that work the same shifts as him often know a little about things with him and Anne, but he keeps his private life quiet at work. The one that would know best is probably Doctor Maycroft, they go for drinks sometimes after shift but I got the feeling he didn't know what was going on either." Allison's eyes followed his to Anne as she spoke, watching to make sure she didn't head over towards their table. Anne seemed to realize they were watching her, and Allison signaled that she needed more iced tea to cover for them.

"Whatever's going on, he's keeping it quiet with all of us too, even Anne. All she seems to know is that something's wrong, and that he's keeping it from her. I was hoping maybe he'd let something slip at work that could help put her mind at ease," Mackenzie took a sip of his coffee now that it had cooled to being slightly warm. Allison didn't answer since Anne came over then with the pitcher of iced tea.

"Everything tasting all right here guys?" Anne asked as she filled up the glass, and for a second she gave Mackenzie a look to let him know she knew something was up. He just gave her a small smile in return, hoping if he acted like they hadn't been talking about her she'd figure that she had just misread their looks.

"Everything tastes great, Anne. Thanks." Anne narrowed her eyes for a moment at this, but then one of her orders were called up by the cook and she turned away to get back to work.

"If she's anything like her brother she's not going to drop that. You're going to be in some trouble later, Callahan." Allison sounded amused by this, and Mackenzie rolled his eyes slightly.

"Thanks, I'll be sure to send some your way 'Miller'," he said, throwing her last name back at her and she laughed quietly. She had a slightly contagious laugh, and he found himself smiling back at her after a second. "Maybe I should tell her you were trying to get information about how serious Blaise was about her out of me. She'd probably kick your ass." Allison gave him a mock look of wide-eyed shock.

"You realize I'd just have to kick your ass then in retribution."

"And you just threatened an officer of the law, young lady," Mackenzie said in a serious tone, and Allison just held her two wrists up towards him.

"Then arrest me..." She grinned at him, and he nudged her hands down back towards the table.

"Don't tempt me. I'm not unfamiliar with handcuffing nurses," Mackenzie said, raising his eyebrow to make sure she got his meaning. She

80

smacked him lightly on the arm for the comment, though he was glad to see that she laughed. They fell into a moment of quiet then that managed not to feel completely awkward as they both picked at what was left of their food. Anne brought their check over after a few moments of this, and he grabbed it before she had the chance.

"You don't have to pay, Callahan," Allison said, grabbing her purse to pull out some cash to give him but he just shook his head.

"Consider it a thanks for meeting with me. It actually helped, I feel more like me than I have the last few days." Mackenzie set enough cash down to cover the bill and to give Anne a nice tip. Allison looked like she was about to protest but Anne picked the bill up before she could, and Mackenzie gave her a quick smile for catching on.

"If you need to talk again, let me know. I get to pay next time though, it was good for me to talk to someone about it too. The other girls try but they don't really get it." She stood and started to pull her coat on and he followed suit, watching her for a moment out of the corner of his eyes.

"No, next time I'm still going to pay. You're going to pay me back by answering a question for me," Mackenzie said, and he saw a moment of hesitation cross her face. He decided to forge forward before she could disagree, wondering what she thought he was going to ask her. "Why do you call me Callahan? I thought before that it was to do with being professional while at your job, but that's not it apparently. I do have a first name, you know." He saw a bit of relief for a second cross her face, and he wanted to ask what question she thought he had had for her.

"Oh, that. I call you Callahan, because to me Callahan is the nice cop that comes around from time to time, does his job well, and does it while seeming to show genuine concern for the people he deals with. Mackenzie on the other hand is some playboy show off that the other nurses talk about all the time, and they will probably some day band together to force into a committed relationship with one of them just to prove they can."

"They really talk about me that much?" Mackenzie said with a hint of pride after staring at her for a moment. She gave him a narrowed look before shaking her head.

"Bye Callahan. Don't let your head get too big." She gave his shoulder a pat as she walked past, and he grinned a little behind her back.

"Bye Miller. Give me some notice if my dates ever decide to unify behind me back." All he got was a short bark of laughter in response before she left. He turned to leave and saw Anne giving him a smirk from across the restaurant and he shook his head to signal her not to comment.

Blaise had been left with the empty house and the need to be alone but active after Anne and Gabriel had left. Anne had told him she'd take Gabriel into work that morning since she had to work at the diner anyway, and he'd accepted her suggestion. He'd then spent the first four hours of the morning chopping wood, falling into a rhythm with the fall of the axe and letting his mind go blank. He couldn't handle not having something to do because his mind would wander back to Taylor lying cold in the bed and the baby crying, but he'd found being around people in town was almost worse. Everyone wanted to ask how he was doing, and there were those he could tell wanted to ask just so they could say they'd talked to someone involved in the incident.

He had gone by the hospital a few times to check up on the baby boy and to just get a sense of normalcy, but one of the other doctors that he'd gotten to be friends with over the years had told him if he kept coming by the directors were talking about extending his leave. He'd taken the warning, but was now left to waste the day alone most of the time. It hardly helped that most nights he would wake up from the nightmares at least once.

He'd cleaned up after chopping a large pile of the wood and was now worn out. He toyed for a moment with going into town to visit Anne at the diner, but it was their busy time so she wouldn't be able to take a break to sit with him for another hour or so. He chose to read then, but he drifted off on his couch quickly after the burst of activity and the long night of little sleep.

At first he thought he'd woken up when he'd opened his eyes and he was still lying on the couch with the book lying on his chest.. When he tried lift his arm to look at what time it was from his watch he found he couldn't move though. Something shifted just out of his line of vision, and a sense of dread suddenly enveloped him as he tried to sit up. She came around to where he could see her and smiled at him, and he closed his eyes to try and wake himself up. It was trying to look like Anne, but he kept catching broken glimpses of whatever it was flickering across her face.

"Hey sugar, I wanted to spend some time with you when Gabriel wasn't here. I have a question I'm hoping you can answer." It was using Anne's voice, but there was a shattered quality to it like she was speaking through a radio who was slightly off in its reception. He still wasn't waking up, and he opened his eyes to find her standing over him. She didn't seem to reach for him but he felt a carass across his cheek. Her weight settled on top of him even before she actually straddled him, and he fought to move again but still had no response from his body.

"I have to wake up." He didn't realized he'd spoken until the words came out sounding heavy to him. It laughed and leaned down over him to press its lips to his, and his head suddenly seemed full of fog.

"No you don't. You're already awake, sugar. Relax, I know you're tired, I can do all the work," she said against his cheek before she leaned back again. She ran her fingertips down along his arms to where they were crossed over his chest under the book, and he could see dark spiderwebs appear then fade under his skin where they touched. "Now, tell me. Does he have it with him or did he hide it?"

"Wake up." He mumbled it to himself again, and she gave him a light slap on the cheek.

"I told you, you're already awake. I thought you'd be happy that I came back to spend time with you." Her hands had stopped at his wrists but he could still feel fingertips running along his arms and down his sides. She shifted on top of him and leaned slightly to look him in the eyes. "You have to know, even if he hasn't told you himself. It's important to me, he stole it when he was out at my place and I need it back, sugar."

"You're not Anne." Her look darkened, and a weight seemed to suddenly lay down on his chest pushing the air out of him. She put her hands into his hair and tugged lightly, pushing her hips down into his.

"Now sugar, who else would I be?"

"I told you he wouldn't fall for it. That's why I said to leave him be." She sat up suddenly when the man's voice cut in, but Blaise couldn't see who was talking. Anne, or at least the thing pretending to be her, narrowed her eyes with a look of annoyance. She sat up to look off to the side, but Blaise didn't see anyone else in the room unless they were just out of his line of vision.

"I'm at least doing something, which is more than I can say for you. I'm getting tired of waiting around."

"I said it wouldn't be much longer, and we'd be getting things done faster if you focused on what I've told you to do. If we get too hasty we'll draw attention to ourselves, and we need to stay unnoticed as long as possible. This isn't going to help, so leave. We're doing this my way, not yours." The argument looked like it was about to continue, but suddenly she decided against it. She looked back down at him and gave him a smile that made him think she would rip his throat out.

"Bye sugar, I'll see you again." With that she was gone, and Blaise sat up suddenly to look and find where she went. He was alone in the room though and the entire house was silent, and he took a moment to remind himself it had been a dream. There was no other explanation for it even if it hadn't been like his dreams before. He ran a hand over his face, trying to steady his nerves before he got to his feet. He suddenly felt like getting out of the house.

Chapter 7 – It's in the Woods -

Anne had headed out that morning for a run with the dogs, free for the day from work and nothing she needed to get done. Things were ready for their Christmas dinner in a few days, at least as ready as she was able to get them until that day when everything would go into the oven. She had all but forced Leo to meet her for dinner the night before, knowing something was wrong with her brother though no one seemed to know what. It was like some disease spread amongst the men of her life. Blaise had been the first and now Leo. Mackenzie was even showing the first signs of it as he was getting a bit distant and irritable towards people. His random but frequent meetings with Allison seemed to pull him out of it for a few days though.

Her dogs suddenly shied to the left and it pulled her out of her thoughts, reminding her she had need to be more diligent and aware than normal. They had been out several times over the last few months, but she had noticed that in the recent weeks the dogs would sense something in the forest that spooked them. She had thought she'd even caught a glimpse of the animal a few times, but never near enough or in open enough space for her to see what it was. It could be something as simple as an elk that had wandered in close to town, but it could also be a number for things far more worrisome. Her first thought was it was a moose, they came around the town all year long and the dogs didn't like them. They were mean and aggressive for an animal that looked so meek.

Now she thought it was a mountain lion after catch hints of its long form slinking along the snow, and it worried her more than a moose did. If the animal was starving it could decide to rush them, and with a mountain lion you couldn't be sure you'd see it before it hit. She called out for the dogs to turn back towards home, eyes catching movement out in front of them and to the right. The thing seemed to follow them, always keeping pace but never approaching far enough for her to catch more than a few seconds of its form flitting between the trees. It had to be a mountain lion, she couldn't think what else it could be. All the bears were hibernating at this time of the year, and it wasn't bulky enough for that. And, even if wolves had made their way this far into Colorado by now it seemed too long for that.

She felt relief when she pulled into the clearing that held her house, though it was followed with a bubble of frustration towards the animal. She had hoped it would have moved on by now, but it was hanging around which made it harder for her to take the dogs on the runs she normally would. It always seemed to follow them once they came upon it, and she never felt at ease then to keep going hoping it would just keep its distance. She wouldn't risk one of her dogs or herself for it.

She had unhooked the dogs and gotten them all into their run before finally trudging up to the front of the house to check the mail. When she turned the corner she was startled by a man sitting on her front step, and she realized it was Blaise. He seemed lost in thought about something and hadn't noticed her yet. She wondered how long he'd been sitting out there, and why he hadn't just used his key to go inside where it was warmer. She watched him for a few minutes, troubled by how worried and worn out he looked anymore. It had been that way for a while now, but it had gotten worse during the past month. She finally went around to the porch to meet him, and Blaise looked up as she sat down besides him.

"How long have you been out here waiting?" She leaned against him and he slid his arm around her shoulders automatically, pulling her close to share some of his warmth.

"Not too long. I just thought I'd stop by..." She nodded, sensing there was more to what he wanted to say so she waited him out. She had learned from Leo that silence was usually the best way to get someone to say something, and she used the tactic from time to time. It was hit or miss with Blaise though since he was so comfortable with lapses in conversation, but even he couldn't help but fill the quiet sometimes. He did so now as he spoke up, though she wouldn't have guessed what he said. "I think you should hold off on taking the dogs out for a while. I know you said you thought there was a bear earlier wandering around your property even after they all should have been asleep, and it might be safer if you didn't go out alone. If it is a bear it's probably starving which will make it more dangerous."

It had been two months since she had mentioned to the other's the thing she thought was a bear at the time, and her instinct was to call Blaise on the fact his concern seemed a bit late. He hadn't met her eyes once yet though, and she got the sense something else had triggered this sudden worry over a possibly starving bear. She followed his line of sight and found that he was watching the treeline, and she felt a heavy weight in her chest as she remembered the feeling of being followed.

"I don't think it's a bear, but I'll hold off for a while until we're sure that it's moved on. Does that work? I'm not willing to keep the dogs in all winter though." Blaise looked at her then, studying her like she'd been doing to him a few moments before. He knew she wouldn't normally agree so easily, taking the dogs out for their runs during the winter was something she rarely allowed to be interrupted.

"Have you seen it since then?"

"I've never seen it Blaise, not really. I just know its there from glimpses of movement and how the dogs react. It doesn't seem to have much interest in coming too close, but it does follow us sometimes. It's never approached the house though."

"Good...if it ever does don't hesitate to shoot. You don't want to wait to see what it's capable of." Anne nodded, glad to see he seemed to relax a little with her easy agreement. He cut her off then from seeing if that was all he was worried over, putting up those barriers that she could glimpse through but had never managed to fully break down. She cursed his father's belittling for giving Blaise those walls and the need to use them when he was young.

"You come out here just to tell me that you wanted me to stay out of the woods, or was there something else?" Blaise gave her a smile then, pulling her close to place a kiss against her temple.

"I was actually thinking of lunch, the 'stay out of the woods' part was just my formal duty as a concerned boyfriend." Anne smiled, standing up and pulling him up alongside her. She was going to accept it then, she decided. She'd accept that there was nothing else behind Blaise wanting her to take a break from running through the woods. It wasn't as much as she thought this was the truth as she didn't want to argue or pry. Right then all she wanted was to go for lunch and spend time with her boyfriend who had the day off for the first time since he'd been allowed to go back to work a week and a half ago.

Mackenzie had been avoiding the church since the man had shown up a second time, not saying much of anything different than he had the first time he'd been there. Mackenzie had a feeling that the man was crazy as he kept seeming to think Mackenzie knew about him, and that a lot of other people did as well. Knowing that he was likely insane didn't change the fact he had made Mackenzie feel the same guilt and despair over the McGully's as he had that first week. Michael was there that morning when he went for an early Christmas mass two days before the actual holiday. He had come and sat down besides Mackenzie just as the service was starting, leaving Mackenzie no choice but to stay seated where he was. They didn't speak to each other through the entire sermon, but Michael followed him out of the church as they left.

"Have you decided that you want to take my offer to save yourself?" Michael asked the question as they reached Mackenzie's car which seemed to have ended up alone in that side of the parking lot. Mackenzie didn't answer, fishing his keys out of his pocket to get the car door open, feeling exposed now that they were isolated.

"You know, I haven't figured out just what it is you want yet. You keep showing up to convince me of my guilt which isn't something I need someone to do for me, and you keep saying you have a way for me to repent but you've never told me how. Just what is it you want me to do?" Mackenzie turned to looked at Michael, frustrated when he couldn't seem to find the right key to get his car door open. The man looked at him mildly, having never really cracked much emotion during their short conversations.

"I want you to understand that I'm giving you the chance to save yourself and the ones you love. If you really must know how I want you to do that, even though you have yet to face the full gravity of your situation I'll tell you. I want you to help me find something that was taken from us." Mackenzie shook his head, finally finding the key and turning to stick it into the lock on his door. He wished he had one of those automatic button locks like he always did at least once every winter.

"And what exactly is it and who took it? Maybe you should go harp on them about saving their souls."

"Don't patronize me. If you really wish to protect your town from trouble then you should find out what he's done with it. Go ask my brother, Gabriel, where he's hidden it. I won't hold them back forever." Mackenzie stopped at the mention of Gabriel's name, and turned to face Michael again only to find that he was alone in the parking lot. On the other side near the doors he could see the last few stragglers from the service pulling out from their spots to head home. He looked around to see where the man had gone, but there was no sign of Michael anywhere and only his footsteps led up to his car.

The last two days before Christmas passed in a rush of trying to get prepared, but right then he couldn't care less if he had everything already wrapped and packed in his car. It wouldn't matter if he couldn't get himself out of work on time to meet the others. Blaise had been glad to come back to work, glad that his physical wounds had healed well and the emotional ones were getting there. Mackenzie had gone back to work as well, and the two of them kept mentioning that they needed to meet for drinks but it never seemed to happen with their schedules. The town seemed to pick up speed the last few weeks, and with the increase of injuries and incidents they both had been working long hours.

The normal lull they got during the winter months didn't seem to be happening this year even with the tourists gone and people nestled inside away from the cold. There had been more accidents, fights and injuries this past few weeks than they'd had the previous two months all together and a lot of times people weren't able to or didn't want to explain them.

Blaise glanced at the front doors, hoping that he'd manage to sneak through them in a few minutes and that nothing else would show up to delay him from getting out to Anne's for dinner. Anne had picked Gabriel up from work for him earlier that day since the coffee shop had closed up early for the holiday, so he at least didn't have to worry about grabbing him on his way out there. Blaise had finished his last check up and was filling in his replacement just then, and finally managed to make his way out of the hospital doors.

The drive out was quiet, everyone else was already with their families and eating their dinner. He pushed it a little to get out to Anne's, hoping they'd all had the sense to start without him. When he finally walked into the house he could tell they'd waited until just a few minutes ago as they were all just starting to eat, and he slid into his seat to join them.

Things seemed like normal for the first time in the last two months as they all ate and talked, opening presents after the dinner was over. It got late without them even realizing it until Leo finally stood up with a stretch.

"I need to head home, guys. Thanks for dinner Anne, it was great," he said, moving to grab a hug from his sister. Anne got up from the couch where she was sitting besides Blaise, and gave Leo a questioning look.

"You could stay since it's late. You usually do." Leo shook his head, giving Anne a tired smile before moving to gather his things.

"No, I need to head into work early to take care of a few things. It will be easier if I don't have to worry about driving to my place first in the morning." Blaise noticed that Mackenzie seemed to stiffen a little, but the other didn't speak up to voice whatever had struck a chord with him. Instead he gave Leo a smile, though there was a bit of bite to it. The two of them had been butting heads recently over something, but neither of them would say what.

"Need me to be there to help out? I didn't realize we had that much extra that needed to be done." Leo seemed to falter, and for a moment Blaise thought he was going to set his coat back down and stay. He seemed to remember something though, and he shook his head as he pulled the jacket on.

"It's stuff I need to do. Going over the hours from the last few weeks since everyone's been working extra. I can handle it, don't worry about coming in to help out. I'll see you guys all later, Merry Christmas." When Leo opened the door Anne grabbed her coat and went outside with him, leaving the three of them sitting there. Gabriel had stayed quiet other than to say a quick goodbye as Leo walked out the door, but he spoke up now.

"What's been going on with him lately?" Gabriel looked at Mackenzie, knowing he'd know the best if something was up with Leo. Mackenzie just shook his head and stood up to grab another beer from the fridge. Blaise glanced at the front door, watching for Anne to come back inside. They could all hear the raised voices that the two siblings were attempting to keep hushed outside.

"I don't know what the hell has crawled up his ass. He won't talk to me about it, and if I ask he just gets defensive. He's probably telling Anne to mind her own damn business right now," Mackenzie said, walking back to his seat and taking a long drag off his beer. Blaise was troubled by how angry Mackenzie sounded. The two had had their arguments in the past, but they were usually short lived. Mackenzie was hard to keep angry and he almost always was able to defuse Leo with a well timed joke, or some sensible reason they should stop fighting.

Blaise had a feeling that he knew at least to an extent what Leo had been keeping secret. It hadn't escaped his notice that Leo had said he'd dreamt of Marie around the same time Blaise had his dream where Marie was devouring Leo, and he worried that the other was still seeing her and she was responsible for the mood he'd been in. Blaise had no idea how to approach the subject though. Asking a guy if he was seeing his dead wife around wasn't the best plan to begin with, and if he was being hostile towards Mackenzie for asking what was up he'd be even worse towards Blaise. It left him feeling like he was floundering for any way to try and stop his dreams from broadsiding them.

Anne came back inside and though she tried to put a smile on he could tell she was very upset. Anne didn't cry much but her eyes were watery and red-rimmed, and he felt a stab of anger towards Leo for whatever he'd said to hurt her.

"Well, no reason to let that asshole ruin our night. How about we get out some eggnog and rum, and we can watch whatever Christmas movie they have going on right now." She sounded just a little too cheerful, and Blaise moved to help her grab the stuff from the kitchen. The movie that they ended up watching was The Grinch, and a couple of them agreed that it was a fitting tribute to their absent friend.

They were all woken up in the early morning hours by the sounds of chaos erupting from out in the dogrun. Anne beat him downstairs, and Blaise was glad to see Mackenzie grab her away from the door of the dogrun to stop her from barging out into a bad situation. Blaise went down the hall, passing Gabriel who was standing in the middle of it looking out towards the living room darkly. Blaise grabbed the shotgun and on his way back past him Gabriel grabbed hold of him.

"Make sure it's loaded." Blaise stared at him for a moment, and then opened the chamber to find the gun was empty. He cursed quietly and ran back to get some shells and loaded it as he went down the hall. Mackenzie was holding Anne back, trying to reason with her why she couldn't just go running out there not knowing what was happening. Blaise made it to the door with Gabriel close behind him, and Gabriel pushed it open while Blaise waited with the gun aimed. The inside section of the dogrun was empty except for one of the younger pups who immediately ran past their legs into the house and under the coffee table.

Blaise moved out, the growls and barks of the dogs mixing with the angry growls of whatever animal had found its way into their enclosure. He nodded to Gabriel who pulled the door that led into the outside pen open, and he moved cautiously through it. The snow outside was churned about and dyed pink, one of the dogs laying on its side motionless just to the left of the door. The others were all trying to defend themselves and each other, lunging at the thing that had somehow torn its way through the metal chainlink fence.

Blaise couldn't move for a few moments as he stared at it. It was focused on a dog that had taken hold of its long, stretched out neck that it was twisting and bending to try and bite and tear at the dog. Another one of Anne's dogs was attacking one of its overlong legs, desperately trying to hold on. The thing itself looked like some type of dog, but one that had been horrible misshapen. Its limbs were stretched out and disjointed, though it fought with an unbelievable strength. Blaise heard Gabriel say something to him as the thing managed to get the dog attached to his throat knocked off balance enough for him to shake it lose.

It noticed Blaise then, and they shared a few seconds eye contact before Blaise raised the shotgun and fired. The thing gave a pained yelp and snarled as it shook the remaining dog loose and seemed to think of lunging at Blaise until Gabriel stepped out of the doorway. It backed off quickly then at the sight of two people instead of just one, and it gave one last snarl at Yakone who tried to nip at its shoulder before it turned off and disappeared.

"What the hell was that thing?" Gabriel sounded about as unsteady as Blaise felt. Blaise shook his head, not really hearing the question as he looked down at the dogs left in the run. Two of them looked like they were already gone, and one looked like she wasn't far behind. The other's were hurt, but didn't seem to be in any immediate danger.

"It was a mountain lion. Come on, we need to get the dogs into town to the vet. Tell Anne to bring the truck around, and get Mackenzie out here to help me," Blaise said, amazed that he was able to sound that assured. Gabriel gave him a long look but he seemed to go along with what he'd been told as he turned around to head inside, the sounds of Anne arguing with Mackenzie about needing to get out there still coming through the door. Blaise heard Gabriel tell the other two the lie about the mountain lion, and then relay that they needed to get the dogs into town. Mackenzie showed up a few moments later and gave a low whistle.

"A cougar did this? How'd it get through the fence like that?"

"Must have been desperate. Come on, we need to try and get them help and have the vet check to make sure the thing didn't have rabies." Anne backed the truck right up to the front of the dog run, and Mackenzie patted him on the back.

"Go pull some warmer clothes on, I'll get started." Blaise realized then that he was still just in his sweats that he'd gone to sleep in, his bare feet going numb to the cold of the snow. He nodded, watched Anne as she got out of the truck and stared at the dogs for a few moments in shock before pulling herself together and taking charge of their loading. He headed in past Gabriel who was on his way back out now with a sweater and boots on.

"I may not have seen one in person before, Blaise, but that wasn't a mountain lion," Gabriel said quietly as they passed, and Blaise stopped to give him a look.

"Well, unless you can explain just what it was then we're not going to tell the others that." It came out a bit short, but Gabriel didn't seem to notice or if he did he chose not to acknowledge the edge in Blaise's voice. He just nodded and headed out the door to help the other two get the dead and wounded into the truck.

Blaise hoped that Anne couldn't tell that his hands were shaking, or that if she did that she'd think it was because of the cold. She had refused to sit up in the cab of the truck, instead wanting to stay with the dogs in the back so Blaise had chosen to sit back there with her. Mackenzie was driving them into town as quickly as he could while being safe. Two of the dogs were already dead, and Blaise had a feeling that one of the more seriously injured dogs, Gemini, was going to be gone quickly. All the dogs were injured somehow except that one that had stayed hidden from the fighting.

Blaise was trying hard to deny what he knew in the back of his mind. He knew he'd seen the thing before, and it wasn't the time he'd been hiking and crossed paths with a mountain lion. He didn't want to accept that what he saw was the creature from his dreams, the one that emerged from Anne's dogrun and into the house covered in blood. It was another step that had come true, and he hadn't been able to stop it, not completely. He didn't know if he'd had a small victory by keeping it from getting inside the house as it had in the nightmares, or if it was something that just hadn't come around yet. Nothing was usually laid out in a perfect timeline for him.

Gabriel had seen it too, knew that it wasn't a mountain lion as he had told them all. He was grateful the other hadn't called him on it in front of Anne and Mackenzie, but he had a feeling that the moment they were alone he'd be asking questions. He looked up as he heard Anne say something over the sound of the wind rushing past.

"I should have been keeping them inside at night. I knew that damn thing was out there, and I didn't do what I should have to keep them safe." Anne looked at Blaise for a moment, seeming to beg him to disagree with her eyes. A hurt look flickered across her face when he didn't speak up right away, though it wasn't because he felt she was right. He was too lost in what he should have done, and it took him a moment to process what she had said.

"Anne, you couldn't have known it would attack much less that it would be able to break through the fencing. They don't normally behave that way." Even to his own ears his words sounded a little flat, and he saw that she didn't believe him. He had to push aside his concern over what he saw and focus more, he knew that and he did his best as he shifted carefully to sit closer to her. "Anne, you can't blame yourself for this. It had to have been starving or sick."

He knew he'd said the wrong thing when her face hardened, and knew that he shouldn't have mentioned that the animal could have been carrying something. If it had rabies and her dogs were exposed it was a possibility that more of them would have to be put down. That was something Anne would have a hard time dealing with, the dogs were basically her life. She had always had them, and to lose all of them at once would be a blow she might not be able to handle.

"Anne, they'll be fine. I was just trying to say that you couldn't go blaming yourself over this."

"Aren't you to blame when you lose a patient?" she said shortly, and he didn't get a chance to respond as they came to a stop outside the vet's house. They had called ahead so that he was expecting them, and as they started to climb out of the car Shawn stepped out of the house. He was a big bear of a man that had moved up here years ago. He looked the very part of a mountain man with his large bushy beard and untamed hair. Mackenzie and Gabriel came around the back of the truck to pull the tailgate down, and Shawn came to take a look at the dogs to decide who he wanted back in the exam room first. He gave a low whistle when he saw the damage that was done, and looked up at Anne and Blaise.

"A mountain lion did all this to them?" He said, and Blaise just nodded in response. He knew that Shawn would be able to tell that the damage wasn't done by a mountain lion when he started to really examine the dogs, and he hoped that he wouldn't start getting questioned about what he saw. "All right, get Gemini into the exam room first. The two that didn't make it you can take into the back to one of the empty rooms. Those two go into the second exam room, I'll need to get to them after Gemini and then the other's can go to the kennel area and I'll get to them as I can. I'm going to call in Ben to come help now that I see how much we'll need to do."

He gave a soft clap of his hands and they started working on moving the dogs into the house that both served as Shawn's home and his practice. Blaise tried to catch Anne a few times to say something about her comment, but she sidestepped him each time until he finally gave up. She went back with Shawn and Ben when they'd gotten the animals all inside, leaving the three of them out in the front room alone. Mackenzie sat down in one of the chairs there giving a tired sigh as he felt the edge of his brain start to pound in complaint. He was surprised it had taken this long for any sign of his drinking and lack of sleep to set in.

Blaise found he couldn't sit, feeling restless as he shifted around the room looking at the different pictures and books that were lying around. He was growing irritated because he could tell Gabriel was watching him, and he finally turned towards the other who had sat down on the couch.

"Can I talk to you?" Blaise said, nodding towards the door that led outside. Gabriel didn't say anything, but just got up to walk outside ahead of him. Mackenzie watched them from where he sat until the door closed, and then he shifted out of the chair to stand at a point he could see them out of the window. Something was going on, and since he was fairly certain that Blaise wasn't completely sober he wanted to make sure that it didn't get going a little too strongly. The last thing they needed was those two getting into a fist fight, though he knew that Gabriel could take care of himself just fine.

"What?" Blaise asked the simple question as Gabriel stepped down from the front porch into the snow. Blaise followed him not trying to keep the frustration from his voice. He shouldn't be feeling angry, but he found that it was coming easy right then. The fear of seeing that thing in front of him when he wasn't dreaming, the hurt from Anne's comment to him in the back of the truck, everything that had been tearing at him over the last month was bubbling up inside him right then.

"Why are you lying about what that thing was?" Gabriel turned around to face him, his own stance saying that he was already on the defensive. He knew well enough that Blaise was pissed off, but he didn't care that he was the focus of all that. He crossed his arms, staring the other man down. Blaise seemed put off by his forward look for a second, but it was short lived before he just returned the hard stare.

"I'm lying because I don't know what that thing was. If I said that some deformed monster had been attacking the dogs I'm pretty certain that they'd all think I was losing it."

"Not if I said the same thing, which I would. I saw it too, Blaise, it wasn't just you. Why were you so worried about it if both of us could tell them what we saw? Whatever it was, it's still out there and do you want to leave Anne out there with no idea what to watch for?" Blaise started pacing through the snow, and Gabriel just watched him from where he was. Seeing the thing had been a shock to him too, but Blaise was more agitated than he really thought the other should be. He had thought it was the mix of shock and alcohol at first, but he was beginning to see that it was something else. "What was it really Blaise?"

Blaise stopped to look at him, and a flicker of something crossed his face for a second. He didn't hide his emotions as well when he had been drinking, and even though he'd had a couple hours of sleep it was still slowing his defenses. It was that moment before he closed up that had told Gabriel all he'd needed to know, and he closed the distance between the two of them.

"What was it Blaise? You know, don't you?"

"No, I don't know. How could I know what that thing was? Why are you questioning me all the sudden, acting like you don't trust me."

"Maybe because right now I don't. Just tell me what it is Blaise, I don't get why you won't if you know. It could help, it could help the vet take care of the dogs, it could help Anne know what she needs to watch for if she's out at her house alone next time it comes around. What I don't get is why you just won't say what the thing is?"

"It's because I don't know, all right. I don't know what that thing is, I don't know why I've been seeing it in my dreams for the past few months. Seeing it ever since you had to pop up in town. I don't know what it is, all I know is that I didn't think it was real until it showed up on the doorstep tonight." It came out in a rush, the anger seeming to go with the words as it tumbled out of Blaise. Gabriel looked at him, his own confidence in confronting Blaise suddenly leaving him as well. He remembered now that Blaise had told him, remembered the dream that the man had explained to him a long time ago and the creature that had lurked in it. He paled a little as they stood there, and Blaise just shook his head in exasperation. "Now do you understand why I can't say that I've seen it before?"

"Yeah….I get it. But, that makes no sense, how can something from your dream just show up out of no where? It's just a dream, it shouldn't be able to come to life." Blaise shifted away, moved to the truck to sit down on the still open tailgate. Gabriel followed him and sat down beside him, the cold air making their breath billow out in front of them. "I can't really explain it, but it's always been this way. If I'm having dreams they always related to something that happens later on. It's been this way since I was a kid. I've been hoping that this time it was just a dream, so much of it seemed so far out there but then things started to happen. I'm at a loss on how to try to stop it all too."

"Tell me what's left, what's left to happen and we can work it out together. I believe you, I can't pretend not to believe now that I've seen it myself. Maybe if we try to work on it together we'll be able to stop it from going any further." Blaise shook his head lightly, staring off into the distance at nothing specific.

"None of it makes sense. I don't know how we're supposed to stop something that doesn't make sense." He told him anyway though, explained what he saw still coming at them. Leo being destroyed and devoured by Marie, the man writing on the walls in blood, and the newest addition of a presence that hung behind Mackenzie. In the end they sat, both at a loss of how they were going to stop things they couldn't fully understand.

Mackenzie had kept an eye on the two outside until the argument seemed to abruptly come to an end and the conversation seemed to fall into a less angry tone. He turned around and found he wasn't alone in the room, Michael was standing back near the door that lead to the stairs as he looked out the window at Blaise and Gabriel.

"He's not what he says he is. You can't trust him, not once he remembers everything. He's getting closer, remembering more each day. Once he knows who he is and why he's here, you won't be able to trust anything he says. When that happens you may not be able to trust your friend either. Though none of them trust you anymore as it is. They won't say it to your face, but they believe that what you did was wrong. They don't trust you not to pull the trigger too soon on someone else."

"You said he was your brother last time. What did he do that was so terrible that you can't trust your brother?" Mackenzie wanted to feel frustrated and angry that the man was there again, that he was there lecturing him and telling him once more that he was wrong for doing what he had done. He couldn't manage to find the energy for that though, couldn't find the desire to argue about whether he was to blame or not.

"He turned his back on his family. He did what you did, pulled the trigger too soon without thinking what his options were. He took something from us, and then decided it was best to try and run from what he'd done. You two are a lot alike, actually. Both with such a sense of righteousness, but all you really do is turn your back on what should be done." Michael focused on Gabriel outside the window, and Mackenzie turned to look back at him. Seeming to sense he was being watched Gabriel turned towards the window, but all he saw was Mackenzie inside alone staring out the window at them. Michael had slipped out of the room again leaving Mackenzie alone, left with a sudden sense of doubt in the pit of his stomach.

Anne had come out from the back after a couple of hours, and she went immediately to Blaise who had come back inside with Gabriel a long time ago. They'd all ended up dozing while they waited until she opened the door, and she curled up in Blaise's lap before she spoke and told them what the result was in the end. Three of the dogs were dead, the two that had been gone before they'd even left the house and then Gemini had needed to be put down. Shawn had done his best, but found that she'd had her gut punctured by deep bite and there was too much damage to repair.

The rest of the dogs were all in back resting after getting their wounds tended, and Shawn had pulled blood samples from all of them to be tested for rabies. Shawn stepped out about a half hour after Anne had appeared, washed up from working on the dogs and he looked at them all with a long sigh.

"Whatever did this it wasn't a mountain lion like you thought. It's bite appeared more canine in origin, though it was more elongated than any I'm familiar with. I'm going to call and ask a collegue of mine if he may have a better idea since he works with wild animals exclusively. The rabies tests should be back in a week or so, until then the dogs will stay here. It will be better anyway so that they can get a chance to heal up completely while I'm close by to help if any problems arise." He spoke to Anne though it was aimed at all of them. Anne shifted out of Blaise's lap, feeling weary and run down both physically and emotionally. She went and gave Shawn a quick hug that was returned. He encompassed her completely when he hugged her, not a hard thing to do for a man quite as large as he was.

"Thank you Shawn for helping. Do you want to just send me the bill once you know what everything will cost?"

"I'll let you know, but don't worry Anne. I know you're good for it, so I don't need a big rush on it. I'll take good care of them, you can come and visit them whenever you want."

As they all filed out Mackenzie pulled out his cell phone to try Leo again. They had been trying him from time to time all night, but he had never answered. Mackenzie was angry at his friend, wondering why he was ignoring every call they tried when his sister needed him right then. He got sent to voice mail again, and he just hung up instead of bothering to leave another message behind. They climbed into the truck, all of them sitting in the cab this time. Blaise and Anne got into the small back seat area while he and Gabriel sat in the front once more.

Anne dozed off now that the tension of the night was wearing off, and her head rested against Blaise's shoulder as they drove. Mackenzie glanced at Gabriel, wondering if what Michael had said was true that the other was remembering things. Worried that if he was that meant that Michael was right about him not being trustworthy as well. He caught Blaise's eye in the rear view mirror for a second.

"Lunch in a couple of days?" Blaise held his look for a second before nodding and turning to look out the window. They both had things they needed to talk about, and they had yet to do so. Now they had even more they were going to need to discuss after tonight, like what were Blaise and Gabriel arguing about outside the vet's. Gabriel looked back at Blaise, but made no comment as they turned in at Anne's house. The torn open fencing and bloodied snow a chilling reminder that stood out on the side of the house.

Leo stood in the shower just staring at the wall. He'd been up all night, she'd made sure of that. There had been a few times when he thought he'd heard the phone ring, but she wouldn't leave him be long enough to grab it. He couldn't even bring himself to argue with her anymore when she woke him as he was just about to drift off. He needed to get to work now, but his head wasn't working right. It was all in a fog, one that seemed full of half-formed warnings and fears. He thought he heard the phone ring somewhere off in the distance again, but then she was there again.

She whispered in his ear, the words not mattering anymore. He was too tired to fight with her, too tired to tell her he needed to get ready and go to work. He needed out of the house, but all he wanted to do was curl up in bed and sleep. *Get out of the house.* It surfaced out of the fog, the thought like a scream and he pushed her away as he climbed out of the shower. He got dressed even as she screamed at him which was followed by pleading when anger didn't work. He was out the door, his head pounding and protesting as the sunlight seemed intensified by the snow on the ground. He could hear her voice in his head all the way down the drive until he'd pulled out onto the main road without anything more than a glance for other traffic.

When he finally couldn't hear or feel her anymore pulling on him to come back he stopped his SUV, his forehead falling against the steering wheel as he tried to calm his shaking. He reached for the cellphone he had hastily remembered to grab, and listened to the messages he'd gotten over the night. He felt a sense of regret and an ache of pain as he heard Anne's voice first begging for him to meet them at the vet's office followed by Blaise leaving a concerned message saying that his sister needed him to answer. The last was an angry message from Mackenzie belittling him for ignoring them when Anne needed her brother the most.

He tossed the phone into the passanger's seat not understanding how he hadn't noticed they'd been calling, wondering how many messages he had on his landline. He felt a bit sick as the night came back to him, first how Marie had been there every time he had heard the phone ring, how she had woken him every time he was about to fall asleep not letting him get any rest. Then he remembered the party, the argument outside Anne's house when he had left because he felt he had no choice. He had heard Marie calling for him, and he hadn't been able to fight it. He remembered the words he had said to his sister, how he had belittled and insulted not just her but all of them.

It's no wonder you feel more comfortable with those damn dogs than with anyone else, you're just a little bitch running around like you're in heat with the fool who killed my wife! Not to mention my incompetent, trigger-happy deputy who needs to consider having the next person he pulls the trigger on be himself. Why would I want to spend time with that mess you call a 'family'?

Even as the words had come out he had been trying to stop, trying to apologize and take it all back. But he had just kept going on and continue to spew worse and worse at his sister until he had slammed his car door in her face and pulled out not caring if she was in the way or not. He didn't know why he'd done it, didn't know what had brought the words that weren't his own out of him. Part of him knew that it had been her, Marie, somehow reaching him even when he wasn't near her. He sat up, forcing himself to focus and push it down as he turned his Chevy towards the direction of Anne's house.

He knew he might not get a very good reception, but his sister needed him and he needed to try. He couldn't let his life crumble apart around him without a fight, couldn't let Marie ruin everything for him. He had to find a way to get rid of Marie, even though that thought made it seem the hole left by her death was being ripped wide open again. It made him feel like he was dying right alongside her.

"What are you doing in here?" He'd entered the room to find his brother standing in the corner, searching through his things. His brother froze for a second before setting the items in his hands down and turning to face Gabriel. "What are you doing?"

"I was just..." The other seemed to flounder for a moment, his usually self-assured brother seeming nervous at being found there. He pulled himself together quickly though, giving Gabriel a smile. "I was just looking for something to leave a note with since you weren't here. We've been called for a meeting in the morning."

Gabriel's brother moved past him, and Gabriel watched his brother go before turning to find if what he kept hidden in his room was still in its place. He'd already known about the meeting, and the rest of his siblings knew that as well. Gabriel didn't know why, but he knew his brother had been looking for something. He felt relief when he found that his hiding place hadn't been discovered.

Chapter 8 – It's in the House -

Anne had asked Leo to leave that morning after the animal attack, and he had done as she asked without argument though he did apologize to her. Did his best to make her understand that he hadn't meant anything that he had said to her the night before, and that he felt like an ass for not answering his phone all night. She had reluctantly agreed for him to come over the next day to take a look at the fence around the dogrun to see if he could fix it. Blaise's car was out in the drive when he pulled up, but he couldn't bring himself to feel annoyed that he wouldn't be able to talk to his sister alone. Leo knew that Blaise was there as a buffer in case he went off on Anne again.

Blaise was the one to let him into the house when he knocked, and he could hear Anne stirring around in the kitchen. The scent of breakfast was coming from that direction as well as the sizzle of bacon. Blaise seemed more concerned about him than angry, and Leo had a feeling that Anne hadn't told him what Leo had said the other night before he'd stormed off. Blaise kept seeming to want to say something though, but in the end appeared to decide against it as he led Leo into the kitchen.

"Hey," Leo said, testing the waters with Anne and getting a tired greeting in return. Leo shifted uneasily, still in the clothes he'd hastily pulled on the day before. He had slept at the station, worried about returning home. If he was honest with himself he was scared to go back to his house, afraid he wouldn't be able to leave again if he walked in there and gave Marie the chance to convince him to stay.

They sat and ate in relative silence before Leo and Blaise headed out through the side door into the dogrun to survey the damage. Leo had gotten a brief look at it as he had pulled up outside, but seeing it close up now he was shocked at the the way the fence was warped and damaged. It had been completely torn apart as though it wasn't made of metal, and bits of fur, blood and flesh were stuck to it.

"How the hell did it do this?" he said, the awkwardness forgotten in his surprise and the sudden fear of what could have happened had the thing gotten to the door leading into the house. The door locked, but it wasn't as strong as the front or back door and if it had been able to do this much to a metal fence, a wood door would have been nothing.

"I don't know. I thought it was a mountain lion when I caught sight of it for those few seconds, but Shawn says that doesn't match with the bite marks left on the dogs. He's going to see if a friend of his knows what it was. I think we may have to just replace the entire section of fence." Blaise stood beside him, doing his best to sound casual though there was a shadow of nerves in his voice. Leo looked at him and realized that Blaise was watching the edge of the woods instead of examining the fence, and Leo looked out amongst the trees as well.

"You think its still out there?" He spoke quietly, not wanting his sister to hear if she happened to be listening. Blaise seemed to think for a few seconds, his jaw tensing and releasing a couple of times.

"Yeah, I do..." The answer was spoken with conviction, and Leo felt anger at the thing stalking out in the woods. If it was still out there it meant his sister was still in danger, and no one and no thing was allowed to threaten his sister and make her feel unsafe at her home.

"Then we're going to have to try and take care of it. Come on, we should get this torn down and then I can come back later to put more fence up."

"All right, I have a few hours but I'm meeting Mac for lunch at about noon so I'll have to leave around eleven. I can help until then though." Leo nodded, and they pulled on work gloves and set about tearing down the old fencing. Both of them kept an eye out towards the woods as they worked, watching for any sign of the thing that they knew was out there watching.

They worked in relative silence through the first few hours of the day, Anne checking on them from time to time and bringing them coffee or tea to warm them up. They'd gotten the torn up area pulled down by about ten-thirty, and were moving it towards the front of the house so it would be easy to load up when they needed it hauled away. Blaise had seemed on the verge of saying something most of the day, and Leo was starting to wish he would just spit it out by this point.

"If you're going to chew me out for the other day then will you just do it? You've been pussy-footing around it the entire morning, Blaise," he finally snapped as they got the last bit of the fencing up by the side of the porch. Blaise looked at him a little surprised, but then shook his head.

"Actually, though I should chew you out about it, I wasn't going to. I'm worried about you Leo." Leo ran a hand over his hairline to catch a trickle of sweat he had felt tickling down to his forehead, and frowned at Blaise. "Are you still seeing Marie?"

Leo felt a bit of a physical shock at the question. Of course, he remembered telling Blaise about seeing Marie that first time out here at Anne's but he hadn't mentioned it to anyone since then. There was also a different sort of hit in his gut that he didn't understand, there was a defensive anger churning in him and he pushed it down.

"No, it was just that one time. It was a dream Blaise, probably brought on by the fact that it was the anniversary of her death," he said the words defensively, but the look on his face must have answered Blaise's question honestly. Blaise was looking at him in concern as he took a step closer; glancing at the house to make sure Anne hadn't stepped outside again.

"It's not her, Leo, and you know that. You can't trust her, and you have to do something to stop her from getting to you. It's not-" Blaise was cut off by the punch that Leo suddenly threw at him, making Blaise stumble back against the side of the house. Leo went to hit him again, but managed to stop himself as they stood staring at each other in shock. Leo's hand was still cocked back for the second hit, and it took all his willpower to lower it down. The anger had been sudden and all encompassing, though not his own at all. Leo hadn't been angry; he'd been relieved that Blaise seemed to get it so easily.

"I didn't do that," Leo said, breaking the moment of silence and Blaise pushed away from the wall though he was keeping his distance from Leo. A look had flickered over Blaise's face at Leo's words, reminding him of what Alex had said to him during those few calm moments in the bathroom. They both looked towards the house as the door opened back by the dog run, and Anne stuck her head out.

"You guys already finished," she called towards them. Blaise nodded at first and then managed to send her a smile and call out to her.

"Yeah, we'll be coming in a second." Anne nodded and disappeared back into the house, leaving the two of them alone again. Blaise looked at Leo, saw the weariness and loss on the other's face. "We need to talk; figure out a way to stop whatever's going on. Let's meet for drinks tonight." Leo nodded numbly, running a hand across his face to try and get the last remnants of her anger brushed aside.

"I'm sorry Blaise, I'm a mess and I don't know how to stop it. It's usually better when I'm not at the house, when I'm there I can't even seem to make my own decisions unless I put up a fight. I don't want that to start happening when I'm away from that place too," Leo said quietly, and Blaise's apprehension seemed to break then.

"Then maybe it would be best if you didn't go home and work the rest of the day, don't go back until after we figure something out tonight. I'm sure you can find enough to do here or at the station." Leo nodded, and Blaise gave him a reassuring pat on the back before heading for the step on the porch. They headed inside; both of them trying their best to act like nothing had happened though Leo could see a hint of a bruise starting on Blaise's jaw.

"Hey Anne, I'm going to have to head out in a minute. I need to at least change before I head into town for lunch." Anne came out of the back where it looked like she'd been repairing something from her sled. She gave Blaise a smile, leaning to kiss him on the cheek. She paused, brushing a finger over the darkening spot on Blaise's jaw.

"What happened there?" Blaise managed not to falter, giving Anne a quick and sheepish smile.

"Sort of wasn't paying attention to where I was when Leo was pulling a piece loose. My fault, not his," Blaise said, adding the last part quickly when Anne glanced at her brother. Anne seemed to debate if she believed the story or not, but then just nodded her head as her hand unconsciously smoothed Blaise's collar.

"Mac called and said he'd be a little late, but I'm sure you had guessed that already. You going to stay Leo; I could make some lunch?" She didn't sound completely sure she wanted her brother to stay, and Leo just shook his head. He'd lost it with Anne once in the last few days and he'd lost it again with Blaise today. He didn't want to stick around his sister and risk a repeat of either event.

"I have to head into the station for a little while; got some paperwork I've been putting off." It wasn't a complete lie, there were things he could do at the station but they weren't urgent by any means. Anne nodded, though she didn't argue or protest that it could wait until after he'd eaten like she normally would have. They shared a look for a moment that clearly said to him that she hadn't forgiven him completely yet. Blaise grabbed his keys, and gave Anne another quick kiss before heading to the door. Leo followed him, and they stepped outside together. Anne waved them off as they headed to their cars before going back into the house.

"If you need to, call Leo. Just don't go back home until we've talked things over," Blaise reminded him, and Leo just nodded. He had no plans to go home just then even if it meant sleeping at the station for another night.

"Blaise…I'm sorry." Leo said the words as Blaise was climbing into his truck, and his friend stopped for a moment to look at him.

"We'll figure it out, Leo." That was all Blaise said before he closed his door, starting up his truck as Leo climbed into his own vehicle.

Blaise pulled up to his house, climbing out of the truck to head inside. He'd gotten out of Anne's at about quarter after eleven, so he didn't have too much time to spend getting changed. Even though he knew Mac would be late, would have been even if he hadn't called to warn Blaise about it, he still couldn't bring himself to be late himself. It only left him with around twenty minutes to get changed and leave his house again so he could get down to the diner in time. He unlocked the front door, tossing his keys aside onto the couch in his rush to head up the stairs.

The sound in the kitchen made him stop, and for a moment he was about to call out a greeting to Gabriel until he remembered that he'd dropped the other off at work early that morning. He froze part way across the living room to the stairs and stared at the small gap of the kitchen he could see to try and figure out what the noise had been. He heard the distinct fall of footsteps, and Blaise thought he saw a figure standing just out of his line of sight in the kitchen.

He shifted quietly to try and get a look at who was in his house, but he saw no one when he moved the few inches that gave him an almost full view of the kitchen. He relaxed then, realizing he had probably just been hearing some animal on the roof or the shift and settle of the house under the weight of the snow. He watched for a few seconds longer to be sure before turning back towards the stairs.

Blaise almost walked into the other man with how close he'd been standing behind him, and he pulled back sharply. He recognized him from somewhere, and it took him a few minutes to realize where from. It was the man from his dreams that painted with blood on the walls, and Blaise found himself unable to react as the man slowly smiled at him.

"Hello Prophet. You're being meddlesome recently, aren't you?" The man took a few steps forward, and Blaise mirrored the movement with his own backward steps to keep the distance. He was closer to the front door than the man, but not by much. He could try to get out and to the car fast enough, but the man would be close behind and he'd have to stop to get his keys if he was going to get anywhere after he was outside.

"Why are you in my house?" He took another step back, but found the man followed him still. Part of him hoped that maybe the guy would just leave, but he had a feeling that it wasn't going to be that simple.

"I was waiting for you to show up, Prophet. My colleagues think that it's time to put a stop to any problems you may cause for us." He started walking again, making a loop and putting himself between Blaise and the front door effectively sealing off that exit. Blaise turned with him, reaching behind him carefully and finding the handle of one of the fireplace tools that were resting in their holder. Blaise got a hold of one, hoping that it was the poker since it would be more effective.

"Why do you keep calling me that?" Blaise tried to keep the intruder talking, hoping to cover the sound of him lifting the iron tool out of its holder.

"Don't play dumb, Prophet, it's unbecoming." The man took a step closer and Blaise raised the poker quickly, swinging it like a baseball bat and hitting the other upside the head. While the man was stunned Blaise pushed past him, dropping the poker as he lunged for his keys from where he had dropped them on the couch. He heard the stranger cursing behind him and dodged towards the door, getting his hand on the handle before he felt a searing pain hit him in the ribs. The man had swung the poker round on him now, and the hooked end had buried itself into Blaise's side.

The guy laughed behind him and pulled sharply back, bringing Blaise with the movement until the end of the poker tore out of him. Before Blaise could pull back again the man reached forward, blood running down the side of his face though he didn't seem to notice it as he grabbed hold of Blaise's shirt and swung him around away from the door. Blaise felt his back hit against one of the bookcases, sending a tumble of books and trinkets down around them. Blaise took a blind swing, trying to push his attacker back from him and was glad to feel the blow make contact with the man's jaw.

The other's hold on his shirt loosened and Blaise tried for the door once more but the man hit him with his full force, tackling him back against the bookcase. The breath rushed out of Blaise's lungs as another blow landed to his ribs. Blaise reached up behind him, trying to grab hold of anything he could use and found a book. He brought it down on the stranger's head and then again on the back of his neck. There was a noise managing to break through over the sound of the struggle, and Blaise realized the man was laughing as though he was enjoying the fight.

Blaise tried desperately to push him away, his new aim being the back door. He'd have to get around the house to get to his car, but the way to the door leading out onto the patio from the kitchen was closest. If he could break free enough to just make it out the door he might be able to make it to the car. He got enough room free between them that he was able to place a kick to the guy's gut and then push him further back. Blaise took advantage of the moment and pushed from the bookcase around the corner into the kitchen. He made it to the door and suddenly found himself outside on the patio without being stopped.

"Go on and run, little Prophet." He heard the words called out to him from inside the house, and pushed himself down the steps. There was a clear trail cut down to the firewood pile and then around the house where they would load it up to take it into town. He followed it, only looking back as he reached the woodpile but no one was behind him. He turned around and didn't have time to react before the piece of wood hit him in the stomach, knocking the breath out of him again and making him fall back into the snow. The man had somehow beaten him to the woodpile, and was standing over him now. He tossed the piece of wood aside as he looked down at Blaise, giving him a bright smile.

"Come on, is that all the fight you have? Get up." The guy kicked at him, and Blaise rolled out of the way of it as he came up to the side of the stack of firewood waiting to be chopped. He was kicked at again, and Blaise didn't manage to completely dodge this one as it grazed his hip. When he came to a stop Blaise found his hand was resting on the handle of one of the axes that must have been forgotten or fallen off the chopping block where they were usually kept. He wrapped his hand around it, slowly getting himself up to make sure the axe stayed concealed behind him from the other.

"That's more like it, Prophet. Come on, let's see if you can get another blow in." Blaise took a couple of deep breaths, his side throbbing from where the fireplace poker had torn a chunk from him. He realized that his shirt was soaking through with blood at the spot, a large tear in it showing the damage. Blaise had a feeling this was the only chance he had left, and he wanted to make sure he made it count. He half turned towards the man, looking at him as they stood a few feet apart. He was in a well-tailored suit, not something Blaise would have thought you'd wear to rough someone up but it had stayed all but immaculate so far other than some blood from the gash in his forehead. "Come on, I'll give you a free try."

Blaise turned to put both hands on the axe, and he readied himself before turning as he brought the axe up in one smooth move. He put all of his weight behind the swing, and it hit home as it dug into the crook in the man's neck where it met his shoulder. The force of it made Blaise's arms and shoulders complain as it reverberated through him. He let go of the handle of the axe with a bit of shock as the other tilted his head at on odd angle to try and look down at it. The head of the axe had sunken down into his flesh up to the very back-edge of the blade, blood was quickly ruining the nice suit.

Blaise felt sick suddenly, a mix of his shock and fear rising up in the back of his throat as bile that he tried to push back down. He took a step or two away from the man as he looked back up at him and heard the choked laugh.

"Didn't see that one coming," the man said, reaching up to take hold of the axe handle with his right hand. His left was hanging dead at his side for the moment, and Blaise was fairly certain that the muscles had all been disconnected. Blaise watched the well-dressed man start tugging at the handle, pulling the axe head out of his shoulder inch by inch as Blaise backed up slowly. The man should be bleeding out, should have already bled out by this point since Blaise could see the arterial spurt bubbling through the wound. With a couple more tugs the axe pulled loose with a sickening slurp, and Blaise felt the burn of bile rise into his throat again.

"How?" Blaise choked the word out, every fiber of his being telling him to run but his legs didn't seem to be able to cooperate. He stood stark still as the man looked at the axe before tossing it lightly so that he was holding it near the head.

"You should be running instead of asking questions, Prophet." The axe was raised, a swing with the handle that hit Blaise aside the head. Blaise heard the sound of the handle shatter as it hit him, and then he knew nothing.

Mackenzie was glad he'd called out to Anne's to let Blaise know he was going to be late, especially now that he was already five minutes past and he was just leaving. Allison had shown up an hour ago wanting to talk while on her lunch, and they had sat down in the café. Mackenzie was starting to feel that she wasn't stopping by so much anymore to talk about what had happened with the McGully's, though she had said she had a nightmare about it again. He'd lost track of time, and had to run upstairs to grab his car keys before he could leave.

He was heading down the backsteps to avoid getting caught in another conversation with someone inside the café, and he came face to face with Michael. Mackenzie pushed past him to head towards his car, but found as he rounded the corner Michael was in his way again. Mackenzie glanced behind him, wondering how Michael had gotten around him so quickly before facing him.

"What do you want?" Mackenzie wanted to get to the restaurant, knowing he'd already made Blaise wait long enough for him to show up. Michael wasn't going to just go away though apparently, and it would be easier to let him say whatever he wanted. The man had been showing up at random times to badger him about Gabriel and how Mackenzie shouldn't trust him. Mackenzie hated to admit it, but the man was starting to convince him that maybe there was reason to distrust Gabriel. He was obviously caught up in something that had followed him here, and it somehow involved his family. Mackenzie's first thought was some sort of mafia tie, but he felt ridiculous as soon as he'd thought it. Colorado wasn't the hot spot of the mob.

"It's on your head. You may have prevented it, but you did nothing but brush me aside. Tell Gabriel it would be wise if he 'remembered' what he had done with it if he doesn't want more to happen." Michael turned and walked away to the front of the building leaving Mackenzie standing surprised by the shortness of the message. Mackenzie followed after Michael, something sick sinking down into his stomach as he tried to catch up, but when he rounded the corner behind Michael the man was no where to be seen.

Mackenzie scanned the street but there was no sign of him. Mackenize thought of going inside the café and asking Gabriel right then what the man was talking about, but he was reminded that Blaise was waiting by the alarm on his phone going off. He'd set it in an attempt not to be late, but now he was even later than usual. Mackenzie turned and walked down to his car, climbing inside and starting it up. He did one last sweep for Michael along the almost empty streets before he pulled out and headed to the diner. He worried the entire way, nervous about the not-so-thinly veiled threat from his personal stalker and afraid that something was going to happen.

He tried Blaise on his way to the diner, but got sent to voicemail. The knot in the pit of his stomach grew, and he pulled up to the diner a few moments later. He parked, not seeing Blaise's truck but telling himself that he may have parked around the side of the diner instead of out front. He went in, hands flipping his cell open and closed as he searched for Blaise sitting at one of the tables.

Blaise woke to his head pounding, the light seeming to blind him and cold soaked through his back. The sky was above him, slowly moving past and he realized he was being dragged. He lifted a hand to his face feeling dazed as it came away covered in blood. His eye on the left side of his face felt strange and he realized it was swollen shut. The edge of the roof appeared above him, and he groaned as his head bounced on the steps of the patio as he was dragged up them. He must have blacked out again since when he opened his eyes next he was staring at his kitchen ceiling. The room spun and Blaise closed his eyes tight against it, trying to roll over but finding the move brought pain. His arms couldn't move, and Blaise tried to look around to figure out what was going on. His hands were tied down with some of the twine he used to bundle the firewood, and his mind slowly processed that he was laid over on the island countertop. His view of the ceiling was obscured by the well-dressed man's face and Blaise groaned as the other spoke, his voice seeming unnaturally loud amongst the pounding pain in Blaise's head.

"I'm glad you're awake. It makes asking questions much easier, and it's a lot more fun as well. Now, don't give in too quickly and just tell me what you know. It would ruin things, and I'd just have to hurt you for the enjoyment of it instead of seriously trying to get you to talk." The man pulled back, lifting a knife up to Blaise's face. Blaise tried to pull away as the edge of the knife dragged along his cheek causing a stinging pain to join the ache of his head. "Let's get started. You can call me Shax, by the way. I think its only polite you know my name since we'll be getting to know each other. Now, first question…Where is Gabriel hiding it?"

"Hiding what?" The words sounded slurred and muffled, but they were distinquishable. Shax 'tsk'ed' at him, and Blaise gave a gasp of pain as he felt the knife slowly sink into his abdomen. He pulled at the restraints, trying to get a hand free but they were tied too tightly.

"Don't worry, I know where to cut that causes the most pain without being immediately fatal. It'd be best if you answer before it gets to the point you'll bleed to death though. So, tell me where he hid it. And we can move on to the next question." The knife twisted and Blaise almost felt like blacking out again. He gritted his teeth, trying again to get a hand free.

"I don't know. He didn't have anything when we found him." He blurted the words out, not caring if they were completely the truth or not. Gabriel had nothing to hide when they'd found him other than the cross necklace he'd been wearing, and that he hardly hid considering he wore it all the time. Shax sighed, pulling the knife out and tapping the tip on Blaise's cheek.

"That's a shame. It would have been so simple if you had known. That's really the only question I had too, at least that's of interest to my business partners. I'm sure I could think of a few more though. How about you tell me what you've seen, Prophet? What good are you if you don't spread the word a little." The knife sunk in again at a new spot, and this time the man didn't pause to wait between choosing other places to run the blade across or to push in up to its hilt. Somewhere far away it sounded like a phone rang, but when it cut off suddenly Blaise figured he'd been imagining it.

"I don't…know what you're talking about," Blaise choked out, and the well-dressed man just shook his head in a disappointed manner before continuing. Blaise didn't know how long it went on, but it seemed like he was lying there for hours. A few times he thought he must have dipped into unconsciousness, but some new pain would pull him awake again. His head was full of fog when Shax seemed to finally stop, standing beside Blaise and looking down at him.

"I can make it stop; we could make a deal. You agree to tell me everything, to work for me and tell me all the juicy bits so that I can be prepared to head off any…complications to my plans. I'll make the pain stop in exchange." Blaise shook his head slightly, less in response to the offer and more in an attempt to clear away the hazy confusion.

"Shax…" The other voice cut in, and the man's face darkened for a second before he looked up with a smile. "You need to finish this. You don't

106

have much time left." Shax stabbed the knife down into Blaise's thigh before disappearing from his sight as he stepped away from the counter. Blaise turned his head, trying to see who else had just come into his home but all he could see was the first man's back. "He's supposed to be dead."

"I think he could be useful. I know you think it's too much hassle, but he barely knows how to use what he has," Shax answered flatly, and there was a moment of tense silence between the two. Blaise fought against the dark edges that were trying to take over his vision, tried not to fall unconscious again. He was afraid that if he did he wouldn't be waking up. He knew enough to realize he was losing a lot of blood, and if the men decided just to kill him it wouldn't take much at this point.

"He's getting too close to realizing things. If he starts to interfere with what we're trying to do-"

"Does it look like he's going to be interfering anytime soon? How about we make a deal since we're at odds over this? He'll bleed out in no more than thirty minutes I'm guessing. If help can somehow get out here and save him before that happens then he'll be out of commision long enough for us to solidify the net we've been trying to lay. If he bleeds to death before then, I guess that God really does smile on you." The well-dressed man spoke lightly, but there was a dark tone carried in his voice that seemed to show some sort of threat. "Or; you could dirty your own hands."

"I'm already putting myself at risk with what I'm doing now. If any of my family realized I knew where he was, much less that I was here myself they'd show up. We can't have that. If you want to deal with the mess he'll make then fine, but don't expect my help if it back fires on you." Shax shrugged his shoulders, turning back to Blaise.

"I'll take responsibility for him then. Shouldn't we leave a little message for Gabriel?" He stopped next to Blaise and gave him a smile before digging his fingers into one of the cuts. Blaise watched as he went to the wall, using the blood to write something there like he had in his dream. The new man stepped intoview, looking down at him with open distaste.

"It would be better for you to die." Blaise looked up at him, recognizing the bright blue eyes though they weren't kind like he was use to them appearing.

"Gabriel?" He wasn't even sure at first if he had gotten the word out, but the man made a flat noise of amusement.

"You aren't so lucky." With that Blaise found himself alone. He tried weakly to pull at the ropes around his wrist but they didn't even budge. A voice in the back of his head said that it would be better to accept it, to let himself slip away into sleep where he'd go without consciously knowing. He wanted to fight though, and he instead tried to hold back the darkness as he hoped for someone to find him.

Mackenzie had become nervous when he'd gotten inside the diner and Blaise wasn't there. He was never late, even if he knew that the other person was going to be. He flipped his phone open and close a few times again before dialing Blaise's cellphone but just got sent to voicemail once more. He tried his house then and the phone had rang a couple of times before the line simply went dead. That had done it for him, trying not to think about what may have happened as he climbed back into his SUV. Mackenzie tried to convince himself that Blaise had just lost track of time or had car problems. It didn't explain why he wasn't answering his phone though.

He drove faster than he should have out towards the house, the anxiety growing as he tried Blaise again on both lines. He got the same result on the cellphone but this time the house phone didn't even ring, but just went to the busy signal. When he pulled up outside Blaise's place he saw the other's car sitting out front and Mackenzie parked beside it. He climbed out and glanced inside the truck and saw Blaise's cellphone lying on the front seat. Mackenzie felt a bit of hope that it was that simple of an explanation and pushed away some of the fear.

That hope disappeared though when he reached the front door and found it closed but not actually latched. He pushed it open gently, wishing that he'd thought to grab his gun from the small safe he kept it in at home. He hadn't thought he'd need it for just meeting Blaise for lunch, but as he entered the living room he instinctively reached for it at his side. He normally would have had it with him, but he had stopped carrying it when he wasn't on duty after the McGully's. He wished that he hadn't let the insecurity get to him now as he saw the wreckage of the house.

Almost everything was knocked off one of the bookshelves, and things were lying all around the living room. He spotted some blood on the hardwood floors, and took care to avoid stepping on it out of instinct from his crime scene training. He made his way carefully wanting to call out for Blaise, but afraid that he'd catch someone else's attention. He headed towards the kitchen and froze when he caught sight of someone lying on the counter. His heart stopped when he recognized the person and Mackenzie headed into the kitchen quickly then, glancing towards the door but finding the room empty other than Blaise.

Mackenzie slipped part way on a trail of blood that led from the backdoor, but he just picked himself back up again and stopped at Blaise's side. Mackenzie thought he was dead for a moment as Blaise stared blankly at the ceiling, but then his friend seemed to notice Mackenzie's presence and took a ragged breath as he shook his head.

"I don't know…" Mackenzie hardly could make the words out, Blaise seeming to be too weak to project any real voice.

"It's me, Blaise. It's Mac. Just hold on, I'm going to get you some help," Mackenzie said, the words rushing out as he looked for something to cut Blaise's hands loose. Blaise stared at him for a long time, but Mackenzie had a hard time returning the gaze. Blaise was covered in blood, and was hardly recognizable as himself with how swollen the left side of his face was. Mackenzie grabbed a knife and turned to get Blaise's hands free, and the other man moaned and shook his head as he tried to pull away. "It's just me, Blaise. I just need to get your hands free."

Mackenzie was trying to figure out what to do. His first instinct was to call for an ambulance, but he was afraid they wouldn't get there in time. Or; that if they did that they wouldn't get Blaise to the hospital in time on the return trip. He had lights in his car though, and could drive faster on the roads than an ambulance could. He could get Blaise to the hospital in half the time that an ambulance could, and that was enough to make up his mind.

"Blaise is it okay for me to move you." Mackenzie tried to get Blaise's attention but the other didn't seem to hear him, and all Mackenzie could do was take that as a yes. He was trying not to panic, trying not to let his emotions get to him when what he needed to do was focus. He made sure he had good footing so he wouldn't slip in the blood again before he lifted Blaise up. The other was dead weight in his arms, but Mackenzie didn't notice as he just pushed himself to get through the house back out to his car.

Mackenzie had left it running out front and was able to get the door opened awkwardly to the backseat. He got Blaise laid down across the seat the best he could, and had another moment of fear when it seemed he may be too late. When he saw Blaise turn his head towards him again it pushed Mackenzie back into action, and he closed the door before climbing into the front seat. He hit his emergency lights and pulled out, heading into town as fast as he could without risking an accident. As soon as he reached the edge of town he took up his radio and made sure it was set on the station that both the hospital and the police station listened to.

"This is Sheriff's Deputy Callahan, I'm coming in hot with a critical to the hospital. I need medical staff to be ready to receive me as soon as I arrive. I'm entering town now, if the roads could be cleared for me. Over." Mackenzie didn't know how he managed to sound so calm or keep from just yelling they needed help. He glanced in the rearview mirror to check on Blaise, and found him staring blankly forward and he had to push back tears. He couldn't let his friend die, Mackenzie had to get Blaise to help because if he didn't it would be on him.

"This is Edenspoint Hospital, we have emergency staff preparing for your arrival. What's the chief complaint of the patient? Over."

"Multiple stab wounds, head trauma, major loss of blood. Over." Mackenzie said the words back, and on the second response the tone of the paramedic on the other end had sharpened.

"Copy, deputy. Do you know patient identity so we can find blood typing in their medical records? Over."

"Patient is Blaise Fairholm. I repeat, it's Blaise." Mackenzie's voice betrayed him then, faltering so that he stopped to clear his throat. "ETA is in three minutes, maybe less." Mackenzie saw the police station rush past, and as he did he saw officers coming out the front doors to their cars. Other cars that had been out patroling had pulled over and moved the minimal traffic aside for him.

Leo had been sitting in his office fighting fatigue when he heard Mackenzie's voice come out of the radios around the station. He turned the

109

volume on his up, listening to his partner's calm and steeled voice and he felt the edge of worry come over him. He knew before Mackenzie said it, knew because Blaise was supposed to be with Mackenzie right then. When Mackenzie said that the critical was Blaise, Leo grabbed his jacket and gun as he moved out of his office and started barking orders.

"Sheila, get Mac on the radio, ask him where we need to go. Tell him I'll be right behind him. Jack get some units together to head out once Mac tells us where this happened." Everyone jumped to, Sheila getting Mac on the other end of the radio quickly and as soon as he said he'd found Blaise out as his house the others moved. Leo was on his way out the door planning on meeting Mackenzie at the hospital. "Sheila, get someone out to my sister's to bring her into the hospital. I don't want her finding out about this from someone else before we find her. I want that house gone over top to bottom with nothing missed, and then I want it sealed off until I can get out there to do my own sweep."

With that Leo was out the door and into his car, heading after Mackenzie down the street as he got the radio call that Mackenzie had arrived at the hospital.

They were there as soon as he pulled up to the front of the hospital, opening the back doors on the car to get Blaise out as carefully as they could and onto a gurney. Mackenzie followed them in through the doors, and would have kept going with them if one of the nurses didn't step in front of him to stop him as they pushed Blaise through the hall leading down to the OR.

"You need to go have a seat, Mackenzie." He recognized the nurse as Rebecca, one of the girls he'd taken out a few times for dinners. He pulled away from her and tried to step around her, and this time was met with Allison.

"I need to know he's going to be okay," Mackenzie said, trying to step around Allison as well but she put her hands on his chest and gave him a gentle shove back.

"All of us need to know he'll be okay, Callahan, but you're not allowed in there and even if you were; you being in there isn't going to help him now. You got him here, he's still alive and that gives us the chance to do what we need to for him. What I need you to do is to try and calm down, and to come with me." Mackenzie looked at her desperately for a few moments, but then just nodded and let her take him by the arm to pull him into one of the back rooms used by the nurses and doctors to change. Rebecca seemed put off by him going with Allison when he had ignored her, but Mackenzie didn't notice the annoyed look that crossed her face.

All the noise from the rest of the hospital seemed to be cut off when they entered the small changing room, the lights flickering on due to an automatic sensor on the wall as they stepped inside. Allison made him sit down on one of the benches, and rinsed her hands for some reason before opening a small cabinet to search out some scrubs for him to wear.

"Go ahead and take off what you have. I'll put it in a bag for you to take," Allison said, handing Mackenzie a scrub top that she guessed would fit him and turning back to find some pants. Mackenzie looked down at himself and saw that he had blood soaked through his shirt and jacket as well as spotted and smeared along his jeans. His hands were covered too and he felt sick thinking about the fact it was Blaise's blood. He realized that the reason Alice had washed her hands was because he'd gotten blood on her when she'd stopped him. He started to peel off his jacket, but stopped as he slouched in the seat.

"I shouldn't have been late. I could have stopped it if I hadn't been late." Allison had turned with some pants in hand, and she gave Mackenzie a sad look though it wasn't one of pity or blame. She set the scrub bottoms on the bench and took his face between her hands.

"You had no way to know that something was wrong. You got to him and you got him to us in time to give us a chance. You're not to blame for this, so don't go beating yourself up over it no matter what happens." She spoke gently but sternly to him, and then pulled her hands away to help him get his jacket off. She helped him get his shirt off next and stopped him long enough to wash off the blood that had seeped through to his skin under the clothes. She worked with precision, nothing behind the act but a detached professionalism as she got all she could off with a wash cloth and some warm water before helping him pull the scrub top on. She had him sit for a moment then, and gently washed his hands clean of the blood as well before having him change out of his jeans.

While he finished dressing she took his old clothes and carefully tucked them into a sealable plastic bag that she sat beside him. He looked at the bag of cloth for a few moments, staring at it and not realizing there were tears running down his cheeks until she brushed them away.

"I don't think I'll be able to get them clean…there's so much blood." She sat down, leaning against his side lightly and the contact gave him some comfort though far from enough to push it all away.

"It might come out, things can be fixed sometimes even when they seem broken beyond all hope," she said softly, and he leaned back against her. She sat there with him until he felt more steady, though he wasn't sure if he could feel completely stable again. Part of him knew now that the adrenaline was wearing off and his mind was trying to process things that he was probably in some form of shock. He felt detached from everything, though at the same time felt like any little thing might set him off. They both looked up when there was a knock on the door, and one of the security guards peeked in hesitantly like he didn't feel right disturbing them.

"The sheriff is here looking for you deputy. I told him I would try to find you." Mackenzie just stared so Allison answered for him.

"Tell him we'll be out in a moment. The deputy just needed a change of clothes," she said quietly, and the man nodded before ducking back out of the room. "You ready to go back out there yet, Callahan, or do you think you need a little more time?"

"I should probably go. He'll just start offending people if he's left out there to worry on his own," Mackenzie said with a quiet sigh, and Allison tried to surpress a small smile as she stood.

"Come on then. I'll stick with you if you'd like, at least until my rounds or they need me for something." She offered her hands to him, and he took them to let her help pull him up off the bench. He picked up the bag with his clothes but chose not to look at them. Even with his hands washed clean he could still feel the blood on them, he didn't need to see it staining the jacket to remember it.

Chapter 9 – Unbound -

Anne had gone out to clean up the inside of the dog run and any scraps left by Blaise and Leo that morning when they'd been working on it with her. The entire time she worked she felt like the animal was out in the woods watching her and she felt on edge until she finally went back inside. Sooli, the youngest dog that had stayed out of the way during the fight, sat inside with her as she tried to find a way to pass her time. She had the day off, and though she felt stir crazy sitting at home she didn't want to go into town either. She had called Shawn to check on her dogs, and he said they were doing well and that the tests would be back for her the next morning to let them know if they had caught rabies from the animal.

It didn't leave her much else to do, and she hoped that Blaise would come back after his lunch with Mackenzie. She glanced at the time and saw that it was about twenty after eleven, and she sighed. What she would normally have done was take the dogs out for a run on her day off, but she was left without that option. Even if they were there with her she wouldn't have felt right taking them out with that thing still roaming around.

Sooli whined beside her on the couch as she flipped through a magazine and gave a sharp bark before the knock on the door had announced a visitor. She felt a small thrill thinking it was Blaise, and she wondered why he hadn't used his key. Her smiled died as she opened the door and she was met with Adam, one of Leo's officers. His partner, Janice, was standing behind him looking out at the woods before turning to face her at the sound of the door opening.

"Anne, we need you to come into town with us," Adam said, and Janice gave him a slight nudge before she stepped forward.

"Anne, there's been an incident and your brother asked us to come out and give you a ride in to the hospital." Anne felt a sense of dread kick in, and her defenses kicked on. Even in their small town she had always worried about Leo getting hurt on the job, and she had had officers call her before to tell her about some minor injury or other that her brother or Mackenzie had ended up getting. Usually it was nothing more than a bruise or broken bone, but Leo didn't normally send the officer's out to pick her up and she worried it meant something worse had happened.

"Is Leo all right?" She stayed where she was, setting a hand on top of Sooli's head as the dog pushed it past her thigh to look out at their visitors. Adam and Janice exchanged a quick glance, and Anne's heart skipped a beat. "Was he shot?"

"Leo's fine, Anne. It's Blaise…he was attacked at his house, but he's at the hospital now so I'm sure they'll fix him up. Leo just wanted us to bring you in so that you didn't hear any rumors before he was able to tell you what's going on," Janice said, and Anne stared at her blankly. Anne wanted to argue, to say that Blaise was at lunch with Mackenzie so of course he wasn't the one hurt. She didn't have to worry about Blaise, he didn't get into situations where he got hurt, much less two within just a few weeks. She had reacted the same way when she'd first heard that Blaise had been hurt when Alex McGully had lost it, but this time her mind was rejecting the thought even more. Blaise didn't get hurt bad enough that her brother felt she needed an escort into town.

"Anne, if you'll just come with us we'll get you into town and Leo will explain-"

"Was it the same animal?" Anne interrupted Adam as her mind found focus on the word attack. They looked at her blankly and she felt a hint of anger that she latched on to. Anger was an emotion she handled better then fear. "The thing that attacked him, was it the same animal that attacked my dogs out here the other night?" Adam cleared his throat, shifting uncomfortably under the steel-edge of her tone. Anne had the thought that he wasn't a very good cop cross her mind.

"Anne, he wasn't attacked by an animal. A person did this. We need to get you in to the hospital now," Janice said, a stern edge coming to her voice to counteract Anne's anger. Anne shook her head, but Janice just pushed past her slightly to grab Anne's jacket for her from the hook by the door; ignoring the soft timid growl she got from Sooli for intruding on her owner's space. "Come on, Anne. Lock up and let's head out."

Anne tried to argue again, fighting against the fear that tried to rise up in her once more by spitting out more anger but Janice quieted her with a single look. She pulled the jacket on and tucked Sooli away in the back room since she couldn't put the dog out in the run before getting into the car with the two officers.

The ride was a quiet one, the two officers not seeming to know what to say when their efforts to comfort her were met with silence. The quiet let her get a better hold on herself, though she still fought to accept that Blaise was hurt. It felt surreal when they passed the turn off for Blaise's house, and the front yard was swarmed with police vehicles.

Leo had been trying to get some word on where Mackenzie was and what condition Blaise was in, but the nurse at the front station was stonewalling him. All she would tell him was that Mackenzie would be out in a few moments, and that Blaise was currently in the OR and that they wouldn't have an update on his condition for a while. He was about to have another go with her when Mackenzie came around the corner wearing a pair of hospital scrubs. Leo veered off from his course towards the nurse's station and headed towards him, noting that Allison was with him. She stepped forward ahead of Mackenzie and cut him off before Leo could start asking any questions.

"Take it easy, he doesn't need you interrogating him just yet," she said lowly, giving him a warning look. Leo gave her a look of his own, put off that she'd think he'd be cross enough to attack Mackenzie with questions right then. She stepped back while giving him one more look, leaving him alone with Mac. Leo noted the bag under Mackenzie's arm, and he carefully took it from him as he motioned towards some chairs in the waiting area. They moved to sit down, and there were a few moments of silence between the two friends. Mackenzie's attitude reminded Leo of how he was after the McGully's though there an undercurrent of anger in how Mackenzie stared down at the floor.

"How are you doing, Mac?" He broached the question carefully, leaning forward to match his friend's posture. He wanted to know what happened, he wanted to know how Blaise was and just how bad it had been, but Mackenzie wasn't the person to get that from just then. Mackenzie picked at a spot of blood under one of his nails that had been missed while cleaning up.

"I don't honestly know right now, Leo. How would you be if you'd walked in and found him lying in a pool of blood?" The question didn't come out defensive, but it was almost like Mackenzie really needed to know how Leo would feel. He looked at him, and Leo just shook his head.

"I couldn't tell you that, but what I feel knowing that you did is angry and scared. Right now I want to be out there finding the son of a bitch who did this, but I'm too scared to leave in case they come to give us some news. I'm doing what I can, I'm staying and trusting our team to start finding the guy responsible." Mackenzie sighed and leaned back in his chair, tilting his head up to look at the ceiling.

"He's a good guy, as far as I know he's never done anything to wrong someone but this still happened to him. Is that why you don't believe in God, Leo? Because he let Marie die?" Leo felt a little twinge at the question, but he pushed it back. Now wasn't the time to let Marie get in the way.

"I don't believe in God because I find it hard to picture somebody who could stand by and watch all that people do to each other. Marie is part of that, but I stopped believing a long time before then Mac and you know that. It always seemed rather hypocritical to me." Mackenzie made a noncommittal sound to this, but didn't ask any further. "Mac, you feel like you're losing faith in things because of this?"

"I don't know. I seem to be getting an awful lot of reasons to doubt lately." Leo was about to respond when Anne came through the doors followed by the two officers Leo had sent to get her. She walked straight to the nurse's station where she was met by Rebecca and Allison, who pointed her in their direction. Leo gave Mackenzie a pat on the knee before getting up to head her off before she could start yelling at the nurses. When he reached her though she was strangely quiet, just asking if they could tell her anything instead of her temper flaring like he thought it would. When his officers saw he had her they turned to head back out at his signal, and he knew they'd head to the house to help with the processing.

"Anne…come wait with us," Leo said, taking his sister by the hand to pull her towards where Mackenzie was sitting looking like he'd rather disappear into whatever back room he'd been in earlier. Anne sat down beside him as Leo directed her, and took Mackenzie's hand in hers which seemed to catch him off guard.

"He's going to be okay, he has to be…" She said it in a hushed tone like she was afraid to jinx it but needed to get the words out either way. Leo sat on the other side of her, and she rested her head against his shoulder while still gripping Mackenzie's hand tightly. "Has anyone gone over to tell Gabriel so he's not waiting for a ride home?" The question seemed to come out of left field and Leo sat there for a few seconds.

"No, I forgot about that..." He hadn't even thought about Gabriel and the fact that he'd be getting off of work at some point and expect Blaise to be there to take him back to the house. He grabbed his radio from his side, adjusting the volume for a few seconds so he could hear it. He'd turned it down completely on his way into the hospital, not wanting any stray conversation about what was going on at Blaise's house leaking through. "Can someone stop by the café and tell Gabriel he needs to come to the hospital."

"We'll head there on our way out to the house, sir," came the response from Janice, her and Adam having obviously gotten back to their car.

"You know he's the one they were after, right? Why else would someone have gone out to Blaise's place with the aim of doing damage..." Leo looked over at Mackenzie when he heard the other speak, but before he could answer Anne did.

"Either way they screwed with someone we love. Having him around just means they'll stick around long enough for us to find them." Mackenzie nodded, and Leo sighed quietly. He wished that it would be as simple as asking Gabriel who would want him dead.

"We'll find them, and when we do we'll make sure that they get what's coming to them in court."

"And if that doesn't work, we'll make sure they get it another way." Anne spoke the thought in a quiet and matter-of-fact way. It was what Leo had been thinking, but couldn't say in his position. He wasn't someone who looked for justice outside the system, but he knew he'd make an exception if it came down to the person who did this just walking away without paying.

The uneasiness had risen in Gabriel before he heard the sirens cut through town, and it was settling in to stay as he tried to focus on making a latte for one of the daily regulars. He'd felt tense and on alert for most of the day, but the feeling of dread had only hit him during the last hour or so. Hearing that Mackenzie's car had come through town with its sirens blaring while it headed towards the hospital hadn't helped him feel any more at ease. Lisa reappeared from the back where she had disappeared a few minutes ago to grab some supplies and she set it down on the counter beside him, making him jump and realize that he was burning the milk he'd been steaming.

"You all right?" Lisa nudged him away from the bar and took over to resteam the milk. She got the drink out quickly and apologized to the customer about it taking a little longer than usual.

"I just feel like something is wrong.... It has me on edge is all," Gabriel said, starting to put things away where they belonged around the counter. Lisa watched him for a few moments before starting to help.

116

"You could always call Blaise to check. I'm sure he'd know what was going on that had Mackenzie going towards the hospital. It may be nothing." She didn't sound completely convinced of this herself, but she was trying to bring that note of reassurance into her voice.

"I might do that, can you handle this?" Lisa nodded, and Gabriel headed into the back to use the phone there. He dialed Blaise's number and listened to it ring several times. It had just gone to voicemail when he heard Lisa call for him from the front of the store, an unknown tone in her voice. Gabriel left a short message asking Blaise to call him back before hanging up and stepping out into the store to see what Lisa needed. There were two police officers standing out in the lobby when he came out, and he gave Lisa a questioning look. "They need to talk to you."

Lisa sounded on the verge of crying, but she turned and disappeared into the back before he could ask what was wrong. The feeling in the pit of his stomach grew as he turned to look back at the two officers again.

"Gabriel, Leo sent us to tell you that you need to head on over to the hospital. If you need one we can give you a ride real quick, but we'll have to go now." Adam was the one who spoke, Gabriel only knowing his name since he came in and ordered the same thing each morning that he worked. Gabriel looked at them both for a few moments before taking his apron off.

"What's happened?" He spoke towards the female cop since he knew Adam wasn't fond of him and likely wouldn't give him a straight answer. Gabriel didn't know her name since she'd only been in once or twice, though Gabriel had a feeling she was the one who drank the white chocolate mocha that Adam usually bought with his coffee.

"Blaise has been hurt, someone attacked him out at the house. The Sheriff wants you at the hospital where he's at with his sister and Mackenzie for now."

"This probably has something to do with you. Maybe if Leo had decided to lock you up instead of letting you stay out there with him-"

"Adam, shut up." Adam's partner cut him off, but he still gave Gabriel a glare. Gabriel couldn't bring himself to care right then what the two officers thought of him. He couldn't deny that whatever had happened may have ties to him, but right then all that really mattered was that his friend had been hurt. If it was somehow his fault he'd deal with that when he could.

"I'll head over there on my own. Thank you for the offer of a ride though," Gabriel said, wanting the two to leave so that he wouldn't have to deal with the angry silence he was sure to get if he took the ride they'd offered. They both turned, but the woman stopped for a moment near the door.

"It'd be great if you could remember something." She turned and left, and Gabriel waited for them to pull away even though he was itching to leave. He turned towards the backroom and found Lisa standing in the doorway looking at him.

"Get going." Gabriel nodded, and as soon as he was out the door he started for the hospital at a run.

The time passed slowly once Gabriel had reached the hospital, the four of them sitting quietly in the waiting room. Leo had asked Gabriel some questions when he'd first gotten there, winded from having apparently ran the whole way. He wanted to know if Gabriel remembered anything, and had felt a flare of anger when the man admitted he did. However, what he did remember wasn't a lot of help other than there was a chance that his brother may be involved. He claimed that he didn't remember his name though, only a face which Leo wanted him to describe to a sketch artist when he got a chance.

Mackenzie had seemed to want to say something when Gabriel mentioned the brother, but whatever it was he had decided to stay silent on it. Leo had noticed it though, and knew he was going to have to talk to his friend when he got a chance. Hours seemed to pass without any news about how Blaise was doing, and every time one of the nurses or doctors appeared they all sat up a little straighter to see if they had come to talk to them. At last Doctor Maycroft came out and approached their small group in the waiting room.

"He's out of surgery, we're getting him settled into the room so it will still be a little while before you can go in and see him. He's not awake though." He didn't wait to tell them his news, knowing that they'd been waiting on edge for it. He did hesitate for a moment before he continued though. "Sheriff, if I could talk to you for a moment. I have somethings that may be relevent to the case."

"Of course," Leo said, shifting out of his chair to follow the doctor towards the nurse's desk. Mackenzie seemed to be ready to follow for a second, but Leo shook his head slightly to indicate he should stay with the other two. He would tell Mackenzie at some point on their own when he knew that Mackenzie was in a better state, but right then he wanted to keep the information close to his chest. Maycroft didn't say anything at first when they came to a stop, and Leo finally prodded him a little with a simple 'Doctor'.

"Whoever did this knew what they were doing, Sheriff. All the wounds were meant to cause pain but not be immediately fatal. It was the amount of stab wounds and the blood loss that was the problem, but any one of the wounds alone would not have been lethal. I can't be completely positive about this, but it seemed whoever did this wanted to keep him alive as long as they could while causing the pain."

"You think the point was torture?" Leo asked the question with a bit of disbelief. This wasn't something that happened in his town, but neither was a husband snapping and killing his wife after the birth of their kid.

"It appears so. I also wasn't sure if I should mention it to the others right away, but we're not sure when Blaise will wake up. He had heavy trauma to his head, and on top of that his heart stopped twice during the surgery and we had to revive him. We're going to run tests, but there's a chance that..."

"He may not wake up?" Leo cut the doctor off, getting the feeling that Maycroft was having a hard time getting to the conclusion of his comment. Maycroft nodded quietly, pressing his lips together into a thin line for a moment. "When it's okay for us to go in, will you let me go first? Give me about five or ten minutes with him alone?"

"Of course, but you're not going to get any information from him, Sheriff. Like I said he's not awake."

"I know, I just want a few minutes if that's okay." Maycroft nodded, and Leo thanked him before turning around to head back to the seats. He couldn't bring himself to tell the others what Maycroft had told him, he didn't want to give them the fear that Blaise wouldn't wake up until the tests had been run.

"What did he say?" Gabriel asked the question when he sat down, and Leo just shook his head lightly.

"Just that whoever did this knew what they were doing. They're going to let me in to see him first, just so that I have a few moments to try and piece some things together and then they'll come get you guys," Leo said, and Anne gave a soft protest at this. "Anne, I just need a few moments so that I can get some things noted for when we start trying to figure this out."

Anne's temper seemed to flare for the first time, but it died away quickly before she spoke her mind to him. It bothered Leo a little, he preferred not to fight right then but Anne was rarely the soft spoken person he saw in front of him. He sat back down beside her and put his arm around her shoulders. He knew he should tell her that Blaise might not wake up, but he couldn't bring himself to do it. He would give it some time for the doctors to do their tests before he dropped that possibility on anyone else's lap.

"This is shit." It was the first time Mackenzie had spoken in a while, and Leo looked over at him. He felt a bit uneasy by the sound of his partner's voice, and he sat up a bit straighter so that he could give him a warning look over Anne's head. "They were after you, Gabriel, why the fuck would they hurt him? What the hell followed you here?"

"Mac-" Leo didn't need this to happen now. He wanted answers too, but it wasn't the right moment to be trying to push for them and Mackenzie wasn't the one who should be doing the pushing.

"Don't, it's fine." Gabriel shook his head when Leo tried to keep Mackenzie from continuing. "I don't know why they would go after him, Mackenzie, though I'm assuming they thought he could tell them something. I do remember enough to know that it could likely be my brother, but why or what his name is I couldn't say. All I remember are bits and pieces, and all that doesn't account for much more than that I did something that my brother thought was a betrayal. If I remember more or if I find out where he's at, you'll be the second person to know."

"I should be the first, goddammit, and you should have told us you remembered anything at all." Mackenzie stood up, and Leo followed suit to put himself between his friend and Gabriel. He really didn't need them breaking out into a fight, but Gabriel stayed where he was seated and met Mackenzie's eyes.

"You'll only be second, because Anne should be first. If I do find him though, I can't guarentee that he'll be alive for long enough for you to interrogate him, Sheriff." The group stopped where they were, and Leo turned to look back at him for a few seconds before nodding his head.

"Whatever you have to do in self-defense, I can't hold you legally responsible for it." Gabriel returned the nod, and Leo looked back to Mackenzie to make sure he was done trying to cause a fight. "Mac."

"I'm fine. He's right, Anne should be first to know." The anger had left Mackenzie's voice as it fell flat again, though it didn't hold quite the same note of despair as it had before. The four of them had made an agreement amongst them just then that whoever had done this wasn't likely to be around to do it again once they found him, and none of them seemed to have any inner quarrels with this. Leo waited until Mackenzie sat down before turning to take his own seat, but he noticed that Maycroft was back and signalling for him.

"Take it easy you three. I'll only be a few minutes, and then I'll have them come call you back," he said as he moved to follow the doctor down the hall. The other three sat there, Anne moving for the first time since the start of the argument as she turned to look at Gabriel.

"Thank you."

Leo was shown into the room and waited until Maycroft had closed the door to give him a bit of privacy before turning to really take a look at Blaise. The other was lying still in the bed with tubes running from him to machines and vice versa, and Leo took a deep breath to steady himself as he pulled his hands through his hair. Outside the room he'd had to approach this as the Sheriff, the older brother and the comforting friend, but now it was just him as the weight of it settled into his chest. He felt helpless as he looked at Blaise, one side of the man's face swollen to where he was barely recognizable.

"Fuck." The word came out louder than he'd intended, and Leo placed a hand over his mouth as he glanced towards the door. When no sound came from the other side to say anyone was near enough to hear he said it again, and then a third time as he felt some relief from the release of it. "God-fucking-dammit, shit, son of a fucking bitch, motherfucker..." The string of words came out almost impulsively as he paced a few short turns in the room, fighting to keep his shaking hands still. He stopped and looked at Blaise almost hopefully, wishing the other would make some smart ass comment about watching his language around an invalid.

Blaise remained silent though other than the beeps and hisses from the machines surrounding him, IV's and tubing that were helping him breathe and take in medication and fluid. Bandages seemed to cover the worse of the damage, and for that Leo was grateful. He pulled a chair from beside the wall over to the bed and sat down now that his small tirade had drained him

"She had something to do with this, didn't she?" The thought came into his mind, but as he spoke it out loud it sounded ridiculous to him. Marie was, as far as he could tell, a figment of his imagination, a sign that he was losing it. But, Blaise had known about her and he hadn't sounded like he thought Marie wasn't really there when they'd talked at the house. "She had something to do with this. It can't be a coincidence that the first time I'm able to really talk to someone about what's going on, you end up like this just a few hours later. Fuck....fuck..."

Leo cursed a while longer under his breath as he pushed the heels of his hands against his eyes, fighting back tears he could feel heavy on his eyelashes. "I wish you'd just wake up and talk to me. I'm trying hard to keep it together for the others, but whatever's going on...I don't know how to deal with all of this."

Leo glanced at his watch to check how much time had passed, knowing that in about five more minutes the others would be coming to join him. He'd need to be the big brother again for Anne when that happened, be the friend for Mackenzie. He pushed out of the chair, feeling jittery as he paced the room a couple more times before stopping to face Blaise once more.

"You better wake up, you know. Anne needs you, and you can't just leave her behind. You're the only one I've ever really trusted her with, I know I've never told you that, but even after all the shit that went on between us after Marie died...you're the only one I've felt okay with her being with. She needs you to wake up, shit Blaise...I need you to wake up. I'm losing it, and I can't be sure I'll be here for them. I can tell already that Mac's starting to fall under the blows, and you're the only one that can keep us all together. You always seem to manage it somehow, and right now you seem to be the only one with some clue as to what's happening. You can't leave us to deal with this without you."

Leo heard the knock of the door and quickly ran a hand over his face to get rid of the tears that had managed to fall before he turned. One of the nurses had poked her head in quietly, giving him an apologetic look .

"Is it okay to send the others in now?" She asked a little timidly, reading that he was upset but Leo just nodded. She hesitated before stepping out of the door, disappearing for a few moments as she went to get the rest of his group. Leo ran his hands over his face a couple more times, taking deep breathes to pull himself back together. When the door opened to let the other three in, Leo was sitting beside the bed quietly with little emotion showing once more.

Mackenzie seemed to hug the wall as he entered, appearing to want to keep distance between himself and Blaise's form lying in the bed. Leo couldn't blame him for his aloofness, he'd seen Blaise at the worst when he'd found him but Leo doubted that made it any easier now. Anne moved to the bed without a word, standing there for a few seconds before Leo saw her shoulders shake in quiet sobs. He stood and slid an arm around her, the older brother comforting her fears and emotions as he moved her to the chair he'd been in. He sat and pulled her into his lap, holding her as he let her cry against him.

He looked up at one point and felt a stir of uneasiness twist through him. Gabriel was standing on the other side of the bed looking down at Blaise, and the look on his face spoke of an anger he'd never seen in the man before. Gabriel looked up and met his gaze, and Leo didn't pity the person who had done this though he did feel relief that Gabriel seemed to be on their side.

He'd found Michael in his room again, and Gabriel stood there watching his brother with fascination. Michael was searching in a desperate manner and had yet to realize that he wasn't alone any longer. Gabriel finally cleared his throat to catch Michael's attention. He was angry with the other for intruding again but was also worried. Michael went ramrod straight before turning to face Gabriel.

"It's not there..."

"Gabriel, you have to understand. It's time to forgive him, you understand that don't you?"

Chapter 10 – A Quiet Storm -

It had taken some convincing by the others, but Mackenzie had headed home to clean up and rest. He had been torn about leaving Blaise and them on their own, but at the same time felt relief at getting away from everyone for a while. He was on emotional overload, and he needed to try and sort it out. He still had his bag of bloody clothes under his arm, though he felt he'd prefer to destroy them. He avoided going inside of the coffee shop on the way up to his place, choosing instead to risk the metal steps leading up from out back. He detoured down the alley way, wishing the last time he'd come this way he'd paid more attention to the warning he'd gotten.

He was careful heading up the steps since the ice had taken a firm hold on them, and he leaned against the railing as he fumbled with his keys outside his door. When he got the door unlocked he stepped inside, leaving the light off for a few moments as he set the bag of clothes down to the side and relocked the door behind him. He was reaching to hit the switch for the living room light when he heard the voice talking to him from the darkness, and he paused before he hit the switch.

"I warned you, but you didn't want to listen." He recognized Michael's voice even in the dark of the apartment and turned to look out into the room towards where his voice came from. He finally reached back and flipped the light on, revealing Michael sitting in one of the chairs in the small living room. Mackenzie didn't answer him right away as he slipped off his borrowed winter jacket to hang beside the door. His first impulse hadn't been one he'd been proud of though it still seemed a pleasant option at the moment. He'd wanted to reach for his gun at the sound of Michael's voice, shoot the other right there even. That wasn't going to solve anything for him though, he wouldn't get answers that way.

"I'd think this would be the last place you'd want to be. I'm not exactly in a chatty mood, especially with you right now seeing as I'm positive you had something to do with this." The smile that Michael gave him didn't reach the man's eyes, and Mackenzie felt the first stirrings of concern for his own safety. He wished once more that he hadn't fallen into the habit of not carrying his gun with him at all times after the shooting with McGully. He knew where it was, but it would do him little good locked in the drawer of his nightstand in the bedroom. Michael seemed to read his thoughts when he spoke back to him.

"You're far from someone I need to be worried about, Mackenzie, even if you hadn't left your gun locked away. I offered you a chance to change how this would go, offered it to you because you seemed the most likely to take it, yet you refused. I can't help it if one of my colleagues decided he was tired of waiting and took action on his own, or that your friend happened to unfortunately wind up in the middle of it."

"Bullshit, you knew that he would-" Mackenzie started towards Michael, and the other stood up to meet him as he cut him off.

"I figured that Gabriel would be the one he'd find in the house, not your friend. It would have been on your head with either of them. I gave you a chance, and when you didn't take it I did what I could to stop an innocent bystander from getting killed." Michael spoke coolly as though Mackenzie wasn't currently in his face. He pressed a hand to Mackenzie's chest to push him back a step or two, and Mackenzie felt like an electric shock had just hit him from the contact. He tried to ignore the pain that was slowly fading from where Michael had shoved him as he refused to back down.

"You could have known with just a look that Gabriel was downstairs in the café at the time, so don't feed me that. You didn't do jackshit other than threaten me and my friends. Am I supposed to believe that you didn't think your 'colleague' would hurt someone if they happened upon him at the house? This is on you, not on me. Your brother seems to think the same from what I gathered today." This seemed to catch Michael slightly off guard, but he covered it up quickly.

"He remembers then?"

"He seemed to remember you, at least enough about you to suspect you had something to do with this." Mackenzie wondered if it was the best plan to be telling Michael this, but he'd already let it slip that Gabriel was owning up to remembering some. If he tried to backtrack now, he had a feeling it'd just do more damage than good. Michael appeared to be thinking the new information over for a few seconds before he moved past the subject himself.

"I warned you that something was coming and I stopped him from killing your friend out right, didn't I? I may have been too late to avoid the situation all together, but he is alive."

"You tried to stop it?" Mackenzie was having a hard time wrapping his head around this, but Michael answered by idly nodding. Mackenzie met his eyes, trying to read something from the man but Michael's gaze made him nervous enough to look away again. "He's barely alive. I find it hard to believe that's due to anything but your 'warning' earlier. You're lucky I don't kill you. I should be taking you in, let you deal with the entire police department for this."

"I'd like to see you try, and even if you managed it you'd just be putting all those people in harms way. You see, you're lucky I don't kill you, Mr. Callahan. Get in my face again, and I may still do so. Now sit down." The blantant threat and the suddenly formal way of addressing him made

Mackenzie listen. This didn't seem to be the same Michael he'd dealt with before, he had a darker edge that was showing through more clearly. He sat down in one of the recliners and Michael sat in the one across from him.

"I want to know exactly why you're after Gabriel." Mackenzie tried to open the conversation his way, but Michael just shook his head. He seemed more relaxed again now that they were sitting, and he leaned back for a moment.

"No, I've already told you what you need to know. If I told you more, you'd just meddle and then you'd stumble into a bad situation like your doctor friend."

"So, you're saying that Blaise knew something and that's why he ended up in the hospital?" Michael stopped and gave Mackenzie a stare as the anger seemed to reappear behind his eyes, Mackenzie wanted to push, wanted to know the truth, but right then it seemed like pushing would cost him more than it would give.

"...I've been patient with you. Patient with you and my brother, but I'm starting to reach the 'end of my rope' as you people might say. Also, I can't keep a leash on my colleagues forever and they're getting restless. One of two things need to happen; you need to get the information I want from my brother, convince him to talk somehow, or we decide to take what we want by force. This is only the beginning of things, Mackenzie. Don't make me feel this is a waste of time."

"Who are you? Not your name, I know that already or at least the first part of it. What I want to know is who you're associated with and why you're all doing this." Mackenzie spoke as Michael stood up, and the other paused for a second to look down at him before giving him another one of those smiles that seemed far from welcoming.

"Perhaps you should consult your priest, Mackenzie, or read the Bible? I'm sure its been a while and if you're going to choose to do this the hard way you may wish to look for some spiritual guidance."

"If you so much as think about hurting one of my friends again, I won't be the one that finds himself in need of salvation" Michael laughed softly as he walked past Mackenzie, stopping to put a hand on his shoulder.

"My, you do get testy when your upset. You should maybe focus on the parts about hell, because with that sort of talk, Mr. Callahan, you might just find yourself there one day." Michael headed towards the door, but Mackenzie never heard it open to let the man out. When Mackenzie turned though he was alone in the apartment, and the uneasiness in his gut told him that the 'what' of what he was dealing with may have been more important than the 'who'.

Blaise hadn't woken up the first day or the day after. Leo hadn't been able to bring himself to tell the others that he may not wake up, but he was starting to get the feeling they suspected it. He was hoping that Dr. Maycroft would break the news to them, but the tests were run but not complete so far and he hadn't broached the subject. Technically, since none of them were family he wasn't even supposed to have told Leo or let them in to the room like they were doing. Leo knew the initial scans were showing promise, and he was letting that give him an excuse to hold off on sharing the information burdening him.

Anne was sitting with Blaise now, and though Leo didn't feel right leaving her there by herself, he needed to go into work to see how things were going with the investigation. What he had found wasn't much. Things were already starting to go a bit cold with a lack of information, and the evidence hadn't made any hits yet. They had found blood that may have belonged to the attacker, but when they'd run tests it came up contaminated somehow. They suspected the attacker may have used something to destroy any DNA evidence, and they were running a scope of tests to find what had been used.

Leo had come out to Blaise's house on a whim after the disappointment and frustration of the news, and he was standing there looking at the mess that had been left behind. His team had gone over every inch of the place, and then Leo had come out late the night before and done it all over again himself. He knew there probably was nothing left behind that could tell him who had done this, but he found himself looking anyways.

He sighed as he finally accepted that things were finished there, and he moved to the laundry room. He dug around for a bit until he found where Blaise kept the cleaning supplies, and he pulled them out into the kitchen. Eventually Blaise would have to come back to the house, and Leo didn't want it to still have all the signs of what had happened left behind when he did.

That wouldn't be until Blaise woke up, and Gabriel was the same. He'd been staying at either the hospital or at Mackenzie's so far, and Leo had a feeling he'd stay there until Blaise woke up. *If he does...*

Leo chided himself for letting the thought slip through, and he set a bucket in the sink and turned on the hot water. He poured some lysol he'd found into it, and let it fill up as he watched the suds build.

He set about cleaning, scrubbing everything down while always keeping an eye out for something that could be of help. He had to empty and fill the bucket a few times as it got too full of blood and grime to be of any use, and he did his best not to focus on the fact the blood belonged to a friend. As soon as he had gotten everything as clean as he could without taking a toothbrush to the cracks, he moved out into the living room. He started trying to organize things back into place, at least those things that had survived the struggle. Some of the items were broken beyond hope of repair, and he set them aside in their own corner. He'd thought of just tossing them out, but he didn't want to before letting Blaise pick through it all.

He worked furiously at getting the house back into proper shape, trying to drain all the nervous, angry energy inside of him with the task. He still hadn't gone back to his own home, had even asked some of the other officers to go out there and get him some clean clothes under the guise of not wanting to be far from the hospital or station for any reason. That part was true, but he knew that the real reason was his fear of facing the woman inside his house.

Being away from that place had given him something unexpected. He was feeling like a small part of himself was returning to him now that he was staying out of her grasp. It didn't make it easier to ignore the part of him that felt torn up about being apart from her though.

When he finished he put everything away where he'd gotten it, tucking the cleaning supplies back into the laundry room. He wanted Blaise to come back to a place that didn't hold bad memories, but as he stepped out into the kitchen he could still see it. Even though he'd washed everything clean he could see the countertop stained with blood, the disorder and the fight that had happened here. If he still couldn't shake the memory then what chance did Blaise have when he'd actually lived it? Leo decided then that he needed to do something more drastic than clean, and once he ran into town to see if there was enough supplies availabile he'd start.

Gabriel was sitting in the hospital room alone other than Blaise. He had come over to sit with him while on his lunch, and he had offered to Anne to stay while she ran home. She had gotten a call that her dogs could come home with her that morning, and she needed to pick them up and take them out there to avoid the extra boarding fees. She had been hesitant to leave, but in the end she'd decided to go. Gabriel was glad that she hadn't decided the dogs could wait longer, because he hadn't had a chance to sit with Blaise on his own yet. He only had an hour for his lunch, but he had told Lisa where he was going and she'd told him to take as long as he needed. She knew where to get a hold of him if she needed him back right away.

At first he just sat there, listening to the quiet rush of the hospital outside of Blaise's room and the hum of the machines that were helping to keep him going. He didn't need them to tell him that Blaise was in bad shape. He could tell just being in the same room as him. He knew that Blaise had at some point been lost, but they brought him back. He knew that being back didn't mean waking up or being okay. He still didn't understand how he knew these things, but he was beginning to get a picture in his head from the dreams and rush of memories that came at him each night.

He knew enough now to know that he wasn't like Blaise or the others, but at the same time he didn't belong where he once had. He remembered very well now that his brother, Michael, was the reason he was here. They had fought, and though he remembered Michael telling him that it was Gabriel that had betrayed him, Gabriel was finding his mind told him differently. He looked at Blaise now, and he felt a pain in his chest. It didn't matter who had done the betraying in his family, either way it had brought this upon the people of the town. Either way, Blaise was still lying there trying to get stronger though still at risk of failing to pull out of it.

"I feel responsible, and I know that you would tell me that I'm not, but…I am. If I hadn't stayed here, you wouldn't be in danger now. None of you would. I'm remembering more, Blaise, and though I still can't tell you exactly who I am or what brought me here I can tell you this. I will find him, whoever did this even if it was my brother, and I will do my best to make sure they get theirs."

Gabriel felt some stir in Blaise, some unsettling in the room that told him something had changed in that short moment. He reached over to set a hand on Blaise's arm, and felt the tension in the man's muscles. It was more a whisper than anything, but Gabriel felt the memory of the man suddenly imprint on him. It wasn't his brother, but Gabriel remembered him and knew that he was the one who had injured Blaise. He had the sense of an ever changing face, though always with the same sort of calm insanity running beneath its features. The thought of the man made him feel sick though he didn't have all the memories to know why. It made him doubt for a moment that the man he'd just had boil up out of his memories could have any ties with his brother, but things were still too fragmented to tell for sure.

"Shax..." Gabriel pulled away as he said the name, and the feel of tension disappeared at the break of contact with Blaise. He wasn't sure whether it was him or Blaise who had made it so he could see the man, though he had a feeling it was a mix of both. That perhaps with his memories, Gabriel was starting to find some of his own strengths again and that it let him get a glance at the prophetic dreams that Blaise seemed to have. Though he now at least knew who had done this, what he wished was that Blaise would wake up. Talking to him would be more of a comfort and a help than just getting a passing thought.

Mackenzie was going through the days in a haze. The hours seemed to go by slowly for him after he'd had his last conversation with Michael, and his only real relief was that the man hadn't shown himself again. He'd gone down to the chapel in the hospital that morning when he'd stopped in to check on things. He didn't go into Blaise's room even though it made him feel guilty and he knew he'd have to visit at some point. He felt uncomfortable standing there in that silent room though.

In there alone with Blaise it felt like he was sitting on death watch, and he felt afraid of the silence that greeted him. He would just rehash finding Blaise again and again, and think of how he could have and should have helped the man more. It was worse with the others there, especially Anne as she sat unmoving besides Blaise talking to him in soft tones. Gabriel would sit lost in his thoughts, a distant expression on his face that Mackenzie couldn't ever read but that he knew made him feel nervous. The only time he felt comfortable in the room was a short period when Allison had come to sit with him. She had sat beside him and taken his hand in hers, and they were quiet together. When she had felt a tremor go through him she had simply squeezed his hand and pulled him closer so he could lean against her.

Sitting in the chapel now he didn't get the same sense of peace he did when he was at the church. It felt more troubled here, but he had needed the familiarity of a religious place. He sat in one of the small pews away from a woman that was praying in the front. No one had said anything, but he'd gotten a feeling from the quiet whispers of the doctors and nurses that there

128

was something they hadn't told them all. Leo had the same air around him, and he wondered if his friend really thought he was managing to hide the fact he knew. Anne might not have noticed since her focus was all on Blaise, but Mackenzie always knew when Leo was hiding something. The woman at the front got up and turned to leave, glancing quietly at Mackenzie as she did.

With her gone Mackenzie moved closer to the front of the chapel, sitting in the front row of pews as he looked at the small makeshift alter there. It was a small thing with a crucifix hanging, and a painting that depicted St. Agatha, the saint of nurses, on one side and St. Jude on the other. Seven angels were along the edges of the painting looking in at them, and Mackenzie studied them. He stopped suddenly as he was naming them in his head as he felt a thought brush through his subconscious. It was gone too quickly though, and he focused back on the painting.

He prayed to St. Jude then, feeling he was the best choice at the time. Things had gone past Mackenzie's control, and the Patron Saint of hopeless causes seemed fitting of their current situation. Blaise's condition, the progress coming to a stand still on finding who'd hurt him, and Mackenzie's own state of mind seemed desperate enough times for him to need the help.

Another day had passed without Blaise waking up, and Leo had decided to start on his project in the kitchen after sitting with him the first half of the day. He'd picked up what he would need, at least the things he could get without having to wait for an order to come in, and headed out to Blaise's house. He'd been in the middle of unloading when it struck him that he didn't have his tool box. He'd thought long and hard about going into town to buy all new tools, but he knew well enough that it would be more than he could afford. Not to mention that he had a few wood working tools he'd need that the store wouldn't have.

That was what had brought him down the road to the long drive up to his house. He was sitting in his car at the bottom of that drive now, and he told himself again that it would be better to turn back. Each time though, he felt like by postponing his plans for Blaise's house he was accepting that Blaise wasn't going to wake up from this. Besides, he wasn't going to have to go into the house. The tool box was in the shed off to the side, and he could get to it without having to get closer than ten feet to the house.

He sighed after a time and started up the drive slowly, waiting to see if he felt her pull on him. He wanted to know as soon as he felt that tug of control she seemed to have over him kick in before it was too strong. If he could tell that being near the house was going to be worse than he was hoping, he'd turn back before the pull was too strong. Yet, all the way up the drive he felt nothing. There was no tug on his subconscious or voice in his ear. This threw him off more than if she'd been standing on the porch waiting for him.

The house seemed silent and abandoned when he reached it, but he still kept his distance as he angled the SUV as close to the shed as he could get it. He didn't close the car door behind him when he climbed out, not wanting the sound to alert her if she didn't already realize he was there. It would also mean an easy entry if he found he needed to leave quickly. He opened the shed with some difficulty since snow had built up in front of it, and he had to wedge the door back and forth several times to get the powdery snow pushed aside and flattened out enough. He hadn't been in the shed the last few months, and it smelled musty as he moved inside to find the tool box along the side of the wall on a bench.

He lifted it up, not wanting to take the time to check that everything was still in it that he'd need. He didn't want to spend more time there than he needed too, and he could feel a stirring in the back of his mind like a warning signal starting. He shifted back out of the shed, side-stepping around some of the organized clutter to get to the door a bit faster. His car was sitting just outside the shed, still idling since he hadn't wanted to risk turning it off. Back out in the open he could feel her watching him, and he knew it had been a mistake to even come this close to the house. He paused as he put the toolbox into the back of the SUV, glancing towards the house and feeling that familiar tug.

He shook his head as he found himself wondering if he should go inside and check if she was still there. He forced himself back to the driver's side door and got back in the SUV, throwing the car into gear before turning back down the road.

He didn't stop until he'd reached Blaise's house, feeling shaky and on edge. He sat outside for a few moments as he took deep breaths, trying to steady himself again. He didn't feel that stirring touch of her in his mind though he still felt anger at himself for risking it.

Leo finally pulled around to the back of Blaise's house where he had unloaded everything earlier onto Blaise's porch. He'd left the back door unlocked, and headed inside to slam the toolbox down onto the countertop. The house answered him with silence as he stood there, and that piercing quiet seemed a welcome thing to him right then. He was itching with the need to do something, anything but think over the renewed thoughts of Marie and the constant worry about his friend. Nervous energy seemed to be overflowing from him, and he needed to do something to get it back under control. He moved out to the back porch and focused on the woodpile where the remaining axe that hadn't been taken as evidence was sitting.

Once inside he let go, hacking at the island countertop until it was in pieces. The axe didn't work as well as a sledgehammer might, but it would have to do. He worked to get every ounce of frustration and fear out of himself, turning the kitchen island into dust on the floor around him with little regard. It was only when he'd taken it down completely, exposing the raw, untiled floor beneath it that he stopped for a breath. He looked around himself for a moment almost wishing there was something else he could tear out, but he'd accomplished his goal.

Instead he focused on cleaning while planning on what he'd do next. He'd need to patch the spot on the floor where the island had sat, and then figure out something to give the counterspace back to the room. He didn't care how as he was just glad to be rid of the old space, glad that he wouldn't have to have another cup of coffee sitting at the damn island ever again all the while knowing what had gone on there even if Blaise did wake up.

He was finishing up the sweeping when his phone rang, and it took him a moment to realize it was in his back pocket. He dug it out as he collected the shirt he'd shed while tearing out the island to wipe at his neck with it as he answered his phone.

"Hello?"

"Come home, Leo. You can't avoid me forever." The voice on the other end of the line made his blood run cold all over again, and he tossed the cellphone away from him quickly. It clattered to the floor somewhere in the living room. The quiet house suddenly felt oppressive around him, and he didn't bother to finish sweeping the last remains of the mess before pulling his shirt and jacket back on to leave.

He stepped outside, turning to lock the door behind him when he heard Marie's voice calling for him inside. He stopped, staring at the wooden surface between him and the voice. A trickle of her laughter came through to him, and Leo felt his hands shake as he turned the key in the lock of the door before he started down the steps to his car. He drove back to the hospital quicker than was probably advisable, but he needed to be around others. He'd managed to let her back in by going out to his house, and he was suddenly afraid that he wouldn't be able to lock her out again.

Leo had been frustrated that it was Gabriel in the room with Blaise when he got back to the hospital, but at the moment he knew he was just glad that anyone was in there. Gabriel glanced at him as Leo came in and sat down; a few seconds of awkward silence passed between the two of them.

"You wanted me to tell you if I remembered anything…" Leo actually startled slightly when Gabriel broke the quiet, and he looked at the other man for a second as he tried to focus himself. Leo sat up a little straighter as it sunk in the importance of what Gabriel may be saying.

"Do you? Remember anything?" Gabriel nodded, glancing at the door as though he was worried someone would come into the room. When he seemed satisfied he turned back, and Gabriel reminded Leo of the man who'd woken up that first time after Anne found him out in the snow. There was an intense determination in the lines of Gabriel's face, and Leo had a feeling the man was more of who he use to be at that moment.

"My brother's name is Michael, I didn't remember it before but I do now. I saw him once while I was here, though at the time I thought it was a dream because I woke up and he was gone. I'm assuming he knocked me out," Gabriel said flatly. It wasn't completely the truth, when he'd seen Michael at Blaise's house he knew now that it was Michael trying to get him to remember something specific. "When I saw him it was out at Blaise's." He saw Leo's temper flare even as the words got out, and he regretted the choice of telling him that detail.

"You didn't think it was important to tell anyone that happened?" Leo said.

"I didn't realize at the time it was anything to tell someone," Gabriel bit back. He thought it was more that he'd actually snapped at Leo in returned that caught the other off guard rather than his tone. Either way Leo's anger seemed to quell itself a little.

"So, you think your brother was the one that did this?"

"No, not directly at least. The man who attacked Blaise is named Shax. You won't find him, not unless he wants to be found. They're looking for something though, that's what I wanted to tell you. My brother tried to take something from me and I hid it. They're trying to find it." Leo shifted, looking at Blaise for a few moments before he responded. Gabriel wished at that moment he could read the man easier. Mackenzie was easy to read, as was Anne, but Blaise and Leo both seemed to shut him out more.

"Do you remember where it is?"

"No, I don't even remember what it is yet. All I remember clearly is the fact that they're looking for something and that if Shax is here my guess is that he's working with my brother."

"Not a lot of help...though we may be able to find something on Shax now that we have a name."

"No, you won't..." Leo looked at him, a subdued hint of the anger coming back in his eyes.

"Then what good does it do me? Right now all I seem to get is a lot of useless information, and nothing that can help. From you, from the crime scene, just about everything dead ends. What am I supposed to do with all of it?" Gabriel felt a moment of uneasiness. Not because of Leo's anger, but because he sensed for the first time a desperation in Leo. The closely guarded, slightly hot-headed sheriff seemed suddenly lost. The moment went as quickly as it came though as Leo ran a hand through his hair. He seemed to reach for his cellphone clip that was attached to his belt, but realized the cellphone wasn't there. "I appreciate the honesty, though if I find you are hiding anything from me I'm counting you responsible."

"I'd expect you to," Gabriel said in return, on more solid footing dealing with the Leo that was threatening to lock him up than the man he'd glimpsed just a moment before.

Gabriel left a few moments after telling Leo what he remembered, and Leo found himself alone in the room. He sat thinking over what Gabriel had told him, and all he could focus on was that it didn't seem to get them anywhere. Leo moved to the chair that Gabriel had vacated and sat back in it as he stared at the wall.

"Do you still think we can trust him?" Leo let the question slip out and hang in the air for a few moments before he shook his head. "Of course you do. And, you're probably right too, dammit." He set his head in his hands for a second before looking up at Blaise.

"I was stupid today. I went out there even after you told me not to. I didn't go in the house, just that shed I have up there but that didn't matter. She found me again because of it...I don't know what to do if she starts following me around outside the house. I was out at your place, and she called me of all things. Told me to come home. I came here instead...that's something at least, right?" He knew he wasn't going to get any advice, but he found it felt good to be talking about it. Voicing it out loud made it seem less like some secret that would choke the life out of him someday.

He realized as he sat there that he'd probably spent more time talking to Blaise now that the other was lying unconscious in a hospital bed than he had over the last few months all together. He felt a hit of guilt wash over him, and he wished he'd done things a bit differently. He could have done a lot of things a bit differently. He gave a quiet chuckle for a moment, though it was hollow sounding even to himself.

"I hope you don't mind, but I kind of tore up your kitchen. Don't worry, I'll get it fixed...just maybe not until I can drag someone out there so I'm not on my own." The small hint of humor died a little from his voice at this. "Mac won't go out there for obvious reasons. I think he's torn up that he didn't go check on you quicker. I haven't let Anne go out there, though she asked once. I don't want her to see that...hell, I didn't want to see it..."

He fell back into silence then, watching Blaise lie there for a few moments. "I'm sorry...you never deserved the attitude I gave you. You've always done right by me, always been a good friend, and all I've done half the time is push you away. Now here I am...lost, haunted by my dead wife, and you're the one person who may be able to help but there's no way to reach you. Maybe this is what I deserve..."

Chapter 11 – Wash the Spider Out -

Leo wasn't sure how long he'd been sitting there that morning so far, the time was slipping past now. Anne had come back the night before, and they'd sat in that strange quiet together. She still seemed fragile like she was going to crack, and Leo wished even more that Blaise would wake up. At the very least he was hoping for something from the doctors soon. He hadn't argued when Anne volunteered to go grab breakfast, though he didn't understand her moods completely. At one moment she didn't seem like she wanted to leave Blaise's side for anything, and then the next she'd disappear without so much as a word and not return for a couple of hours.

When Marie had gone Leo was too far lost in his own haze to know if this was how Anne had acted back then, though he did remember a few arguments they'd had when he felt she wouldn't let him be. It troubled him now, he didn't like to see his sister seem so vulnerable when she usually was so strong and independent. He sighed as he glanced at his watch, and saw she'd only been gone a few minutes. She'd said she was going to get something from outside the hospital because she was tired of the food in the cafeteria, but he felt it was an excuse to be alone for longer.

Leo looked up when he heard the door open, surprised she'd be back so soon but found Mackenzie hesitating in the doorway instead. Leo understood Mackenzie's actions better than his sister's, the other seemed to be decidedly avoiding Blaise's room though he was constantly at the hospital itself. When Mackenzie was in the room it was obvious he felt guilty, and he'd only glance at Blaise but never really take a good look at the man. Leo motioned for Mac that it was all right if he came in and sat down. Mackenzie pulled a chair up to the other side of Blaise's bed, and settled himself in it. He chose to look over Blaise at Leo instead of focusing on their unconscious friend. They sat like that for a while, Leo trying to count off the minutes in his head.

"He's not going to wake up, is he?" The question brought Leo around, and he looked up to find Mackenzie staring at Blaise. Leo looked back at Blaise himself as he leaned forward in his chair slightly, shifting uncomfortably at being put on the spot.

"There's a chance he won't. They told me the first day but...I haven't been able to tell anyone. The results to everything aren't back or finished...I was worried if I said it out loud it might make it happen." Leo's leg jumped a little in a nervous fashion before he forced it to be still. "I should have said something..."

"Alice told me when I was here last night down in the chapel. She was upset that no one else had talked to us about it, even though she knows that with us not being family...Did they tell you his heart stopped?" Mackenzie spoke like he hadn't heard half of what Leo said, his voice low even though they were the only two in the room. Leo understood though, the potential death of a friend wasn't something you talked about in normal tones, it was something that called for hushed voices.

"They did...they said it happened twice." Mackenzie nodded when he answered, and looked away from Blaise. They both stared at the floor then for a while, wishing everything could just return to normal. "I'm worried Mac...I was out at his place cleaning up-" Leo wasn't sure at first what it was that cut him off, but he realized quickly that it was Blaise gasping for air. The man had sat up suddenly in the bed, and was in a panic as he pulled at the tube that ran down his throat to help him breathe.

"Holy shit..." Mackenzie stuttered out the words as they both moved to grab Blaise to stop him, not sure if he could hurt himself pulling the tube out. By the time they took hold though he'd already managed to tug it free, choking and gagging the whole time.

"Blaise, I don't think-" Leo had set his hand on Blaise's arm, and at the touch Blaise's panic seemed to rise up out of him. Leo barely managed to miss the backhanded blow that Blaise threw causing Leo to stumble back a step. Mackenzie tried to move to grab Blaise as the man started pulling free from the IV's, and Mackenzie got an elbow to the face for doing so. Mackenzie let a muffled string of curses loose as his nose started to bleed and swell right away.

Leo tried to get Blaise to stop and calm down as the other managed to get the IV's torn out of his arm and Blaise moved to deseperately scramble out of bed. Leo was worried Blaise was going to injure himself, and he tried once more to get a hold on the man only to have Blaise slip out of his reach across the bed.

"Blaise, calm down.." Mackenzie's words came out awkward as he lunged after Blaise who was heading for the door. Mackenzie got an arm around Blaise's chest to try and hold him back, and this seemed to set Blaise onto the defensive again.

"No!" Blaise choked the word out though it was barely audible, his voice broken and rusty from disuse and the abuse of having the tube ripped out of his throat. He fought against Mackenzie, twisting them around and slamming Mackenzie back against the wall. Another string of curses broke out of Mackenzie as Leo moved to block Blaise from making a run for it, pushing him back by the shoulders to pin Blaise between himself and Mackenzie.

"Blaise, it's me. Calm down, it's just me. It's Leo." Leo grabbed the sides of Blaise's face trying to get the man to look at him while failing to avoid a kick to the shin. Mackenzie managed to keep a grip on Blaise, holding the other's arms back so he couldn't do more than kick which wasn't as effective since he had no shoes on. Leo finally just pushed his forehead against Blaise's forcing the other to look him in the eye. "Blaise, it's just me. You need to calm down, it's just me and Mac." The wild look in Blaise's eyes seemed to turn to confusion as he looked at Leo, and his struggling slowly stopped though he stayed tense like he was ready to snap if he found it was a lie.

"Leo?"

"Yeah, it's just me and Mac," Leo said with a slight nod, his hands falling to Blaise's shoulders though he kept a firm hold just in case. Blaise looked past him as Leo pulled back some, and he seemed to be trying to get a sense of where he was.

"What happened? Where?" Blaise's voice was stronger now though it was still harsh and ragged sounding.

"Mac found you. You're at the hospital, you've been out for a few days." Blaise gave a short nod, and he seemed to let himself relax a bit. Mackenzie let his grip loosen now as Blaise seemed more aware of his surroundings, though he quickly grabbed hold of the man again when Blaise started to sway to the side. Leo took Blaise's shoulders too to try and help him keep balanced and upright.

"I guess...being in the hospital...explains the cathater," Blaise said, and Leo stared at him for a second before he started to laugh quietly.

"I really don't want to know how else you were going to explain that to yourself," he said, patting Blaise's cheek affectionately.

"I'm just glad that bag didn't break. If you'd managed to break my nose and get piss all over me, I'd think I'd have let you go run around the hospital and embarrass yourself," Mackenzie said, and the three of them laughed more out of relief than humor.

"Can we get the patient back in the bed now?" They all looked up at the sound of the voice, and found a few nurses all standing in the doorway. Allison had nudged her way to the front, and was the one that had spoken up to them. She nodded towards the bed, and Leo and Mackenzie moved to help Blaise get back into it since he was unsteady on his feet. After that though they were kicked out by Allison so that Dr. Maycroft could check Blaise's vitals and make sure he hadn't torn any stitches open. Leo and Mackenzie went down to the waiting room to call Anne and Gabriel to let them know Blaise was up, Leo borrowing the phone at the front desk to call his sister since his cellphone was still out at Blaise's house.

Leo headed back up to Blaise's room after getting a hold of Anne, leaving Mackenzie to get his nose checked to see if it was really broken. Mackenzie had said he'd meet the others when they got to the hospital once his nose was taken care of. Blaise was hooked back up to some of the machines, but in place of the tube that had been down his throat he had a small one that just fitted under his nose to supply extra oxygen. He'd been lucky, and they hadn't found that he'd torn anything open during the struggle. His oxygen levels were still low though, and Leo could tell that now that Blaise was awake he was feeling some pain.

"You look like shit," Leo said, moving to sit down beside the bed. Blaise chuckled a bit roughly at this, though Leo could tell the humor was at least partially put on.

"Thanks, I feel like I was hit by a train." The attempt to be cheerful came off a little hollow, but Leo let it slide. He couldn't blame Blaise for not being in a great mood, especially if the other remembered clearly what had happened to him. He wondered for a second if the hospital had advised Blaise to talk to someone, the local therapist at least. It made him hesitate for just a second before asking what he had come to ask.

"Blaise, had you seen the guy before? Could you give us anything that might help us find him?" Leo dropped his own pretense of being cheerful. He was glad and incredibly relieved that Blaise was awake and alive, but he couldn't be truly happy until he knew they had the guy who had done this. The guy was still out there, and there was the risk that he'd come after Blaise again if he found out the other had survived. Blaise sat for a few moments before giving his answer, and Leo couldn't read his expression which usually meant Blaise was hiding something or some emotion. Leo leaned forward so he could catch Blaise's gaze, and seemed to bring him out of some thought. "Come on, Blaise. I need to find the son of a bitch…is there anything you can give me?"

"I'd seen him before, but it's not going to help you out Leo. I saw him the same way I knew that 'Marie' was hanging around you." Leo shook his head at the answer, not understanding what Blaise was getting at. Blaise fidgeted a little, which wasn't something that Leo was use to seeing him do and he seemed about to speak up again when Anne came in. She was followed by Mackenzie and Gabriel a few seconds later, and Leo sighed to himself. He had to push back the annoyance at the conversation being interrupted as his sister moved to cover Blaise in a hug. She had every right to be there and to see him, and Leo wasn't going to deny that. It didn't help that nagging feeling that his time to figure this out was being wasted.

Blaise shot him a quick look, and Leo understood it meant they'd talk about it later. Whatever it was Blaise wasn't about to bring it up in front of the others, at least not in front of Anne. Leo nodded though he wasn't in the mood to wait for later. The last time they'd agreed to talk later Blaise had almost been killed.

"I'm so sorry I wasn't here when you woke up," Anne was still holding Blaise in a hug, mumbling against his neck for a second before she pulled back to look at him. "Are you all right? Are you feeling okay?" Blaise smiled a little at her, taking hold of her hands gently to stop her nervous fretting with his bedsheets.

"I'm fine, a little worse for wear but I think I'll be all right." Blaise was trying to put on a cheerful façade again, but he wasn't quite managing to pull it off for once. There was still a crack in his normally perfect wall he put up in defense, and it was enough to let some of the trouble and turmoil leak through even with his best attempt. Leo glanced over at Mackenzie and Gabriel who were standing just inside the doorway. Mackenzie had gotten cleaned up though his nose was still a bit swollen looking and had a couple of bandages over it that made him look slightly ridiculous. Mackenzie was smiling, though he could tell Gabriel and he were both thinking the same thing Leo was. Anne seemed to be the only one able to just focus on Blaise being awake and okay, the rest of them were thinking about how the person who had done this was still out there.

Anne was whispering quietly to Blaise, and Leo moved to nudge the other two out of the room. He wanted to talk with Blaise, get the full story from him, but he'd give Blaise some time with Anne first. They left the two of them alone, stepping out into the hall and closing the door.

They all silently agreed to head downstairs to get coffee, the three of them stepping into the hospital elevator. The doors had closed before Gabriel spoke, seeming to startle the other two out of their trains of thought.

"He's still out there. If he hears that Blaise is awake…" Gabriel had a feeling that Shax wouldn't have left Blaise alive if he hadn't at least half expected the man to survive. What the point of that was Gabriel hadn't fully worked out yet, but he'd had an idea of what it may have to do with. The other two didn't know about Blaise though, didn't know that the man had dreams that came true or what it could mean if someone else figured it out.

"You still sure it was this Shax guy? You can't tell us what he looks like though…" Mackenzie glanced up at the two of them, and Gabriel realized that Leo hadn't talked to him about what he'd shared. It struck him as odd that it was kept from Mackenzie, and he glanced between the two men for a second.

"No, I can't. He's good about…disguising himself. You didn't tell him?" Gabriel nodded at Mackenzie, and Leo seemed genuinely surprised himself when he realized that he hadn't in fact told Mackenzie. The two friends seemed to share silent words, and Gabriel was able to tell that there was something off.

"Have you run the name through the database?" Mackenzie asked the question, and there was a hint of anger when he did. Gabriel shifted slightly, now hoping the elevator would move a little quicker down to the café.

"Yes, I did. It brought up the usual, no one stood out. I even googled the damn name, and all I got was a hand full of companies and a bunch of shit on some demon that appeared on a tv show about witches." Leo bit the words out in frustration, though it seemed to leave him more deflated. Mackenzie glanced at him as Leo rubbed at his eyes.

"You been sleeping?"

"No." The answer was short, and as the elevator doors opened before Mackenzie was able to ask more. Leo stepped out into the main atrium of the hospital quickly to avoid the questions, the joy of Blaise waking up sufficiently snuffed for the time being. Gabriel followed the other two down the hall towards the cafeteria but hung back to let Mackenzie and Leo pull a little ahead of him. Gabriel watched the two from a slight distance and could tell they were arguing, but where Mackenzie had seemed the one upset at first it was Leo that now seemed angry.

"Look, will you stop pushing, there's nothing wrong other than the obvious. I'm sorry I forgot to mention it, I've had a lot on my mind." Gabriel heard Leo snap at Mackenzie when he caught up to them at the start of the line where you grabbed your trays. Mackenzie held up his hands as if to say he was backing off, and he let Leo go ahead to grab some food.

138

"I'm sure he didn't purposely not tell you I'd talked to him," Gabriel spoke, and got a look from Mackenzie in return. "Right now isn't the time to be fighting, we need to be working together. Whatever the issue really is, you two need to work it out."

"Think I don't know that? He'll get over it, he always does. Now stop making us sound like some old married couple who needs counseling please." Mackenzie took his own tray and moved ahead to decide on what he wanted and Gabriel sighed as he followed suit.

Anne hadn't wanted to leave Blaise's side, but Leo had finally been able to make it work out that he had a chance to talk alone with Blaise. He'd reminded Anne that she needed to check on the dogs now that they were back out at her house, and after a lot of back and forth she had finally left. Mackenzie had already excused himself, seeming even more uncomfortable now that Blaise was awake and thanking him for finding him and saving him. Gabriel had been the last one, but he'd seemed to understand as he'd left. Blaise had drifted off by the time the room had emptied, and Leo stepped out into the hall to grab some coffee before he woke him.

The hospital was quiet and still since it'd gotten late, and there was only one nurse sitting at the nurse's station. Leo gave her a small wave as he passed then stopped at the coffee maker to pour himself a cup. He had reached the nurses station again by the time he noticed the man that had made his way into the hall. Leo watched him closely, unconsciously picking up his pace as he saw the man stop outside of Blaise's room for a second before slipping inside. The door was closed behind the man, leaving only a small crack of space to look in to. Leo felt a twist of fear in his chest, and he set the cup of coffee onto a cleaning cart he passed.

He slowed to a stop just outside the room, not hearing anything from inside. He pushed the door open slowly, wanting to take the man by surprise. Leo saw the him standing beside Blaise's bed with his back to the door, and Leo stepped inside quietly. Blaise was still asleep and the man wasn't doing anything but watching him but Leo noted the gun the stranger had on his hip. Leo reached for his own weapon, setting his hand on the heel of his gun as he unclipped the holster to slip it free.

"Excuse me…" Leo spoke up so the man would turn to look at him, and when he did Leo found himself frozen to the spot. The person he was looking at was himself, and Leo couldn't do anything but stare in horrified confusion. His twin didn't appear to be as startled as he was, and Leo tried to react as he saw the other him suddenly draw his gun. All Leo had time to do was get his gun halfway raised before his twin had turned and pressed his own gun under Blaise's chin as he pulled the trigger. The sound of the gun went off around him and Leo felt the floor drop out beneath him as he suddenly found himself almost falling out of a chair.

Leo caught himself barely before he fell and hit the floor, and his mind reeled as it tried to catch up to what was happening. He turned to look at Blaise and found the other awake in bed watching him. Leo pushed himself up out of the chair when the voice suddenly spoke in his ear, scanning the room for its source.

"Shoot him for me, Leo." He turned again as he heard her speak, but his scan of the room revealed that it was only Blaise there with him. "Kill him for me, shoot him Leo." Blaise was watching him, seeming a little uneasy but more worried than frightened.

"Is it getting worse?" Blaise speaking up seemed to cut through Marie's voice ringing in Leo's ears and she faded as he turned to look at Blaise. Leo had to stand and think for a few moments to process the question. When things fell back into place around him, Leo pressed on his temples to try and dull the pain that was now thumping behind his eyes.

"It had been better. I hadn't gone home, and things seemed almost normal..."

"But then you went home?" It wasn't an accusation, Leo knew that but he couldn't help feeling guilty like he'd just taken the last cookie out of the jar without permisson. He sat down again, though one of his legs jittered up and down beyond his control.

"I didn't even go in the house. It was stupid, but I just needed some tools from my shed. I thought...I don't now what I thought. It's like she's in my head now though, I heard her out at your place and now here. I don't know how to stop this, it's feels like I'm going crazy Blaise."

"You're not going crazy, Leo. From what I've seen, she's real. She's not Marie though, Leo, you have to remember that. I don't know how to get rid of her, I was hoping I could have helped you with that but now..." Blaise motioned at the hospital room in general. Leo knew that Blaise had been asking to leave the hospital basically since he'd woken up, but they wanted him to stay at least for a few more days for observation. Blaise did the fidgety thing with his hands again that he'd done when they'd been talking about the man who'd attacked him. "Maybe you need to confront her. Tell her she has to leave...it's the only thing I can think of without being able to look into it further."

Leo could hear the doubt in Blaise's voice, and he realized for the first time that Blaise didn't know any better than he did how to handle this. Leo had been thinking for some reason that when Blaise woke up he'd just have the answers for him. He felt lost now as the truth presented itself to him. Blaise had no better plan than anything Leo could have thought of himself.

"I don't know if I'm strong enough to tell her to leave if I go out there..." Leo spoke quietly, looking up at the ceiling for a moment like it may offer some fresh advice to him.

"You can't avoid going home forever, and she's obviously not going to leave you alone if something isn't done..." Blaise sounded as lost as Leo was feeling, and there was an apology in his tone. Leo just shook his head, and looked back at the other.

"I think I'm the only one that can figure it out. You're right that I have to confront her, but I need it to be on my terms. I have to find a way to be

140

prepared for it." Blaise nodded, though he seemed to hesitate before speaking again.

"I know you're not religious, but maybe you should ask Mackenzie if there's something that may help. It can't hurt to have someone else know what's going on at least, and I can't imagine something like that could make things worse."

"Blaise, you know I have no faith in all of that. It won't do me any good, and the last time I confided in someone you ended up in here. I can't even be sure this is a spiritual thing to begin with, maybe it really is just a mental problem." Blaise shrugged and seemed to drop the subject, but Leo could tell he had more to say. Leo sighed as he pushed a hand back through his hair. "I'll ask him. I'll say I'm having a crisis of faith or something. It will get him all a twitter to think he may be able to save my soul." Blaise made an amused noise, and Leo could tell he relaxed a little.

"I've never seen Mackenzie be the type to run around saving souls. He does have a lot of faith in religion though..." Blaise trailed off as a frown crossed his face, and Leo watched him with a bit of concern that something was wrong. "You know what a prophet is, Leo?"

"I know that much, Blaise. I was raised Catholic even though you wouldn't guess it. Prophets spread the word of God, and they usually can see visions of the future. Why?" Another round of the hand fidgeting where Blaise didn't seem to know what to do with them or where to set them.

"The guy kept calling me that. I thought...maybe that's the closest I'll come to explaining what I am..." Leo lifted an eyebrow at the suggestion.

"If that's the case, Blaise, then I don't know what God is trying to tell us through you."

"You don't know it all..." Blaise trailed off, and Leo sat watching him. His friend was staring at the wall with an expression that made the pit of Leo's stomach drop a little.

"How much worse?"

"I don't know for sure, but I'm thinking pretty bad..."

"I'll talk to Mackenzie." Leo looked down at his hands, working at a hangnail on his thumb. He couldn't imagine it would change anything, but the way Blaise was acting made him worry and feel like he needed to give every option a chance. "She was telling me to shoot you."

"Huh..." Blaise said it like he wasn't surprised by the confession, which almost bothered Leo more than anything else. "I don't think she's the only one that wants me out of the way." Leo made a quiet noise of agreement.

Leo was left feeling on edge and nervous after the incident at the hospital with Blaise. Even the relief of Blaise being released after the fourth day of him being awake didn't ease the tension Leo seemed to carry around on his shoulders. He still heard Marie from time to time, and despite another conversation to try and make a plan things had still boiled down the same. Blaise and him could only see a confrontation as a clear way of dealing with it. Blaise had encouraged him again to talk to Mackenzie, and he had tried to a few times but always stopped himself. He felt ridiculous asking the other if he had anything to help rid himself of the spirit of his dead wife.

Blaise has also asked Leo not to go out to the house on his own, even when he decided that it was time for the confrontation with Marie. Still, Leo couldn't stomach the thought of putting someone else in her path. He was sitting at his desk now, most of the station empty this late at night other than the few officers that worked the third shift. He looked up when he heard the knock on his door and saw Mackenzie standing there.

"Hey, I figured you'd be here." Mackenzie leaned against the doorframe, not just inviting himself in like he usually did. Leo motioned that he could come inside, a little confused and caught off guard by the hesitation. Leo knew he should have expected it though, things had been strained between the two of them for a while and it had only been made worse by his omission about his conversation with Gabriel.

"Trying to get some things done. What are you in so late for?" Mackenzie sat down across from him, leaning back in the chair and for a second things were almost normal. Almost was the operative in that thought by far, and it was made even clearer by Mackenzie taking a few moments to think before he spoke.

"It's been a rough few weeks, I thought you might want to talk. You've been here night and day since Blaise got attacked, but he finally got to leave and is out with Anne now. It may be good for you to go home too, get some rest..." Leo paused in setting some reports on the completed pile that he'd formed on his desk. Mackenzie was there to tell him that the rest of them had noticed he still hadn't gone home. He'd been trying to find a way to bring up the subject himself, and now he had it set in front of him.

"I can't..." Mackenzie looked at him expectantly, waiting for a reason why. "Look, what do you use to rid yourself of bad memories or spirits or whatever you want to call them? Holy water or something like that?" Mackenzie gave him a confused look as he leaned back in his chair, seeming to try and gauge if Leo was being serious or not.

"Are we having a crisis of faith all of the sudden, Leo?" Mackenzie made it sound light hearted, but Leo could hear that if he said yes that Mackenzie would take him seriously.

You're such a coward, dragging him into this. Her voice was in the back of his mind, and it seemed to derail his thoughts. Leo pushed himself up from his desk to pace the office a couple of times while Mackenzie watched him. *Really, you've always been a coward.*

"Leo, whatever it is you can talk to me." Mackenzie prompted him again, watching Leo as he made his path back from the right side of his office to the left.

"I just need to know..." *I should have left you for him back then. He was always the better man, not to mention a better fuck.* Leo stopped in his tracks, and Mackenzie shifted uncomfortably in his chair.

"What do you need to know, Leo?" Leo looked at him, and Mackenzie could tell that something had changed in the last few seconds. Leo seemed

142

almost angry at him, and Mackenzie stood by instinct to be ready to meet that anger.

"Did you sleep with my wife?" Leo watched Mackenzie ; saw the surprise hit him like a blow. The desk was still between them, but Leo found himself calculating how easy it would be to get over it to the other man.

"What? Leo-"

"Did you...sleep with my wife?" The question seemed to baffle Mackenzie the second time as much as it had the first, and Leo felt doubt work its way into him. He would have answered already if it wasn't true, but part of him knew that even if Mackenzie had denied it immediately he would have thought he was protesting too quickly to be telling the truth.

"Leo, what the hell is going on? Does this have to do with that dream you had of Marie a few months ago?"

"Did you sleep with my wife!" Leo only realized he'd yelled the question when he noticed one of the third shift officers that was sitting out at the front desk look back towards his office. Mackenzie had froze where he was at; staring at Leo like he'd finally lost it.

"Never, Leo. She was yours from the first, and I always knew that. I never slept with Marie. Can we calm down a little now?" Leo felt the anger deflate out of him to be replaced with guilt and regret, and he heard her laugh at him in the back corner of his mind. He realized his hand was resting on his opened holster, and he dropped it away in shock. He knew Mackenzie had noticed it too, but his long time friend didn't acknowledge it as they stood in silence. Leo couldn't do this, he couldn't risk bringing someone else into this and having her manipulate him into hurting them. He had to face her on his own, and he knew that now even more than before.

"Yeah...I'm sorry...look, I think you're right. I need to go home, get some things done and get some rest." Leo grabbed his jacket from the back of his chair, and turned to face Mackenzie again. The other seemed uncertain if he was going to drop it, and Leo stepped around the desk to leave before Mackenzie had a chance to ask what was going on. Mackenzie still stopped him though, stepping in front of him to keep Leo from getting out the door.

"Leo, we can talk if you need to. Whatever is going on, whatever made you think-"

"I need to sort some things out on my own first, Mac. I'll call in the morning, we can grab breakfast or something and talk then. Right now I just need some time to deal with things." Leo thought Mackenzie was going to argue as he continued to stand in Leo's way.

"First thing in the morning?" Mackenzie didn't really want to let it wait til morning, but it was clear that Leo wasn't in the right frame of mind. He almost told Leo to just crash on his couch until he remembered Gabriel was already camped there.

"First thing." Leo gave a short nod, and Mackenzie hesitated for a moment more.

"You're first question, about the religion stuff. Holy water can work, there are prayers and rituals too. You have to have faith in them for them to really do much though." Leo stared at him like he didn't know what Mackenzie was talking about, but then understanding registered in his eyes.

"That's what I thought," he said, and Mackenzie moved out of his way so Leo could reach the door.

"Leo…" Mackenzie stopped him as he was stepping out into the bullpen area, and Leo looked back at him for a second. "We're good, right? You know I'm telling the truth, I never even tried for Marie."

"I know, we're good." Leo leaned to give Mackenzie's shoulder a rough pat before he turned and left quickly through the front. Mackenzie watched him going, not able to fight the feeling that he needed to do more but at a loss as to what. There was something else happening beneath the surface, but whatever it was Leo wasn't sharing. Mackenzie knew he wouldn't sleep that night, so instead he went to his own desk and started keying in the reports in his own 'To Do' file. He'd work the few hours that were left of the night, and then if Leo didn't contact him early enough for his liking he'd call him instead. He noticed he had a file with Blaise's name sitting on his desk that Leo had already signed off on. All their leads had gone cold on them, and now it seemed like that would continue to be the trend. He sighed and dug through the file to pull out the description that Blaise had managed to give to Leo the other morning, entering it into the database to see if any hits would come back to them.

Leo was sitting in his car outside the house, staring at the front door as he tried to think of all the reasons he shouldn't just turn around and go back. There seemed to be a lot more reasons to go though than there were to stay, but in the end he couldn't take it anymore. He couldn't take hearing her in the back of his mind, having her drive him mad while holding his life hostage. He could tell that she knew he was there. He had seen her watching from one of the windows when he pulled up, and he could feel her hold trying to slip around him.

He was here. He needed to do this now so he could clear his head of her. She was ruining everything, including his ability to focus on finding out who had attacked Blaise. She was trying to turn him against his friends, and had nearly managed it with Mackenzie back at the station. He could remember the rage that had filled him at the thought of his best friend betraying him with his wife. It scared him that he may have hurt Mackenzie if he hadn't gotten an answer he liked, or one that he'd found convincing enough.

Leo took a deep breath to steady himself, and finally stepped out into the cold to head up to the porch of his house. He watched for any movement inside as he approached, and he felt a small rush of longing hit him as he made his way up the stairs. This place had always been home to him, but now it felt threatening as he unlocked the door and stepped into the dark living room. He reached to the left and hit the light switch there, and the space lit up around him. He stayed close to the open door, ready to turn and leave as he scanned for her. He found that he was alone in the living room and he hoped that it was a sign he had the upper hand somehow.

He stepped further into the house, but didn't close the door behind him. He didn't want to leave himself feeling trapped there, and having the feel of the cold air rushing in at his back comforted him. His hand reached for his gun a second time that night, though it was with purpose now. He didn't think it would do him much good in this situation, but it was the same as the open door to him. He didn't know anymore what it was he was dealing with, but he knew for sure that it wasn't his Marie. He knew he needed to remember that, it was the most important thing. He stopped at the main junction of the house, one way leading to the kitchen while the stairs lead to the bedrooms and his office.

"I love it when you wear your uniform home, sugar." He heard her voice behind him, and turned to face her quickly. The front door was shut now, and either way she was between it and him. He wasn't sure if being away from her for so long had opened his eyes to it or not, but Leo realized with a wave of guilt that this thing wasn't anything like his Marie. She didn't talk like her, nothing about her body language spoke of his wife. All that he'd seen is that she looked like Marie, but now it wasn't enough to fool him. "You've been gone so long I thought you had forgotten about me. You should have come home."

As she spoke she moved to put her arms around him, and he felt that mental tug she had on him try to dull his sense of purpose. For a moment he just stood there as she pulled him into her embrace, but she didn't even feel right held close, not fitting to him as Marie use to. He was torn between that influence that tried to wash everything from his brain except the content feeling of having her close, and the utter wrongness of her. He stepped back then, and she gave him a look of anger before she smoothed it over with sad eyes. He realized she'd been talking the whole time, and he focused on hearing her words.

"If he had died, it would have just served him right. You should have killed him for me a long time ago for letting me slip away from you." The words helped push back the illusion that she'd tried to cloud him in. She was talking about Blaise, and hearing her wishing he had died confirmed for him that this wasn't his wife and that he should have realized that a long time ago. Marie had adored Blaise and had become friends with him quickly when he moved to their town. Even after she'd died she wouldn't have wished him ill, and he should have known that before.

"You're not Marie. I know that now."

"What are you talking about, sugar?" She stepped towards him, lifting a hand to press against his cheek and he knocked it away as he moved back from her.

"She never called me sugar. She never called anyone that. I don't know who or what you are, but you're not my wife. She's gone, and that kills me but I can't change it. You need to leave." She stared at him with sad concern for a few seconds, but when he didn't seem to back down the look darkened. She still had Marie's face, but the familiarity of it was washed away by the personality behind it.

"It's too late to start fighting now, sugar. You should know that, I've got myself too wrapped up in you. You are right about one thing though, this whole thing is going to kill you." Leo pulled back as she suddenly lunged at him, his hand going for his holster but as soon as the gun was freed from it she knocked it aside as she swung at him. He threw his own blow, but she ducked low and wrapped herself around his center and took them both down to the floor. He fought and twisted to get her off of him, but as soon as he was free and tried to get up she jumped onto his back. She clung there as he tried to break her hold, but his movements were becoming sluggish. He felt like he was drugged, like everything was draining out of him and leaving his mind in a haze.

He heard her laugh as he caught sight of their reflection in the window and it seemed like she was sinking into him. A moment of panic broke through the haze, and Leo tried to tear himself free again as she seemed to claw her way into him. His arms only managed to get tangled in her though as she disappeared further inside him. Pain cut through it all like a knife, shooting up his nerve endings and into his brain as he seemed to lose all ability to move. It blinded him as he fell to the floor, and then all he knew was a silence unlike any he'd ever experienced.

"Hey Stranger." Leo had been trying to make sense of some chicken scratches one of his officers had put down on a report when he heard the knock at his office door. He looked up, a grin coming to his lips as he saw Marie there.

"Hello ma'am. Can I help you with something?" It was a litte game they played when Marie visited him at the station, and it had yet to grow tired between the two of them. It hadn't escaped him that Mackenzie rolled his eyes when he was around for the charade though.

"Yes, I seem to be missing a husband. He was supposed to be home for dinner, but then he called to say he had to stay late at work." Marie stepped into the office, a large bag on one arm as she nudged the door closed. Leo caught the scent of pot roast, and his smile grew a little more.

"Well, you're husband must be some sort of fool not to come home to you, ma'am." Leo got up from his desk, taking the bag of food from his wife with one hand while wrapping the other arm around her waist. She pressed up against him as they kissed. "Sorry I made you drop dinner off. Things are a bit hectic today."

"I know, Leo. I wanted to bring you something to eat though or you'd waste away. I figure I can stay and eat with you." Marie smiled up at him, patting his cheek before pulling away to reclaim the bag. Leo sat back down as his wife pulled out the containers of food, organized and neatly divided portions for each of them. He wouldn't have guessed in high school that Marie would be so domesticated after they married, but she'd fallen into the roll without him expecting it of her. He'd have been happy even if she hadn't insisted on cooking so much.

146

They ate together, going over their days and Leo picked up that Marie was waiting to say something. He knew not to push when she got in a mood like this though, and he just sat it out until she decided she was ready. She gathered the dishes back up in silence, and Leo started to worry that something was wrong for the first time.

"You all right, sweetheart?" Marie looked up at him when he spoke, and a smile crept to her lips. She moved to slide into his lap, placing a kiss on Leo's cheek as she curled up into him.

"Well, I've been thinking about something."

"Mm-hmm?" Leo mumbled it against her temple, resting his lips there for a second. She shifted in his lap, straddling him a little and Leo found he was glad they'd closed the door. The feeling that something was wrong came back as she looked him in the eyes seriously and took a deep breath.

"I think we should try for a baby." Leo stared at her, saw the smile tug at her lips and he gave a quiet laugh.

"What? Here in my office?" Marie frowned at him, giving Leo a light smack on the arm though there was an amused look in her eyes. Leo fell into a more serious mode though as he tried to gauge his wife's mood. "You being serious?"

"I am. I know I've given you every excuse under the sun why we're not ready yet the last few years, and you've been so patient with me even though I know you really want one. I've been thinking about it though, and I realized the reason I was making excuses was that I was scared."

"And...now you're not?" Leo asked it tentatively, afraid that if he pushed she'd suddenly change her mind. It wasn't like Marie to say something if she didn't mean it, but the topic of kids had always seemed to make her nerves jump.

"No, I still am. I'm not sure if we're ready, I don't know if I'll be a good mother or not, but...I realized something. I realized that I don't need to be scared when I know I'll have my Lion at my side." Marie leaned in to give him a kiss, Leo letting the silly smile slide to his lips. "Besides, why wouldn't I want a little you running around?"

"Cause you know what a pain in the ass he'd be?" Marie laughed, but the clear memory cut out suddenly to the sound of sirens. Lights flashing outside a hospital as Leo felt panic tearing through him. He pushed his way through the doors, wanting and needing to find Marie standing there waiting for him. What he found was two gurney's in a hall though, nurses pushing them further away from him as he tried to catch up. Blaise looking shellshocked for a moment as he realized it was Marie that had just been rolled into his ER before he managed to pull it together and start giving orders.

"You make sure she's all right, Blaise? Do you hear me?!" Leo yelled it after his friend as Blaise started down the hall after the gurney holding Marie's broken body.

"I will, I promise," Blaise called it back, but Leo knew that it would be a promise broken. He knew that Marie was already lost.

"Don't worry sugar, the worst part hasn't even started yet." Her voice seemed to echo all around him, and Leo slowly became aware of the present again as the memories of that day faded away. Feeling returned slowly though it was a distant sort of sense of the world around him.. Even as he sat up he knew it wasn't him controlling the movement, and he watched from some side corner of his mind as the thing stretched and stood.

She could feel Leo fighting her for control as she stood, fighting to understand what had happened. She languished in the feeling of having a solid body, finding the mirror that hung down at the end of the hall near the kitchen. He had let himself go while he'd been away, a layer of scruffy stubble taking hold on his face. She'd take care of that first, they needed to look their best. They had a job to do in the morning, and she assured Leo in the back of their mind that he wasn't going to like it.

He couldn't tell much about his surroundings other than that they were in a large room. He was sitting alone in the quiet, and for a moment it seemed he was watching himself. The sound of a door caught his attention, and he looked up to watch the man who'd come into the room. The other man looked a bit run down, dark hair a mess with pieces hanging down over his deep set eyes. Gabriel watched him as he came to a stop by the table and set something down in front of him.

"He's decided it's yours to keep. You'll be the one to use it when the time comes."

Chapter 12 – Losing it -

Mackenzie had fallen asleep at his desk at some point, and the sound of someone coming in through the front entrance of the station woke him up. He looked at the time and saw that it was a few minutes before seven, and he ran a hand over his hair as he attempted to wake himself up completely. He was actually glad he'd stayed the night at the station, as they had started to get several calls about domestic disputes a little after Leo left. People in town seemed antsy about something that no one could put a finger on, and it had managed to lead to a lot of fights that needed sorting out. On top of that there'd been reports of animals stalking along people's properties, and a few pets had gone missing overnight. All of it added up to a stack of paperwork for them to all finish when they got time. It had calmed again about three in the morning, but the sound of a phone ringing somewhere down the hall made him feel a stab of worry it was starting once more.

He jumped slightly when his phone rang beside him, and he felt a moments relief when he saw that it was Leo. He had half expected the other not to call, forcing Mackenzie into tracking him down. He'd felt uneasy with the conversation from the night before, and he couldn't deny he felt a little guilty that he hadn't pushed Leo to talk to him the first few times he'd noticed his friend trying to bring something up. The conversation still didn't make sense to him, how Leo had asked about religious help before accusing him of sleeping with Marie.

"Hey Leo." He answered the phone, giving a short wave as he saw some more of the day shift come in through the doors up front. He heard more phones ringing down the hall, and knew that things were going to be hectic all day from the sounds of it. Not what he needed or wanted when he'd be trying to get Leo to fess up to what was going on. "I'm glad you called, I was about to call you."

"Hey, yeah…sorry about last night. Things were just…look, I was hoping you'd meet me out at Anne's. I'm on my way there now, I got a call from her but the line went dead and she's not answering when I try her back. It's probably nothing, but with all that's going on I'd feel better if the two of us headed out to check on her and Blaise. Afterwards, maybe we can grab breakfast and talk about things." Mackenzie frowned when he heard another phone start ringing but so far things appeared under control in the station. Leo still sounded off, maybe even more so than he had the night before and Mackenzie didn't want to put off talking for fear that his partner would clam up again.

"I'll head out. It was a little crazy here last night, but things are under control now so I can slip away. Do you want me to try and give her a call?" A long silence followed the question, and it was enough of a pause that Mackenzie was about to ask if Leo was still there or not when the other finally answered.

"No, just meet me out there. Like I said, I'm sure its nothing but I'd feel better if we just went out to see." Mackenzie tried to read the tone of Leo's voice, but he couldn't place a finger on it. It didn't really sound worried like he expected, and it came off as unusual for him. But, things weren't right between the two of them right then and he knew that could be a factor in Leo's tone and behavior towards him. He stood up to get his jacket off the back of his chair as he glanced around the station one more time.

"I'm on my way now. I'll see you out there." Mackenzie was greeted with the sound of Leo hanging up without any other acknowledgement, and he sighed. Apparently things were worse than he'd thought, and he hoped that Leo had believed him the night before when he said he'd never touched Marie. It was the truth, but he didn't know how to convince Leo of that especially since one of the people involved couldn't exactly confirm or deny his story anymore. Mackenzie couldn't shake the feeling that there was something more going on though and he hated to ignore it but he wouldn't know for sure what it may be until he saw Leo. Going out to Anne's was the fastest way to do that right at the moment, so he'd follow through.

He heard a few sirens as he headed out of town, and it confirmed his suspicions that his town was continuing its turmoil from the night before. He had faith in their team though, and he was technically checking up on his own possible problem at the moment so he avoided the guilt. He toyed with his phone for a second as he debated about calling Anne even though Leo hadn't asked him to. It couldn't hurt if he tried, and maybe he'd manage to get a hold of her and find out what the problem was if there even was one. At the same time though, he knew that at this point Leo should be getting close if not already out at his sister's. Mackenzie was approaching Leo's own drive when he finally hit the contacts list on his phone, Anne's number resting up at the top of the alphabetical list.

The morning was still dark, and clouds were making it gloomy headlight weather for driving. The car that was suddenly coming out of Leo's drive and straight towards Mackenzie's car hadn't had their headlights on until the last moment, and when they flipped on it was the only reason Mackenzie even noticed the vehicle. He had just enough time to drop the phone and grip the wheel to try and manuever out of the way before the SUV broadsided him. He slid at first, but then he lost all bearings as he was pushed off the road and started to flip down the slope of the shoulder and into the trees.

When Mackenzie regained consciousness he was hanging upside down from his seatbelt, his airbag had deployed at some point and white dust was settling around him. Someone was approaching the car, their shoes visible as they walked towards him and Mackenzie followed their progress. He already knew it was Leo before the other crouched down to look in at him through the broken driver's side window, and Mackenzie had the idle thought that his head had probably broken it.

"Leo…" The pain from the wreck was starting to set in on him, but he found that nothing hurt too horribly. Considering the world had flipped on him, it was surprising that he may have escaped serious injury. Leo had a few cuts and bruises, but nothing that seemed life threatening in the least.

"No sugar, not Leo. You should have listened to him, you know. Michael was trying really hard to approach this whole situation from a different angle. For some reason he hoped you would make this easier for us, but I can't complain. I get to play now, and not just toy around with your friend, really have some fun. I don't know why he bothered, when we get what we want it will be over for you all anyway. It's almost a shame." Mackenzie stared at Leo in confusion, but the tone and pace of his friend's voice was wrong. Everything was wrong, and that small feeling he'd pushed aside before was now a screaming voice trying to warn him. *Not Leo. That's not Leo!*

Mackenzie flinched when the other reached in to pat him on the cheek hard enough that his head jolted with pain and a spike of nausea went through him. Leo stood then, leaving Mackenzie hanging upside down as he started to walk away and Mackenzie was about to call out to him when something stopped the words from escaping his mouth. His head had cleared enough to understand the warnings that were going through his body, and he waited as Leo's feet disappeared from view. When he knew that he was alone, and that whatever was masquerading as Leo had gone for good he started to try and get himself loose. He needed to get out of the car and get to Anne's, which was unfortunately the same direction the fake Leo had gone. He needed to warn the others that there was someone else walking around in Leo's skin.

Gabriel was supposed to have gone into work that morning, but instead he was sitting in Mackenzie's apartment in the dark. He had woken up sometime in the early hours of morning when everything was still and quiet, and he'd been left feeling sick to his stomach by the knowledge that something wasn't right. Everything had seemed off, even the air tasted wrong to him. He had sat there over the hours until sunlight started to turn the darkness into a grey haze, going over his thoughts and the dreams that had made his nights sleep a fitful one. He kept getting close to something that sent every fiber of him on alert, but the dream or memory always pulled back when he tried to focus on it. None of the things he could remember had made clear sense to him, and he knew that missing piece was the answer why.

He clung to the last dream he could remember having before waking up, one that had given him a sense of falling and had brought back the searing pain in his chest where the scar ran. He forced himself up in frustration as whatever clue he was reaching for slid away again, and he went into the bathroom to splash some water on his face. When he looked up his eyes were drawn to the scar and the cross that hung around his neck just above it. They were the only things he'd had with him, the only parts that tied him to who he use to be. He studied the cross with a small glimmer of hope that it would trigger something, but other than a stirring sense of sadness he couldn't find any memories clinging to it.

When he looked up again he met his own gaze in the mirror, and suddenly could see his brother looking back at him with those same eyes. The last time he had seen Michael face to face he had the same look Gabriel had now. Anger, frustration, sadness and a lack of understanding all turning in the similar bright blue eyes. It was that which triggered it, that shared look so alike between the two of them that made Gabriel remember. With it came an urgency that told him what he was up against, and what he needed to fight it.

He got dressed on auto pilot, making sure to slip out the backway of the apartment to avoid being seen and questioned by Lisa. He could have brushed it off by saying he was getting some medicine, but he didn't want to waste the time. He could hear sirens in the distance, and at one moment there was a sudden burst of loud pops that sounded like gunfire from the other side of town as he walked quickly down the back streets.

It was quiet when he finally reached the church, but every now and then some sound of trouble would drift over from a different part of the town. It was bitter cold, and the clouds that were looking down at the town didn't seem be planning on leaving during the day. He stepped inside the church, looking around to make sure he was on his own before he moved forward towards the door that lead to the private chambers that sat at the rear of the building.

Gabriel heard the slightest hint of sound behind him, and turned to face whoever had followed him. Michael was sitting in the pew that Gabriel had just passed even though he hadn't been there a moment before. He didn't look at Gabriel, but just shifted over in the pew to make room for his brother. Gabriel was hesitant to sit, but right then the invitation didn't appear to hide any malicious intent. He sat down beside his brother, and they both chose to look up towards the alter of the church rather than each other.

"You remember then?" Michael was the first to break the silence, and Gabriel felt a twinge of joy over that small victory against his brother.

"I do." Gabriel pulled his eyes away from the altar and looked at his brother beside him, though Michael didn't meet his gaze. "Though, I still don't understand why. I never would have imagined that you would work with them, least of all Shax."

"I only brought them in once you refused-"

"Refused what? To betray our family all for some sentimental bullshit you decided to act on without consulting the rest of us? To go against my own intuition just to please you?" The anger came out in a burst from

152

Gabriel, and Michael finally turned to look at him with his own fury breaking out.

"You're the one that betrayed me, Gabriel. You betrayed us. What I was asking was only for your help in bringing our family back together, and you turned your back on me. You turned your back on us, and refused to even consider-"

"What you wanted wasn't reasonable, Michael. It would have destroyed all of this if I had agreed, and I'm not willing to do that. I didn't betrayed anyone Michael." The anger seemed to seep out of them as quickly as it appeared, leaving the air between them charged. Silence fell between the brother's, and Gabriel looked up towards the alter and studied it as he mulled over his thoughts. "You could stop this all right now."

"I still stand by what I believed before, Gabriel. He's our brother too, and I feel that we did wrong by him. Besides, it's too late to call Shax and Lilith off now unless you hand it over. They won't stop until you do."

"You brought Lilith into this too?" Gabriel looked at Michael sharply with disbelief, and shook his head in disgust when his brother let his silence answer the question. "You know even if I did hand it over, those two won't stop if you've let them loose."

"I can control them, you forget who I am."

"How could I forget that?" Gabriel gave a sharp, humorless laugh. "I won't give you the key, Michael. It wouldn't do you any good even if I did, it will only work for me. You keep clinging to this notion of getting our brother back so we can be a family again that you don't see it, do you?" Gabriel's voice dropped down to a quieter tone as he looked down at the floor, waiting to hear Michael's answer.

"I thought out of all of them that you would have understood. If you won't hand it over then I can't be responsible for what happens here. It will all burn, Gabriel, because of you." There was the sound of air igniting from above, and Gabriel looked as the roof of the church went up in flames. "It's already too late for the sheriff, but you could have saved the rest of them from suffering at their hands."

Gabriel turned to look at Michael, but his brother was already gone. Smoke was starting to fill the church in a fast, greedy curl from the flames above. He heard the doors from back by the altar open, and saw the priest come out in a fearful rush.

"We can't be a family now that you've cast me out, Michael." Gabriel spoke quietly to himself before he stood. He called for the priest, moving to help the man out of the church before turning back into the building as the priest called after him. He needed to get some things if he could before they were destroyed or beyond reach, and then he needed to get to the others. If Michael had really set Lilith and Shax loose on his friends, the two of them would tear them to ruins in their futile search for the key.

Chapter 13 – Where has Leo gone -

Anne was humming quietly in the kitchen while pulling down the box of pancake mix from the small pantry set against the back wall of the space. She glanced out at Blaise who was asleep on the couch still. It was early and she didn't want to wake him up if she could avoid it. He'd fallen asleep there the night before while listening to some music as she'd read, and she had wanted to let him get as much rest as possible. Blaise was complaining about how he could do things on his own often now that he was out of the hospital, but she noticed that he still wore out quickly. Every now and then he seemed to be in pain as well, though she only caught it when he thought she wasn't looking. The headphones were still in his ears, but without knowing if music was still playing through them she was trying to be quiet in making breakfast.

Anne watched the rise of fall of his chest for a few moments before stepping back into the kitchen to inspect the mix box to see what she needed. She opened her fridge door to see if she had eggs and milk, and cursed quietly when she remembered that she'd run out of eggs the day before. Anne wasn't someone who was bursting with ideas for what to make, and she quickly settled on a bowl of cereal instead. She stepped out of the kitchen a few moments later, and nearly dropped the bowl onto the carpet. Leo was sitting in one of the chairs having pulled it up beside the couch near Blaise.

"You startled me, I didn't hear you come in..." She was talking quietly, and restrained the urge to say a few curses at Leo as well for scaring her. He didn't normally just let himself in, and though she'd always made sure he knew where the spare key was he'd never used it before. She took a few steps forward intending on sitting in the empty chair beside him, but stopped when she noticed that Leo had his gun out hanging in his hands between his knees. "Leo, what are you doing?" Leo looked up at her, and the sense that something was wrong hit her like a train when he gave her a small smile.

"I need you to do something for me, sis. I'm sure I've asked before, but...what did Gabriel have with him when you found him?" Anne shifted a little uneasily, eyeing the gun that spoke against her instinct that Leo would never hurt Blaise or her. Leo didn't casually carry it around outside the holster, and it made her glance towards the front door. Leo would only have himself readily armed if he thought there was some danger coming, and she hoped he'd thought to lock the door behind him.

"I've told you that the only thing he had was the cross around his neck. I didn't see anything else when I found him, and you saw yourself that he didn't have anything but that when I got him to the house. What's going on Leo?" She motioned towards the gun, taking a few steps to sit down but Leo shook his head at her when she did and he switched the safety off the gun. "Leo...?"

"I'm going to need you to take me out to where you found him, sugar." Leo didn't use pet names, and now that she was thinking about it she couldn't remember a time he'd called her 'sis'. Anne frowned, glancing at Blaise who was still asleep. The music must still be playing or he must have been more

154

tired than she thought, but a part of her felt better that he hadn't woken up. Leo was making her nervous, and though she was sure the danger would be coming through one of the doors he seemed more focused on Blaise himself.

"I don't know if I could find it again after all this time, Leo. When the dogs went off course I was paying more attention to getting them straightened out than where exactly they pulled off at."

"Then we'll take the dogs and they can lead us back there. I'm not in the mood for arguments." As Leo spoke he lifted his hand so the gun pointed momentarily at Blaise. It was a casual gesture, but it spoke against everything Anne knew about her brother. He never aimed his gun at someone on accident or without meaning, and it was enough to get a point across to her. There was no argument in his tone either like she'd be use to him having if he felt she was lying or holding out on him.

"Leo, what the hell are you doing?" She hissed the words at him, fighting against the anger and fear that had shot up her spine. She didn't know what had happened, but something must have. Leo was acting wrong, even the posture he was sitting in was wrong for her brother and it made her feel suddenly like she was in the room with a stranger.

"Go get the dogs ready. I need to have a few words with your boyfriend." The gun made its casual lift again but stayed aimed at Blaise this time instead of dropping back down. Leo had ignored her question, and was making it clear that her only choice was to listen right then. She almost opened her mouth to argue, but a slight shake of Leo's head made her close her mouth once more. "Go on."

"I don't know what's going on, Leo, but if you hurt him…"

"If you don't go then I might just do that." Leo said it sharply, and the words seemed to cut into her and assure her that she was right. Something was wrong, and whether it was something that had happened to make Leo upset or if Leo had just lost it in general, this wasn't the man she was used to dealing with.

They had argued before dozens of times to the point of them both being furious with each other, but she had never heard this dangerously calm tone from Leo before. It silenced her in a way that was against her nature, and she backed towards the door that lead to the dog run. She paused there for a second, afraid to leave Blaise alone with this stranger that looked like her brother. She was more afraid at the moment of what Leo would do if she didn't listen however, and in the end she stepped outside with a quiet prayer to no one in general for help.

Leo shifted so that he was sitting on the edge of the couch besides Blaise, and he tugged sharply on the cord of the headphones to pull them free of his ears. The motion woke Blaise up, and he opened his eyes to see Leo sitting next to him in silence.

"Leo, what's going on?" Blaise shifted to try and sit up, but the motion was abruptly put to an end when Leo shoved him back down against the couch cushions. Leo kept his hand pressed against Blaise's chest to keep him from moving to sit again, and it made the sore areas that were still healing ache. "I'm pretty sure it's worse for you to push me back down than it would be if I just sat up, Leo." He was getting a little annoyed with the doting that he'd put up with since he'd ended up in the hospital, and tired of being treated like he couldn't even cut his own food up on his own.

"Did you really think he could stand up to me? Maybe if he'd done it at the beginning he would have had a chance, but he was too eager for me to be his dear little wife back from the dead." Blaise tensed when he heard Leo start to talk, the frustration at what he originally thought was Leo treating him like an invalid changing to worry. There was an anger in Leo's voice, an undercurrent of distaste that seemed to spike his words as he looked down at Blaise. "Really though, I owe you my thanks for convincing him he needed to come back out to me. It gave me the chance I needed to gain control. He was much more difficult than that new father at the hospital."

Leo's words made something click into place for Blaise, and he realized that he'd failed again. This wasn't Leo in front of him anymore, but the imposter Marie that he'd seen devouring his friend. Blaise felt something fall apart inside him as he tried desperately to think of a plan to fix this, but deep inside he suspected that Leo was lost. That thing had swallowed him up and taken Leo's place, and it was because Blaise had told Leo to confront it face to face. He focused his words on the comment about the hospital instead of leading them down the path of his guilt. He needed to not let his failure to act on the fear that Leo would go and do something on his own direct things.

"That was you that did that to Alex? That's why he said it wasn't him who killed Taylor." Blaise talked to buy himself time to think, to try and find some answers around himself. He glanced around what he could see of the house to try and pinpoint where Anne was, but couldn't find her.

"Smart boy though you're also the one with the mental cheat sheet. That was for fun though, I was bored waiting around to get the cue to act and I needed something to pass the time. Plus, it gave me a chance to take a stab at you. I don't like you, sugar, and I really think this is a waste of time. But, I have a job to do and you're going to help me get it done." Leo's fingers drummed against Blaise's chest as he spoke, reminding Blaise not to try anything.

"And what makes you think I'll help you?"

"Because, you have an idea of the things I'll do to you and to your little dog bitch if you don't. Now, Gabriel brought something with him when he landed his pretty little ass here and I need to find it. You're going to help me do that." Leo's tone switch from spiteful and dangerous to sweet and innocent after the threat. He gave Blaise a smile that was just a touch too crazed. Blaise wondered if he could be bluffing, if Anne had gone out to get something and wasn't even there at the moment.

"I already told your friend that I don't know what you're talking about-" Leo's fingers stopped drumming abruptly, and a look of disgust crossed his face.

"Shax is hardly a friend," the words were spat out at Blaise, but the next moment the tone had switched back to being sweet again, "he's more of a business partner. And, I know you don't know where it is. You're little lady though, now she can at least lead me to it and you're the perfect motivaton for that. Now, unfortunately, although I can threaten it, I can't kill you. Shax has decided you're useful, and though I don't agree I'm not quite stupid enough to blatantly go against that either. He has a temper, as you might have seen." Leo gave him a wide smile that put a twist in Blaise's stomach. He also had a moments hope though in knowing that something was holding the monster inside Leo back. "But, your Anne doesn't know that I have that little roadblock in front of me and we're not going to tell her. Besides, there's no rule set about not hurting you…badly if I wanted to." Leo shifted off the couch, giving Blaise some space at last though he didn't get a chance to act on the freedom as he shortly found Leo's handgun pressed against his chest.

"What if she can't lead you to whatever it is you're looking for? It may not even be out there. Neither of you seem to have any idea where it is."

"Then, she won't be of any use to us at that point and there won't be any reason for me to tolerate her anymore. I have a very low tolerance level for useless women."

Anne had debated getting into her truck and driving to get help, but the fear of what may happen if she just left kept her from doing so. She had never been afraid of her brother, and feeling that anxious undercurrent was alien and unnatural to her. She kept trying to tell herself that she was overreacting, and that it was Leo she was thinking about. But, Leo wasn't acting like himself and she couldn't shake that feeling that she wasn't dealing with her older, slightly hotheaded brother.

She was worried that something had caused Leo to lose touch with things, and she couldn't deny that he'd been acting off since winter started. He'd still been her brother though, still been himself just acting like he did when something was worrying him or wearing on his mind. He had been acting a bit like he had when Marie died actually. But, now the person inside the house no longer seemed like Leo. The measure of his words and the set of his posture was wrong, and she didn't know how to deal with the situation other than do as he asked. Inside the house were the two most important men in her life, and she was terrified something might happen that would make her choose between them.

Anne worked on getting the dogs harnessed, and they seemed to be picking up on her emotions. They were quiet and anxious where they would normally be barking in excitement about the chance to go for a run. Yakone whined at her when she got her hooked up to the lead, and she scratched the dog's ears in assurance. She turned back towards the house after making sure the brake was in place, dug down deep into the snow. She found she didn't want to go back inside, but she hadn't heard anything happen in the house while she worked. She wasn't sure if this comforted her or scared her more.

As she stepped towards the door a sound caught her attention towards the front of the house, and she backstepped to see what it was. Someone was approaching the house cautiously, and when he got into a stream of light from the front windows she recognized Mackenzie. Anne felt a wave of relief at first, her instinct being that Mackenzie had always managed to talk Leo down from his anger and that he'd be able to fix this as well. When she processed that there was blood running down Mackenzie's face from a gash on the side of his forehead and the limp in his step, that relief melted away into concern. He had seen her by now, and was heading towards her while glancing around like he was watching for someone else to appear.

"Mac, what happened?" Anne took a hold on Mackenzie when they met, looking him over with concern and afraid that he might collapse. He seemed to be sturdy on his feet despite the injuries though, and he waved a hand of dismissal at her.

"Leo ran me off the road." He said it nonchalantly as though it wasn't important, and before she could respond he cut her off. "Something's wrong, Anne. He's not acting like himself."

"I know, did he hit his head in the accident? That may be why he's acting off?"" Anne cut in, taking his face between her hands to try and get a look at the gash, but at her words he froze and brushed her hands aside again. The move frustrated Anne, her mind now having a reason for Leo's odd behavior. It was a reason that could be handled, but the look on Mackenzie's face was serious and stiff.

"Where? Where is he?" Mackenzie's voice had dropped lower as though he was afraid Leo would hear them even from inside the house. Anne gave Mackenzie a look like he was being silly, though she found she dropped her voice too.

"He's inside with Blaise. He's still acting weird, he's worrying me a little. I didn't know what was going on, but if he bumped his head in the accident then he might have a concussion. We need to get you both to the hospi-" Anne had started to step away from Mackenzie to head back into the house, but the other grabbed a hold of her arm to pull her back to look at him.

"Anne, it wasn't an accident. He ran me off the road on purpose. Do you understand that? This isn't because he bumped his head." Anne tried to pull away from Mackenzie with a shake of her head, not wanting to listen to the other.

"Mac, you're confused. Leo wouldn't have caused the accident on purpose. You both just need-"

"Anne, listen to me." Mackenzie cringed when he realized he'd said the words louder than he'd meant, and his tone dropped down again almost immediately. "I know it makes no sense, but that's not Leo in there. We're not dealing with Leo, we need to get out of here."

"You're right that makes no sense. Besides, if something's wrong with him then we need to get him to the hospital. I'm not just going to leave Blaise and him in there." Mackenzie's jaw tightened in frustration, and he glanced up towards the window on the side of the house. He knew well enough that

158

arguing with Anne was like arguing with a brick wall, and right then the look on her face made it clear she had her mind made up. He shook his head a little, regretting it when a pang of pain shot through his brain.

"You stay out here. If anything happens I want you to go. You head to get help and bring it here, do you understand?" Anne's look darkened, and not for the first time in his life Mackenzie wished that everyone in the Briggs family wasn't born with the natural inclination to fight. "Anne, please just listen to me for once. Stay out here, and leave if it sounds like things go bad. Where in the house were they?" Mackenzie prayed silently that Anne would just do as he asked, and he let a sigh of relief go when she answered him.

"The living room. They were both in the living room, Blaise was asleep on the couch. Look, he wants me to take him to where I found Gabriel. I don't know what's going on, but I know my brother and he wouldn't go hurting people intentionally like you're suggesting."

"You know I know that, Anne. But, I really don't think normal Leo rules apply right now. Remember, go if things sound bad."

"I'm not just going to leave." Mackenzie was going to protest further, but by the look on Anne's face he knew it would turn into a long back and forth between them if he did. He didn't think they had time for that, and so he just ignored that she had talked back in the first place.

"Stay out here, listen for if anything goes south. I'll come out and let you know if I get him to calm down and get things under control. Anne, if things go bad though you know the best thing to do is go get help instead of rushing in there." Anne was about to say something more, but there was a sudden crash from inside the house that pulled their attentions away from the conversation. Mackenzie felt Anne's grip on his arm, and he put his hand over hers reassuringly when no further sounds came from inside.

"Get Blaise out of there." She said it quietly, and the fight was gone from her voice suddenly. He had a feeling she knew that what he'd been saying was true, that Leo wasn't himself right now and that meant they couldn't guess what he would do. Mackenzie nodded silently in response, nudging her towards the dogsled.

"He slashed the tires on the cars. You're going to have to take the sled if you need to go." For a moment when she opened her mouth Mackenzie thought she was going to argue again, but she closed it quickly as she glanced towards the front where her and Blaise's cars were sitting sunk down in the snow. Mackenzie made sure she was going to stay with the dogs and then headed back towards the front of the house, doing his best to ignore the throb in his head as he heard another crash from inside.

The confirmation that Anne's life was basically viewed as disposable to the thing controlling Leo was enough to push Blaise to risk a fight. He couldn't let them get out into the woods only to find that Anne couldn't lead them to the spot or that the thing they were looking for wasn't there at all. He couldn't let Anne be placed in the situation where she was defending herself against her own brother, even if it wasn't mentally him anymore. Blaise

159

pushed the gun aside to get its aim off of him, and he rolled himself off the couch while taking Leo with him. He'd been hoping to make Leo lose his hold on the gun, but the other managed to keep it in hand. Leo took a swing at him with the handle of the gun, managing a hit to his jaw but Blaise was already kicking at Leo. Blaise got him knocked aside, and scrambled to put some distance between them but Leo snagged him by the back of the shirt. He pulled Blaise back and used the momentum to throw him into the coffee table which broke under his weight.

Leo came at Blaise almost immediately with the gun, and Blaise had a moment to be concerned he'd overestimated the monster's desire to keep him alive. When Leo hit him in the chest he felt pain shoot through his nerves, the thing he'd thought was the gun turned out to be a tazer Leo had pulled from his belt. Blaise had never been hit by one before, and he wondered how he was still able to scream as it knocked the breath out of him. It felt like it went on forever as his body jerked under the shock, but then both the pain and Leo seemed to disappear.

Blaise rolled over onto his side, sucking in deep breaths as he tried to steady himself.When he was able to focus he saw Mackenzie and Leo wrestling back and forth. The stun gun had been dropped just a few feet from him, and Blaise pushed his body to reach out and grab it. He had to abort the effort to curl and cover his head as Leo and Mackenzie almost tripped over him though.

"Leo stop, you have to stop," Mackenzie forced the words out as they struggled, Leo's gun between them. He hadn't realized the other had had it in his other hand when he'd lunged to get him off Blaise, and now they were fighting for control of it. Leo was winning at the moment as it angled towards him, and he hated that he couldn't gauge whether his friend would actually pull the trigger or not.

"Leo's not here to stop anything, altar boy." Mackenzie glanced away from the gun for a second to look at Leo, and he saw how dark his friend's eyes had gone and for a second he thought he understood. He didn't have long to absorb the thought that shot across his mind though as his back hit the wall and the gun sounded between them. Everything seemed to freeze in place as Mackenzie looked down at himself in confusion. He'd been hit on the left side just above his hip and blood was starting to soak into his shirt underneath his jacket. Blaise stood a foot or two away having gotten a hold of the stun gun and seemed to have had the intent of using it before the gun had gone off.

Mackenzie looked up again as he felt Leo tremble, the other's hold on the gun loosening a little as Leo's forehead came to rest on Mackenzie's shoulder. Mackenzie thought the man was laughing at first, but he slowly started to realize through the shock that Leo was crying. Mackenzie let the gun go and it hung loosely in Leo's hands between them as Mackenzie instinctively put an arm around his friend's shoulders to pat him on the back.

160

"I'm sorry Mac, I tried...I tried.." The words came out choked and strained like Leo was having to fight to talk, and Mackenzie had that moment of clarity again where he understood that Leo was doing just that.

"It's okay, Leo..." Mackenzie could feel it now, the throb of pain that was radiating out from his hip. It hurt, and he found that reassuring for some reason despite the fact he could only guess at what damage the bullet had done. Leo shook his head, still apologizing as he pulled away. Without his support Mackenzie's leg gave out and he slid quickly down the wall to the floor. Leo looked almost sick as he looked down at Mackenzie, and Mac tried to get him to understand again. "It's okay."

Blaise was beside him then, hands trying to push aside the fabric of his clothes to assess the damage. Leo watched them, and Mackenzie winced when he felt Blaise press his hands down onto the wound to try and slow the bleeding. Mackenzie glanced up at Leo again and saw the change happen in his friend's eyes suddenly.

"I think if we keep pressure on it-"

"No, Blaise!" Mackenzie had seen the smile slide onto Leo's face as the man raised the gun towards the back of Blaise's head. Mackenzie tried to push Blaise a little as the man turned at the same time, and Leo corrected the aim of the gun with the movement so that it went off right besides Blaise's ear. Blaise's hands went to his head as he fell back beside Mackenzie on the ground.

When Blaise lowered his hands again there was a trickle of blood starting to come from his left ear. Blaise couldn't hear Mackenzie as the man tried to get a response from him. Instead, he rocked slightly as he tried to push himself up but the room spun around him. Blaise tried to focus through the pain and the high pitched ringing that was suddenly overlying the world, muffled sounds coming through on the right side but just that ringing on the left. Below the sheer pain and nauseous vertigo he knew that his eardrum had ruptured, and he fought to steady himself with the knowledge that the room wasn't truly spinning. Something grabbed his hand and he tried to pull back as he saw Leo putting the handcuffs around his wrist. When Leo tried to grab his free hand he fought, and Leo boxed him along his left ear and the world almost went sheer white with the pain.

"You're coming with me," Leo said flatly to Blaise as he locked the man's wrist together with the handcuffs, ignoring Mackenzie as the other struggled to get up but couldn't as his leg buckled beneath him. Leo turned and aimed at Mac as a warning while he pulled Blaise up to his feet.

"Leo, don't do anything to him." Mackenzie tried to reach the rational being inside of Leo instead of this thing that was controlling him, but he could tell by the sneer he got in response that Leo was buried again. Mackenzie desperately wanted to do something to stop this, but he failed to have the upperhand and Blaise was between him and Leo now. Leo pulled Blaise towards the door, and the quick movement seemed to throw Blaise off balance. Leo smacked him aside the head again in frustration, and half dragged Blaise until the man could manage to get his feet underneath him. "Leo!"

"Leo's not the one calling the shots, sugar." Leo turned towards Mackenzie quickly as he snapped at him, and they stared at eachother for a few minutes before Mackenzie gave him a little smile.

"Don't be so sure. Leo's not one to take someone hurting his friends lying down." The thing laughed at him, turning to shove Blaise through the side door of the house and out into the dogrun. Mackenzie's confidence drained as he was left in the living room alone, hoping Anne had listened to him and left. He needed to try and find a way to drag his ass up and stay standing. They needed help, but Mackenzie wasn't sure he was up to the job any longer as he looked down at his blood soaked shirt.

Anne had felt her bones go cold when she heard the first shot inside the house putting an end to the shouting that had been filling her with dread. It didn't matter who the bullet may have hit, everyone inside that house was someone she couldn't stand to lose. She was standing on the rungs of the sled, torn between leaving to get the help they seemed to need or going inside the house to try and stop things on her own. When the second shot went off inside and she heard Mackenzie yell for Blaise everything had gone numb. She nearly fell when the sled suddenly took off beneath her, and she gripped onto the handles desperately. The dogs had started without her cue, and were quickly going at a dead run while dragging her behind them. She had to run a few paces to get her feet back onto the rungs, and she barely managed that. She yelled for the dogs to stop, but they were beyond listening to her and she felt a bit of helplessness set in. They weren't heading towards town, they were taking her out into the woods, running their old familiar path and leaving everything she cared about behind in the house. Her cheeks felt hot and slick and she realized that she was sobbing as she clung to the sled, not sure if she should abandon it and let them run without her or stick with them.

The dogs weren't barking or making a fuss like normal, instead running in focused silence through the trees. She never let go, unable to make herself willing to walk back and see what had happened. Unable to get to town without going back into the house if she abandoned the dogs to their run. She was stuck trying to pull herself together, carefully using the back of her sleeve to wipe away her tears so she could see clearly which direction they were heading. She tried to call to the dogs again, but they reacted as though they'd gone deaf to her commands. She was going to call once more in desperation when the dogs veered to the right, and she realized where they were going.

She had thought the dogs were just running what was familiar to them, but now they had gone off course like they had that first day of the season. They were heading towards where they'd found Gabriel, and Anne fell silent behind them. It seemed to take forever for them to pull into the clearing, and when the dogs came to a stop they all looked back at her.

"I don't even know what we're looking for," she said to them at a loss for what they wanted, and her voice seemed to break their focus on her as they started milling around or nesting down into the snow. She didn't know why they had come out here, and she felt that panicky need to do something productive itching at her. Her options were to walk back to the house on her own and by then who knew what she would find there; or she could try to find why the dogs had brought her here. It was where Leo had wanted her to bring him as well, and there had to be some correlation. The dogs wouldn't have headed out here for no reason, she had enough faith in them to know that. She climbed off the sled, her feet a bit unsteady at first. The snow was higher now than it was that first time, but she could clearly tell it was the same spot. There was no sign that anyone had been here, the only thing of note were some animal tracks in the snow. She crouched down to look at them for a second, and felt the lump of fear in her chest solidify a bit further. The prints weren't right, and she knew they didn't belong to any animal from the area though there was a familiarity to them.

They looked almost like the tracks her dogs left, but they were much larger and further apart than any of her dogs' strides. She stood up, backing away a few steps towards the sled as she felt that finding what was out here was less important than avoiding what could be out in the woods. She moved besides the sled, watching the trees around her as she got back on the rungs.

"Hike!" She tried to call out the word to the dogs, but her voice came out as a whisper as the fear of alerting something to their presence dug at her. The dogs stayed as they were, and Yakone looked back at her for a moment before giving a soft bark. They rarely didn't listen to her other than at times where one would have a stubborn streak, but there had only been once that all of them had disobeyed her at the same time. She tried again, but they stayed lying in the snow looking at her silently. She cursed as she got off the sled, staring at the trees as though they may come to life around her.

She knew they weren't that far from the house, and if she found the river that ran through her property it would lead her back through the trees. It would be the quickest route, but it would require her finding it and wading through the snow that had climbed in height over the winter months. Leaving the dogs wasn't a comfortable thought for her either, and despite their disobedience they still offered her some protection.

For a moment she thought she heard a shout from somewhere out in the trees, and she had almost called back before she stopped herself short. She didn't know who it was out there, and though a part of her still couldn't fathom being afraid of her brother her better senses kept her quiet. She stood near the dogs, a hand reaching down to pat the closest one on the head, fingers twisting in its fur out of nervousness. She felt the dog nuzzle her back, and got some relief from the comfort.

She tensed again as she heard something out in the woods, not shouting but an animal noise. It had almost come off as a bark, and she felt the agitation rise in her dogs. Anne decided that it was time to get the shotgun from the sled, keeping her back turned towards her dogs. She let them watch in one direction as she took the watch in the other, making sure the shotgun was loaded and taking the safety off.

Gabriel stared at Michael for a few minutes in silence, studying his brother with apprehension. He'd known it had to be something like this, but he hadn't expected Michael to go behind his back. Michael hadn't been happy when it became apparent Gabriel would be the one to hold the key, but in the end he'd agreed to it. Gabriel didn't understand why Michael was doing this now though. He would have understood at the beginning when he'd been unhappy with the decision, but it had been a long time ago now.

"I have forgiven him, Michael. But, just because I forgave him for what he did doesn't mean I feel he should be welcomed back." Gabriel stepped into the room a little further, closing the door behind him so the conversation could happen in private. He didn't think at the time that a simple closed door could be what doomed him.

Chapter 14 – Caught in the Fall -

Blaise stumbled as Leo pushed at him in an attempt to get him to walk faster through the trees. They had started by following the trail of the sled that was cut through the snow, and Blaise realized quickly that it was the trail Anne normally rode. She had taken the dogs out for a short run the day before, and since no snow had fallen since then there were two sets of tracks left behind. Leo hadn't given him a chance to grab a coat before pushing him out of the house, though out of necessity he'd given Blaise a few moments to pull on an old pair of work boots that had belonged to Anne's grandfather that still sat out in the dog run. The cold was biting through his shirt at him, and he did his best to keep his arms moving as they walked so the blood would stay circulating.

He'd regained some of his balance at this point, but his head was still aching and no sound reached him through his left ear. It wasn't helping their progress that the snow was deep, and even along the cut trail of the sled they sunk knee deep into it from time to time. Blaise hoped that Anne had kept going and that she wouldn't choose to turn back around or stop. He knew her too well to really believe that she would, but he didn't want to know what would happen when they came across her. He was at least grateful that the thing inside Leo had fallen silent, seeming to be focused on trudging through the snow.

The quick walking pace had helped block some of the cold by the time they reached the fork in the trail, and they had to come to a stop. Blaise hesitated, doing his best not to show his thoughts as Leo moved ahead of him to contemplate the two different directions. The way that continued to the left was the normal direction Anne took during her rides which meant that the right side of the fork was where she'd headed today. Blaise felt a stir of unease as he watched Leo look down both trails. He had a feeling Leo knew where Anne had gone from how she had described the day she'd found Gabriel to him. If she'd managed to find the clearing again and had stopped it meant they couldn't be far behind her now. Leo turned to look back at him, and Blaise did his best to look blank other than being cold and miserable.

"Let's go." Leo motioned towards the trail on the right, either figuring out their direction from Leo's own memories or due to some hint in the trail. When Blaise didn't move Leo sighed like he was dealing with a child, moving back towards him down the trail as he pulled the stun gun free from his belt again. Blaise didn't give him a chance to use it though as he threw himself at Leo, knocking them both off their feet as they rolled down the enbankment of the hill they'd been steadily heading up. They tumbled for what felt like a long time, but when they finally came to a stop Blaise did his best to disentangle himself from Leo to get on his feet. The fall had sent the world spinning again for him, and he only managed to stumble to his knees when he tried to stand. He felt the tazer hit him in the center of the back and he wasn't able to bite back the scream.

Leo pulled back when a voice suddenly called to them through the trees, and he stood up while keeping a hold on Blaise. The voice called a second time, and Blaise heard it himself then and it spurred another attempt to pull away from Leo. He couldn't lead Leo right to Anne, he'd been hoping to do the opposite but now he knew Leo would use him to bring her to them if he could. Leo kicked at him when he fought, and pulled Blaise up to his feet to drag him a short distance before slamming Blaise's back against a tree to pin him there. The thing gripped Blaise's jaw to make him meet Leo's eyes.

"Scream for me again, sugar," Leo said with a grin, and Blaise did as the stun gun met his temple and fireworks exploded behind his eyes.

Blaise was suddenly not there anymore, though he found himself still watching Leo. They were in a clearing and everything around him seemed to be on mute as Leo spoke words that Blaise couldn't hear. Sound exploded around them out of no where then, and blood began to pour from Leo's shoulder as Blaise felt himself falling straight down. He was plunged into water, and Blaise was staring at the lifeless face of the man who'd attacked him in his house. Blaise struggled to get to the surface that he could see above, snow covered ice frosting the sky that seemed to grow further and further away.

Blaise was brought back to the present by the sound of Leo's voice calling his name, and what felt like too many hands pushing at him to hold him up. His knees felt like jelly beneath him and he fought to push back the bile that rose in his throat as he tried to focus his eyes.

"Blaise, talk to me, please." There was panic in Leo's voice, and the words were strained and heavy. Leo came into focus for Blaise again as he tried to help the doctor lean back against the tree, hands on his shoulders to keep Blaise standing. Leo asked again if he was all right, and Blaise finally got some bearings on his surroundings.

"Leo?" Blaise was ready to push the man away if he got some sign that it wasn't his friend talking right then, but there was earnest concern on Leo's face. Blaise couldn't describe the relief he felt at this, because right then he knew that he'd probably just fall face first into the snow without Leo's support.

"God, I thought...I don't think I can keep this up for long." Leo's words were stumbling out of him, and he rested his forehead against Blaise's as though he couldn't hold it up without something to lean it against. "Are you all right? What was that?"

"Vision...I think..." Bile rose into Blaise's throat again, and he did his best to push it down once more. He took a few gulps of air, trying to get his body to stop feeling jittery and like it was going to implode on him. "Leo..."

"Don't. I know...I'm pretty much fucked, I can feel her tearing me up inside." Leo cut Blaise off, guessing correctly from Blaise's tone of voice. Blaise stood there, watching the exhaustion and determination on Leo's face as he struggled to stay in control, and he couldn't find any words that seemed sufficient.

"I'm sorry...I should have talked to you sooner or went out there with you that first day I got out of the hospital. You may have had a chance..."

"Don't." Leo said it again, but this time there was a strict sort of anger in his voice as he looked at Blaise. "Don't you dare blame yourself for me, jackass. I screwed myself over on this one." The words were harsh and pointed, and Leo gave him a little push for emphasis. A small tremor went through Leo, and Blaise tensed until he heard Leo's tone again still cutting through. "You still have a chance. I can't do this much longer though. I need you to find Anne, get her out of here."

Blaise didn't catch himself in time, and Leo caught the look that flickered across his face. Leo's own expression darkened, but it did so in a familiar way as Leo shoved him gently again against the tree.

"Don't you dare say that whatever this is gets my sister." Blaise shook his head to this, and it took a second for Leo to understand as he stared back at him.

"I don't care what you've seen Blaise, she can't lose us both. You have a chance to fight still, and whatever it is you think is going to happen you fight it." Leo spoke quickly, the words a bit mumbled together as he spoke them. Blaise shook his head, but Leo just gripped his shoulders tighter. "You fight it."

"I don't know if I can. Every time it's been the last thing I've seen." Leo shook his head sharply, refusing to hear Blaise out. "It always ends the same way, Leo, and it's getting clearer."

"I don't care, you can change these things they don't have to be the way you see it every time. You find a way to fight Bl-" The words died quickly on Leo's lips, cutting off midsentence as another tremor went through him and his face screwed up in pain. "Go...go...go now..." The words were choked out and barely audible as Leo spoke; his hands still gripping Blaise's shirt tightly. Blaise tried to pull free, watching another tremor rattle through Leo as he tried to get out from between his friend and the tree. Blaise finally managed to get loose as Leo seemed to go still, and Blaise didn't bother to wait to see who had won the small war for control as he took off. His legs were still unsteady, but he forced himself to keep moving even at a tripping uneven pace until he was able to get his footing.

"Get back here you pain in the ass." The tone made it clear that Leo was gone, and Blaise cursed at his legs as he forced them to move one in front of the other until he had a pace going. He crashed his way through the trees and snow, not caring which direction he was heading in as long as it was away from Leo. He look back behind him after a few moments, and was suddenly knocked to a stop when he ran into something in his path.

Blaise turned forward again to get around what had blocked his way, but instead stumbled back a few steps when he saw the well-dressed man standing in front of him. Shax gave him a smile as Blaise turned to try a new direction. Leo had already caught up to him though, the sheriff hitting him hard and taking him down into the snow. Leo grabbed Blaise's hair to pull his head back, hissing into his ear.

"I'm going to tear your throat out, and I'll enjoy every minute of it darling." Leo's free hand pressed against Blaise's throat, and that same nausea he'd experienced that day during his dream about the thing pretending to be Anne hit him.

"Lilith..." The word was spoken casually enough, but there was a clear threat held in the tone. Leo seemed to freeze in place while gripping Blaise, and then the hand on his throat disappeared. Leo kept a grip on Blaise's hair still, and the man wished desperately that Leo would have been distracted enough to let him go entirely.

"Shax...I wasn't expecting you..." Leo stood straight and dragged Blaise with him back onto his feet. There was a tension in the air, but Shax's eyes never left Blaise as he stood there awkwardly. Leo nudged Blaise ahead of him as he let him go, and the doctor now found himself in the middle.

"You've damaged him..."

"It's just an ear, maybe a few bruises." Leo spoke in a dismissive voice, sounding as though he was trying to glaze over the fact that he'd just said he was going to kill Blaise. Every fiber in Blaise's body was screaming at him to get away, but standing between the two men didn't give him much of a chance. Leo stepped around him casually after a moment, the move putting him between Shax and Blaise. "I doubt it will make him any less of a nuisance." Blaise caught the slight shudder in Leo's step as he stepped directly in front of Blaise and he realized he was being given a chance. Blaise waited a beat, watching for the right time to act and hoping that Shax hadn't noticed the change as well though this hope was short lived.

"Really, Lilith, can you not keep control of one pathetic man? You've lost your touch." There was a pause after Shax spoke the words and before Leo threw himself at the man. The moment Leo made his move Blaise made his own, taking off in the other direction. Blaise pushed himself as hard as he could, stumbling and sliding a few times but managing to stay upright. He fought against the vertigo and the stiffness that was trying to settle into his muscles from the cold and just ran. He felt the edges of self-hate starting though, creeping in and eating away at him for leaving Leo behind. He had no idea how to help his friend now, no way to save Leo from what had him in its hold. All he could do was try to do what Leo had asked, to find Anne and get them both away from there safely.

Shax caught Leo by the neck before the other could manage to tackle him, and he gave Leo a disapproving shake of his head.

"Did you really think that would work? You aren't strong enough to face me even when you aren't fighting Lilith at the same time." Shax frowned when Leo started to laugh, and he smacked him on the cheek to stop the laughter.

"He still got away, didn't he?" The words were followed by more laughter, and Shax looked over Leo's shoulder to where Blaise had been. Rage crossed Shax's face, and he threw Leo aside into one of the trees with a growl. "Lilith, I expected better from you. Find the girl, find the key or I swear I will lock your useless ass away." As Leo picked himself up a look of pure spite was on his face.

"And what have you done, Shax? You fucked things up by not killing the one fucking idiot that may have a chance of keeping us from succeeding all because you thought you could use him. How is that working out for you anyway?" Lilith spat the words at Shax, and sent him off with a high squeal of laughter as Shax stormed off through the trees. "That's real good, Shax. I'll go do all the real fucking work on my own!"

Mackenzie had to struggle three times to get to his feet before he managed it, and even then any movement he made sent pain shooting through his hip. Once he was standing he had to lean against the wall for a few moments to get his breath back before he could attempt anything else. He wasn't going to be able to walk after them, that much was obvious. He couldn't just sit there though, waiting to see what happened to everyone that he considered family. He knew that Anne had the snow mobile in the small shed outback, and he hoped she had it in working order. She only used it when things got bad enough that the snow plows weren't even able to get through to clear the roads, and it wasn't always reliable.

He pushed himself with the help of the furniture to make it into the kitchen where he dug the first aid kit out from under the sink. He'd already left a trail of blood dripped along the floor, and he did his best to tape one of the larger cloth bandages down around the wound to try and slow the flow. He wasn't sure how much blood he had lost so far, but if he couldn't get it to at least slow if not stop then it was going to take him out before he'd even have a chance. He was pulling his already ruined shirt back down over the bandage when he heard the front door open, and tentative footsteps started across the living room.

Mackenzie quietly reached to unhook his gun from its holster, but if it was Leo returning he didn't know if he could bring himself to use it. He shifted as quietly as he could manage to see if he'd catch a glimpse of the intruder, and for a few seconds could see nothing in the small section of living room visible to him. A man stepped into view as he walked through the living room cautiously, and Mackenzie raised the gun towards the person. His first thought had been that it was Michael, and he could have almost brought himself to pull the trigger. When the man looked towards him though Mackenzie realized with a start that it was Gabriel. The other stopped where he was, and Mackenzie knew that Gabriel had seen him sitting there against the kitchen cabinet taking aim at him. Mackenzie lowered the gun with a sigh, and Gabriel moved once he wasn't in the crosshairs.

"Mac?" Gabriel stepped into the kitchen, and paused for just a second when he saw the blood on Mackenzie's shirt before he was helping pull him to his feet. Gabriel kept a steadying hand on Mackenzie's elbow once he'd gotten the deputy up.

"We have to find the others. Leo's not himself anymore, and Anne and Blaise are out there with him somewhere. I don't know what else is out there though I can't imagine they sent only one for whatever the hell they're here for." Mackenzie didn't waste time in trying to limp his way out of the kitchen and down the hall to the mudroom at the back of the house. Anne would have the snow mobile keys hanging back there, and he hoped they were well marked so that he could find the right one. Gabriel picked up a small bag he'd dropped beside the hall and followed him, seeming to try and help keep Mackenzie on his feet.

There was a key rack in the mudroom big enough for six pairs of keys, but only two hung on the rack right then. The first pair of keys Mackenzie recognized as Anne's spare car keys by the emblem on them, so he grabbed the second set of keys and hoped it turned out to be the right set. Gabriel was watching him wearily, seeming unsure if he should be protesting about Mackenzie going out there to find the others.

"We should call you some help, Mac. I can go find the others, I know how to deal with these things and you're hurt pretty badly right now." Mackenzie leaned against the doorframe that lead out the back of the house, and turned to look at Gabriel. The look on the man's face spoke clearly his thoughts on being left just waiting for help even before Mackenzie vocalized them.

"That's my family out there right now, Gabriel. I'm not just going to sit here waiting to see if someone I'm not completely sure I can trust anymore will bring them back. I'm on my feet and I'm moving, and I'm going to keep moving until I know they're safe. If you want to come along, that's fine, I can keep a better eye on you that way." Gabriel was hurt by the distrust that he heard in Mackenzie suddenly, but he didn't feel he could blame him for it. Everything that was happening was because of Gabriel, and so far he'd not done much to help stop it.

"I want them back safe as badly as you Mac. I understand why you may not want to trust much of what I say, but you have to know that at least. I need to know that if I ask you to go, if we find them and I tell you to get them out of there that you'll do it without questions. This is my mess to clean up." Mackenzie seemed to size Gabriel up for a few seconds, but then he turned to open the door carefully while still bracing himself against the frame.

"Come on, Anne's snow mobile is out back in the shed. We'll catch up with them faster with that." Gabriel followed, helping Mackenzie through the snow when the man seemed to stumble. It took some effort to get the snow mobile out of the small shed, but the two of them managed. While Mackenzie kicked it on and checked the gas Gabriel secured the small bag to the side of the snow mobile and then they were heading out towards the woods. The vibrations from the snow mobile made the ache in Mackenzie's hip grow worse, but he was just glad that he was at least moving instead of stumbling around in the snow and tiring out before he could even reach the trees.

They rode in silence most of the way, though Gabriel felt some need to explain. He couldn't think of how to do that, how to make Mackenzie understand what was happening. They had come across a fork in the trail after a ways, and they had followed the fresh set of tracks down to the right. The sound of a scream broke over the hum of the motor, and the snow mobile came to an abrupt stop.

"It came from behind us," Gabriel said, both of them listening for another sound to come out from the trees. Another shout came from in front of them, and Mackenzie recognized Anne's voice. They heard Blaise behind them again after a few seconds, and Mackenzie found himself torn. He didn't know how Blaise and Leo had managed to fall behind them, but it was obvious that they had passed the two at some point along the trail. Anne didn't call out again from ahead, and the seconds seemed to pass slowly. "Keep going. We'll find Anne, and then we cut back. She's most likely still on the trail, but we don't know where the other two are."

"We could split up. I can go ahead to Anne, and you…"

"It's better if we stick together. It will just make it easier for them if we split up."

There was hesitation in Gabriel's voice, letting Mackenzie know that he was worried about leaving Blaise behind as well. Mackenzie understood the reasoning though, and he said a silent apology to Blaise as he started down along the trail again. He had a feeling Blaise would understand them going to Anne first, but he couldn't shake the sinking feeling that he was leaving Blaise behind for good. When they pulled into the clearing they found the sled and the dogs there, the animals lifting their heads to look at them silently before going back to watching the trees. Anne wasn't there though, and Mackenzie stopped the snow mobile beside the sled.

Gabriel climbed off first and stood close by so that if Mackenzie needed to take a hold of him he could. Mackenzie ignored the unspoken offer of help; wincing as he forced himself to stand on his own two feet. Mackenzie drew his gun, feeling uneasy as they stood scanning the trees until Gabriel nudged him and nodded off towards the way they'd come. There was a smaller trail through the snow leading off to the left of the sled's tracks, and it disappeared into the trees.

"I'll go look. You stay here and keep an eye out. If you see something, and it's not one of our own you shoot it." Mackenzie tried to protest about being left behind, but Gabriel ignored it and just started off down the trail that

Anne had created. Mackenzie took a few steps after him, but after the second or third his hip gave a dangerous twinge of pain in warning that it would give out. He stopped and tried to put most of his weight on his uninjured leg, and looked up to find Gabriel was already out of sight.

Anne hadn't made it as far into the woods as Gabriel had been afraid of at first, and he felt a small bit of relief when he saw her sitting in the snow just down a slope from the clearing. He carefully slid his way to where she was, her hand pressed over her mouth as though she was trying to keep herself from making a sound. Gabriel stopped beside her, crotching down to get her attention while hoping not to startle her.

"Anne." She shook her head sharply when he spoke, her hand grabbing his sleeve to pull him lower down. Gabriel looked up to follow her gaze and saw Leo about a yard or so away. He was picking his way through the snow, following the meandering trail of something that moved between the trees in front of him. Leo had blood on his clothes, and Gabriel had to fight a sense of anger for a second. Leo seemed to be alone other than the thing leading him, and Gabriel slipped his arm around Anne's waist to try and pull her back towards the slope as carefully as possible. "Come on, we have to go." He spoke in a whisper, leading her gently back up the hill. They needed to go before Leo got to the clearing, and then they needed to find where Blaise was.

"He killed him...didn't he?" Anne spoke as though she'd read Gabriel's thoughts, and he found he couldn't answer right away. He focused on getting them up the last bit of the slope, Mackenzie coming into view near the dog sled. "Tell me...did he kill Blaise?"

"I don't know." Gabriel said it with a shake of his head, nudging her towards Mackenzie as he looked back over his shoulder. He couldn't see Leo through the trees anymore, and instead of giving him a sense of comfort that there was more distance between them it made him more alert.

"You're hurt..." Anne was talking to Mackenzie now, their voices still low out of fear of being overheard. She had tugged Mackenzie's jacket up to try to get a look at the wound, but he pushed her hands away with a frustrated shake of his head.

"I'm fine. We have to get out of here, Anne." Mackenzie was trying to direct Anne towards the sled to get her to take the dogs out of there, but she firmly shook her head and stood her ground. Gabriel moved over to them hoping to get them both moving, looking around for any sign that they weren't alone in the clearing anymore.

"They won't go...I won't go, not until I know..." Anne said with a little more force, this time looking at Gabriel as he approached them.

"We can't stay. Anne, that's not your brother down there. I can't tell you where Blaise is or what's happened right now. We need to get out of here," Gabriel said, seeing Mackenzie tense at the mention of Leo being close by. Anne's anger started to flare, but Mackenzie's hand on her arm made her stop as he tugged her behind him towards the snow mobile.

"Anne, I'm sorry but Gabriel's right. We have to go. If Leo's down there we can't stay. He's already shot me, I can't say what he'll do right now." Mackenzie hissed the words at her, trying his best to talk through a new twist of pain in his hip. It was wearing on him, and his normally mild temper was beginning to flare because of it. Anne seemed to freeze for a moment, and then looked down at Mackenzie's blood covered shirt again and the fire in her seemed to drain as she paled.

Gabriel turned when the dogs stirred at the ends of their leads. They had all stood up from the snow, and were watching a spot in the trees that was now on the opposite side of the clearing. They'd already waited too long, and Gabriel stepped to move past the two to put himself between them and the thing he knew was in the woods. Mackenzie was trying to talk Anne into attempting to get the dogs going again since all three of them wouldn't fit on the snow mobile, but his words trailed off when he saw Gabriel's stance.

"Where?" Mackenzie asked the question tensely, his hand going to pull his gun from its holster as he tugged Anne a little closer to him. Mackenzie stumbled from the movement, and Anne put her arm around his waist to be his support as he scanned the trees in the direction Gabriel was watching. Leo stepped out of the trees, his hands held up in the air in mock surrender as he gave them a slow smile.

"I see you finally found your brain, little scarecrow. I figured your big brother would be babysitting you." Leo spoke to Gabriel, ignoring the other two as Anne's dogs gave a chorus of low growls. Yakone pulled at the line, turning a tight circle before breaking out in barks at Leo. "Hush." The word was a sharp command, and all of the dogs fell quiet at it with their tails tucked between their legs. Leo looked back towards them and gave Mackenzie a small wave over Gabriel's shoulder. "I see you haven't died, that's a shame."

"Where's Blaise?" Anne was the first of them to speak, and Gabriel shook his head to try and keep her quiet. The question was already out though, and Leo lowered his hands back down to his sides as he leaned to look at her. Mackenzie clicked the safety off on his handgun, but still couldn't bring himself to take aim at Leo. He didn't think he'd be able to fire at his friend, and he hoped that it wouldn't come down to that. Protecting Anne was his main priority in all this though, and he knew he'd have to find the will to pull that trigger if the time came.

"He's dead…or maybe still dying. He got on my nerves, so I ripped his throat out and left him out there somewhere. Don't worry, he should bleed out soon if he hasn't already." Leo's words were tinged with amusement, and he laughed at the look on Anne's face. Anne went rigid next to Mackenzie, and he pressed against her side with his weight a little more firmly. If she went for Leo he had no doubt that the monster inside her brother would respond with force in return. He knew Leo was still in there somewhere, but he wasn't sure his friend could gain control again. "So, you came out here. Did you find it?"

"There was never anything out here to find, Lilith." Gabriel shifted as Leo started to circle around the edge of the clearing, keeping himself in Leo's path if he wished to get to the other two. Leo's look darkened for a second, but then the amused expression returned. One of the dogs risked a low growl, but Gabriel didn't look to see what had emboldened the animal once more. Mackenzie felt Anne tug at his shirt and glanced to the side where something was coming out of the trees to their right. The thing froze him to the spot as it moved in its own circular path towards Leo. It looked almost like a dog that had been pulled and twisted out to impossible dimensions, and it took a snap at the string of dogs attached to the sled before looking at the three of them.

"Gabe…"

"I know." Gabriel spoke quietly, not taking his eyes off of Leo despite the thing that was stalking through the clearing with them.

"There you are, sugar. I was wondering where you'd wandered to." Leo practically baby talked to the creature as it came to a stop at his side. He reached down to pet affectionately at its ears. Mackenzie raised his handgun towards the creature, taking a careful step up beside Gabriel. "Don't you go pointing that thing at my baby, darling." Leo turned quickly with a snarl, drawing his own gun to aim at Mackenzie. Gabriel pushed Mackenzie's arm down, trying to defuse the situation before things got out of hand and Leo laughed. "Aw, go ahead Gabriel. Let him shoot me. We can see who's faster, Mac. It will be like our own little cockfight."

"Lilith…" Gabriel gave a warning tone, but all it did was make Leo laugh.

"Please, that doesn't work anymore. You don't have the juice that you used to Gabriel." Anne was still tucked behind the two men near the sled, and Gabriel heard her searching for something. He didn't dare to look behind him, not wanting to draw attention to her as Leo's aim shifted to him from Mackenzie. "You're just one of them now. All it would take is one bullet. Come on, Mac…think you can hit me before I get a shot in Fly Boy here? Let's try in three."

Leo dropped his gun down to his side as he cocked it. He started counting slowly, and Gabriel took his hand away from Mackenzie's arm.

"As soon as he fires, you grab Anne and you get out of here." Mackenzie looked at Gabriel like he'd misheard him before shaking his head. "Mac…you said…" Gabriel didn't get a chance to finish as Leo suddenly got up to three, but Mackenzie was faster. Leo jerked back as the bullet hit his shoulder, and a second later the dog-thing had come at them both and knocked Gabriel and Mackenzie apart.

The animal knocked Mackenzie down hard into the snow, but its attacked focused on Gabriel as it tried to wrap its elongated neck around him and land a bite at his throat. Leo was looking down at his shoulder in surprise before he started to laugh, starting towards Mackenzie. Mackenzie tried to get to his feet again, but the jolt from hitting the ground had sent a fresh wave of pain through him. Leo reached him first and pulled Mackenzie up, kicking at one of the dogs as it tried to get a bite of him. He turned to drag Mackenzie a

174

little further from the sled, but stopped when he found himself face to face with Anne.

Anne had pulled the shotgun out of the sled from where she kept it tethered and had it currently aimed at Leo's chest. Leo kept a hold on the collar of Mackenzie's shirt for a second before dropping him and giving Anne a grin.

"Go on Anne. You can do it." Anne seemed to hesitate, but then pulled back the hammer of the gun though she still didn't rest her finger on the trigger. "Come on...are you really that weak or did he just mean that little to you? Shoot me." He took a step forward as Anne continued not to act, and she mimed him with a step back. "He begged for you. He cried and screamed for you while I tore his throat out, and then I left him there. He died alone out in the cold, and you'll probably never even find his body to take back." The shotgun shook in Anne's hands, but she took a breath to steady herself and finally put a finger on the trigger.

"You're not my brother..."

"You just finally figured that out?" Leo snarled and quickly backhanded Anne across the face with his own gun, following it with a kick to the ribs as she stumbled and fell. She raised the shotgun and fired a shot, but it went wide as Leo grabbed the barrel and yanked it to the side. Leo pulled the gun out of her hands, it's shots now spent so it was useless to her either way. He kicked at her ribs again, following her as she tried to scramble away to get distance between them.

Mackenzie was struggling to get back on his feet while trying to dig his own gun up out of the snow, hoping it would still function. Anne had finally curled up into a tight ball in an attempt to protect herself from Leo's kicks. Mackenzie heard Gabriel call his name, and he looked to see the man still fighting to get away from the creature. The thing was tangled around him, trying to tear at Gabriel as he did his best to push its head away. Mackenzie found his gun, hesitating between hitting the creature or Leo, and then finally raised it and took aim. The thing went still as the gunshot went off, and for a moment they all seemed to hang there until Leo turned to look back at Mackenzie.

"How dare you..." The words came out in an angry growl, and Mackenzie suddenly wished he'd made a different choice. The canine creature hadn't gone down with the shot either, though Mackenzie had at least managed to hurt it. It's attention turned away from Gabriel as it snapped at its own side like it was trying to attack whatever had injured it. Gabriel was trying to get himself freed from the weight of the distracted creature tangled around him as Leo stalked towards Mackenzie. Anne moved as quickly as she could, grabbing Leo's leg and taking him down into the snow where she pinned him. Anne was cursing as she punched at Leo, landing a couple of good blows before Leo managed to kick up a leg and roll them over. He pushed Anne down into the snow, digging his knee into her back as he pressed her face into the powder with one hand.

Gabriel managed to get loose, moving toward Mackenzie at a pained limp. There was a large bite taken out of one of his thighs, but Gabriel seemed to be ignoring it. The creature had recovered, and tried to make a lunge for Gabriel before one of the dogs grabbed hold of it. The animals erupted into a pile of chaos as the sled dogs all went at the creature at once, emboldened by the actions of the one. Gabriel kept his distance from the fighting the best he could, but he had stopped at the snow mobile beside the sled and was trying to dig something out of the bag he'd placed there. Mackenzie fought to get up to get over to Anne, and finally got to his feet as he felt a twinge of frustration at Gabriel for not immediately jumping in to help them. Mackenzie could feel the fresh blood running down his leg, and he knew the bandage he'd put in place had either slipped or been bled through. Mac tried to take aim at Leo, but the gun just misfired when he pulled the trigger this time giving a dull click.

Mackenzie cursed and dropped it to the side, instead placing an arm around Leo's neck to pull him off his sister. The move forced Leo to let go of Anne, and she rolled over taking large, gulping breaths. Leo reached back to scratch at Mackenzie's neck but Mackenzie ignored the attack and tried to pull Leo further back from Anne. His hip gave out at the attempt to carry the extra weight, and the two of them fell back into snow. Leo reached back towards Mackenzie again in what Mac assumed was another attempt to scratch him, but instead Leo just pressed his hand flat against Mackenzie's neck. Mackenzie felt the sudden wave of fatigue wash through him with a mix of complacency and relaxation. He tried to fight against it but Leo pulled out of his grasp easily, and for a confused minute Mackenzie thought he heard Anne call his name but found he couldn't focus on it. He tried to brush Leo's hand away, but Leo just gripped his wrist with his free hand to stop him.

Anne had moved to get Leo off of Mackenzie, not sure if the other had been hurt again by the fall back or why he'd suddenly stopped fighting her brother. As she got closer though she saw the black streaks spreading under Mackenzie's skin from where Leo was touching him. Leo dropped Mackenzie's wrist and then pressed both hands against Mackenzie's cheeks, and the same black lines starting to spread from there as well. All sound started to fade for Mackenzie, even the sounds of the dogs snarls and barks as they pinned the creature down in the snow. The thing was torn open in several places, but it was still moving and fighting against them despite it.

"Not feeling well, Mackenzie?" Leo asked with mock concern, but his words seemed to echo around in Mackenzie's head like a woman was echoing what he said. "You would have been more fun to toy with than your friend. He was so busy wishing his dead wife had come back to him, but you…oh, you just like to have fun, don't you?" Leo leaned in close and Mackenzie tried to shake him off as an uncomfortable warmth seemed to start burning inside him. "See, now you it works wonders with, unlike the prophet. You're so very human."

Mackenzie wanted to pull back, but nothing seemed to be working for him as his head filled with fog and the woman's voice. He didn't recognize the voice at first, but it seemed to slowly change and morph into something else as it rolled around in his mind. *Why don't you kiss me, Callahan? You can be mine for good then...* The voice suddenly belonged to Allison, and Mackenzie felt the desire to fight slipping away when Leo was pulled sharply away from him. The fog seemed to lift from his mind as Mackenzie blinked his eyes a few times; managing to get his bearings back. Anne was there with him, shaking him lightly to try and get a response.

Behind Anne, Mackenzie could see Leo struggling against the hold that Gabriel had on him. Gabriel was saying something in Leo's ear, and it sounded familiar to Mackenzie but he couldn't place the words exactly. Leo was fighting against Gabriel though, thrashing and spitting curses at him angrily. The creature had stopped fighting against the dogs, but was instead struggling to get free of them as it almost keened towards Leo like a dog calling for its owner.

"Leave him Lilith," Gabriel said angrily, the words coming out in English suddenly and the monster inside Leo laughed.

"You're far from what you used to be, Gabriel. Are you scared you can't beat me? You know that at the least you can't save him." Gabriel took a small bottle he'd had in one hand, and forced it to Leo's mouth to quiet him. Leo kicked, trying to fight harder as he seemed to register some danger the bottle contained.

"I'm not what I use to be, Lilith, but I can still get rid of you." Gabriel slipped back out of English, and Mackenzie realized with a start that he was speaking Latin. Anne was gripping Mac's hand tightly, seeming to be torn between helping Leo and letting whatever was happening just happen. Gabriel poured whatever was in the bottle into Leo's mouth while the monster inside him tried to keep his lips pursed shut from it. As Gabriel was able to force some past Leo's lips the air was suddenly filled with a the scent of sulfur.

A lump of flesh bulged suddenly; growing out of and then separating from Leo's back as Gabriel tried to pull the thing free. The creature finally managed to break loose from the dogs and started struggling to its feet but having to drag itself towards Gabriel and Leo. As the lump of flesh got further out of Leo it seemed to change shape until at last it was almost free, and it formed into a woman who turned to try and claw at Gabriel. The woman's skin seemed to smolder and burn as Gabriel got her upper torso free from Leo and she twisted herself towards him, bending her back at an unusual angle. She seemed for a moment to be clinging to Leo and Gabriel both, unwilling to let go of either one as she gripped Gabriel's face in her hands with an angry scream, her waist down disappearing into Leo's back.

Gabriel did his best to avoid the touch that sent black streams running under his skin, his eyes turning inky with it as he forced the latin from his lips. His vision began to sink into darkness, but he made himself continue saying the words. Even as he heard her start to speak through his mind, as the feelings of surrender tried to cloud his judgement, he made the words form patterns.

Pain suddenly seared through his temples as the voice became clearer to him, changing and shifting as Lilith tried to find the voice that would affect him the most. The pain faded into feelings of relaxation and indifference tugging and pulling at his will.

"Come, Gabriel, you can't win. Give in, give up...you've already lost so much, what's one last thing? Gabriel..." She cycled through his memories hoping to hit on the right trigger. First it was Anne's voice, then Lisa's, different women from the town followed but all the while Gabriel fought against the pull and kept his words coming until Lilith finally pulled clear of Leo. She seemed to sense that her chance was ending, and the pain reared its head again. It burned through Gabriel's head, and the words stumbled for a second, slurring and halting until he choked out the last syllables.

"You aren't winning, Gabriel. He'll be dead, and by the end of this; so will you," the woman's words came out as a harsh hiss until finally she burst into smoke and ash leaving Gabriel standing there covered in soot. At the same time a cry came from the creature who hadn't made it in time, and the thing collapsed down into the snow as it coughed out a cloud of smoke and ash that settled around it.

Gabriel stumbled a step when he was freed of the burden of the demon's weight, burn marks along his cheeks and forehead where she had touched. The ink-black lines drained away slowly from sight, his vision returning to show the other three left in the clearing with him.

Leo stood in front of Mackenzie and Anne for a few seconds looking shellshocked before he coughed, blood trickling out of his mouth as he collapsed. Mackenzie pushed himself up the best he could and barely caught Leo before he fell, and they both went down hard into the snow. Anne was at their sides immediately, trying to help Mackenzie prop Leo up, resting him back against Mackenzie's chest as more coughs wracked his body. More blood came with each spasm until they finally seemed to slow. Anne cupped Leo's face in her hands, calling his name as she tried to get him to look at her. He finally seemed to focus on his sister's face, and a small smile came to his lips though it faltered when a sickening gurgle broke from his throat.

"Love you, sis..." The words were barely audible, but they had no trouble hearing them as they were focused so strongly on Leo. Anne gave a quiet sob, shaking her head at her brother as she ran a hand over his hair.

"Love you too, moron."

"You're going to be okay, Leo. Hold on, we'll get you help. It will be all right." Leo didn't seem to hear Mackenzie though as he looked up at Gabriel. The man seemed to be keeping his distance while hovering at the same time, and for a moment he met Leo's eyes.

"Thanks...." Gabriel nodded sadly at the words, but didn't say anything in return. He knew what the other two didn't, and he also knew that there had been a time he'd have been able to save Leo. He couldn't anymore though.

Leo tried to push himself up suddenly, but Anne stopped him and pushed him gently back again. "Blaise…"

"No, you shouldn't move, Leo." Anne spoke to keep Leo from trying to get up again, but stopped when she realized what her brother had just said. Gabriel stepped forward at the name, kneeling down beside Leo and putting his hands on the man's shoulders to help Anne with keeping him from moving.

"Blaise…he has Blaise…" Leo spoke the words a bit frantically like he was trying to get them out before he didn't feel he could.

"Who does?" Gabriel asked it calmly, trying to get Leo to calm down himself though he could hear an edge still leak through in his voice.

"Shax…" Gabriel went still for a moment, but chose not to speak whatever thought went through his mind. Leo seemed to relax a little though he continued watching Gabriel closely.

"I'm sorry I couldn't help you more." Gabriel said it quietly, and Leo started to respond but more wracking coughs started to run through him accompanied by the bright stain of blood. Anne pushed Gabriel away angrily at his words, cursing at him.

"Shut up! Just shut up, he's going to be fine. Don't talk like he's dying!" Anne all but screamed it at him, and Gabriel stepped away as she turned back to Leo and cupped his face in her hands once more. "You're going to be fine. We'll get you help, and you'll be fine. We can find Blaise, and he'll fix whatever it is that's wrong and it will all be okay. It will be." Mackenzie was watching Gabriel silently, and when the man shook his head at him there was a flicker of pain that crossed Mackenzie's face before he pushed it away.

"Anne…" Mackenzie spoke gently, feeling Leo's weight growing heavy against him. His friend tried to say something, but his mouth moved without making any sounds. Gabriel shifted away from the three of them, moving to sit off to the side silently as he looked away. It was a private moment he wasn't entitled to, and he did his best to give the three their time. Mackenzie felt a tremor go through him as Leo became deadweight against his chest, and he rested his cheek on the side of Leo's head as he tried again. "Anne…"

"Mackenzie, don't. He's going to be fine. Help me get him onto the sled, and then he'll be fine." Anne pointed at Mackenzie angrily to hush him, and Mackenzie just shook his head sadly at her. Hot tears were rolling down Anne's face, and she shook her head furiously at the look Mackenzie gave her. "No, he's fine…he's my big brother and he's fine."

"He's gone Anne…" Mackenzie felt his own tears, and he reached an arm out for Anne. She smacked it away at first, but when he insisted a second time she collapsed into his hold. The two of them sat there, Leo's body hugged between them as Anne sobbed and Mackenzie let his own tears fall. Mackenzie looked up when he heard Gabriel clear his throat, the man standing up and brushing snow off his jeans.

Leo seemed to have been the thing holding the two of them up, and now that he was gone they seemed slightly deflated. The behavior struck Gabriel as wrong, and part of him wondered if he left them behind if they'd just continue to sit there with Leo until they froze. He shifted, determined to get them moving in the direction he wanted.

"You two need to get back to the house. I'll go find Blaise, its better if you're not there. Shax is…worse than Lilith, and that was all the Holy Water I could get." Anne clung to Leo for a moment longer before she sat up and brushed her tears away the best she could while they were still falling.

"No, we're coming with you. I need to know he's all right." Gabriel looked at her silently as a flicker of her old determination came back to her eyes but shook his head. It wasn't a good idea, and the two of them were emotionally in shatters. Anne was trying to pull herself together, but he could still see the turmoil and loss swirling beneath the surface waiting to break free. He couldn't risk them anymore than he already had.

"I'm sorry, but I-"

"We're coming with you, Gabe. You're not going to shake us." Mackenzie spoke up, shifting himself out from under Leo a little. He looked at his friend and for a moment felt some doubt. They couldn't leave Leo out there, but he wasn't sure how they would get him back to the house either with or without going to help Blaise. Anne glanced at Mackenzie and then down at Leo, and seemed to have the same thought. Gabriel frowned at them, seeming to be weighing the options of arguing with them now or just allowing them to do what they saw as best. He knew for sure that he wouldn't just leave them to their own devices if they refused to listen to reason.

"I'll get him on the sled. But, you two are still going back to the house," Gabriel said with a quiet sigh, shifting down to lift Leo up from between the two. He felt a moments disturbance at how empty Leo felt when the Sheriff had always been such a heavy weight in the lives around him. He carried Leo to the sled, the dogs watching him from where they were lying in the snow. The remains of the deformed hound was lying not far, seeming flattened out and empty like it was a sack that had been drained of whatever had been filling it. "I'll take the sled. It will be easier for me since I'll be on my own."

"We're not going back to the house, Gabriel." Mackenzie spoke for them both, Anne helping him up to his feet. Mackenzie sounded more defiant this time, but Gabriel chose to ignore them while getting Leo settled in securely. He looked down at the man, silently asking Leo why he had to have such stubborn friends before he carefully lifted the basket cover over him and tucked it into place. "If you try to go without us, we'll just follow you or go look on our own." Gabriel stood and looked back at them for a few seconds.

"It's strange…you're all very different than what I would have thought back then. I always knew you were more than what some of my family believed, but you seem to do nothing but drive me crazy." Gabriel didn't speak the words with anger, but more with a curious amusement. Anne looked at him confused as though she wondered if he'd lost touch a little, but Mackenzie just stared at him.

180

"Maybe you could tell your brother that." Gabriel studied Mackenzie in return, and got the impression that Mackenzie knew more about what was going on than Gabriel would have assumed. He shook his head lightly.

"Michael's past listening to me. If you two insist on coming along, then you stay back some. Remain in eyesight but don't follow too closely, I can scout ahead since I'll be quieter. If we do get separated I expect you to head back to the house." Anne was shooting a look at Mackenzie, but he ignored the question that was held in it as Gabriel changed the subject. Anne's attention was pulled back to Gabriel as she gave a short shake of her head, shifting to stop him when she saw him move to pull the brake out of the snow.

"They won't run for you." She said it a little deflatedly, and it sounded as though she was stating a simple fact instead of trying to argue more. Gabriel looked up at the dogs who were watching him expectantly before he pulled the brake free. He hoped he'd be able to figure out how to direct them, but he had a feeling they would listen.

"Make sure not to fall out of the line of sight. If I see anything I'll signal you to stop. If we find them then you're to stay out of the way." Gabriel made sure the dogs were staying where they were with the brake off, and stepped back over to help Anne get Mackenzie to the snow mobile. She hesitated at first, but then the two of them worked together to help Mackenzie get himself situated. Mackenzie took his first good look at Anne, and could see the bruising along her jaw where Leo…Lilith had hit her. She moved tenderly as well as she got on the snow mobile in front of him, being careful about her ribs. He was worried she had at least a few badly bruised ones if not some that were broken, and he was careful about how he rested his hands on her sides.

Gabriel returned to the sled, getting himself ready on the rungs. He didn't even call out to the dogs before they started off through the trees back in the direction of the house. Anne waited a few seconds, perhaps a few longer than she intended due to her surprise at the dogs easy reaction to Gabriel and then she followed him to help search for Blaise.

Blaise pushed his way through the woods, fighting to stay on his feet as the world tilted randomly beneath him. The tug of vertigo from his ear was making it hard to keep a hold on his sense of equilibrium. He forced himself to keep running though, ignoring the burning in his lungs. At last, some root or rock under the snow caught him unexpectedly and sent Blaise tumbling down to his knees. He looked around, trying to get some bearing on where he'd ended up. Blaise glanced behind him, but he couldn't see any sign that he was being followed.

He let himself take a few moments to catch his breath then, though conscious of stopping for too long. Blaise stayed low near the ground until he was ready to go, pushing himself up to stand. He was cold and damp from the snow and the moisture in the air, and he knew he needed to keep moving as much to stop himself from freezing as to get away from the man following him.

As he stood and looked around he could see the dip in the snow, the change in the landscape letting him know he had reached the river. He looked along the cleft and saw wider areas where the snow was thinned out and Blaise quickly knew where he was. The river that ran through Anne's property widened in a section, and it formed three deep ponds that had been made by some beaver dams.

He felt his blood run a little cold at the realization of where he was, but he tried to keep focus on the fact that it meant he wasn't far from the house. If he could get there he might have a chance, though part of him knew he was fooling himself with that thought. Blaise moved a few steps towards the frozen water's edge, making sure to keep enough distance he wouldn't risk stepping out onto snow-covered ice by accident. The river would lead him to the house the quickest, as well as making sure he didn't get turned around.

Blaise froze when he heard a noise and he turned to his right to try and track it, but couldn't see anything. He scanned the trees but there was no sign that anyone was there. He turned to check all around, tensed and ready to run if he caught a glimpse of Shax. The voice spoke directly in his ear causing Blaise to wheel around quickly back towards the ponds to confront whoever was there.

"You've always been a disappointment." Blaise recognized the voice when it spoke, and it caused his breath to hitch slightly. It wasn't Shax, but another man who had terrorized him at one point in his life. "I can't believe I have such a fool for a son." His father's voice came from behind him once more, but as Blaise turned to search he only found the trees around him. Blaise backed away from the water a few steps, starting down along the bank towards the house. "I should have known that any child that your mother produced would turn out an idiot. You're probably not even my son."

Blaise stopped when the voice came from in front of him amongst the trees, and he had to stop himself from taking an involuntary step back towards the ponds. He stood undecided for a few moments, trying hard to pinpoint where the voice was coming from when it spoke so he knew which way to make his escape.

"Nothing but a fool. You think you're a man now, do you? Think you're strong enough to take on your father?" Blaise's hands fisted at his sides, and he tried to remind himself that this was a trick as the words from the night his father had finally physically taken his anger out on him echoed back from the woods. "Why don't you take a swing?" The voice was right behind him again and Blaise turned to swing at it only to find empty air. His foot slipped beneath him as it hit the edge of the ice and he scrambled back from it nervously. When he'd put a few feet between him and the pond he stood ramrod straight, trying hard to get a handle on his breathing.

"What kind of man uses the word 'fool'? Where did your father get his vocabulary; the A team?" Blaise found himself beside Shax then, the man standing behind him and to the left. Shax gave Blaise a condescending smile before taking a step towards him. Blaise moved as well to keep the distance between them, though he was painfully aware of the ponds behind him as he tried to turn their movements so that he could keep some distance from the water's edge. "Then again, I do think he had a point. You haven't been able to do anything effectively, have you? You failed to act on your dreams, failed to avoid me...you've fucked things up rather well. I have to thank you for that, though you have still managed to be an annoyance. You got close with the Sheriff, but in the end you failed at that too. No wonder your father pushed you down a flight of stairs."

"What do you want? I still can't tell you where Gabriel hid what your looking for. I'm no help to you..." Blaise could feel the cold starting to set in on him now that he wasn't moving at the quick pace from before. He'd slowed down for too long and the sweat and moisture on his shirt was starting to freeze and stiffen against his skin. He refused to show his discomfort though, not wanting the man to see any weakness to pick at.

"You're wrong.... You can be of help if molded right. Have you rethought my offer, Prophet?" Shax spoke lightly in an amused tone, though there was a warning note in his words as he continued to follow Blaise in a lazy circle. Blaise was finally away from the edge of the pond, the still immaculately dressed man now between him and the water.

"What offer?" Blaise tried to bluff though he remembered better than he'd like. He would have preferred that he didn't since the memory came with the feel of a knife cutting into him. He had tried to hide how much of the actual pain he remembered from his friends while giving them what information he could. The man's offer to him was one of the last things he did remember about that day before it melted into a painful blur.

"Don't. I enjoy the games we play, Prophet, but I don't have time for them today. I want an answer, if I don't like the one I get then I'll find some way to get the one I want." The sharp undercurrent cut through more clearly this time as Shax stopped to stand and watch Blaise. "What answer is it going to be?"

Blaise's ears had started to ring and the sound was getting louder by the moment. He tried to ignore the buzz as his mind raced through his choices. Shax turned towards the trees as though he too could hear the buzzing hum, and Blaise realized that it wasn't a ringing in his ears but something coming through the woods. He froze when his mind identified the sound as one he knew, a snow mobile's engine cutting through the forest. "Well, if you don't want to give me an answer now we could always wait for them to get here. I'm assuming its your friends…"

It took only a couple of seconds for the decision to be made in Blaise's mind and for him to act on it. He remembered the image of the man's blank, dead face under the water with him from his vision and realized he didn't really have a choice at all. He refused to let Shax get a hold of the others even if it might mean he ended up in the icy water with him. Shax seemed genuinely surprised as he looked back to Blaise with a smile that faded quickly as the man hit him at a full run. Blaise's shoulder hit Shax in the midsection as he tackled him, and they both fell back onto the ice of the middle pond. Blaise had braced himself for the surface to crack immediately under their falling weight, but instead they were met with a solid impact that left them lying there on top of the ice in stunned silence before Shax started to laugh. As if in response to the sound, the pond's surface sent up a cracking noise beneath them that failed to deter Shax in the least.

"I didn't realize you wanted to be so close, Prophet. Shall I take this as your answer then?" The ice protested loudly beneath them, and Blaise tried to pull himself back towards the safety of the shore. The movement seemed to be the trigger the surface needed though as it suddenly let go. Blaise tried to lunge away from the hole that had appeared beneath Shax, but he felt the man's grip take hold on his shirt and they both plunged into the frigid water.

The cold hit Blaise first but the pain followed closely behind as his shattered eardrum was flooded by the bitter water. It almost managed to knock the breath from Blaise's lungs, but he struggled to keep the air from escaping. He pushed back at Shax, attempting to get free of his hold and back to the surface. His lungs were already starting to burn in his chest by the time he succeeded in landing a kick to Shax's ribs, a spurt of air bubbles breaking free from the other man's lips. Blaise felt Shax's hold loosen and he pulled away as Shax tried to take an instinctive breath and instead sucked in water. Blaise kicked at the man again, watching Shax struggle to pull in air as his movements went sluggish before slowing and then stopping completely.

Blaise tried pushing upwards towards the sky he could see above the water, hoping that he wouldn't find himself sealed beneath the water by a layer of reformed ice.

Blaise's chest was screaming at him that he needed a breath, and it was getting harder and harder to fight back that impulse to draw in air. There was a moment where he thought he would black out before he managed to break through the surface of the water, but he found himself suddenly pulling in a long breath of air. He reached for something solid to pull himself out of the pond with; the relief from reaching the surface wearing away when all he found to grab hold of was ice. Each time he tried to get a purchase on the edge of the brittle layer the ice would break away, the hole widening further.

Blaise finally managed to get a grip on a solid piece of ice, and took a second to rest as his muscles protested against holding him up. Something unexpectedly took hold of his ankle from below, and Blaise found himsef pulled under for an instant before he was able to get himself back above water. He kicked in an attempt to get himself loose from whatever he was tangled on, but it tugged down on him sharply in return and he found himself back under the water. Blaise bent to get a look at what had caught him and pulled back in surprise as Shax gave him a smile from below. The man pulled Blaise down deeper to his own level on the bottom of the pond, the surface only a couple of feet above them, but it seemed far enough away for panic. Blaise pushed at the other man, feeling stupid to think that Shax may have actually drowned after his previous experience with him. They struggled under the water, Blaise fighting to get himself free only to have Shax abruptly let him go.

Blaise pushed himself up to the surface, and had just enough time to take in another deep breath before Shax dragged him under once more.

They'd been silent as they traveled through the woods, Gabriel leading the way on the sled about a yard ahead of them. Mackenzie knew that Anne was crying in front of him on the mobile, his head resting against her shoulder and feeling the tremble go through her. Mac forced himself to straighten up, focusing himself on watching for any sign that they weren't alone on the trail. He didn't say anything to Anne, knowing her well enough to understand that she didn't want him to acknowledge her tears if she wasn't.

They were getting close to the house again with no sign of Blaise other than the set of tracks they'd picked up on a few moments before. They'd heard Gabriel call for him at one point when he'd had them stop, but there had been no answer. Though no one had spoken the concern out loud, they each knew that Blaise may already be lost as well. Mackenize didn't register that Anne was asking him something over the hum of the snow mobile until she'd asked the question a couple of times and he leaned forward to hear her better.

"What was that? What took my brother from me?" Anne's voice was steady despite the wet tracks that Mackenzie could make out on her cheeks when she turned her head to glance back at him.

"I think I know, but I don't know if I'm right...and I don't know if you'd believe it." Mackenzie was hesitant to speak his thoughts, to say that he thought Leo had been possessed by something. Even after what they'd seen during Gabriel's impromptu exorcism, he felt almost afraid to speak like it had been real. He knew he'd have to face that it was eventually, his friend's dead body that was currently traveling on the sled with Gabriel was evidence of that truth.

"Tell me, Mac...I need to know..." He could hear Anne's own thoughts in her voice, her own suspiscions and worries flooding out. Mackenzie relented then, telling her what he could about the things that had happened with Leo the days and months leading up to his death. The reasons he felt that his friend had been taken over by something unnatural. Before he realized it he was even telling her about his meetings with Michael, and for a few minutes he could feel her anger radiating off of her. The backlash didn't get a chance to play out though as Gabriel came to a sudden stop ahead of them, and Anne slowed to a stop as well to keep the distance between them.

"You should have told someone." The bitter words were the only chastising he got from her as they sat waiting for some sign. Gabriel seemed like he was listening for something, and Mackenzie found himself straining to hear whatever the man had picked up on. Gabriel turned back to them, motioning for them to stay where they were before he started off through the trees without them. Anne cursed under her breath as they sat there waiting to see when Gabriel would come back.

Some noise made its way to Mackenzie through the trees, and he turned to look down the small slope to their left. When the sound of a laugh cut through the silence Anne turned her head towards it too, and they sat completely still. Mackenzie looked forward again when they heard the start of a shout that got cut short, but Gabriel was no where to be seen. The two of them came to a silent agreement as Mackenzie rested his hands on Anne's hips again and she started them down the slope towards the noises. Gabriel would be able to follow their tracks when he got back if they weren't there.

As they went along they realized the trail they'd been following cut back in this direction and led down into a clearing they both recognized. It was the beaver ponds that sat out a little ways from Anne's house, and the tracks meandered through the area in an erratic pattern. Anne pulled to the center of the clearing and stopped, climbing off to try and tell in which direction the footprints led back out of the area and into the woods. Mackenzie sat, trying to steady himself so he could get off and help as well. Sitting on the snow mobile had caused his leg to stiffen further and he found it was taking him longer to get going again.

Mackenzie looked over towards the ponds, trying to see from there if the trail moved along the stream towards the house when he noticed that the surface of one of the center ponds was broken. He stared as his mind worked on some thought that wasn't willing to solidify, and it wasn't until he caught sight of the hand breaking out of the water's surface and trying to get a hold of the ice before slipping under again that he grasped what his subconscious was telling him. With a curse Mackenzie pushed himself off the snow mobile, almost collapsing into the snow but pure determination managed to keep him on his feet.

Anne called out after him in confusion as Mac pulled himself towards the pond, his left leg dragging behind him as it refused to properly function. Anne watched him for a few moments as he ignored her, and then looked towards the pond herself. When things clicked into place she was following after Mac, the two of them hitting the water's edge at the same time. Mackenzie let himself fall to his knees and then down onto his stomach,

186

pushing himself out over the ice to where the cracked edge was and hoping that he wouldn't end up in the freezing water as well. He felt Anne's hold on the waist of his pants, holding on to help pull him back if need be as he reached down into the water.

He didn't know if it was Blaise, but Mackenzie wasn't going to risk it if it was. He didn't find anything at first, and then something grabbed hold of his wrist and he clamped his hand around it.

"Pull Anne, now," Mac said, trying to reach down with his other arm to get a better grip but not able to quite yet. Mackenzie propped himself up with the free hand instead, pushing back to try and drag whoever he'd gotten a hold of up out of the water. When he felt Anne pulled back on his belt to help him he had to fight back a wave of pain as the fabric tightened over the gunshot wound. He must have made some grunt or cry though, because he felt Anne almost let go until he snapped back at her not to. They both pulled, seeming to be fighting a tug of war with something under the surface. The hold on Mackenzie's wrist was weakening under the water, and he called back at Anne to pull harder as he fought to get the person above the water line. He prayed it was Blaise, his mind refusing to accept any other possibility. Finally, whatever had been pulling back against them seemed to let go and they dragged Blaise up out of the water. Mackenzie and Anne hauled him up along the ice and then away from the water's edge, laying Blaise out in the snow for lack of a better place to put him.

Mackenzie had to sit back hard in the snow as Anne leaned over Blaise beside him. He had to fight back the stars that were filling his vision, a numbed throb going through his hip to the beat of his heart though oddly enough he didn't feel any real pain. A warmth was spreading down over his thigh, and he knew that he was bleeding fresh once again as whatever clot had formed over the wound had been torn open.

"Mac, he's not breathing." Anne's words as she looked up at him desperately made Mackenzie do his best to push back the haze in his head, and he did his best to focus. He shifted closer to Blaise, sitting across from Anne who was on his other side, and Mackenzie tilted Blaise's head back.

"You breathe when I tell you, all right Anne?" Anne nodded, though she gave Mackenzie a strange look that made him wonder if his words had been slurred. Mackenzie ignored the look, doing his best to steady himself as he checked for a pulse in Blaise's neck. There was a faint one, and Mackenzie felt a moment's relief both that Blaise's heart was still beating and that he didn't have to attempt the difficult act of chest compressions with his injury. Mackenzie counted off between breaths for Anne, keeping track of Blaise's pulse in case it stopped before they got him breathing and his worry grew as he felt it slow and weaken. After the fourth or fifth breath though Blaise started coughing, water coming up out of his lungs as he came to life under their hands. Anne turned Blaise onto his side quickly so he wouldn't end up choking, and Mackenzie let himself sink back into the snow again.

Anne was telling Blaise to breath in a calm voice though she seemed far from relaxed with the shaking in her hands as she rubbed his back.

Mackenzie looked up over her head as movement caught his eye, and he froze when he made eye contact with the man. Mackenzie didn't have to be told that this was Shax, the description they'd gotten from Blaise after his first encounter with the man had been close to spot on though he was perhaps shorter and slightly less built than Blaise had said. It was a common thing though, someone seeing their attacker as larger than they really were. Mackenzie tried to get to his feet, his struggle pulling Anne's attention to him as he managed on the second try though his vision threatened to go dark around the corners for a few seconds as he stood. Shax gave him a crazed-looking smile before glancing over at Blaise who had sat up in the snow as he pulled in deep breaths.

"After almost chopping my head off with an axe the first time, did you really think that was going to work Prophet?" Mackenzie chanced his own glance towards Blaise as the man spoke, and could see his friend fighting against tremors from the cold. His lips were slightly blue too, and Mackenzie recognized the first signs of hypothermia starting to set in. It was going to get worse if they didn't get Blaise away from here and into somewhere warm. Anne had moved herself to be a barrier for Blaise, but he was looking around her at Shax. The two of them seemed to be having some sort of contest of who would flinch first, but Mackenzie doubted that Shax flinched often.

"Had to give it...a try," Blaise managed to speak, the words an airy rush as he still took in large breaths of air. Shax gave a grin as though he'd just told an amusing joke before gazing at Anne. Mackenzie stepped over Blaise's legs to get himself between his two friends and Shax, and felt the man's eyes turn on him though Shax had lost some of his amused attitude. "Mac..." Blaise's tone was a warning even over the slightly harsh rasp and the stutter from the cold.

"You should listen to him, Mackenzie. Only your sheer bullheadedness has made you last this long. I'm surprised you're still conscious. Besides, even if you weren't slowly bleeding to death you wouldn't be a threat to me." Shax stepped up to Mackenzie, stopping at an uncomfortably close distance as they held each other's eyes. Mackenzie did his best to sqaure his shoulders, making a point of the fact that he was taller than Shax and had a bit more power behind him. A smile was the only response he got in return before the man grabbed hold of his side, digging his thumb down on the bullet hole through Mackenzie's shirt and the soaked bandage. Mackenzie blanched as his body jerked to pull away, but the man held him in place easily making it clear that the size difference didn't much matter.

Mackenzie heard Anne say something, catching her movement towards them from the corner of his eye. He shook his head, desperately willing her to stay back and not get involved.

Shax pressed harder, pushing down directly on the wound as Mackenzie tried to reach out and push the man away. His attempt to fight back ended up with him gripping the man's shirt in pain instead, and Shax finally let go with a slight shove backwards. Mackenzie fell back into the snow and didn't get a chance to react before the man kicked him in the hip, causing him to curl up reflexively to try and protect his injured side. Mackenzie tried to reach up and grab ahold of the man as he stepped over him, but he was too weak to hold on tight enough to stop Shax from just pulling free of him.

Anne had moved towards them, but either Mackenzie's motion to stop or her doubts about leaving Blaise exposed had stopped her part of the way. She stood her ground as Shax moved towards them. Blaise made an attempt to get to his feet but his shaking was worse now with the cold. His limbs had started to feel stiff as they seemed to try to hold him down. Shax made a sort of disapproving tsk towards Anne, shaking his head as he stopped a short distance away from her.

"It's very touching how loyal you all seem, but really now?" Anne didn't respond, and Shax gave a bored sigh as he looked her up and down. "At least you're nice to look at." Anne managed to block the first attempt Shax made to grab her, but as she went to duck below the swing he reacted by taking hold of her hair at its root. He pulled her back up to look at him for a moment, dragging her away from Blaise who had managed to get to his feet. Shax pulled Anne's head down then, meeting it with his knee before he pushed her away. She staggered but managed to stay on her feet, taking a few moments to steady herself before she lunged at him in a blind manner. He was faster though as he grabbed her by the wrist, twisting it back and up behind her. He pulled harder as she tried to break away, and she felt something in her shoulder pop and her bruised ribs complained against the movement and strain.

"Stop it." Blaise had managed to stay standing and was almost to them before Shax pushed Anne towards him. He caught her and they almost both went tumbling down into the snow before she was able to steady them. Blaise's whole body had chills and shakes running through it, but he still managed to push Anne back behind him as he turned to look at Shax.

Shax took a step towards them; a leisurely step that trended towards the side like he was going to start circling the two of them. "I'll do it, just let them leave." The words were a bit stilted as Blaise got them out through the chatter of his teeth, but even as he spoke the shakes wracking his body slowed. Blaise knew enough to understand this wasn't a good sign but instead one that hypothermia was setting into its next stage.

"You will?" Shax said in mock surprise as he stepped closer, but Blaise didn't back down from him this time. He reached up and straightened out Blaise's collar carefully before looking him straight in the eyes. "If you're serious then I'm willing to let them go. Is that a deal?" Shax held out his hand towards Blaise, watching him hesitate for a moment.

"I tell you what I've seen, and they can leave without any interference from you or anyone working with you?" Anne tugged on Blaise, trying to say something but he gently pushed her back away from him without taking his eyes off Shax. He was trying to find some sign of deception in the man's face, but he couldn't get any clues to what his intent was.

"That's the deal." Shax continued to hold his hand out between them, and Blaise finally took it. They shook for a second, but when Blaise tried to remove his hand Shax wouldn't let him. Instead, he tightened his grip and looked over Blaise's shoulder at Anne. "You two, leave now."

"Blaise-"

"Anne, go. You need to get Mackenzie some help, get out of here." Anne had steadied herself for an argument, but the sound of Blaise's voice cut her short. The words sounded final to her as though Blaise was expecting this to be the last thing he got to say to her. It froze her to the spot, and she reached out to touch his shoulder only to have him shake his head without turning to look at her. "Go on Anne, it will be all right." The tone was gentler now, but that only scared her more. Blaise finally broke his eye contact with Shax to look back at her and it left her with no doubt. "Please Anne."

Anne took a step back, afraid to face the look in Blaise's eyes. Her mind was denying it stubbornly even as she moved besides Mackenzie, watching Blaise as he turned back towards the man who was going to steal him away from her. She reached down to try and help Mackenzie to his feet, feeling detached and numb as a part of her emptied itself of feeling. She couldn't leave him, she knew she couldn't leave him but she was on autopilot as she supported Mackenzie by hugging him to her side with one arm. His injured leg no longer seemed to want to hold weight at all, and she tugged him along towards the snow mobile even as he started to fight against her; to try and intervene about leaving Blaise.

Shax had finally let go of Blaise's hand, but he'd rested his hands on the other's shoulders as though to keep him from trying to bolt away. He looked at Blaise with fake concern, ignoring the other two as he no longer saw them as a threat or worth his time.

"You look cold, Prophet. I'd let you borrow my jacket, but then I would just be cold instead and that wouldn't do us any good. Now tell me, as a show of trust that you're not going to try and go back on our deal, what you've seen happening now?" Anne finally stopped beside the snow mobile, standing there silently with Mackenzie who was watching the other two in the clearing. She couldn't make herself turn around, afraid that if she looked back at Blaise again that she'd lose whatever force was supporting her.

"Anne..." she shook her head when Mackenzie said her name, but he managed to throw his weight so that they twisted and fell back against the snow mobile. He nodded his head towards Shax and Blaise, and she told him no until he reached over and made her look by tilting her chin upwards. Mackenzie wasn't looking at Blaise and Shax anymore, but beyond them past Shax's shoulder to the woods.

"You..." Blaise hesitated, at a loss of what to tell Shax. He hadn't seen anything that occurred past the point of being trapped below the water, he had nothing to give and the other two were still in range of Shax's anger if he found out. Blaise's mind was sluggish on trying to come up with a good lie, something to hold him over long enough that he'd be the only one to receive the backlash of rage from Shax when he found out the truth.

"You're trying my patience, Prophet. What have you seen?" Shax spoke as though he was talking to someone he thought of as slow or perhaps a child.

Blaise shifted uncomfortably, glancing behind him for a second and seeing that Mackenzie and Anne weren't leaving. The two of them were leaning against the snow mobile watching, and he looked back at Shax in desperate hope of something coming to mind. Movement caught his eye over Shax's shoulder, and he focused on it for just a second before dropping his eyes. He felt Shax tighten his hands on his shoulder, pressing down on his collarbone as a warning that he was taking too long.

"You get your ass kicked..." Blaise looked at Shax then, and the man stared at him for a few second before chuckling and ruffling Blaise's damp hair.

"By who? You?" Blaise took a second to react, his mind not staying as clear as he needed it as the cold ate away at him but after a moment he smiled at Shax. The look seemed to finally disconcert the man as he narrowed his eyes at Blaise.

"No...him."

"What we did to him wasn't fair! What I did to him…" Michael was talking earnestly now, the calm conversation having quickly deteriorated. Michael seemed desperate, even angry at Gabriel, and it left Gabriel at a loss on how to handle his brother. Michael never talked about the brother they had locked away, and they all assumed it was because Michael didn't feel he was worth mentioning. None of them had thought that it may be guilt; guilt over the fact that Michael had been the one to do the final deed.

"What he did to us wasn't fair, Michael. He turned against us, was conspiring against us and the people we've been told to watch over. If we let him free he may well do the same thing all over again, he won't have changed back to who we once knew." Gabriel tried to take control over the conversation again, but knew it was a lost cause when Michael's sword appeared at his side. "What are you doing, Michael?"

"Give me the key, Gabriel."

"You know I won't. I won't risk our family or every person on Earth for this."

"You wouldn't be risking our family. He is our family, Gabriel. Now give me the key!" Michael took a few steps towards him, and Gabriel backed towards the door. He felt the first hint of concern for his safety, and he wished he'd left the door open.

"Fine, maybe you're right and I won't be putting our family at risk. However, I still won't risk those people. Not for him, and not for you, Michael."

"How could you choose them over me Gabriel? You're willing to tear our family apart for their sake." Gabriel steadied himself, hoping he was wrong about what was coming but he had seen Michael's anger before. He had seen how quickly and strongly it would burn, blinding him to anything but his goal. The first time he'd really seen it was when Michael sealed away the brother they rarely spoke the name of anymore.

"I told you I won't give it to you, Michael. It's my decision to make, and I've made it. Now leave, please." Gabriel saw the movement, and turned to try and get the door open but he wasn't quick enough. Michael hadn't hesitated for even a second, and the sword had driven through Gabriel's back, the blade slicing through and back out of Gabriel's chest. Michael pulled the sword free, and Gabriel turned to look at him stunned. The two of them stood in shocked silence, and then Michael looked Gabriel in the eyes.

"What have you done, Gabriel? Why couldn't you understand that I was trying to save our family? You betrayed us." Michael could see Gabriel's rage flare, a rare thing to see in his brother and it was a hot enough anger to make Michael step back. Gabriel tried to speak but the words seemed caught in his throat as he stumbled a step towards Michael, grabbing hold of his brother. Michael noticed the key hanging on the strap around Gabriel's neck with the cross, reaching for it but grabbed thin air as Gabriel disappeared from the room.

Blaise said the word as he tried to react by pulling back, but his movements weren't fast enough. When Shax turned to face Gabriel coming up behind him, Gabriel was ready with a hard hit to the face with the butt of the shotgun. Shax stumbled into Blaise, almost causing him to fall back if Gabriel hadn't reached out and pulled Blaise forwards onto his feet again. Gabriel continued the movement to swing Blaise behind him before cocking the gun quickly, taking a shot as Shax tried to get back his balance. He was hit in the chest by the shotgun's spatter, and it sent him stumbling back down into the snow this time; giving them a few seconds to react.

"Anne, the sled is just in the trees. I suggest you take it, the dogs will run easiest for you. Blaise, get Mackenzie on the snow mobile, you all need to get out of here now." Gabriel shouted the orders to them, pulling Blaise along with him towards the snow mobile while turning every few seconds to see how quickly Shax was recovering. Gabriel shoved Blaise towards the other two when they got closer, and turned to fire another shot as Shax started towards them. Any amusement at the situation was gone from Shax's face, replaced by a look of pure rage as the second shot hit him. He didn't get knocked down this time, but it still slowed him. Anne grabbed Blaise's hand when Gabriel pushed him towards her, and she pulled him along towards Mackenzie who was trying painfully to get himself onto the snow mobile.

"We can't leave him."

"Trust me, he can take care of himself," Anne said, shoving Blaise onto the vehicle behind Mackenzie who'd finally managed to get settled. Gabriel was managing to move fairly well despite his own injuries, the large bite marks and scratches from the creature Lilith had sicced at him earlier still oozing some. The shotgun was now empty as he moved to intercept Shax and he used it as a club this time, swinging it towards the man to hit him in the ribs.

Before Blaise could argue more, Mackenzie had gotten the snow mobile running and Anne was turning to run off towards the trees where Gabriel had indictated the dogs were. Blaise tried to get off the snow mobile, but his movements had grown too slow and sluggish to do so before Mackenzie took off and made Blaise grab hold of him to keep from falling off backwards.

A few moments later they caught sight of Anne through the trees behind them, the dogs tugging urgently at their tethers despite most of them looking like they'd been run ragged and injured from their own fight. Blaise saw Anne glance back towards the clearing at one point, and when she looked forward again there was guilt on her face as they left Gabriel behind.

"Gabriel…"

"Shax." Now that they were the only two in the clearing the determined drive of their fight seemed to have eased. The two men stood a few feet apart, Gabriel wishing he'd thought to grab more shells for the shotgun from the sled before he'd intervened. He'd been worried he didn't have time though, and now he'd have to do without. Gabriel watched Shax closely as the man straightened his suit jacket despite the holes that were preforated into it by the shotgun blasts.

"I thought that you'd remembered everything, I was hoping I was part of those memories. Now that I know I am, this should be much more enjoyable. I have always wanted to kick your ass, and now here you are without any of your old strengths and a whole basket full of new weaknesses." Shax gave him a wide smile, standing his ground though not approaching him yet. "Look at you!" He spoke like he was talking to an old friend who's grown through the years unexpectedly, holding his arms wide to indicate Gabriel as a whole. "I'm amazed you even managed to take out Lilith and her little hellhound, though I suppose that didn't end the way you probably wanted it to, did it? That sheriff dying wasn't part of your plan." Gabriel raised the barrel of the shotgun when Shax took a couple of steps towards him, hoping the man wouldn't call his bluff. Shax paused and looked at the weapon between them, but then shook his head lightly. "You know that won't do anything."

"It will knock you on your ass for a few moments and give me time to prepare something that will." Gabriel made himself sound confident as he spoke, but Shax just took another couple of slow steps through the snow.

"No it won't. You're out of ammo or you would have pulled the trigger already." Gabriel swung the gun around in his hands again to try and club at Shax when the man lunged at him, and he felt it make contact though it was more a glancing blow than the direct hit he'd hoped for. Shax recovered too quickly for him, and Gabriel felt himself slam back against one of the trees at the edge of the clearing. Shax had him by the throat with one hand while the other pulled the shotgun away from him, tossing it back into the snow. "Those things are so impersonal. As I'm sure you remember, I prefer a more intimate way of hurting people."

Shax produced the knife from some pocket in his jacket and toyed with it near Gabriel's chest. Gabriel tried to kick out at Shax, but they were too close together for him to get a good enough swing. He tried to push the man back which only caused him to tighten his hold on Gabriel's neck.

"Where is it, Gabriel? This all would have been over so much quicker if Michael had let me at you. But, he didn't want anyone hurting his damn baby brother so we had to try to pry at everyone you surrounded yourself with." Shax spoke casually, but there was a telltale hint of distaste in his voice as he mentioned Michael. He smiled quite brilliantly all of a sudden though, a hint of malice in the look. "Not that I minded prying at your doctor friend, slicing him up was the most fun I've had in a long time. Once I'm done with you, I'm going to find him again. I'll hold him to the deal we made after I show him how I feel about someone trying to trick me out of what they've promised."

"You're not going to leave this clearing, Shax."

"Yes, I can tell. You're doing an amazing job at stopping me, Gabriel. How silly of me to think that I would have a chance to escape," Shax spoke with heavy sarcarm as he pushed against Gabriel. The air was cut off completely from Gabriel's lungs as he felt his feet leave the ground, the bark of the tree biting into his back even through his jacket. "Now tell me, where is-"

Shax's words fell off as the knife broke through the skin where he was pressing it against Gabriel's chest. He stared at the spot for a second as though it had just spoken to him, and then he gave an incredulous laugh. Gabriel attempted to use Shax's string of laughter to his advantage, trying to hit the man's elbow to weaken the hold on his neck. When this failed Gabriel went for the eyes, but Shax just laughed louder as he pulled away. Shax's hold loosened a little with the movement, but still not enough to give Gabriel a chance to break away.

"You made it a part of you? That's why you lost all memory and connection with your Grace, you drained what was left to make it a part of you. I knew there was something off about this whole thing, not all of your fallen brothers have lost their memories in the past but here you were completely oblivious. Its because, you fucking beautiful moron, you used it all up." Shax laughed again, reaching up to pat Gabriel on the cheek with the flat side of the knife. "You realize Michael's going to tear you limb from limb when he finds out, don't you? He'll rip your heart out and take the key back just from sheer anger that you would do something so...I can't even decide if you're an idiot or a genius."

Shax pressed the knife to Gabriel's chest again, his laughter dying down though he was still grinning ear to ear. "I could save your brother the trouble of realizing you wasted any chance you had at getting home again. I could just cut it out of you now." Shax pressed the blade of the knife between Gabriel's ribs near the scar that had formed across his chest. A noise behind him made Shax pause quickly, and he turned to see Michael heading towards him already only a few feet away from where he'd appeared out of no where.

"I told you that no one harms my brother, Shax." Michael's voice was full of rage, and Shax dropped Gabriel quickly as he shook his head and backed away.

"Michael, he has the key in-" The rest of the words never made it out of Shax's mouth as Michael's hand met his forehead. A scream ripped out of Shax as the body of the man he'd possesssed separated from his real form, and then he was gone as he dispersed into a puff of smoke that left an empty shell behind. Gabriel caught himself before he sunk down into the snow, a hand going to his chest to press against the reopened wound. Shax hadn't gotten a chance to sink the knife deep enough though, and the blade hadn't reached its goal. He kept his eyes on Michael who stood a few feet away looking at the body lying at his feet in disgust before meeting Gabriel's eyes.

"You certainly have a way of turning on the people who trust you," Gabriel said a bit roughly.

Mackenzie was doing his best to stay focused on the path ahead of them and keeping the snow mobile from running into a tree. He wasn't feeling right anymore though. His left side was slowly going numb, the feeling seeming to radiate out from his hip. Even with that he could feel the pain, a strange sensation of it in the background like a mild discomfort. Blaise was heavy against his back, the other's speech having dropped into a slur even as he tried to convince Mackenzie again that they needed to turn back around. When they finally pulled into the clearing with the house, Anne was beside them on the sled watching with concern. Mackenzie was a little slow to react on stopping the snow mobile, but he managed it before it hit the porch.

Anne helped Blaise off the snow mobile first before offering Mackenzie help. He didn't want to admit that he couldn't stand on his own without support, so he chose to lean back against the sled once he was off of it while Anne kept Blaise steady.

"Get him inside and call for an ambulance or two. I'll get Leo in." Anne gave Mackenzie a doubtful look, hesitating to take a step towards the house.

"Mac...I don't think you're in any shape..."

"Anne, go get Blaise inside and warming up. We can't let him get any colder, he's already bad as it is. I'll be fine." Anne looked at Mackenzie before glancing at Blaise who had gone quiet. He seemed to be having trouble keeping himself awake, and this seemed to make Anne's mind up for her as she turned to half drag him into the house. She left the door slightly ajar, but she didn't reappear right away and Mackenzie said a small prayer for this. Blaise was already dangerously hypothermic, he could tell that from dealing with it before in people who got themselves lost, not to mention the risk of frostbite. Mackenzie managed the couple of steps over to the sled and then sunk down into the snow next to it with his back resting against the wooden frame. Yakone pulled the line of dogs around so he could lick at Mackenzie's face, and Mackenzie set a hand on top of the dog's head. Yakone responded by lying down beside him with his head resting on Mac's leg, the dogs closest to them following his lead and lying down around Mackenzie in the snow.

"You need help, Mac." Mackenzie looked up at the sound of the voice, and saw Leo sitting there on the edge of the sled. Yakone whined slightly but didn't seem to otherwise acknowledge the man sitting there.

"I'll be okay, I think. I just needed to rest for a moment..." Mackenzie looked back towards the house, trying to figure out how many steps he'd have to force out of himself to get inside.

"Mac, I shot you...she shot you," Leo was quick to correct himself, though there was a hint of pained guilt in the comment. "You're losing too much blood, you can't keep pushing yourself like you have been." Mackenzie sat quietly for a few moments before he looked up at his friend.

"I know...just a little longer. Just until I know the ambulance is here and that they're going to be all right..." Leo sighed, setting his hand lightly on Mackenzie's shoulder. They sat like that for a while as Mackenzie looked down at the dogs around him blankly. When he looked back up at Leo he found that he was alone sitting with the dogs and his friend's corpse. "Plus, I still have to get you inside..." He said it quietly with regret that Leo hadn't stayed, and he looked at the front door of the house again as he scratched idly behind Yakone's ears. "I'm working up to that still."

Anne had called for help as soon as they were in the door, and then had set about helping Blaise get his wet and mainly frozen clothes off. She was scared with how pale his skin was and how cold he felt, scared that he was too far into hypothermia already and that if he wasn't he'd have frostbite that couldn't be helped. She glanced towards the door a few times waiting for Mackenzie to get inside, but got distracted as she worked on getting Blaise wrapped in warm clothes and blankets as quickly as she could. Blaise didn't seem as confused as she'd first thought when they'd ended up outside the house, though his words were still slurred to the point of difficulty.

Before Anne realized it she could hear the sirens of at least one emergency vehicle in the distance, and she looked towards the door again with startled concern as she realized Mackenzie still hadn't come inside. She left Blaise with a hot water bottle pressed close to his chest as she moved and nudged the front door open. Mackenzie was sitting against the sled, the dogs all lying around him like a furry barrier. He wasn't moving though, his back lying heavily against the sled and his head tilted against the frame like a pillow. He had zipped his coat up at one point, and it hid some of the blood she knew stained his shirt and the thigh of his pants so it almost looked liked he'd just sat there for a nap.

"Mac?" Her voice came out weak at first as she tried to get the man to stir, but when she didn't get a response she felt her chest tighten almost painfully. "Mac!" It came out as a high cry now as she tried to speak louder, still afraid to approach and confirm the worse as the sirens grew louder. From where she was she could still convince herself that Mackenzie was just not hearing her, or was even just unconscious. The delusion kept her in place, terrified of shattering it by going closer and finding that he was gone. She'd been handling her emotions the best she could, had been keeping the thought that Leo was gone for good pushed back as far as she could to keep functioning. The additional weight that hit her at the thought that Mackenzie may be gone too was bringing everything down around her though, the carefully built walls cracking apart.

Two ambulances pulled into the yard with a final loud blast of their horns, and she found her breath rushing back into her lungs as she saw Mackenzie start. He stirred more as he saw that help had arrived, and even managed to get to his feet though it was painful to watch him do so. Anne stepped back into the doorway, moving quickly to get Blaise to his own feet so they could get him into the back of one of the vehicles. She was assured with the knowledge that the paramedics would take care of them, all of them.

As Blaise was put in the back of one of the ambulances she saw Mackenzie sitting on the bumper of the other as they loaded Leo's body into it still hidden by the cover from the sled. She watched as Mackenzie followed him in, a paramedic climbing back out to talk to another. Anne looked as the woman beside her nudged her gently to get her attention, helping Anne up into the back of the ambulance with Blaise. She would have preferred for them all to go together, but as the woman got into the back with her she realized that room constraints would keep that from happening.

"Gabriel is still out in the woods somewhere. He might need help." Anne spoke to the paramedic, but the woman just nodded as she worked on getting more blankets wrapped around Blaise and his hot water bottle.

"We have someone calling that in. Stan from the other ambulance is going to hang back and stay until the police get here. He'll watch so that if your friend gets back to the house he'll be able to help. Once the uniforms are out here they'll make the decision to start a search if its still needed." The paramedic spoke gently to Anne, and she found herself surprised that she could still feel a sting of anger at being treated like a child. Anne reached over and took hold of Blaise's hand tightly as the doors to the ambulance were closed. Theirs left, and she could see out the back window that the other was following closely behind as a man headed up onto the porch of her house to wait.

Chapter 17 – Are you there God?

"Shax never trust me just like I never trusted him. The way he saw it I was a means to an end for him. I told Shax you were off limits to Lilith and him, obviously he got overly ambitious." Gabriel forced himself to stand straight and stop leaning back against the tree as his brother talked. He was already starting to feel worn down, and he didn't need anything to be blocking his path if Michael came at him. Gabriel doubted that his brother had a happy reunion in mind after everything, and Shax had been right about Gabriel not having the strength he'd had before. He'd barely been able to fight Shax as he was, which meant it would be impossible for him to stand against Michael.

"You know what my answer is going to be if you ask where it is Michael. I'm not going to tell you." Michael seemed to ignore this as he started on his own tangent, not approaching Gabriel though there wasn't enough distance between them as it was to make Gabriel feel safe.

"I remember what it was like back then. All of you seem to remember the things our brother did wrong, but I still remember what he did right. Who were we to condemn him just because he didn't listen to what our Father said, Gabriel? We know barely more about our Father than these people do. All we've got are stories told to us and orders passed down. Lucifer was just trying to make things clearer."

"Even if I felt the same way, Michael, I'm not willing to throw these people into turmoil and death. It won't be like their books and religions say, it could all be destroyed if Lucifer is angry enough to lash out at them. We can't know what he'll do, the last we saw of him he was furious with us all."

"And he had every right to be! We turned ourselves against him, we followed our orders blindly. What does it matter what happens to these people, Gabriel? They are nothing compared to us, they are not a part of our family." Michael spoke passionately, his passive stance breaking as he moved towards Gabriel to take him by the arms. "Our family is what's important."

"But, I'm not a part of your family anymore, Michael. You made sure of that." Michael stopped, seemed to freeze in place before lowering his eyes from Gabriel's.

"What happened with you was unfortunate-"

"What happened to me is your fault, Michael. Don't make it sound like some accident that happened while I was being careless. You were the one to choose this for me, you were so eager to get one brother back that you've thrown another away." Gabriel was surprised at the bitterness in his own voice, but he wasn't able to hold it back now.

He knew what it was he had lost and couldn't ever get back, and that pain had been driving him until now. He could tell the moment that Michael chose his own anger over the feelings of guilt, knew the second his brother had made up his mind to avoid facing what he'd done. Michael took a step back from Gabriel before he seemed to produce the sword out of thin air, and

Gabriel pushed himself to move quickly to the right to avoid the swing that was thrown upward at him.

"You betrayed us, Gabriel. You did this to yourself, you chose not to be a part of our family anymore." Gabriel had to duck this time as Michael came at him, rage and pain coming through his brother's words. Gabriel was almost too slow at reacting to one of the blows, and he felt the sword swing past his right shoulder. He managed to duck low under Michael's arm and past him at one point, moving to find the shotgun in the snow. He knew that it wouldn't help him much, but he needed something to try and block the blows with.

"You betrayed me, Michael. You were the one that demanded I go against my own will and judgement, you were the one that made a decision for all of us without consulting any of us. You're the one that betrayed us," Gabriel shouted the words back, rolling to the left to avoid a low strike from his brother and found himself beside the shotgun. It was half buried in the snow, and he took hold to pull it up over himself to block another fall of the sword. Michael put his weight against the swing, trying to break Gabriel's hold on one side or another of the shotgun.

"Tell me where you've hidden it, Gabriel!" Gabriel managed to push Michael back for just long enough to put some distance between them, blocking his brother's attacks even as his moves slowed. At some point Michael was going to be too fast or the shotgun would break, and at the thought Gabriel knew he couldn't win. Gabriel made the choice then and dropped the shotgun down to his side right as Michael made another thrust at him with the tip of the sword.

The two brothers found themselves suddenly face to face, standing in an eerily silent clearing. Michael's hands still gripped the sword that was buried up to the hilt in Gabriel's center as he looked at Gabriel in shock.

"Gabriel…" All the anger was lost from Michael's voice, fear and pain flooding through instead as he let go of the sword. Michael grabbed Gabriel's shoulders to stop him from falling, pulling his brother close to him. Gabriel thought he'd have to fight against the pain, but he found there wasn't any. He could feel bile rise in the back of his throat, taste the blood that was flooding into his mouth with it before he pushed it back down. "You were supposed to block, Gabriel."

"Why are you upset, Michael? Isn't this what you wanted…" The words came out hushed, but with the stillness of their surroundings Michael had no trouble hearing him. Michael sank down while still holding Gabriel close, lowering his brother into the snow near one of the trees to lean him against before hesitating and pulling the sword from Gabriel's stomach as gently as he could.

"This was never what I wanted, Gabriel." Blood spilled out onto Michael's hand when the sword was freed, and he stared down at it for a second as though the shock of it was hitting him a second time. When Michael looked back to Gabriel's face his brother gave him a sad smile, though Gabriel's focus was a bit distant over Michael's shoulder.

"It won't work for you even now, Michael. It was always his right." Michael turned to face the owner of the voice and found that there were two new additions to the clearing. The man had messy auburn hair that went with the rest of his disheveled look as it hung over his deep cut blue eyes. He looked as though he'd neglected himself for a couple of days as the rough beginnings of a beard were growing in. He stood a short distance behind the woman who had spoken, her chin lifted defiantly making her dark red curls a frame around her face. They were both watching Michael, the woman in a prepared fashion while the man seemed hesitant about the fight they seemed to expect.

"Uriel…" Michael stood as he spoke, holding his hands out in front of him with their stain of Gabriel's blood like an admission of guilt. The man shifted uncomfortably behind the woman, eyes moving to Gabriel where he sat against the tree behind Michael.

"You closed us off from you, Michael. I didn't understand at first why you would choose to do that as we searched for Gabriel, but I see you've found him." Uriel spoke softly though there was no mistaking the authoritative tone in her voice. Micheal took a step back from the two, standing between them and Gabriel as the man leaned forward to talk into Uriel's ear. She nodded softly at what he said, letting her eyes drop for a second as she listened though never turning away from Michael. "Raphael's right. You lied to us, Michael. You said that it was Gabriel who went against us."

"I was only-"

"Yes, we know now what you were trying to do. I miss Lucifer as well, Michael, but he had to be punished for the wrong that he did and at this point he isn't the same angel we knew back then. He was lost to us a long time ago, and now you've lost us another brother." Uriel let her eyes drop to Gabriel for the first time, a flicker of pain that passed quickly crossed her features. Gabriel met her gaze, but it was obvious he was struggling to keep focus on what was going on around him. "We can't repair what you've done here, Michael."

"Raphael-"

"Raphael may be able to heal a lot of things, but even he can't bring Gabriel back to us." The words were snapped out in anger, and Michael nearly took a step back but managed to stand his ground. "What you've done Raphael can't fix, he can't heal and restore Gabriel to what he once was." Raphael reached forward to place a hand on Uriel's arm, and the touch seemed to pull her back from her anger. She sighed as though she was suddenly tired, and took a step towards Michael. "We can fight Michael, but you know that you will lose against both of us. You will come with us to face what you've done and perhaps you will find that you'll see our condemned brother sooner than you'd hoped." There was a bitterness in the last phrase as she watched Michael to see which course he would chose to follow.

Michael moved to reach for his sword, but froze when he turned to grab it and was met by the sight of Gabriel in the snow. Michael dropped his hands to his sides, staring silently down at Gabriel for a second before looking back at the other two.

"Come with me, Michael." Uriel held out her hand with a slightly pleading look, wanting her brother to come without a fight between them. Michael reached and took her hand in his and then the two of them were gone, leaving the air with a static feel for a few seconds before it faded away. Gabriel was left in the clearing with Raphael who looked at him silently before moving to sit down beside him.

"Raph..." Gabriel tried to speak, but the other shook his head strictly to cut his words short.

"I know, Gabriel. If it helps, I never believed you had gone against us. We couldn't find you, all signs of your Grace had disappeared. I understand why now, but you don't have to worry. It will be kept between us..." Rapheal's voice was quiet and strained as though he wasn't use to speaking loudly, and he reached up to toy with the scar that ran under the collar of his coat and across his throat. He gave up massaging it after a moment, and reached over to place a hand over Gabriel's in the snow. "You're afraid of dying...I don't know what it might bring either. Don't worry though, whatever does happen will and there won't be anything to do about it by then. I'll leave you your gift though, it was your responsibility to hold that key before this and I believe you are still capable of making that choice."

They fell quiet then, Raphael sitting with Gabriel a while longer before leaning to pull his brother's coat around him tightly. He pressed a hand over the wound that still wept blood from his abdomen, and then all signs of Gabriel's family was gone.

Mackenzie hadn't even realized that they'd left the house before they hit the edge of town. He'd been looking down at Leo as the ambulance screamed down the road when he heard his friend's voice again. He knew Leo was sitting at his side without having to look up.

"Mac, the others are safe, as safe as you can get them. You have to stop pushing yourself. You need to let them know how bad off you are." Mackenzie had told the paramedics that the blood was Leo's when they'd asked, and he had kept his jacket zippered shut. It had allowed him to ride with Leo, and it had also made it possible for the paramedic that would have been riding back with him to stay at the house waiting for Gabriel.

"You doing all right back there, Mackenzie?" It took him a second to realize that it was the man driving the ambulance that had asked this, and not Leo. He looked up to where the paramedic was glancing back at him while trying to keep his eyes on the road at the same time. "You sure you're okay?" The man was looking at him strangely, and Mackenzie glanced down at himself to see the mess he was.

"Fine." He said it with an attempt at a smile that didn't seem to convince the man, and a second later Mackenzie heard him say something into his radio. Mackenzie glanced at Leo beside him and found that the sheriff was staring at him a bit angrily.

"It's all right. It doesn't even hurt anymore." Time seemed to skip suddenly as he spoke, and Mackenzie realized that at some point they'd come to a stop outside the hospital. He said the words to Leo, but there was a shock of cold hands cupping the sides of his face gently that made him realize Leo wasn't there anymore. His friend wasn't sitting next to him and his body was gone from the back of the ambulance as he'd already been taken inside. Mackenzie instead found himself looking at Allison who was kneeling between his legs as she looked up to him.

"What doesn't hurt anymore, Callahan?" She let her hands fall to rest on his thighs as she looked out the back of the ambulance to the paramedic who was stating that Mackenzie had said his injuries weren't serious. She gave the man a look that clearly said what she thought of him taking that as the truth without checking himself before her attention focused fully back onto Mackenzie. She patted his thigh, trying to get Mackenzie to look at her again instead of out the back of the ambulance and stopped when she realized her palm was coated in fresh blood. "What's this blood from?"

"He said that was the Sheriff's-"

"I'm not talking to you." Allison snapped the words at the paramedic who backed off immediately, watching instead for the stretcher they'd called for to take Mackenzie inside once it was clear something was wrong. Allison looked up at Mackenzie, and asked him again what the blood was from.

"It doesn't hurt…" Frustration mixed with Allison's concern as she tugged at Mackenzie's zipper; pulling it down so she could get a look at his side where the blood seemed concentrated. It took her a couple of tries, the zipper snagging twice before she got it down and pushed the jacket back out of her way. Mackenzie was watching her quietly as the look of angered shock crossed her face, and he lifted his hand to hers for a moment to get her attention. Allison saw that for the first time Mackenzie looked scared and completely focused as he held onto her. "It's not good that it doesn't hurt anymore, is it?"

Allison gave Mackenzie's hand a squeeze, not sure who she was trying to reassure more at the moment. The bullet wound was clear now that the jacket and shirt had been pushed back, and a string of curses were going through her mind as she pressed her free hand over the wound.

"No, Callahan, it's not. You idiot, why didn't you tell them you'd been shot?" Allison spoke over the sound of the stretcher making it out to them, but when she pulled back to let the other nurses and the paramedic get Mackenzie out onto it he wouldn't let go of her hand. She moved with him instead, staying beside him as the rush started up around them to get him prepped on the way to the operating room. "Where did it hurt, Mac? When it was hurting before, where was the pain focused at?"

"Hip…" Mackenzie wasn't sure if he'd actually spoken the word or not, and tried to wave to indicate his hip. Allison just looked down at him sadly as they moved down the hall, the clatter of voices a muffled sound in the background to him.

"You're going to be okay, Mac." Allison was the one speaking, but Mackenzie looked over her shoulder at Leo instead. Leo shook his head slightly, and then Mackenzie didn't remember anything after that.

Chapter 18 – Proluge -

He leaned carefully to set the flowers on top of the headstone beside a small litter of other objects. There was the beer he'd set down just a moment before, some other flowers he knew were from Anne, and a letter tucked under a rock with the ink smearing slightly from the damp snow. Allison had sent the flowers with him as she had last year, asking him if he wanted her to give him some company. Mackenzie had told her he'd go on his own and she hadn't argued with him about it, instead she'd given him a quick kiss goodbye before he left. She'd be getting ready for work now at their house that he still couldn't stop himself from thinking of as Leo's. He'd been surprised that his friend had left it to him in his will, in truth surprised that Leo had had a will though his friend was always more organized than Mackenzie'd ever be.

The beer he'd brought was for Leo, Mackenzie knowing if his friend had been there he'd much prefer that than the flowers. He vaguely remembered his conversations with Leo that night, how it hadn't seemed unusual that his dead friend had been talking to and watching over him while he struggled to survive his own injuries. Mackenzie hadn't seen Leo again like that since waking up in the hospital several days later to find Anne and Blaise sitting near by with Allison. He hoped Leo was with Marie now, the real Marie. The rest of that time had passed in a flurry of activity which included the FBI showing up in their town due to the description he had managed to enter before things went to hell. Apparently the man who'd gone by Shax was their missing person from a few states over who'd walked out on his family one night and never returned. What the FBI had failed to mention before was the man wasn't a witness but their main suspect in the death of his family.

Mackenzie cursed quietly under his breath as he took a moment to lean heavily against the cane he had with him. He didn't need it everyday, didn't even need it most days, but he had found that when the cold set in his hips tended to stiffen and cause an aching pain. That pain was his reminder of what happened, just like Blaise and Anne each had their own. It was a miracle Blaise hadn't lost more then a couple of toes to frost bite after being out in the cold as long as he was. Anne had admitted to Mackenzie after he'd woken up that there was a short period where they didn't know if Blaise would lose some of his fingers, and she had been terrified that loss would be more than Blaise could cope with. In the end he hadn't lost them though, but they could tell there had been something lost inside Blaise with how quiet he fell around this time of year.

The letter was from him, something he'd done the year before as well. Mackenzie and Anne had talked about it, both curious and worried about what was written on the pages, but neither of them felt comfortable reading them. They were meant for Leo, not for them, just like the one he left for Gabriel was no one else's to read. At the thought Mackenzie looked towards where the headstone they'd all pitched in for Gabriel sat. They'd never found him out in the woods, and he knew that uncertainty was what ate at them. In the end they'd assumed he'd been killed. Anne didn't take the dogs out into the woods in that direction anymore, seeming afraid of what she may find someday.

Mackenzie paused as he realized that someone was standing at Gabriel's grave, a piece of paper in his hands and Mackenzie realized the man was reading Blaise's letter. Mackenzie felt a twinge of anger at the thought that someone else was carelessly reading the words, and he started to say something when a hint of recognition stopped him. The man looked like he was a few years older than him, his hair a slight mess around his head and dropping into his eyes. The beginnings of a beard had started to take shape on his face, and though Mackenzie couldn't be sure behind the rough exterior he thought he knew the man.

Mackenzie stood there, stuck to the spot until the man folded the letter carefully back up as though making sure not to tear it. He set it under the rock that Blaise had used to pin it in place before looking up towards Mackenzie, revealing the blue eyes under his fringe of hair. The man gave him a kind smile as he nodded his head in acknowledgement.

"Sheriff." The man said the word both as a greeting and a farewell as he turned to start back up the hill towards the front of the cemetary. The voice had been what confirmed it for Mackenzie, what had hit a string of memory in his mind and he tried to start out after the man.

"Gabriel!" He called it after the man's retreating back, but either the man didn't hear him or chose not to respond as he continued up the hill. Mackenzie cursed at his leg as he tried to catch up, but the man had disappeared over the top of the hill even as Mackenzie called after him again. A few moments later Mackenzie got to where he could see the layout of the cemetary around him standing on the ridge of the hill that it climbed up around the sides of. There were footprints all along the main paths here, but as others had been coming and going since the last snow he couldn't tell in which direction the man had gone. He looked all around, calling out Gabriel's name once more but seeing no one even near the gates of the cemetary.

The man was gone, seeming to have disappeared into thin air, leaving Mackenzie standing alone in the center of the graveyard as the snow began to fall once more in the Colorado mountains.